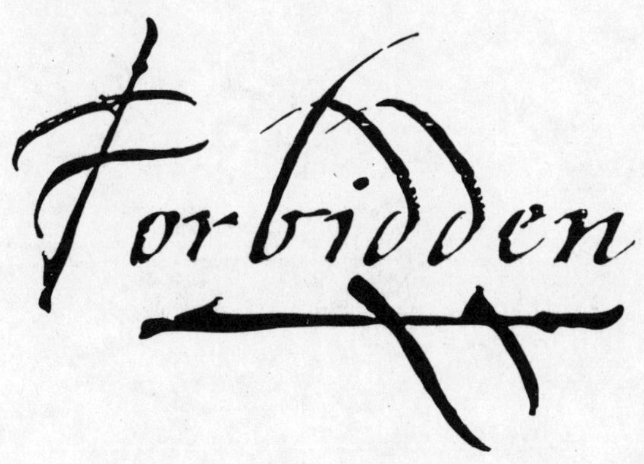
Forbidden

D0109346

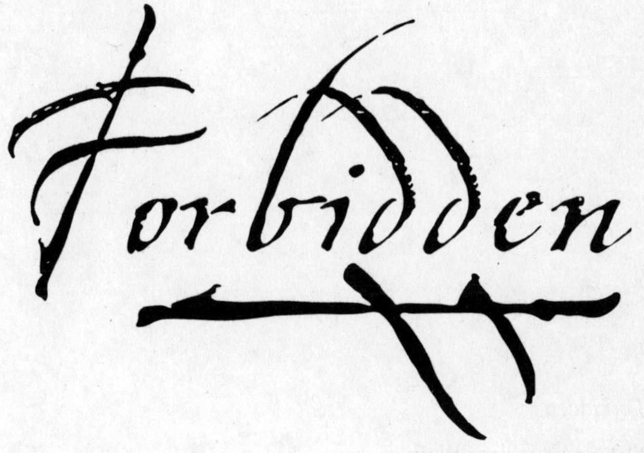

Wilma Wall

Forbidden

Published by Kregel Publications, a division of Kregel, Inc., P.O. Box 2607, Grand Rapids, MI 49501.

Cover design: John M. Lucas

ISBN 0-8254-3947-7

Printed in the United States of America

04 05 06 07 08 / 5 4 3 2 1

To survivors of World War II and the brave men and women who served—both in the armed forces and in alternate service.

Acknowledgments

I WOULD LIKE TO THANK ALL THE wonderful people who made it possible for me to research, write, and edit this book.

Dave, my best friend and husband, for his patience and long suffering.

My family and support group: daughters Jean and Margie, for their expertise in nursing; Judi, for her good critique; Ed, Rick, and Don; Mike, Eric, Robyn, Jeff, Carrie, Micky, Tami, Richard, Terra, and David, who all had faith in me; and my sister Verna, who has always encouraged me.

Elnora King and the Tuesday Afternoon Writers' Workshop, for their insight and guidance.

The staff at the Reedley and Fresno libraries, who have provided me with many resources.

All my Mennonite and Japanese friends who have answered my pestering questions.

Dr. John Hayward and Dr. Jake Friesen, who gave me information on medical schools and hospital procedures of the 1940s, and Dr. Donald Yoshimura who filled me in on neurological problems.

Much appreciation to The Writers' Edge Manuscript Service for their worthy efforts.

Special thanks to Kregel: editors Sue Miholer and Paulette Zubel for keeping me on track; and Stephen Barclift, Janyre Tromp, Wendy Widder, and Dennis Hillman for giving me the chance to share this story.

Except for political figures mentioned in context of historical events, all characters in this book are a product of my imagination. Any similarities to real people are unintentional. The fictional town of Rosemond is a composite of the many small towns surrounding Fresno, California.

All Scripture is quoted from the 1928 King James Version, since that was the source most used in the World War II era.

Glossary

German

Note: These are Low German *(Plautdietsch)* words, unless otherwise noted. They have been spelled phonetically to assist with pronunciation.

ach. An exclamation, comparable to "Oh, dear!"
Anchen. Pet form of Annie ("chen" used after a name is an endearment).
be'duzzled. Confused.
be'soped. Drunk.
Bist rehd? "Are you ready?"
borscht. A hearty soup, served hot. Mennonite **borscht** is composed of cabbage, beef, and potatoes, as opposed to Russian **borsch,** which is made with beets.
"Danke lieber Heiland für dies essen. Amen." "Thank you beloved Savior for this food. Amen." A grace spoken before meals. Often said in unison by the children in the family after a more formal prayer by the father.
deef. A mispronunciation of *deaf,* common among the uneducated.
Doch nicht! "But no!" An expression used to show disbelief, sympathy, censure, etc., depending on the tone of voice.
eiyah pie. Egg custard pie.
faspa. A light meal—generally served Sunday evening—consisting of **tvehbock,** cold cuts, cheese, and coffee. Canned fruit is often added.

In Mennonite households, the traditional Sunday noon meal was always big, and there were often guests and extended family members present. Because no work was done Sunday afternoons, no one was very hungry by evening, but by the time the visiting women had cleaned up the kitchen after the noon meal, it was often time to put on the coffee again. Guests could eat a little something before they went home to do their farm chores and then go to the evening church service.

fe'rekt. Crazy.

fest committee. A committee elected to prepare meals for church dinners.

husfrue. Housewife.

heyna sup. Chicken noodle soup that is usually made with homemade noodles.

Jugendverein. (High German, pronounced "Yu-gunt fe-rine.") Originally, it meant "Young People's Society," but later it referred to a more relaxed Sunday evening program enjoyed by the entire church. It included music by various ensembles, quizzes, and readings.

kinderfest. (High German.) Literally, children's festival, it was the name given to the church Children's Day picnic, which actually included the entire family.

kindt. Child.

kleen baitya. A little bit, a pittance.

klopps. Hamburger, meatballs.

levenstiet. Expression that means "for the love of time."

liebchen. Beloved. Also used in High German.

na. An exclamation, similar to "Well!" or "Oh, dear!"

Na, gote. "Well, good!"

Neh, obah! Literally "No, but!" An expression of disbelief, frustration, scolding, or even sympathy, depending on what tone of voice is used.

niedrich. Not quite up to standard, second-rate.

"O Tannenbaum." (High German.) "O Christmas Tree," a German Christmas song.

peppaneht. Peppernut cookies. Tiny square cookies made especially at Christmastime.

Plautdietsch. (Low German.) An oral Mennonite vernacular that reflects the years Mennonites have lived in different countries like Holland, Germany, Prussia, and Russia. In recent years, efforts have been made to standardize it into a written language. High German was used in Mennonite church services, in formal settings and correspondence, but **Plautdietsch** was—and still is—the much-loved, relaxed, everyday talk of the people.

pluma mos. A thin purple pudding made from prunes and raisins.

prips. A hot drink made from barley; it is a caffeine-free substitute for coffee.

rollkoaka. A deep-fried cruller.

ruggebrot. Rye bread.

schaubel sup. Green bean soup, made with ham, onions, potatoes, and summer savory herb.

schups. Hair rolled into a bun in the back. During the mid-forties most mature Mennonite women wore their hair in this style.

schuzzle. Someone not quite up to standard, sloppy, silly.

Taunta. Aunt.

toots. Little paper bags, usually filled with candy, an apple, an orange, and nuts in their shells and handed out after the church Christmas program.

tvehbock. Double-decker yeast roll.

"Und Gott spracht." (High German.) "And God spoke."

verenikya. A large flat pocket of dough that is filled with cottage cheese or hoop cheese and then boiled and sometimes fried.

yauma. Misery.

yo. Yes.

Zionsbote. *Zion's Message.* The Mennonite Brethren conference's magazine, written in High German until the magazine was discontinued in 1964.

Japanese

Baachan. Family or children's term for grandmother.
goban. The board for the game of **goh.**
goh. A board game using black and white stones.
gohan. Rice.
hai. Yes.
hakkujin. A white person, Caucasian.
Jiichan. Family or children's term for *grandfather*.
kamikaze. Literally, "divine wind." A member of a Japanese air attack corps in WWII assigned to make a suicidal crash on a target; an airplane containing explosives to be flown in a suicide crash on a target.
Konnichiwa. A Japanese greeting.
On. An unrepayable debt of obligation. The respect and loyalty Japanese traditionally have toward parents and other people in authority, especially to their government. In the United States, the immigrant Japanese *(Issei)* tried hard to instill that kind of respect in the second generation *(Nisei)*, but sometimes the casual American lifestyle filtered it out.
picture bride. A woman selected from a picture and brought from Japan to the United States for the purpose of marriage.
sake. A Japanese alcoholic beverage made from rice.
Shikata ga nai. "It can't be helped"; "Accept the inevitable."

Miscellaneous References

CLOC. Christian Life on Campus. A club on college campuses for Christians.
cotton rat. A wad of cotton-filled material, 2 or 3 inches in diameter and about 4 or 5 inches long. Used by young Mennonite women as a base for a curved roll of hair at the nape of their necks.
CPS. Civilian Public Service. During World War II, an alternate service

for those with religious convictions against using weapons. Men served in forestry camps, dairies, mental hospitals—all without pay except for a pittance given by their churches.

fifth column. Secret sympathizers with the enemy.

GI Bill. Financial help from the government to help veterans pay for schooling and/or to help them buy a house. A way of expressing appreciation for their service in the armed forces.

"Hubba, hubba." An admiring comment about girls, comparable to a wolf whistle. It was considered a compliment.

MB. Mennonite Brethren. Used among members.

MDS. Mennonite Disaster Service. A nationwide relief agency to rebuild communities hit by disaster.

spinning hookers. Speeding a car in a circle, then slamming on the brakes to cause it to skid. Done in vacant lots or fields by exuberant boys.

Chapter One

Fire sirens wailed over Rosemond, piercing the hot stillness of August.

Annie Penner, posting the afternoon accounts at McGinnis Furniture Store, stopped her work and listened.

The sirens shrieked on and on, and she wondered if the whole town was on fire. Then the bells of the Presbyterian church added their chimes, car horns honked in the streets, and people on the sidewalk shouted as they rushed by the store window. Now Annie knew—something important had happened.

Pulse racing, she jumped up from her desk and clicked on the little radio that sat on the counter. Mr. McGinnis, salesman Bob Taylor, and the deliverymen all clustered around her. A woman who'd been looking at sofas left an opened Hide-a-bed and joined them as they listened to the news.

". . . Japan accepts the surrender terms of the Allies. The war is over!"

"Wahoo!" Bob jammed his fists into the air, index and middle fingers of both hands stretched into triumphant Vs.

The truck driver pounded the counter. "About time! They knew they were licked."

Annie held her breath, hardly daring to believe it. The war is over? Would life finally get back to normal?

For more than three long years—since early 1942—everyone had pulled together: buying ration stamps and bonds, saving scrap metal, some even making huge balls from gum wrappers. People had done without, trying not to complain about all their favorite foods being rationed. And all that time the radio reported the news about bombing and fighting—battles won and lost—while everyone hoped the GIs would be lucky enough to make it through with bodies and minds intact.

Mr. McGinnis clicked off the radio. "The store is now officially closed," he announced. "Take tomorrow off, too. Harry'll be coming home soon, and my wife'll want to celebrate."

"But what about my couch?" the customer asked.

Bob steered her toward the door, promising, "Don't worry, I won't sell it out from under you."

Annie felt sorry for Bob. This woman had come in every few days for several weeks, trying to make up her mind. Bob had been patient with her, but how could anyone think about sofas at a time like this? The boss's son and all the other men would be coming home! A whole new world had just begun.

Annie dumped her ledgers into a desk drawer, tossed papers into a pile, then grabbed her purse. She'd have to walk home—her mother was saving gas rations so they could visit relatives at Christmas.

She was too excited to drive, anyway. In the street, traffic crept bumper to bumper—a pandemonium of cars, pickups, and motorcycles. A cacophony of horns mixed with the cheers and screams of the people. Teenagers were crammed into cars to drive around town. In one convertible some of them perched on the seat backs, shrieking and waving hastily scrawled banners.

They're lucky, thought Annie. *Their lives won't be disrupted after all.*

At the beauty parlor next to the furniture store, operators huddled around the radio on the front counter. A customer, her curlers still harnessed to long wires, lifted herself as far as she dared, craning her neck. Her eyes were wide, her mouth a perfect letter "O."

It seemed like the entire town had poured onto the sidewalks that August afternoon. Everyone smiled, shouted, cried, and hugged anyone within reach. Annie pushed her way through the crowds and got more than her share of hugs.

The elderly owner of the dress shop peered out her store's front door. Annie waved to her and shouted, "The war's over!" But the crowd carried her along before she could say more. She was jostled past the five and dime, Dr. Entz's office, and the Ford garage with its used car lot.

The residential section of town lay just beyond the Presbyterian church. The crowd thinned there, and as she walked past the houses, people burst out of front doors, scurried down porch steps, jumped up and down, danced on the sidewalks. Annie dodged blow-out noise makers, children, and barking dogs. Someone grabbed her and twirled her around, and then a man in uniform—a guy she'd barely known in college—kissed her smack on the lips.

Tasting the salt of tears, she flashed him a victory sign and said, "Welcome home!" But he'd already grabbed another girl and was making his way in the opposite direction.

The entire neighborhood seemed to have gathered on the McGinnis front lawn, singing "When Harry Comes Marching Home." Her boss, already there, pulled her into a conga line and they snaked around the yard.

Joy bubbled inside her as she felt the years of tension, fear, and waiting melt away. Life would begin again. She didn't even worry that someone from her Mennonite church might see her dancing! Today, she let the line carry her along, as though she'd been dancing all her life.

All the Mennonite young men were gone, too. But most of them were scattered through the states in civilian public service camps. When they came home from CPS, would their lives return to normal? So much had happened. What would "normal" be now?

The impromptu dance ended with wild cheers, and Annie tugged furtively at the garters that held her sagging rayon stockings—she hoped nylons would soon be available again in the stores. That part of "normal" would be nice.

Annie found Mrs. McGinnis, hugged and congratulated her, then went on. Many windows displayed flags with a blue star for each serviceman in the family—one house had four—and she breathed a prayer of thanks. They'd be coming home, too.

But as she passed the windows with gold stars, Annie's tears of happiness mingled with grief. She'd known some of those boys. Their families would never welcome them home again.

In another four blocks, just before peach orchards and vineyards stretched into the countryside, Annie reached her house. Her mother was on the front lawn, talking excitedly with neighbors. When she saw Annie, she held out her arms. "I wondered if you'd come home early!"

As Annie embraced her mother, she noticed a smell coming from the house. "Is something burning?"

Her mother gasped and ran inside. Annie followed. In a pot of hot fat on the kitchen stove were four twisted rectangles of *rollkoaka,* burnt beyond redemption. On the bread board lay the last few rolled-out slices of dough.

"*Yauma,*" her mother wailed in exasperation. Turning off the burner with one hand, she moved the pot off the stove with the other, and explained, "I wanted to have a quick supper so we could get to prayer meeting early. The church will be full."

Annie grabbed a fork and poked at the ruined *rollkoaka.* "The neighbor's chickens will love them," she laughed. "There're still enough good ones, though, for us."

As she carried plates and utensils to the table, she saw the mail in the center of the table and sorted through it. The telephone bill, a store advertisement, the Mennonite *Zionsbote* magazine, and a letter for her.

It was postmarked Placerville and was from Jonah Krause, a conscientious objector who was in the CPS camp in the mountains near Sacramento. Annie gave a wry smile at his crooked printing on the envelope, then jammed it into her skirt pocket and finished setting the table.

"*Kindt,* aren't you going to open it?"

Annie hated being called a child, but instead of protesting, she just said, "Later."

Three years ago, a different letter, from another young man, would've sent her running to her room to tear it open and devour it. That letter would have been postmarked from the desert of Arizona.

Her mother poured the blackened fat into an old lard can. "Such a nice boy, that Jonah. A hard worker. And so handsome! He'd be a good husband."

Annie had heard that too many times, with several different names—Ben, Aaron, Pete . . .

Not answering, she went into the cool cellar and brought up a watermelon to complete the meal.

As for Jonah, he was okay. A good friend. Sometimes it seemed as though he wanted more, but she couldn't see herself married to him.

Most of the girls in her church had married right after high school. Here she was, twenty-two—practically an old maid.

Somehow, none of those good-looking men had been right for her. And once she'd met Donald Nakamura, no one else had measured up—not in personality, not in manners, not even in intelligence. Now, with the war over, maybe she'd meet someone as special as he.

Her mother put the platter of salvaged *rollkoaka* on the table, and they bowed their heads as she thanked God for the food: "*Danke lieber Heiland für dies essen. Amen.*"

Annie loved the crisp, salty *rollkoaka,* but today she was too nervous to eat.

Her mother didn't seem to notice. After her third slice of watermelon, Mrs. Penner got up to dump the rinds into the bucket under the sink. "I guess now the CPS camps will close. It'll be good to have all the young men back in church," she said. Then she sat down at the table to spread jam on a last *rollkoaka* for a dessert.

Annie nodded. The town would probably have a parade and a band concert to honor all the returning servicemen—maybe even fireworks afterward. But there'd be no special fanfare for the conscientious objectors. The church would welcome them back into the fold and praise God for their obedience, and then they'd pick up their shovels and hoes and go back to work. "At least their families are taking care of their land, and the church pays them a little," Annie said.

Her mother curled her lip. "Just a *kleen baitya.* Five dollars a month!

Not near enough to support a family. Poor Frieda Schmidt has to leave her baby with strangers and work as a telephone operator. Then she has to drive home in the middle of the night on winding mountain roads."

"Well, that'll be over, too." Annie never had understood why everyone felt so sorry for Frieda. It'd been her choice to marry at seventeen and follow her husband to Placerville. Her life would have been a lot easier if she'd had the patience to wait for marriage until the war ended. Still, Annie thought it must be wonderful to love someone that much.

While washing the dishes, Annie listened to the radio. The station replayed President Truman's words: "This is a great day, the day we've been waiting for . . . free governments . . . restore peace to the world."

After the weather report—rain predicted after the long, dry spell—the station switched to ballroom music. Annie closed her eyes and moved her shoulders dreamily to the music.

Her mother cleared her throat. Dutifully, Annie clicked off the radio and went to her room to get ready for church. But oh, that smooth melody reminded her of Donald, the way his deep, rich voice broke into song whenever a chance word reminded him of some lyrics.

As her mother had predicted, the church was filled. In the fervency of the occasion, the kneeling people didn't wait their turns. Instead, in an unusual rush of openness, several prayed aloud at once, weeping, praising, thanking, even singing snatches of songs.

Annie prayed, too—but silently. Her petition was for *all* the boys to come home safely, especially those she'd known in college. Surely God didn't love only Mennonites. And through the whole evening her heart begged, *Please—wherever he is, please bring Donald back. He mustn't be just another gold star.*

After church, Annie and her mother were quiet on the drive home. Once there, Annie kissed her mother on the cheek and went right to her bedroom.

Her college yearbooks were on the lowest shelf of her bookcase. When she pulled out the 1942 edition, the pages fell open by themselves, right to the page where his senior picture was.

Donald Nakamura. Thick black hair mounded over his forehead. There was that slight tilt of his head. His eyes were so dark they shone like onyx, and seemed to be smiling at her. Her mind whirled, and memories flooded over her—memories she didn't have the strength to escape.

Annie met Florence Nakamura during their freshman year at the college just outside of Rosemond. Annie had recently moved to the area and Florence was a Baptist minister's daughter. She and Annie became best friends. They made a lot of other friends, too—both guys and girls. But after Annie met Florence's brother, Donald, all the other boys seemed to fade. Donald—slim, handsome, broad shouldered—his distinctive walk radiating confidence.

When Florence introduced Donald to Annie, he said in his deep and mellow voice, "You're new, aren't you?"

"Is it that obvious?" Annie felt a flutter just below her sternum. Hoping she looked presentable, she resisted the urge to make sure her blouse was tucked in neatly.

He cocked his head and raked back his already smooth hair. "It's just that I'm sure I would've noticed you before." As he left, she heard him sing softly—something about a "strawberry blonde." Puzzled, Annie wrinkled her forehead at Florence.

Florence shrugged. "A senior. Thinks he's too grown-up for us lowly freshmen."

But Florence was wrong. The next day Donald and his friends joined them for lunch under a huge oak tree on the school lawn—and Annie's whole life changed.

She told her mother about Florence, that the Nakamuras had acres of the best strawberries in the valley. But she saw no reason to mention Donald.

At first he was just one of the guys, the leader of the Christian Life on Campus Club, known as the CLOC Club. And later—well, there was never a "right" time to tell her mother about him.

Then the evacuation of the Japanese swept him away, but he'd written from the internment camp.

When the letters stopped, she waited—wondering and grieving. Then she tried to forget him. *With all the pretty Japanese girls in the camp,* Annie reasoned, *he probably lost interest in me.*

It's for the best, she told herself. *Maybe I read more into his letters than he intended. Maybe it's God's will.*

But if it *was* His will, why couldn't she fall in love with one of the Mennonite guys—a nice, fun-loving, dependable German boy who met with the approval of both her mother and the church?

Everyone knew that Mennonites married Mennonites. That's why Annie's mother moved to the farm community of Rosemond. Annie's father died when she was still in grade school, and when Annie grew old enough to date, her mother chose a large Mennonite Brethren church full of young people.

Annie tried to get interested in the boys in her church. She even dated several of them. She admired their cars, praised their fine tractors, and asked about their favorite sports teams. She laughed at the jokes she heard over and over. But none of the boys made her feel the way Donald did.

Please, Lord, do I have to settle for less? Isn't there one German boy who can light up my heart and make it flutter? Someone whose slightest touch can set my senses on fire and send me floating up into the clouds?

She'd kept his letters—just three of them—hidden in her closet. For three years they'd been sitting on the shelf behind boxes of out-of-season clothes. Not to deceive her mother, she told herself, but to keep from hurting her.

Now, she wondered, *Is God punishing me for hanging on to the memories?* If she got rid of the letters, would he bring her the perfect Mennonite guy? Annie laid the open yearbook on the bed. Standing on a chair, she reached to the closet shelf and shoved the boxes aside. There they were—the letters in a thin packet tied with a red ribbon.

Her heart skipped a beat. She'd been so thrilled to receive them and had read them over and over until she knew them by memory. Still, she ached to see the words again, and couldn't help taking the packet down. Settling into the chair, she caressed the envelopes with her fingertips, then slid the paper out. The familiar handwriting again hurtled her backward through the years.

Chapter Two

DONALD'S FIRST LETTER ARRIVED. It was dated August 28, 1942, and enclosed in the same envelope with Florence's letter, postmarked from the Gila River internment camp. It arrived two weeks after that, and by then it had been over a month since he'd left—a long, long month. During that time Annie wondered where he was, how he was getting along, whether he really would write as he'd promised. Annie tore open the envelope and found Donald's letter. She carefully unfolded it, and just the feel of the paper, the faint smell of ink, brought him close.

Dear Annie:

I hope you enjoyed your summer vacation and are ready to get back to classes. I miss all those swell times we had, eating lunch together on the school lawn under the oak tree.

Before the internment, Florence told Annie that Donald liked her. Annie casually answered, "I'm glad. He's a nice guy."

But Florence shook her head. "No. I mean he *really* likes you. When he looks at you, he gets all goo-goo-eyed."

At first, Annie didn't know what to think. He certainly didn't fit the category of "a good Mennonite boy." Still, she felt honored that such a popular guy thought so much of her. But it wouldn't be right to lead him on either.

The next time they were together she watched him a little more closely. Sure enough. When he talked to her, his face took on a beautiful golden glow and his eyes turned soft—almost adoring. She got a funny, tingly feeling and could hardly breathe. She'd seen that expression before—on the faces of couples who were in love. She'd seen it in Frieda's blue eyes—and on her entire face—when she looked at Dan Schmidt.

She shivered, wondering if that was what love felt and looked like. But then she gave herself a mental shake. This couldn't be happening. Not to her. Not with a Japanese boy. She'd be the talk of the church, and her mother would have kittens.

But all during that fall of 1941, whenever their group of friends spent time sitting on the lawn under the trees, she noticed that he usually sat next to her, sometimes asking others to scoot over to make room for him.

And there were other little things. Things she thought at first were accidents—the touch of his shoe against hers or his hand brushing against her arm. Soon the others noticed, and one of the girls advised Annie, "Watch it, kiddo; don't get in too deep."

The problem was, she liked the feeling and looked forward to seeing him. She missed him when he wasn't around.

But she never dreamed that she'd miss him the way she did now—now that he'd been sent away.

His first letter described the camp at Gila River, Arizona, as a desert with the hot wind blowing sand into their faces. They lived in barracks that had been divided into several small rooms, with entire families assigned to one little room. Although there were no closets, Donald had found scrap lumber and built shelves for their clothes. People worked in vegetable fields under the hot sun while others built a school and a machine shop. Some had even talked about leveling an area for an athletic field so the kids would have something to do.

I was lucky to get a job in the hospital. With thousands of people here, there's always somebody sick or hurt. We treat everything from scorpion bites and sunstroke to chicken pox and childbirth.

I would have written a lot sooner but there just isn't any privacy here. And with my father gone, I have to take care of my family. We still haven't heard where he is, so please pray that he's all right and will be released soon. I'm holding on to that verse you gave me.

Annie wiped away tears. Donald wrote just the way he talked, and she could hear his voice as she read. It was as if he were beside her, walking with her on the way to her psychology class in the science building, where he took all his premed classes.

The first time he'd caught up with her, she felt tongue-tied and could hardly speak. But he kept the conversation going, never running out of things to say. After that, she looked forward to those few minutes alone with him.

He'd read a lot of the authors she enjoyed—Charles Dickens, Mark Twain, John Steinbeck, Sinclair Lewis, Lloyd C. Douglas—and even suggested other books she might like.

He enjoyed studying the Bible and said it opened up his mind, gave him direction, and helped him solve problems. Like her, he loved classical and sacred music. One day, when she admitted to playing piano at church, he asked her to accompany him for the solo he was singing at the next CLOC Club meeting. "My favorite song is 'His Eye Is on the Sparrow.' Do you know it?"

When she nodded, he added, "It'll be practice for 'Showers of Blessing.' You know, the radio program. Saturdays at 10 A.M. Ever listen to it? The ministers in town take turns preaching. Once a month, my father gives the sermon. Sometimes I get roped into singing."

"'Showers of Blessing,' hmm?" Florence had told Annie about her father and the Japanese Baptist church he pastored, but she hadn't mentioned a radio broadcast. Annie decided to tune in at the first chance.

Donald asked her about Mennonites. "I thought all the women wore little caps, but I haven't seen any of those around here."

She shrugged. "Some do, some don't." She explained about the different branches of Mennonites, that the Old Order followed a strict ruling on clothes, but the modern denominations were more concerned about personal relationship to the Lord. "The MB's, Mennonite Brethren, doctrine is pretty close to that of the Baptists, except for our nonresistance."

"What's that all about?" he asked, his eyes widening.

"Well, instead of going to war, Mennonites believe in nonviolent ways to serve both God and country. Like forestry, working in hospitals, that sort of thing. Wherever help is needed. Otherwise, we're about the same as other people."

She thought a bit, then laughed, embarrassed. "Well . . . maybe we're a few years behind in clothing styles. I guess hairstyles, too. The older women slick their hair back into a tight *schups*."

"*Schups?*"

"You know, a knot." Pulling her hair back, she twisted it into a ball at her neckline to demonstrate and then shook it loose.

He cocked his head, studying her. "You sure have pretty hair." He reached out and touched the ends of it, his fingers grazing her neck.

She felt an electric thrill throughout her body. Startled, she drew back.

He gave an embarrassed laugh that turned into a cough, and his face colored. "Sorry. Didn't mean to be fresh. Just wondered how you'd look with a—what did you call it—a *schups?*"

They reached her classroom door. She leaned against the wall for support, holding her textbook against her chest while they finished their conversation. "I'll never have one," she protested. "Not even if I get kicked out of church." She knew she was babbling, and she hoped he couldn't hear her heart pounding.

He frowned. "They'd do that? Your church?"

"No, just kidding. But there are so many rules—customs from way back—and people look at you funny if you don't follow them."

"There aren't many Mennonites here in college, are there?" said Donald. "What makes you different?"

He seemed to know her better than she knew herself. "Maybe it's because of my dad. He felt bad about having to quit school to support his family, and he wanted me to get a good education, to learn more than just how to cook and keep house."

He looked at her with a funny little smile. "Can you?"

"Can I what?"

"Can you . . . um . . . cook?"

Her legs felt shaky, and she curled her toes to tense her leg muscles. "Oh, sure. When it comes to food, I'm right there with the best of them. *Borscht, tvehbock, verenikya*—"

"Whoa, whoa. I know *borscht* is cabbage soup, and *tvehbock* are double-decker buns. But that last one—"

She started to explain that *verenikya* were pockets of dough filled with cottage cheese, but Donald looked around and noticed the empty hallway. "Uh-oh. I'm going to be late to class. See you later," he called back to her.

In psychology, she collapsed onto the nearest empty seat and tried to concentrate on the lecture. But she still tingled from the touch of Donald's fingers on her neck, and his voice echoed in her mind. Tomorrow she would tuck a flower in her hair. And someday she'd bring him a *verenikya* for lunch.

But then came December 7. Japan bombed Pearl Harbor, and everything changed.

Highway 99 was a dividing line. West of it, which was closer to the coast, was designated as Zone 1, and the east side of Highway 99 was Zone 2. All the Japanese who lived in Zone 1 were evacuated.

Rosemond was in Zone 2, and the Japanese in that area were not considered a threat. Nevertheless, Florence dropped out of school. Donald still attended, but Annie could tell he was worried. Some kids called him a "dirty Jap"—even to his face. Although he held his head high and kept a polite face, she knew he felt humiliated. Annie and his other real friends told him to consider the source and assured him he was as American as anyone else. But she knew the slurs still hurt him.

One day in history class, the girl behind her hissed, "Jap lover! If you know what's good for you, you'll stay away from that guy."

Shocked, Annie turned and stared at the girl, and for the first time realized how hard it was to follow the Bible's command to love one's enemies. "I'm German," Annie said evenly. "Are you afraid of me too?"

The girl slumped back into her seat, glancing at the students around them. Most of the class watched, saying nothing.

Finally the girl mumbled, “Forget it.” But after that she sat on the opposite side of the room from Annie.

The day before Christmas vacation Donald met her in the hallway between classes. His face was pale and his eyes had trouble meeting hers. She knew something was terribly wrong.

He spoke softly, choking on the words. “My father . . . he’s been arrested!”

“What?” Surely she’d heard wrong.

“The FBI.” He ran his hands through his hair. “In the middle of the night . . . they hammered on our door, and when he answered, they put handcuffs on him. My father!”

“Why?”

“They wouldn’t say. They searched our house from top to bottom . . . left everything in a mess. Took his short-wave radio, my grandfather’s Japanese newspapers, my binoculars, my camera—”

“But . . . but . . . your father’s a minister!”

“Some people object to his broadcasts. Maybe those same people turned him in.”

“For a Christian message? That doesn’t make sense.”

“At the end of his regular message, he always gave a short sermon for our older people—in Japanese.”

Annie stared into his eyes. “What’s wrong with that?”

“Maybe the FBI thought it was in code . . . for the enemy.” He sighed as he leaned against the wall, his hands in his pockets, his head down.

Annie felt cold all over. If the FBI arrested his father, would Donald be next? “Where is he now?”

“They wouldn’t say. Just told us to stay home. Keep off the highway.”

“How are you going to finish school? You’ve got to graduate!”

He lifted his shoulders, then let them slump. “What’s the use?” he sighed.

Annie watched him, silently hurting for him. What should she say? How could she encourage him? Then she remembered a passage they’d read in CLOC Club recently—Psalm 46:1. She touched Donald’s arm.

"Remember the verse: 'God is our refuge and strength, a very present help in trouble'?"

For a minute he didn't answer. Then he nodded and reached for her hand. Stroking it with his thumb, he murmured, "Thanks. You always know the right thing to say." He released her hand and they moved apart as a group of students came toward them.

The next spring, Donald graduated earlier than the rest of his class. His teachers were worried about the growing hostility toward the Japanese. They gave him clearance papers to show any suspicious vigilante that he had a right to be on the road. With all the rumors in the air, they also let him finish his classes ahead of time and take the exams, in case there might be more trouble.

Annie looked back at the letter and re-read the last line. He closed with, *I miss you and your way of cheering me up. It sure would be nice to have a picture of you.*

Yours truly, Donald

She sighed as she read his name, smiling at the way he signed with a flourish.

Florence's letter went into more detail about life in the camp. The sand was everywhere—in their hair, in their faces, and even in their food. It blew in through cracks in the buildings. Never any privacy—not even in the communal rest rooms, which had no separate stalls.

Florence worked as a typist in the community office and took night classes in painting and baton twirling.

My grandmother's been sick. She can barely walk to the mess hall, and then she hardly eats anything. The doctor doesn't know what's wrong, but Donald thinks her heart is broken.

Annie answered both letters that very evening and mailed them in the same envelope the next day. She tried to sound cheerful—told them about her summer fruit-packing job, the tough old forelady barking at the packers and the prissy little fruit inspector poking into the boxes of peaches. Just for the fun of it, she and her coworkers even speculated on a romance between the inspector and forelady, and they lamented that all the machinery breakdowns would keep the packers from earning enough money to buy them a wedding present.

She gave Donald and Florence more Scripture promises as well, hoping to encourage them. In Donald's letter, she added a little red strawberry heart next to her signature, hoping he wouldn't think her too bold. Then she slipped in a snapshot of herself sitting on the empty loading dock of the packing shed. Her feet dangled over the edge of the dock and one arm was wrapped around a supporting post. *To Donald. Wish you were here,* she wrote on the picture.

School started again right after Labor Day, and she so missed both Florence and Donald. It just wasn't the same without them on campus.

Donald's answer, again included with Florence's, reached her a month later, during the first week of October. His father had been located in a prison in New Mexico, and people were trying to get him cleared. At camp, sports leagues and a drama group had been organized. The different Protestant church groups had combined their services, with pastors from Phoenix and Mesa taking turns preaching. After he sang a solo in one of the services, Donald had been asked to help form a choir.

But I have so much bitterness and confusion about my future. I was so sure I was called to be a doctor, but what medical school would admit a prisoner? You're right, though. I must trust in the Lord for strength and courage. I'll try to follow your advice and stay close to him.

At least my work in the hospital is good experience, even though the equipment is old and the doctors don't seem to know what they're doing. Sometimes they even ask me for advice!

Annie loved that part. Back in college, soon after she'd met him, she asked, "What do you want to be when you grow up? A farmer like your grandfather or a preacher like your dad?"

Just then the civil defense siren shrieked, and they all jumped up from the lawn, grabbed their lunch sacks, and filed into the hall where they lined up against the wall. As they stood there, Donald threw his shoulders back—Annie noticed he was nearly a head taller than she—and murmured his answer to her last question. "My father would like me in the ministry. But I'm going to be a doctor. Ever since I was little, I've wanted that." Flexing his nimble fingers, he added, "The Lord can use doctors, too."

Florence, on the other side of her, whispered, "Not if you make mistakes, cutting people up."

Donald pointed his finger at his sister and clicked his tongue. Winking at Annie, he said to Florence, "I won't make mistakes. I'll just take out your tonsils and plant them next to your appendix."

Annie could imagine him working in the camp hospital, giving advice to the doctors, and she smiled. It was so typical of him. He was confident, but not cocky. Not when it was important. The doctors must have appreciated his insight. How terribly sad if, with his talent and brains and all the years of preparation, his lifelong dream were to be shattered.

Thanks for the picture. When I look at your lovely face, I remember your sweet smile and the good times we had together. If only the war would end so I can get out of this concentration camp and see you again.

Please write soon. Your letters mean so much to me. Don't forget the meetings under the oak tree. When I close my eyes, I dream I'm with you again.

Love, Donald

Love! Annie held the letter to her face. Inhaling deeply, she could almost smell his freshly starched shirt and the faint scent of Brylcreem.

His last letter was dated October 1, 1942.

Good news! My father's here. He doesn't talk much about the prison, but I know it must have been awfully hard on him. And he's sad his ministry was suspected. Now he's counseling the discouraged and helping with the combined services.

When he arrived, my grandmother seemed to improve at the sight of her son, but now she is slipping again.

Donald's grandmother. Annie remembered her, too. She and her mother had bought their first strawberries from the Nakamuras right before the evacuation. Annie had nearly died of embarrassment while her mother quibbled over the price and questioned the amount of change. And all the while, the elderly woman had been friendly and patient.

My father's pleased that I'm leading the choir. It's big, about fifty members. No problem getting them to come to practice—there's not much else to do in the evenings. And it's fun. Besides singing Sunday mornings, we perform pop music at socials.

When I'm not working at the hospital, I teach biology in the high school. It keeps me awfully busy, but that's what I need.

I carry your picture with me always and pretend I'm that post you're holding. At night I hug my straw pillow, but it's a poor substitute for you. Remember the song "I See You in my Dreams"? It's true. But then I wake up and realize how far apart we are, and it nearly drives me crazy. I think of you day and night.

Annie closed her eyes and wished that he were beside her, their arms around each other. She still felt the thrill, the complete joy of being near him.

Those times under the oak tree were so special.

The last day she'd seen him, they stood under that oak tree. His eyes were sad and his lips tense. "Have you heard? All the rest of us 'Japs' are being sent to those concentration camps. Zone 2 . . . east of the highway . . . makes no difference. Everyone's got to go." His voice was harsh.

"But you're an American citizen!"

"Right now, that isn't worth a plugged nickel."

"When . . . when are you going?"

"We register right away."

"No." She grabbed his arm. "Where will you go?"

He shrugged. "All I know is we've got six days to get ready. Sell or store all our stuff and leave. Six days!"

"You can't leave!"

It happened so naturally. She was in his arms, his face nestled in her hair, and it felt so right. "I don't want to go," he'd murmured. "You're the best thing in my life. But there's nothing I can do about it. Not a thing."

Hot tears streamed down her cheeks, and then suddenly his lips were on hers—soft and tender—and she was swept away with a passion she'd never felt before. At that moment, she knew she'd never love anyone else the way she loved him.

Then he was gone.

When I get out of here, I'm coming to see you. We'll celebrate with a picnic. You bring the sandwiches; I'll bring strawberries. Did you know strawberries are called the fruit of love? It is because they're heart-shaped. And sweet, like you. Darling Annie, you're always in my thoughts.

Love, Donald

Now, Annie read the last paragraphs over and over, picturing his face—his shining dark eyes, his soft, smiling lips. After saying all those intimate words, how could he have stopped writing?

But three years is such a long time. She'd been young and naive, thrilled by his attention. In his letters, Donald had never mentioned any new friends, but surely he'd been as popular in the camp as he was at college. By now, he'd be twenty-five. A grown man. He must have met a lot of pretty Japanese girls. What if he'd fallen in love with one of them? What if he was married? He could even be a father!

The thought stabbed through her heart.

She could never destroy his letters. He said he'd come see her, and she'd wait until he did. There had to be a good reason why he stopped writing.

Florence had written:

I don't know when or if I'll finish college. I wish I could be there with you, sitting next to you in bookkeeping, studying in the library, laughing about silly things. Maybe next year.

As usual, she replied to both Florence's and Donald's letters the same evening she received them and mailed them in the same envelope the next day.

A month passed and she didn't hear from them, so she wrote again.

After she wrote three letters with no answers, she asked some of Donald's college friends about him. But by then, only a few of them were left on campus, and they'd lost touch with him. They smiled at her with a look of pity, as though she was foolish to hang on to a little college flirtation.

One evening after church, she even stopped Menno Bartel in the parking lot. He'd been the Nakamuras' neighbor and was tending their farm. "Have you . . . um . . . kept in touch with the Nakamuras?"

"*Yo,* I send them reports on the farm. Told them the strawberries are doing well."

"Do they . . . have they written back?"

"Vell, *yo,* the rev'rent, he writes thanks." Mr. Bartel removed his hat, scratched his head, then put the hat back on. "How do you know them?"

Her face grew hot, and she was glad they weren't standing under a light. "Their daughter Florence and I were friends in school. I just wondered, uh, how the family was doing."

"He says nothing about the family. Just thanks me for news about the crop." He looked toward his car. "The missus is waiting. I must go."

"But . . . do you know if they're still at Gila River?"

"Sure, Gila River." He nodded. "Same as always."

That night, Annie wrote again, but this time just to Donald. She asked about his choir, his hospital work, and what it was like teaching high school kids. He'd have to answer all the questions. Maybe he'd explain why he hadn't written.

But she never heard from him again.

If only there'd been someone for her to confide in. She'd often wished that she could tell her mother about her feelings, her worries. But her mother wouldn't have understood. Annie knew that her mother wanted the best for her, but only if the best was a Mennonite. And nothing was more important than what people thought of you. Had her father lived, would he have understood?

Loneliness had washed over her, and she wondered if she would ever be happy again.

The war had turned life upside down. Every week at least one student was drafted, and blue stars on the college bulletin board kept being added. Annie felt sad when gold stars appeared.

She'd avoided the oak tree. Just seeing it made her cry. And without Donald's leadership in the CLOC Club, attendance had dwindled.

To boost servicemen's morale, girls were encouraged to write them, and Annie's classmates corresponded with long lists of grateful soldiers. Annie had done the same for young men in the civilian camps, but their answers were usually boring. Jonah's spelling was terrible, but at least he remembered to whom he was writing. One guy got mixed up and signed his letter, *Your son, Henry.* It made her wonder what he'd written in his letter to his mother.

Nineteen forty-three and forty-four came and went—and Annie still heard nothing from or about Donald. In April of 1945, with her senior year nearly over, she was in the school library studying. The student across from her was reading the *Rosemond Recorder,* the town's newspaper. On the page facing Annie was a letter from an overseas soldier. He'd met a Japanese-American boy from home who was ". . . serving in the 442nd Regimental Combat Team, an all-Nisei regiment."

Nisei! American-born, second-generation Japanese. Like Donald. If he still hadn't been accepted into medical school, could Donald possibly be in the Army?

Annie had sat back in her chair, wondering what her church would think of that—Japanese-Americans fighting an American war. Mennonites didn't believe in fighting—period. All their young men were advised to register as conscientious objectors, Class 4-E. Some had compromised and joined the Army, but as a noncombatant, Class 1-A-O. A few dared to go straight 1-A, available immediately for military service.

She'd even heard of one family that had escaped to America from Russia to avoid military service there. Out of gratitude to America, three of that family's sons had enlisted in the United States Army.

She respected the conscientious objectors, if that was their own belief and not just what they were told to do. But *somebody* had to stop Hitler and his terrible Nazis, as well as Tojo and his *kamikazes.* And those who were brave enough to risk their lives deserved to be honored.

If Donald had enlisted, she'd be proud of him. He wouldn't go in as a noncombatant. She knew he'd go all the way and do the best he could.

But the thought of him in danger made her freeze. What if he'd been sent to fight? What if he had been wounded, captured . . . or killed?

The rest of her senior year and graduation went by in a blur. She was hired at the furniture store after graduation, and her days were filled with columns of numbers.

But throughout the war she'd faithfully listened to radio news and scanned the papers for familiar names. One of Donald's friends was missing in action, another was killed in Germany, and still another in the Philippines. But where was Donald?

Now, finally, the war was over, and she still didn't know.

Dear Lord, bring him safely home. The thought of seeing him again filled her with excitement and yearning, but those feelings were mixed with dread for what she might learn—about where he was or what had happened to him.

Footsteps clicked in the hall. With trembling fingers, Annie slid the letters into the yearbook and closed it. She opened the envelope from Jonah and took out the page of ruled binder paper just as her mother opened the door.

"You didn't eat much supper. Want a crust of *ruggebrot?*"

Usually she would have jumped at the chance for a heel of her mother's freshly baked rye bread. But tonight, food didn't interest her. "Thanks. I'll wait until breakfast."

Annie resented her mother's popping in without knocking. She'd complained several times over the years, but her mother always acted hurt. "Just the two of us. We've no secrets. Why be formal?"

No secrets—not until Donald. "You were right," she said as she scanned the letter from Jonah. "He says they'll be closing down the camps as soon as the war is over. So some of the guys will leave in a week or two."

Her mother smiled. *"Na, gote.* About time we get our men back. It's not right for young women to be alone. Maybe now we'll hear wedding bells."

Annie thought of her friend Malinda, who was a year older than she. Malinda had an on-and-off romance with a man sent to New Jersey to work in a mental hospital. Would he come home now, or decide to stay there and work a regular paying job? Where did Malinda fit into his plans?

Her mother still stood there, an eager look on her face.

Annie raised her eyebrows. "Did you want something?"

Her mother's cheeks flushed and she shrugged her shoulders. "Just wondered what your young man had to say."

"Mom! He's not *my young man.*" She handed the sheet of paper to her mother. "Here. Read it yourself. There's nothing personal."

Chapter Three

A FEW MILES SOUTH OF FRESNO, Donald Nakamura stepped out of a battered Ford sedan. He thanked the driver and stepped off the road onto the shoulder. Shifting his duffel bag, he watched the car drive off, then he sighed deeply. He'd thought the war would go on forever, but finally Japan had surrendered.

It had taken two more months for his points to be calculated, qualifying him to be discharged. With all his medals, his wounds, and extra service in the Philippines, he'd been released before many of the others. They had to stay and mop up.

Now, after ten long hours on the road, he was on the last leg of the journey home. Even the oleander bushes bordering the highway looked like old friends.

He squinted into the afternoon sun, recalling how chilled he'd been much earlier in the day.

It was cold as Donald started out in the early morning, up north in Marysville where he'd been discharged. He walked briskly along the 99—after all the action he saw in the army, all the marching and maneuvers, he was in good physical condition. He could probably double-time all the way, but hitchhiking would be faster, and he was eager to get home. To his real home—not Gila River this time.

Some sparrows chattered and flitted past overhead, landing in three rows on the power lines ahead. They reminded him of his favorite hymn, and he belted it out to the whole universe.

"I sing because I'm happy. I sing because I'm free!" Free from the internment camp, free from the war, free in his own country. "His eye is on the sparrow—and I know He watches me."

Donald wore his uniform, thinking it would help him get rides. But traffic was light that time of day. He walked over a mile before a Filipino truck driver stopped and took him as far as Stockton.

There, he found a pay phone and called his folks to tell them he was on his way home. It was great to hear their voices, and he could hardly wait to see them, his grandfather, the strawberry farm . . . and Annie. No matter what, he had to see her, had to learn what had happened to her.

He'd mentioned her to a couple of his army buddies and, after they pestered, showed them her picture. But when she didn't answer his letters, they told him, "What you expect, man? She's *hakkujin*—a Cauc. You want a real woman, someone to stick with you; get one of our own kind."

He couldn't explain it. It wasn't because Annie was Caucasian that he wanted her, but because she was . . . well, she was Annie, the girl he loved. And when he got home he would find out why she stopped writing.

He walked into a café near the highway just outside of Stockton, slid onto a stool at the counter and folded his cap on his knee. The waitress, a gum-chewing teenager, looked at him funny and asked if he was Chinese.

He said, "I'm an American."

She looked doubtful, but when the cook yelled, "Two sunny-side up on ham!" she quickly handed him a menu and turned to take the food from the cook.

The wonderful smell nearly made him drool. He shoved the menu aside and pointed to the plate the waitress was carrying. "I'll have the same." It'd been a long time since he'd had fresh eggs and real meat.

When she brought him the food, she said, "I couldda sworn you were Chinese or something."

He winked at her. "That's okay. You Caucasians all look alike, too." It wasn't true, certainly not for him, but it got a smile out of her as she refilled his coffee cup.

He paid his bill and headed out the door, passing a large man who was coming in. The man turned and stared at him through the glass door, but Donald waved and went on. He walked back to the highway, his stomach pleasantly full. He savored the leftover taste of freshly buttered toast and salty ham, the stickiness of egg yolk on the roof of his mouth. The coffee had been good and strong, freshly made.

The sun climbed, warming his back. Switching his duffel bag to his other shoulder, he marched down the highway.

This time his uniform had attracted plenty of attention. People skidded to a stop and backed up to him. But when they caught a good look at his face, they peeled away as though they'd seen a ghost. Did they think that the war was still on and that he was the enemy?

Maybe he really would have to hoof it all the way. Well, he'd had plenty of that in Italy, up and down bare scrubby mountains. At least here he didn't need to watch for land mines. Or dash into the line of fire to rescue the wounded, patching them up until he could get them to the battalion aid station.

All he had to carry now was the pack on his shoulder. Before his promotions, he'd hoisted plenty of wounded—mostly on stretchers, but some onto that very shoulder—rushing them to safety. Too many hadn't made it.

But they'd all proved their loyalty to the country. Brave men, the 442nd. They fought as a team wherever they went. Earned a good reputation. At discharge, they were handed medals as freely as pieces of candy. They pinned them on, like all the other guys—Italian, Irish, whatever. They even were given a dress uniform with the diamond-shaped honorable discharge patch—that squatty little eagle in a wreath the guys called a Ruptured Duck—glued on the chest. He thought then,

"I'll finally be accepted as an American." Now he wondered if he even had a country.

He spotted a Giant Orange stand in the distance, realized he was thirsty, and walked faster. An old Buick was parked off the shoulder and an elderly couple stood at the counter drinking their juice.

But when Donald reached the huge round hut, the man behind the counter glared at him and turned away. "No Japs served here."

Heat flooded Donald's body, and his fists clenched. Bile rose into his throat, spoiling the flavor of his breakfast.

He forced his hands to relax, squared his shoulders and faced the scornful man. "Sir, I'm an American. Staff Sgt. Donald Nakamura. Fought the war for you, both in Italy, France, and the Philippines. Received a Bronze Star and a Purple Heart." He fingered his top shirt button. "Want to see my wounds?"

Ignoring him, the man opened the little wooden door, spit on the ground, then closed the door again. He muttered to the other man, "A Jap's a Jap. We got too many of 'em around here."

Donald stood frozen. He'd given up three years of his life. Even after finishing off the Germans, he and several buddies in his outfit had been assigned to another unit. They risked their lives for another go at the enemy in the Pacific, just so guys like this would be free to run their business and sneer at him.

He felt like socking him in his arrogant mouth, but what would that prove? That Japs were no good?

The man wiped the counter, then asked the couple, "You guys done? I'm outta orange. Gotta close up."

The woman put down her half-full cup. "Yeah." She glanced at her husband. "Let's go." She looked back at Donald, and he saw the fear in her eyes. Just like the drivers who hadn't picked him up.

She believes I'm dangerous, too. That I'll attack them. It's a good thing I didn't lose my temper.

He tipped his army cap. "God bless you, ma'am, sir," and walked away, trying not to think how good that cold drink of juice would have tasted.

In a few minutes the old Buick passed him, and the woman turned back to stare at him, her mouth open. Donald shook his head. Some people wouldn't be very comfortable in heaven. "A lot of Japs are there, too," he muttered.

As he walked along, he wondered if he was really free. He helped win one war. Was there still another one to fight?

He thought back to the day the recruiters came to the camp. An all-Nisei battalion, they said. Good pay, benefits, Uncle Sam wants you, too.

He signed up right away. He'd show everyone he was a loyal American. The government had arrested his father, corralled his family, and caused his grandmother's illness. But it was still his country and he would defend it with his life—especially if that would get him out of the miserable camp.

A lot of guys argued with him. "You're crazy. Why fight for a country that stabs us in the back?" Some even challenged him to fight them, but backed off when he flexed his muscles. Working on his family's farm had served him well.

The sun bore down, and Donald's throat was parched. He took off his jacket, smoothing it over his arm. He'd forgotten how hot the San Joaquin Valley could be, even in October. But it was a good dry heat, not humid like the Philippines. There, after weeks of wearing the same clothes, he'd had to practically scrape them off with a knife. But even that had been a relief after the cold, forbidding mountains of Italy and the freezing rain in France.

He came to a farm with a bubbling standpipe and reached for his canteen. After filling it, he trudged to a nearby tree and threw his duffel bag onto the ground in the shade. Sitting on the bag, he upended the canteen, allowing the cool water to trickle down his throat.

His thirst quenched, he leaned his head back against the tree trunk, and suddenly a memory caught him by surprise, stabbing him in the heart.

An oak tree, so much like the one at college where he met Annie. Where he kissed her good-bye.

For months in college, he'd dreamed of kissing her, imagining how it would be, but never thought he'd get up the nerve. Then suddenly it just happened, and it had been more wonderful than he'd imagined. She fit into his arms as though God had made her for him. Her strawberry-blonde hair was soft against his cheek, and he was lost in its sweet, natural fragrance.

Donald shut his eyes and took a deep breath, exhaling slowly to ease the pain of losing her. At the internment camp, her letters pulled him out of despair into delight. He'd known her mother wouldn't be thrilled about him writing, so he persuaded Florence to add his letters to hers. No sense making problems for Annie.

He'd been so excited to get her answers. He remembered each one so vividly—especially the first one. She said she missed him and hoped he was well. Told him things about school. Then she reminded him of the verse she gave him when his father had been arrested—"God is our refuge and strength, a very present help in trouble." She encouraged him to stay close to the Lord, and it was the Lord who had helped then and all through the war. Donald knew he would give him the endurance to get through these bad times, too.

The ending of that letter was the best part:

You look so handsome in your senior picture. Since I can see it every day in our yearbook, I thought it was only fair that you have one of me. If you look at it at ten o'clock in the evening, I'll look at yours. It'll almost be like being together.

He'd studied the black and white snapshot she enclosed, memorizing every feature, imagining the green of her eyes and shining gold of her hair. Finally he slipped it into his wallet, tore out a page from his notebook, and poured out his heart to her.

All of her letters had meant the world to him. But in the last few he received, she sounded different, as if she were holding something back. And she hadn't answered the questions he'd asked. Had he been too pushy? Maybe she wasn't ready to get serious. Maybe that was why she stopped writing. He asked her what was wrong, but after that, she never answered. And as the months went by, he accepted that she'd forgotten him.

But he never stopped looking at her picture at night. The ache in his heart was still there, even when he gave up and spent time with Shirley Otani, the young lady who taught Florence's baton-twirling class.

Shirley was very pretty with long black hair and delicate features. She was slimmer than Annie and moved like a floating feather. But it was soon obvious that he and Shirley had different goals.

With Annie, he'd been able to discuss anything. She understood about spiritual doubts and problems, and they often shared verses of comfort and reassurance.

Instead Shirley had challenged him about God. She sneered, "If there was a God, there wouldn't be any internment camps."

He told her that God's thoughts were far above man's understanding.

"If he's so smart, why doesn't he run the world better?" she shot back. "Why are we here instead of me in Hollywood and you in medical school?"

He hadn't seen much of her after that.

But at the camp hospital where he worked, some of the nurses—both Japanese and Caucasian—had been friendly. One even reminded him of Annie—only she turned out to be married.

He wondered if, by now, Annie might be married, too. A buddy once wrote saying he'd seen Annie with a guy from her church—a Mennonite named Jonah Krause.

Well, it figured.

I have no claims on Annie. Can't expect her to sit home and twiddle her thumbs waiting for me. But she could have written and told him.

He'd met Jonah Krause a few times at Trager's farm equipment store and around town. Nice guy, good-looking, big and blonde with blue eyes. He could see why Annie might fall for him. But that didn't make it hurt less.

The honk of a car horn made him jump. "Wanna ride, soldier?" called a cheerful female voice.

He turned to look and saw that a middle-aged couple in a Ford sedan had pulled up beside him. He gladly accepted their offer. They took him past fields of sugar beets, cotton, and alfalfa, before dropping him off just a little past Fresno.

And now he was nearly home. He crossed the highway to the county road that led eastward to Rosemond, threw his jacket over his shoulder, picked up his bag, and started walking. If he had to, he could hike the twenty miles in three or four hours. It might be hot, but the scenery was great.

After all the ruined cities in Italy, the bombed-out buildings and bridges, the torn-up country and hillsides, the San Joaquin Valley looked wonderfully fruitful and lush. Peach and plum trees lined the road on both sides, resting now that their season was over. They gave way to row after row of grapevines, a few still heavy with green clusters of Thompsons. Other rows were divided by wooden trays heaped with dark, sweet-smelling raisins. Peaceful and perfect. Did America even realize what war was like?

While Donald was at camp, Menno Bartel wrote that the strawberry farm was doing fine. Donald hoped it was still true. He quickened his pace, suddenly more homesick than ever.

His family had been lucky. Although they lost their savings and investments, they still owned their land and their home. Some others had been forced to sell everything. Everything! And people had taken advantage of them, buying up houses and furnishings for a penny on the dollar. He didn't blame those who'd just boarded up their businesses and left them vacant. At least they'd saved face. But now, with nothing left, where would they go?

Donald walked for about half an hour, then an old flatbed pickup rattled to a stop beside him. An elderly man in overalls leaned out the window. "Hop in the back, soldier, if you don't mind the bags of fertilizer. The cab's all full of junk." A glance through the rear window revealed that the man wasn't fooling. Boxes and sacks were piled high, occupying all but the driver's seat.

Donald wiped the sweat off his forehead and looked at the dusty sacks on the bed of the truck. Glancing down, he smiled wryly, realizing what the ride would do to his uniform. What a hero's entrance—coming home, sitting on a throne of manure!

Oh well, anything to get there quicker. He thanked the man and tossed his duffel on one of the sacks. Then he jumped in, dangling his feet over the side as they bumped along.

The old man craned his neck out the window and shouted over the noise of the motor. "Where you headed?"

When Donald told him Rosemond, he said, "I thought you looked familiar. You the Nakamura kid? The strawberry farm?"

Donald yelled back, "That's me."

"I see you got home in one piece. My grandson wasn't so lucky. He's shot up pretty bad."

Donald nodded to the faded blue eyes in the side-view mirror. In spite of the fertilizer, this man meant well. Not like that guy at the Giant Orange. "How was your grandson wounded?"

"Land mine. His leg was the worst. They tried to save it, but . . . you know." His voice trailed off and his eyes blinked rapidly.

"Too bad. That's really hard." He sat listening to the chug-chugging of the pickup. A lot of his buddies hadn't made it. He'd had many close calls himself.

After a while he added, "I got hit in the shoulder, but a couple of weeks in the hospital took care of it."

"Yeah. Nobody gets off free in a war. . . . That your place with the trees in front?"

"That's it. Thanks a lot. And I'm sure sorry about your grandson." When the pickup slowed to a near-stop, he jumped off and waved.

The man raised his hand in response. "Good luck, kid!" The truck roared off, blue smoke pouring from the exhaust.

Donald walked down the dirt driveway, gazing at the house. It was shabby and weather-beaten, but it was home. He felt a flood of joy to finally be where he belonged. The strawberry plants looked healthy, the newest crop thriving and the oldest plowed under. The next field was also plowed, and he wondered why his grandfather hadn't planted squash and carrots.

"Donald . . . my boy . . . Donald!" He turned, to see his mother burst out the back door and run to him, arms out-stretched. "You home!"

He hugged her, lifted her up and twirled her around, then set her down. "You're still the prettiest little picture bride of all. I'm glad my father chose you!"

She straightened her apron, and her fingers darted to her hair, tightening bobby pins. "And you still the bad boy you always was." She grabbed his arm and turned him around, brushing his uniform trousers. "How you get so dirty?"

"Almost as bad as Gila River, huh?"

She wrinkled her nose. "Nothing as bad as Gila River." Then she smiled and patted his arm. "But now we home, praise God."

Donald hugged her again and nodded, swallowing hard and blinking his eyes. He would never forget the fierce combat, the mines and booby-traps, and his valiant buddies. But maybe now he could move on with his life.

He looked back at the strawberry field. "Where's *Jiichan?*" It was strange not to see his grandfather weeding, watering, or doing whatever the plants needed.

His mother's smile faded. "Inside. He . . . not so good."

"Oh? Is he sick?"

"Maybe so. In heart. He not want leave *Baachan* at camp cemetery. We had to push him on to bus. Now he sit all day in chair. Mope." She pulled the sides of her mouth down to demonstrate his sadness.

Donald nodded. He'd never seen his grandfather openly show affection to his grandmother, but the two had been married over fifty years. No wonder it was hard on him.

Donald felt tears pricking his eyes. His dear little *Baachan.* The camp doctors had said it was cancer, but what did they know? If her spirit hadn't been broken at Gila River, she would have survived. When she died, he'd been overseas and wasn't able to get a leave to come back. He wouldn't have made it in time for her funeral, anyway.

He walked with his mother to the house, his arm draped over her shoulder, her arm around his waist. "Where's father?"

"Where you think? Church."

He wished Florence were home. He'd like to talk to her about Annie. But he was glad she'd been accepted at a Christian college, even though it was way back in Kansas.

He heard a car honking, and turned to see his father driving into the yard. He gave his mother another hug and bolted off to meet him.

His father slammed on the brakes, jumped out, and met him halfway. "Good to see you, son." He threw his arms around Donald and patted his back. "God answered our prayers and brought you safely home."

Donald felt blessed by the rare show of affection. "I hear grandfather's—"

"Depressed. We pray he'll recover soon. Physically, he seems all right." His father smiled, but his eyes were sad. "Remember the verse I gave you when you enlisted?"

Donald nodded. "Psalm 91:11: 'For he shall give his angels charge over thee, to keep thee in all thy ways.' I really depended on the one you gave me for camp. Deuteronomy 33:25: 'As thy days, so shall thy strength be.'"

"And God kept his promises, didn't he? Now we must trust him to heal your grandfather's spirit and give him strength."

⌒

The next morning, it was Donald who needed strength. As he entered the bank in Rosemond to open an account for his service paychecks, he saw long lines at the tellers' cages. He hadn't realized how busy the bank would be this time of morning.

As he got in one of the lines, he scanned the people. Recognizing several, he nodded greetings, even shaking hands with some that came over to him.

The first man in the line next to Donald finished his business. As the others moved forward, Donald saw from across the room the flash of strawberry-blonde hair. He nearly shouted, raised his hand to wave, even began to leave his place in line to go to her. Then he noticed she wasn't alone. She and a tall, handsome blonde man—Jonah Krause—were laughing together, their heads bent over a savings account book.

Chapter Four

Annie had been walking toward the bank building when she heard Jonah whistle. He caught up with her at the door, his own cash bag in hand. His blue eyes sparkled as he ran a hand through the blonde wavy hair, which threatened to spill over his forehead. Now, after making the furniture store's deposit, she stepped aside to wait for Jonah.

When he was released from the CPS camp, the church had elected him assistant treasurer. His current assignment was handling a special fund to purchase an organ. Some of the older people objected to such a big investment. "Isn't a piano good enough for singing?" several protested.

But Annie hoped enough money would come in. Maybe she could even take lessons. She'd heard it was easy to adapt piano skills to the organ.

As she glanced at Jonah, she bit her lip to keep from laughing. He might be good in math, but his spelling was as bad as ever. He'd proudly shown her the growing balance in the savings account book. And there it was, in bold black ink. Instead of "organ fund," he'd written "orgun funned." She couldn't resist teasing him about it.

When Jonah finished at the cage, he and Annie hurried out of the bank. With a smirk on his face and laughter in his eyes, he jabbed her in the ribs with his elbow. "I'll drop you off at the store, if you can stand riding with a guy who flunked spelling."

She patted him on the shoulder and clicked her tongue. "I don't know if I dare. You might lose your way." But she went with him to his car, an old blue Chevy coupe.

He got in first and reached across to open the door for her. "Now that the war's over, won't be long and we'll see new models at the dealers. I'm saving for a Super Deluxe."

Annie nodded. "That'd be nice." A lot of things were now available—gas rationing was over, people were going more places and taking vacations again. And she'd heard that when a store in Fresno got a shipment of nylons, the line had been two blocks long, waiting for the store to open.

Jonah drove past the street to the furniture store, and Annie looked around. "Hey, I was only kidding about getting lost. Where are you going?"

Jonah grinned. "Just taking the long way around. Gotta show you something."

"I need to get back to work!" she protested. "You want me to lose the best job in town?"

Then she spotted the Japanese Baptist church and caught her breath. She saw a car parked there, and someone was hoeing weeds in front. Was the church preparing to hold services again?

"Wait a minute. Stop, stop!" she shouted, her hand on the door handle.

"Oh, no you don't. Can't get away from me that easy." He stepped on the accelerator. "I want you to see something in the next block. A new music store. They'll have sheet music and records, and Bibles, too, I think. And they'll order instruments from a catalog. Maybe they'll make us a good deal on the church organ."

Annie, still looking back at the Japanese church, hardly listened. The flowerbeds had been cleared of weeds, and a few straggly geraniums huddled next to the steps. Were the church people back already? She'd heard some Japanese families had come back, but hadn't recognized any of the names.

Jonah parked and gestured to the buildings to their right. "Well, what do you think?"

Annie looked around. In front of them were the Sweets and Treats sandwich shop, a shoe store, and an empty building. "About what?" she asked, puzzled.

"Are you deef or something?" His uncultured pronunciation of the word made her cringe. He pointed to the empty building. "That's the music store I was telling you about."

She peered at it, still wondering why it was so important to Jonah. The windows were covered with big paper signs, announcing their opening in December.

Jonah frowned. "I thought you'd be excited. You won't have to go all the way to Fresno to buy your tinkly tunes."

Annie took a deep breath and let out a sigh. *Tinkly tunes?* She'd poured her soul into the pieces she played at church, and all he heard was tinkly tunes?

As if Jonah's spelling wasn't bad enough, he couldn't tell a music trill from a chicken cackling. Good thing there were four other people on his committee. If it were up to him alone, they'd end up with a cheap pump organ. What was that he'd said? Something about buying it through a catalog?

Just like him. He didn't know anything about tone quality and registers, or the importance of touch and the response of the keys.

But it *would* be nice to buy music here in town, as long as the store stocked a decent selection.

Annie glanced at her watch. "Well, thanks for showing me. It'll be swell. But I've got to get back to work. Please?"

Jonah looked around. "There's nobody out here. How about a kiss first?"

Annie frowned. "Jonah, I've told you. I don't want to get serious."

Jonah hit the steering wheel with the heel of his hand. "Boy-oh-boy. How long do I have to wait? You sure led me on in your letters. What changed your mind now?"

She stared at him, shocked. "Led you on? How? I never promised you anything!"

"You don't remember saying you wished I was home again, and how much fun we had Christmas caroling? Or," he added with a wolfish growl, "the time you let me hold you on my lap?"

"What could I do? The car was crowded. I didn't know all those other kids were coming along. And sure, I wanted the war to be over, and to have all you guys back home. But—"

"And what about that kiss at the Rempel house? Huh? You didn't squirm away that time."

Annie remembered all too well. Jonah had been home on leave, and she'd given up on Donald. She'd *wanted* Jonah to kiss her, to see how it felt, but mostly to see if there was any chance of falling for him.

But she'd felt nothing—absolutely nothing. It was like kissing the back of her own hand, the way she and her cousins did when they were little. They'd wondered why big kids made such a big deal about smooching.

She glanced at Jonah and then looked straight ahead again. How could the best-looking guy in her church have so little charm and personality? Especially compared to Donald, and that unexpected sweet farewell kiss under the oak tree. Thinking about it made her face grow hot.

"See!" Jonah was practically crowing. He jabbed her twice, and she was sure she'd have bruises by tomorrow. "You're blushing. You liked it, you know you did!" He put his arm around her shoulder and jerked her closer.

Annie rolled her eyes. "What could I do? The kids held me under the mistletoe." She pushed his arm up and slipped away from him. "Jonah, I just don't—it's not that I don't like you as a friend."

His face turned dark and his lips curled. "Well, thanks a lot! If that's all I am to you, why do I bother?"

Why indeed? Annie threw the car door open, hopped out, and slammed it shut. "Good-bye, Jonah. I can find my way to the store."

"Annie!" She heard him yell. "Come back here. I didn't mean—"

She hurried away, not looking back. Maybe now he finally got the message.

When she came near the Japanese church, she slowed down and

crossed the street to look at it more closely. Nobody was in front now, but she heard a faint metallic clink and followed the sound to the side of the building. There she saw an elderly Japanese man bent over and twisting a hose onto a faucet.

"Pardon me—" Annie started.

The man quickly stood up and rubbed his back. "Yes, miss?"

"I'm sorry, I didn't mean to startle you. I just wondered . . . have any of the church people come back yet?"

"Some come, some later maybe."

"What about . . . the Nakamuras?"

"Yes, yes, Nakamura. Pastor here tonight."

So there must be enough people for a service. But Donald? Had he come back too? Or was he in the army or medical school? She wanted to ask the man those questions. But her heart beat so fast and her throat became so tight that her mouth refused to form the words. What if he told her that Donald was married and had moved to his wife's town? She couldn't bear to hear that. Not now—and maybe not ever.

"Thank you," she said and hurried back across the street. She'd call Florence now that she knew the Nakamuras were back, and casually ask about Donald.

She checked the time again and was shocked to see how long she'd taken for her trip to the bank. Mr. McGinnis would be wondering what happened to her.

As it turned out, he wasn't even in the store when she returned. Bob Taylor was showing a dining set to a couple, and he told Annie that the boss had taken a Sealy mattress representative out for coffee.

She entered the bank deposit into her ledger and balanced the columns. By that time Bob brought the customers to the counter to fill out a contract for the dining set. He handed Annie their check for the downpayment, and she rang it into the cash register. Next, she started a new page in her accounts receivable ledger.

By noon, the store was empty. Annie reached into the desk drawer, took out the sandwich she brought from home, and started to eat.

Bob told her, "I'm going to the stockroom. Buzz me if anyone comes in."

It wasn't long before she heard laughter from the stockroom area. She wrinkled her nose. He and the deliverymen were probably swapping girly jokes.

Then she realized that as long as she was alone in the store, this might be a good time to call Florence. She lifted the receiver.

"Number please!"

Annie tried to keep her voice from trembling as she told the operator, "6-7-F-1-2." Her heart beat a crazy rhythm while listening to the one long ring and two shorts.

After three tries, Annie heard a click. "Florence?" No one answered. Another click, and the rings continued. Someonc else must have picked up on the Nakamura's party line, then hung up again.

After several more tries, the operator said, "They don't seem to be answering."

"Thank you. I'll try again later." Annie hung up the receiver, her palms sweaty. She knew she wouldn't get up the nerve to call again today—not on a party line with people listening in. *Dear Lord, if it's your will, please let him be home . . . and still single.*

But if he *was* home, why hadn't he looked her up?

And why did the thought of him still make her melt inside? She'd prayed for God to take that desire away from her, but he hadn't. Wasn't he listening? Or did he *want* her to love Donald?

Life was so complicated. Annie thought about Jonah. After he came home at the end of summer, he took her to a few church-group socials. He acted as though he was crazy about her. Church people said they made a good couple, and she sure knew her mother's opinion of him. But none of that had kept her from missing Donald—or comparing Jonah to him. Jonah always came up short.

If she'd never met Donald, would Jonah seem more desirable? She certainly didn't feel anything for him now. They had so little in common. Sure, Jonah was a Christian. At least he'd been baptized when he was twelve, along with all of his friends. But he didn't like to study the Bible. Maybe it was because he didn't enjoy reading, which was another thing hard for her to accept about him.

But he also didn't like to *talk* about spiritual things. Whenever she mentioned a verse that touched her or an answer to prayer, he made a joke out of it. Or steered the conversation to farming, cars, or how pretty she was.

If I have to end up with him, Lord, help me understand him. And make us stop arguing. But oh please, Lord, bring Donald back soon. No matter what, I have to see him. Need to see him.

Donald was the only guy she'd ever felt close to. And after three years he'd now be a man. Even if he weren't married, he might have changed a lot. Maybe that's why he stopped writing. Maybe he decided a "strawberry-blonde" didn't fit into God's plan for him.

Annie heard a clicking noise and looked up. Her boss was standing at the counter, snapping his fingers at her. "Lost in a daze, huh? I'd like you to meet Mr. Ross Bentley." He turned to the man with him. "This is my right-hand girl—usually—Annie Penner."

Annie smiled sheepishly and rose quickly from her chair. "I'm sorry," she said, closing her ledger. "The war ending makes my head spin. So many things are happening." She went around her desk to the counter and reached out her hand. "Pleased to meet you, Mr. Bentley. Your company makes the best mattresses."

They chatted a little, then the two men found comfortable seats, and Mr. Bentley opened his sales catalog. Annie knew they'd be occupied for quite a while.

A customer entered the front door, and Annie buzzed Bob. Then a couple came in while Bob was still busy, so Annie showed them around until Bob was free to help them. It wasn't until closing that she had time to think about herself again.

As she walked home, Jonah's blue coupe squealed to a stop against the curb next to her. He called out, "You're not still mad, are you?"

Annie shrugged. *Mad* wasn't the right word. Frustrated, maybe.

Jonah reached over the seat and opened the passenger door. "C'mon, I'll take you home."

She sighed. Might as well; it would save a little time.

Jonah didn't say any more about their squabble earlier that day. He was excited about a piece of land his father wanted to buy for him and a tractor they'd been looking at.

His father was known for shrewd bargaining, and the family had always been well off. Jonah was like his father and would be as prosperous and dependable. In reality, he was probably *the* Mennonite "catch" of the season. Was she being stupid for not encouraging him? If she tried hard, would love and passion come in time?

Jonah pulled up in front of her house. "Don't forget. You promised to go to Youth for Christ with me tomorrow night. They're having a special guest, a ventriloquist."

She *had* forgotten. *Oh, yauma,* she thought. How would she get through another whole evening with him?

But she *had* promised. And people could change. Maybe this time the service might get through to him and bring him closer to the Lord. "Okay," she said, getting out of the car and thanking him for the ride. As he drove off, she got the mail out of the box and hurried to the back door.

Shuffling through the bills, letters, and magazines, she thought of Donald's letters, still safely stashed in her closet. What a thrill it had been, three long years ago, to see his familiar handwriting, to open the envelopes and know he was thinking about her.

Her mother had supper ready, and Annie chattered about things at the store. She told her of Mr. McGinnis introducing her to the mattress salesman as his "right-hand girl." She didn't mention the "usually." She wished she could talk to her mother about the Japanese Baptist church, and the way she felt—or didn't feel—about Jonah. But she knew it would only worry her mother.

After supper and the cleanup, her mother settled into her chair in the parlor and busied herself crocheting a shawl. Annie felt restless. She couldn't forget what the Japanese man had said.

His family was back in town, but where was Donald?

Suddenly she remembered a piano book she'd borrowed from the preacher's wife. She'd planned to keep it a little longer because the hymn transcriptions were so beautiful. But maybe Mrs. Loewen needed it since she often played solos in church. It was getting dark, so Annie borrowed the car keys from her mother and drove the four blocks to the Loewen home. There was no answer to her knock, so she slipped the book inside the screen door. After that, the car just seemed to know where to go.

The Japanese Baptist church was lit up. Two cars were already parked in the lot beside it, others were turning in.

Annie drove slowly, practically idling. Her heart was in her throat.

Then she saw Donald. He was getting out of his car, sheets of music in his hand. She slammed on the brakes and her car squealed to a stop.

Donald looked up. For a long moment, they stared at each other. Then he started toward her. Although the distance was only a few yards, it seemed like an eternity before he was beside her.

Chapter Five

DONALD'S PULSE RACED. FOR SEVERAL MOMENTS, he could do nothing more than stand and stare at Annie. Framed in the window of her mother's old black Chevy, she was even more beautiful than the picture he'd cherished all these years.

Her blonde curls glowed, fluffed over her forehead, and in back swept down in waves to her shoulders. Her eyes, green with gold flecks, were fastened on his, and moments went by in silence.

Then her lips parted and she lifted a trembling hand to cover them. He caught a faint whiff of a fragrance that reminded him of roses.

Not able to help himself, he reached for her hand and held it in his own, never letting his eyes leave hers.

Then a car honked. He realized they were stopping traffic, so he cocked his head, motioning for her to pull over to the curb.

After she parked, Donald, his legs like rubber, walked back to her. With all his military training and combat, his body was strong and firm, but the sight of her made him feel as weak as a jellyfish.

His palm still tingled from the feeling of her hand in his. It had been her left hand, and he noticed there wasn't a ring on it. So she wasn't married, or even engaged.

But he couldn't forget seeing her in the bank with Jonah. He cleared his throat. "How've you been?" he stuttered. What a dumb question. In the army, he'd been known as "The Mouth," always knowing what to say, *But look at me now*, he thought.

"Okay. When did you get back?"

Hearing her voice made his heart skip a beat. "Yesterday afternoon." He'd never been so tongue-tied in all his life. "What are you doing these days?"

"I . . . I work at McGinnis Furniture Store. Bookkeeper."

"Bet you're good at it."

She shrugged. "You? Did you get into medical school?"

"No. I've been in the army."

"I wondered. The paper had an article . . . I thought you might have enlisted."

"Don," a soft female voice said, "aren't we going to practice before the service?"

He turned. Grace Miyamoto stood behind him, smiling, her eyebrows raised as she repeated the question.

Donald glanced down at the music in his other hand. He'd completely forgotten. He gave the sheets to Grace and said, "Be there in a minute. Pass these out, would you please? And get the group started for me, okay?"

She looked from him to Annie and back, then nodded and left.

Annie's eyes followed her. "She's very pretty."

Automatically, Donald turned and glanced at Grace. "Oh . . . I'm sorry. I should have introduced you."

To please his father, he'd agreed to help with the special music tonight. Now he could kick himself. How could he leave Annie, after all these years apart? "Do you want to come in for the service? We have a good speaker—"

Annie shook her head. "I've got to get home."

He looked back at the church. People stood in the doorway, staring, holding their hands near their mouths. He was sure they were whispering to each other, gossiping about him. "I'd like to talk longer, but I promised to help the singers. I'll . . . see you again? Soon?"

"Sure." She kept looking at him, her eyes sad, her fingers trembling on the steering wheel. Then she shifted into first, grinding the gears ever so slightly.

He watched her drive off—watched until her car turned a corner and was out of sight.

Why is she sad? What will she tell me the next time I see her? What's wrong? The questions ricocheted in his head. He felt a loss, as though she were leaving his life again.

As Donald lay in bed that night, thoughts of Annie filled his mind. While hitchhiking home, he'd looked forward to his comfortable room. After muddy foxholes, army cots, and the straw-filled mattresses of Gila River, his familiar bed would be luxury. But now Annie's face was etched into his mind, and he felt sick with yearning for her. Sleep wouldn't come.

He thought of her letters. They had become so precious to him and were such a life-saver in camp.

Remember God's eye is on the sparrow, and he cares even more for you. He'll keep you safe. That time under the oak tree was so special. When you come home, I'll take you up on that picnic.

During all those months overseas, he'd watched other guys get mail from sweethearts and wives. He'd waited for her letters. Needed them—badly. In spite of what her answer might have been, he should have asked her tonight why she stopped writing. If only Grace hadn't interrupted.

The whole service at church had passed in a blur. He and Grace ran through the special music with the dozen or so people who volunteered to sing that evening, but several times he failed to bring in the voices with his cue, and Grace had to lead with her piano accompaniment. Thanks to her, the performance must have gone okay since several people had said they enjoyed it.

He'd been looking forward to hearing the speaker, a former missionary to Japan. But after the message was over, he couldn't remember much of it.

How could he still be totally consumed by a girl so far out of his reach?

In the past three years, surely she'd made a life for herself with her own people—a life that didn't include him.

Donald sighed, turned on his bedside lamp, and reached for his Bible. "Father in heaven," he prayed, "tell me what to do. Guide me in your paths and show me your will."

He opened to the psalms, and the beginning of Psalm 37 caught his eye. "Fret not thyself because of evildoers."

His father had told him to forgive the authorities for evacuating all the Japanese, but he hadn't yet been able to do that. They tore him away from Annie, from his future, and caused all his studying and hard work to go down the drain. Was the Lord speaking to him through this verse?

He read on through the third verse: "Trust in the LORD, and do good; so shalt thou dwell in the land, and verily thou shalt be fed."

That was comforting, but it still wasn't enough. Then he came to the fourth verse and caught his breath. "Delight thyself also in the LORD; and he shall give thee the desires of thine heart."

His greatest desire? He took a deep breath and sighed. *Annie.* Was it God's will for them to get back together? Did he have the right to tell her about his love for her?

The words echoed in his mind: *The desires of thine heart.* Suddenly he felt so much joy he could hardly stand it, and he knew what he had to do.

⌒

At the furniture store the next morning, Annie's mind spiraled far from her duties. She made mistake after mistake, until the eraser on her pencil was worn to the metal rim.

Often she caught herself staring at the wall. Instead of the mountain scene that hung there, she saw in her mind's eye Donald's face. He looked so mature, so manly—his thick black hair now parted on one side and above his lip a narrow, Clark Gable mustache. To her, he was even more handsome than the movie actor. But if his looks had changed, had he changed in other ways? His eyes still had the same warmth, the touch of his hand was tender, but was he still free? What about that pretty girl at the church? She had seemed very confident, very familiar with him.

"Annie?"

She looked up to see Mr. McGinnis staring at her, his entire face a puzzled frown. He put some letters on her desk. "Better type these over. I've circled the errors."

If it weren't Saturday, their busiest day, he probably would have sent her home long ago. She hung her head. "Sorry. I'll take care of it." Because he continued to stand by her desk, she added, "I'm just tired. I didn't sleep well last night," and busied herself putting the paper in the typewriter. She didn't explain that she'd lain awake remembering every word she and Donald had said, every movement he'd made, the thrill of his hand holding hers.

After her boss left, her thoughts went back to Donald. That girl—what if she was his sweetheart? Or worse, his wife? Her stomach knotted at the thought. If he'd worn a ring, she would have felt it. But then, not all married men wore rings. Perhaps it wasn't a Japanese custom.

She thought of his last letter—about working at the camp hospital and teaching biology to high school kids in the barracks. She pictured him in front of a class of kids; they would have loved him.

She would have.

Last night, he said he'd see her again. Soon. But did that mean when they happened to pass each other on the street sometime, or that he wanted to spend time with her? It just didn't make sense that he stopped writing to her. If only she'd had the courage to ask him why!

Annie corrected the letters and posted the week's receipts to accounts receivable. The hands of the clock dragged across the minutes, the hours, until it was noon. She reached into her desk drawer and took out the sack lunch she brought.

"Can I interest you in a picnic?"

Annie looked up, then blinked, wondering if she was still imagining things. But there he was, Donald in person, smiling in that special way she couldn't resist, his eyes dark and mysterious. Her heart shot up to her throat and landed back in her chest with a thump. Was she even breathing? He wore a white shirt with the sleeves rolled-up, and she stared at his arm muscles, so manly and virile.

He wouldn't have asked her out if he were married. She felt excited but nervous—ecstatic, yet afraid. After three years of silence, how could he still affect her this way?

Trying to keep the quiver out of her voice, she said, "Sure. Just give me a minute." What a mess she must be. Grabbing her purse, she hurried to the restroom to comb her hair and tuck in her blouse.

Donald's car was parked outside—the same old Plymouth coupe he'd driven to college, now washed and waxed to a sparkling finish. He opened the door for her and, one hand lightly under her elbow, helped her in before going around to the driver's side. His touch on her arm made her shiver, and she couldn't help thinking of Jonah, who reached over the seat to open the door for her. What a difference.

As he drove down the street, Donald told her his family had been very fortunate. "Menno Bartel honored his handshake and gave us back our land that he rented while we were gone. He even stored our cars in his barn.

"People kept telling us we were crazy; the man would steal us blind. Too many were forced to sell out at rock-bottom prices. Their backs were against the wall. What else could they do? Some who leased their farms or businesses came home and found they'd been cheated out of everything."

Annie felt sad for those who were treated badly, but glad for the Nakamuras. "Mr. Bartel would never cheat you. Mennonites might be tight, but their handshake is a promise."

Donald nodded. "He's a real Christian. He took good care of the strawberries, like they were his own, and kept the farm in my name. Always sent my father our fair share of the crop proceeds. And when my parents came home, they found the truck waiting in our barn. The cars were still up on blocks at his place, the tires stored on dry cement."

Annie watched Donald's face as he talked, his smooth cheeks, his soft lips. She wondered how the mustache would feel to her fingers.

When he turned the corner, Annie knew exactly where they were going. In a few minutes she saw the buildings of Rosemond College, the towering oak tree shading the side lawn.

Their celebration picnic. But how would she ever be able to eat?

He parked in the closest lot, opened the trunk, and took out a blanket and a basket covered with a white cloth. She'd brought her lunch, too—after all, in her letter she'd promised to bring sandwiches—but was embarrassed because she'd brought only one.

She glanced over the grounds. Hardly anyone around. It was Saturday, so the out-of-town students were probably in the cafeteria or had gone home for the weekend. In the distance, two people whacked tennis balls back and forth on the cement court.

A janitor, Mr. Bailey, pulled a floor waxer out of the maintenance shed and headed up the steps toward the back door of the nearest building. He glanced their way, then turned again to stare before finally going in. Through the ground-floor windows, Annie saw him enter a room and go about his work.

A cool breeze fluttered the leaves, and Annie remembered the radio news had predicted more rain. Dark clouds were piled up in the northwest but were too far off to be threatening.

Donald spread the blanket on the grass and unfolded the white cloth on top of it. Pulling out a bag of fried chicken, two bottles of Coca-Cola, and a bunch of Thompson grapes, he placed them on the white cloth. "That's the best I could do," he apologized. "It's too late for strawberries."

"That's swell." Annie took out her carrot sticks and egg sandwich and handed him half of it, hoping he wouldn't notice her hands trembling. "Sorry I don't have much to contribute." She settled down on the blanket and leaned against the tree.

Donald sat down beside her and smiled. "Doesn't matter. Your being here is what counts."

Annie felt her heart skip a beat. She knew she was blushing.

"Ready?" he asked as he folded his hands to pray. When she nodded, he bowed his head and thanked God for the end of the war, for bringing him safely home, for keeping Annie safe and giving her a good job, for letting them meet again on this beautiful day, and, finally, for the food.

No flowery words, no theological terms, just talking to God straight from his heart, the way he had in CLOC Club. At least that part of him hadn't changed.

He looked up, smiled, and bit into the half-sandwich. "Mmm! Homemade bread! Did you bake it yourself?"

Annie nodded and mumbled, "Yes."

"Wonderful!" he proclaimed as he tore off a small bunch of grapes and handed it to her. The touch of his fingers was electrifying.

She asked him about Florence, and he told her about the college in Kansas that had accepted her while they were still at the camp. "Didn't she tell you? It's a Christian school. They gave her a full scholarship. She'll graduate in the spring with a teaching credential."

Why hadn't Florence written her that good news? "What will she teach?"

"High school English. She hopes." He smiled wryly. "Isn't that something? A Japanese teaching English? Think she'll find a job?"

His tone was light, but Annie heard hurt in his voice, saw it in his eyes, and she felt sad for him. She knew he was having a hard time getting over the internment and all the prejudice. Maybe there was some way she could help him, but she didn't know what it might be, and she simply answered his question with a question.

"Why not? She always got top grades. She'll be a good teacher." She felt Donald's eyes on her as she searched for something else to say. Annie finally asked, "Was she home this summer? If I'd known, I could have called—"

"No. She stayed there and worked in the school office. My parents haven't seen her since she left the camp." He stretched out on the grass just like he had during college and popped a grape into his mouth.

"That's a long time." Annie nervously pinched little pleats into her skirt, then smoothed them out. "How are your parents?"

"They're well; they're adjusting. My father enjoyed working with other pastors in the camp; you know, all the denominations were together in one church. But he's glad to be home with his own congregation. My grandfather—" he sucked his breath in through his teeth and shook his head. "He's having a bad time. Ever since my grandmother died—"

"She died?" Annie felt a pang, and wondered why he hadn't written her about that. "I'm so sorry. I only met her that one time, when we bought strawberries just before the evacuation. She was so sweet and friendly. I remember Florence saying she was sick, but I didn't know it was that bad."

"But I wrote you! I was overseas and couldn't get a pass to come home for her funeral. Don't you remember?"

"You wrote me from overseas? I never got any letters from overseas."

"You didn't? None?" Donald sat up and stared at her, his dark eyes widening in disbelief. "I wrote you dozens of letters." He thought a minute. "What about the one saying I enlisted? The ones from basic training at Camp Shelby? Not even the one saying our troops were being shipped out?"

She kept shaking her head. "Nothing like that. I only got three letters from you . . . total. In the last one you said your father had been released from prison and had joined you, and you were leading the church choir." She didn't mention all the sweet things at the end—things that she'd cried over night after night, wishing he'd write again.

"But that was way back—"

"October 1, 1942."

"Nineteen forty-two? I'm sure you wrote me after that. You told me about school, the music you were playing, the CLOC Club. You even said you missed me." He moved closer. "But it was strange . . . you didn't comment on any of the things I told you, didn't answer any of my questions. I wondered why."

Avoiding his eyes, she reached down, pulled up a blade of grass and shredded it to bits. "I kept writing for a while. Kept watching the mail." She didn't dare look at him. "I thought maybe you were just too busy . . ." Her voice drifted off.

Surprised beyond belief, he looked at her intensely and shook his head. "Oh, Annie . . . no matter what, I always have time for you." Then he stared off into the distance, frowning. "At camp, the government tried to stop our newsletter because it printed some of the stunts they were pulling, like not delivering our meat. Do you suppose they destroyed my letters because I complained about something?"

"I don't think so." She shrugged her shoulders as she looked toward him. "The letters I did get mentioned conditions at camp, but nothing was censored. And that still wouldn't explain the ones I didn't get from overseas." She thought a minute. "Are you sure you had the right address?"

"Same as always—thirty-nine, twenty-eight Haynes. You haven't moved, have you?"

"No." She bit her lip. "I finally wrote one asking if you'd forgotten me, but I was afraid to send it. Afraid of what you might say." She looked away and hoped she wouldn't start crying.

Donald scooted even closer. "I never forgot you. *Never.*" She heard the fervor in his voice and turned to face him. As she stared at him, she saw such intensity, such yearning in his eyes that her heart ached for him. He touched her shoulder, and as though drawn by a magnet, she leaned toward him.

A heavy door crashed open, interrupting their reunion. Looking around, they saw the janitor hurry down the steps and stride toward them.

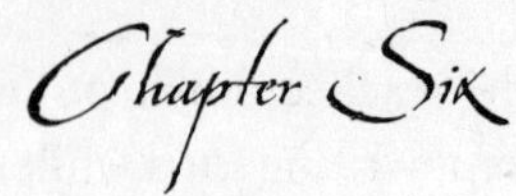

Chapter Six

JUST LIKE OLD MR. BAILEY TO PICK this moment to ruin their time together. Donald moved away from Annie and gathered the remnants of their lunch, packing them into the basket. He breathed deeply, trying to slow his pulse.

Donald had noticed Mr. Bailey watching them through the window and knew he'd better be careful. But he'd hoped that the tree hid them from the janitor's prying eyes. And then Donald had almost lost control of his emotions.

Even back in their college days, Donald had noticed the janitor eyeing them—when they walked together to the science building, or laughed and teased each other at lunchtime under the oak tree. Mr. Bailey always gave Donald that scornful look, as though saying, "Who do you think you are, Jap—fooling around with a white girl?"

Now the janitor stopped at the edge of their picnic blanket, glanced first at Annie, then at Donald. "Hey, aren't you the Nakamura kid? Used to come here—science classes?"

Donald nodded. "That's me." He kept his face smooth and expressionless, politely cool—just as his father and grandfather had taught him. "Don't do anything to call attention to yourself," they'd said. But never had it been more difficult.

Annie looked up at Mr. Bailey. "I went here, too. I guess you could call this an alumni meeting."

The man stared at her for a moment and nodded. Then he turned to Donald. "Were you in that Jap army?"

Donald gave himself a few seconds, mentally uncurling his fists. Then he coolly stated, "No, sir. I was on *our* side. The 442nd." He stole a look at Annie. She bit her lip, looking down at her folded hands. He followed her gaze, saw her raise a thumb and then let it drop.

Mr. Bailey shrugged. "That's what I meant. I heard you fought like the dickens."

Donald nodded ever so slightly as he folded the white cloth and smoothed it over the basket. He didn't think the comment needed any further answer.

Mr. Bailey gabbed a while. He made a comment about the good strawberry crops while the Japanese were gone and added, "See, you're not the only good farmers." He mentioned the arrest of Donald's father, concluding with, "Guess he won't be preaching Japanese over the radio any more!" With a laugh that was almost a sneer, he asked, "Okay, kids, about finished with your—*meeting?*" The way he spit out *meeting* let them know he thought they had no business being there.

Donald didn't answer. Annie glanced at him and saw he didn't intend to speak further to Mr. Bailey. "Soon," she responded curtly.

The janitor had already spoiled their closeness. But Donald couldn't let Annie take the brunt of the insinuations. Through tight lips he added, "Yeah, in a few minutes."

Mr. Bailey walked away a few paces, then turned back, "Well, make it snappy. I'm turning on the sprinklers." Looking at his watch, he added, "In ten minutes. Sharp."

Donald glanced up at the sky. The dark clouds were coming closer; it should rain by evening. There was no reason to water the lawn, not now that it was fall. But the janitor still stared at him, as though daring him to argue.

By the time Mr. Bailey finally left, Donald was ready to explode. If it had been his buddies—just guys—here with him, he might have let go with a few choice words.

But Annie leaned back against the tree, touched him gently on the arm, and smiled. "You were great. I'm so proud of you for staying cool. The guy's a louse and not worth losing your temper."

He looked into her lovely green eyes and slowly shook his head. She actually understood how he felt! "I don't deserve a wonderful friend like you."

"Oh, Donald, don't run yourself down. Some day you'll show the whole world what great things God can do through you. Just let him direct you."

As peace and hope flooded through him, he sensed a new strength and courage, and now he didn't care if ten janitors stood watching. He took Annie's hand in his. "Second only to God, you are my guiding light, my shining star, my rainbow of happiness."

Then they heard gurgles of water. He and Annie stared at each other for a split second, then scrambled to their feet. He grabbed the basket and she quickly wadded up the blanket. The gurgles turned into sputters, then water spiked and weaved around them. Squealing and laughing, they scampered across the lawn.

When they reached the car, Donald put the basket in the trunk, then patted her arms and face dry with the edge of the damp blanket. Annie shivered.

"Are you cold?" he asked.

She shook her head, looking up at him, her eyes shining. He wanted to kiss her cheeks, her chin, and oh, those sweet lips. Just as he had when they said good-bye, three long years ago. But did he have the right?

A clanking noise from the classroom area interrupted the moment, and he pulled away from her. Mr. Bailey dumped wastebaskets into the outside trash barrels, looking their way and shaking his head.

Donald opened the car door and helped Annie in, but when he was settled, too, he didn't start the motor. Instead, he asked, "Do you need to leave?"

Annie looked at her watch. "Fifteen more minutes."

They sat quietly for a bit. As she studied her folded hands, he gazed at her face, her curls, the smoothness of her neck. After all these years of cherishing her picture, he still couldn't believe he was right there beside her, seeing her in person.

Without looking up, she asked, "What was it like, being a soldier? Where were you?"

He hadn't thought he'd be able to talk about those days, but now he wanted her to know. He told her about the men in his unit, how they bonded into a close group of friends no matter where they came from. How he used what little knowledge he'd picked up at the camp hospital and ended up in the medics. The K rations, the ill-fitting uniforms.

"I was in Naples, Anzio, Livorno and other places in Italy. Marseille, Avignon, Lyon in France—even managed a pass to relax a bit in Nice. Then while most of the guys stayed to mop up, a few of us got attached to other units and ended up in the Philippines."

But when Annie asked about the battles, he shook his head. "Someday I'll tell you about those times. Not yet." He looked away so she wouldn't see the sadness in his eyes.

He mentioned he'd been wounded. "Shrapnel," he added. He socked himself on the shoulder and jerked back. "I thought I was a goner. But a couple of weeks in the hospital, and I was back with the platoon." He added casually, "It did get me a Purple Heart, though."

Her eyes widened. "You earned a medal?"

He shrugged. "Yeah. Several, actually. I'll have to show them to you."

Annie drew a deep breath and let it out. "Wow! You're a hero!" She stared at him for a moment, her eyes wide and sparkling. Then a sober look came over her face as she glanced at her watch. "I guess we'd better go," she said, her voice full of regret. "It was a great picnic. Thanks."

Not wanting it to end like that, he asked, "Would you like to do it again sometime?"

Her smile was his rainbow after a storm. "I'd love to," she answered.

He reached down, picked up her hand and pressed it to his lips. She moved a little closer, and it felt so right to him. All the months, the years of wondering if she still remembered him, still cared for him. . . . All the hurt rolled away and nothing mattered except that they were together again.

It was almost closing time at the furniture store when Annie remembered the Youth for Christ meeting. Jonah would be picking her up at six-thirty!

How could she go out with Jonah now that Donald was back? Now that she knew Donald still cared for her, when being with him made her feel as though she'd died and gone to heaven?

Her mother would be upset if she didn't go to the meeting. Ordinarily, she wouldn't mind going with him just as friends, knowing it didn't mean anything. But if Donald showed up, saw her with Jonah, what would he think? No, she had to break the date—immediately.

She grabbed the store telephone and asked for Jonah's home. The operator rang the number at least ten times, but no one answered.

He's probably out in the field, she realized, *rolling paper trays of raisins or boxing them.* If it rained hard before the raisins were covered, he could lose his crop to mold. Annie knew he always picked grapes as late as possible. He took pride in their high sugar content.

When Annie got home from work, her mother was outside taking trash to the incinerator, so she hurried inside and tried calling again. This time Jonah's mother answered, and Annie gave her the message. "Tell him I won't be able to go to Youth for Christ with him tonight."

"I'll tell him, *Anchen,* but I know he'll be disappointed. He's got his dad and all his brothers working extra fast to get done in time." Jonah's mother spoke warmly, using the affectionate form of her name, and Annie felt sad. She was sure his mother had the same hopes as did her own mother about her and Jonah.

She tried to ease the rejection. "He'll probably be relieved; this way he'll be sure of beating the rain."

His mother sounded doubtful. "Well, sure, maybe." Then her voice brightened. "But there'll be plenty other times, *yo?*"

Now Annie felt really guilty. A lot of people were going to be disappointed. But it wouldn't be fair to lead Jonah on.

She avoided the question. "Thank you. See you in church Sunday."

Her mother came inside just then and looked sharply at Annie. "Who was on the phone?"

"Jonah's mother."

"Oh? What did she want? Is she starting on your quilt?"

How could she tell her mother that she'd just broken a date with Jonah because of Donald? Ever since she started writing to Jonah at CPS camp, and especially now that he was home, the two mothers had become very close. And Jonah's mother had mentioned piecing a quilt for each of her children as they got married. Jonah was the youngest—his quilt would be gorgeous, her best work.

Annie bit her lip. "She didn't say. But Jonah's trying to get his raisins in before the rain."

Her mother nodded. "Supposed to be quite a storm. He's a fine boy, Annie. A good hard worker. Don't let him slip away."

Annie turned to the kitchen table and idly shuffled through the mail her mother had brought in. She knew there wouldn't be anything interesting. From the corner of her eye she saw her mother watching.

After Donald's letters had stopped, she told her mother that she'd been corresponding with him, acting as though it was nothing important. After all, she'd written to other boys away from home, just to cheer them up. But maybe her mother had seen more in her face than Annie realized, especially since Annie always checked through the stack several times and sometimes even went out to the box—just in case something had gotten stuck in the back.

Now when Annie glanced up, her mother quickly looked away, turned abruptly, and pulled pots and pans out of the cupboard to prepare supper.

After dinner that night, Donald's father motioned him to come into his study and gestured for him to sit down. Donald thought his father wanted to talk about the farm, or maybe counsel him about his lingering bitterness over the internment.

His father did start out with the strawberries. "As you can see, your grandfather is no longer able to work the fields. With the land in your name, it is important that you step in and take charge. I believe you could run the farm and still serve the Lord as my assistant pastor."

Donald swallowed hard. What about his lifelong desire to become a doctor? He breathed a quick plea for the right words, then cleared his throat.

"With due respect, Father, I can only promise to work the land through this next spring's strawberry harvest."

His father frowned. "I don't understand. Surely you don't still expect to attend medical school? After all this time and the many rejections? I was under the impression you had given that up."

How could he give up everything he'd worked for, all his hard study and training? "I don't know. There are other schools. I still feel called." At camp, the hospital had needed him. In the army, it seemed a miracle that God placed him in the medics. After that, how could he just forget it?

His father steepled his fingers under his chin. "Being a doctor is a most honorable profession. But be very sure this is God's call and not just your own wishes." He tilted his chin lower. "And that leaves us still with the problem of the farm. Must we let it go to ruin after our neighbor was so kind to keep it flourishing for us?"

Donald wished life weren't so complicated. The honorable Japanese way would be to observe *On*—the unrepayable debt of obligation, the respect and loyalty that the Japanese give to parents and other people in authority. The Japanese part of him knew that he was expected to obey his father without question. But the American part couldn't give up his dreams, his love of medicine and healing. Not yet.

Hadn't he already given up enough? If it hadn't been for the internment—*concentration*—camp, he could be in medical school by now. In spite of the hospital work, those crucial months had been wasted in that stark, isolated desert.

In the army, he'd been respected by his fellow soldiers and honored by all those medals and citations. He'd proved himself by his bravery. But he never expected that to be an end in itself. All the time, he hoped someday, somehow, he'd still reach his goals.

His father pointed a finger at him. "You are twenty-five years old. It is time you settled down. Get married. Have children to carry on the family name. Forget about going back to school."

During the church service the other evening, Donald saw his father watching him and smiling as he and Grace Miyamoto consulted about the music. He knew nothing would please his parents more than for him to marry a Japanese Christian girl. Grace played the piano well and was active in the church. When he'd asked for volunteers to form a choir that would practice weekly and sing regularly in the Sunday services, Grace was one of the first to meet him at the front of the church after the service. She was very pretty, very nice, and very friendly to him. He probably should be flattered.

The Bible plainly taught that a condition of long life was honoring one's parents. The fifth commandment agreed with Japanese culture. If he married the girl his parents chose, would he in time learn to love her?

His grandparents hadn't seen each other until their wedding, and their marriage had been solid. His father and mother had learned to love each other over the years. What did God want him to do with his life?

The desires of thine heart. Was it really *Annie* that God meant for him?

Donald leaned his face into his hands, his heart gripped by agony. He couldn't lose her again. She was so sweet, so lovely. She cared about people—he could tell she cared for him. Even back in college, she always encouraged him, brought out the best in him. They liked the same things—literature, good music, nature—and she could talk intelligently about anything—from spiritual things to world events. It seemed she'd been created just for him. And now, in spite of those three miserable years of separation, in spite of his believing that he'd lost her, God gave him the miracle of finding her again, of allowing him to see the love shining in her eyes.

Then he remembered seeing her in the bank. What were her feelings about Jonah? She hadn't mentioned the guy, and he'd meant to ask her about him. All during their picnic, the thought of Jonah hovered in the back of his mind, but he didn't want to spoil their near-perfect time together by asking about him.

He pictured the two of them standing at the teller's cage. Jonah so tall and blonde, Annie so beautiful—a matched pair. To be brutally honest, she'd be far better off with Jonah than sharing a life with *him*—a life full of uncertainties, hardship—and always, always prejudice.

But oh, how he loved her.

His father watched him. "Then it is true."

Puzzled, Donald stared at him.

"There is gossip that you have been seen with a Mennonite girl, Florence's friend." His father shook his head. "My son, my son. Wasn't the internment bad enough? All the hatred shown to our people? It is one thing to accept the inevitable, *shikata ga nai.* But this—you are asking for problems far above your imagination." He stood up and turned on his desk radio, and Donald knew the discussion was over.

He wondered how long his father had known about Annie. Had he also known about the letters? Could he have—

No. His father was honorable. He would never have tampered with someone else's property. That was unthinkable.

Chapter Seven

Malinda poked Annie and whispered, "Page forty-eight."

Sitting in the church choir loft the next morning, Annie tried hard to concentrate on the sermon. But somehow Rev. Loewen's description of the ten lepers and their cleansing ritual drifted away, and Saturday's picnic played itself over and over in her mind. Donald's every word, every expression, his gentleness and good manners, the tender way he'd held her hand . . .

Now, she breathed a sigh of relief for the closing hymn.

On the way out the side door, Malinda asked, "What's going on? You're not even half here."

Annie wanted to tell her—to tell *somebody,* but it was too soon, too precious. She murmured something about "working things out," hoping Malinda would think she was talking about a musical arrangement and let it drop.

But Malinda stared at her. "What things? What are you talking about?"

"Oh . . . you know . . . I have to . . ." Annie looked around for a distraction and saw Frieda Schmidt and her baby surrounded by admiring friends. She pointed. "Look—isn't he cute? The suit he's wearing, isn't that the one you gave Frieda at the shower?"

Malinda followed Annie as she headed over to the group. When the others were occupied, Annie slipped away to the parking lot to wait in the car for her mother to finish visiting.

Usually, her mother invited someone for dinner and fixed something special. But today they went home alone and ate leftover *borscht* and *tvehbock.* When they finished and her mother went to take a nap, Annie relaxed with a new library book.

She turned about a dozen pages, none of the words registering. Then she heard a loud rhythmic knock at the front door. That "shave-and-a-haircut, two-bits" kind of knock. Her first thought was of Donald—but no, that didn't seem like something he'd do. Besides, he'd never been to her house before and wouldn't drop in without an invitation.

When she opened the door, there stood Jonah, still in his navy pin-striped Sunday suit and oxford shoes. He'd taken off his tie, and his starched white shirt collar stood open.

"Got a full tank of gas. I'm taking you to the mountains!" He rubbed his hands together, grinning, his blue eyes shining. "Gotta celebrate getting all them raisins rolled."

Annie felt trapped. That time at the music store, hadn't he gotten the hint that she wasn't interested? Especially since she broke the Youth for Christ date. But how could she turn him down now, after he and his family had worked like crazy all night?

Going anywhere with him was out of the question. Her heart was still so full of Donald. Her mind was dreaming of him, every nerve in her body wanting to be with him again.

She leaned weakly against the doorjamb and hunted desperately for an excuse. "I . . . I've got a headache. And there's quartet practice."

"Ach, levenstiet!" her mother scolded impatiently as she entered the room. Jonah's knock on the door had awakened her. Annie turned and saw her mother coming toward them, smoothing stray hair back into her *schups.* "That's not until five. You've been working too hard, adding up all those numbers. A ride in the fresh air is exactly what you need. Here," she said, handing a sweater to Annie. "Take this in case it gets chilly."

Annie stared at the sweater and then at her mother. Had this been planned—maybe even with Jonah's mother—to make up for that broken date? Was that why her mother hadn't invited someone over?

She glanced down at her dress. She'd changed into an everyday one and slipped into a pair of tennis shoes. Her mother looked at her sternly, gave her a nudge and whispered, "You look fine. Now go."

She'd have to make the best of it. Maybe this would be a chance to call it quits for good. Gritting her teeth, Annie took the sweater and followed a beaming Jonah to his car.

After the night's rain, the sun shone in a nearly cloudless sky. They rode past orchards of peach and plum trees, vineyards, then grove after grove of citrus that looked like fat Christmas trees decorated with oranges. Eventually they rose into the foothills, with live oak trees and pasturelands, all looking fresh and green.

They talked casually about church activities and mutual friends. Jonah laughed about a guy who could tie vines faster than anyone else but always tripped over his own feet.

Annie remembered the Sunday school lesson that morning. "Mrs. Kroeker told us God can use whatever talent a person has." She chuckled, "I guess Barney's talent is using his hands."

"Talk about hands. Roger Esau bought himself a guitar. Wants to learn hymns on it," Jonah snickered. "Imagine—a guitar in church! Just like a cowboy."

Annie shrugged. She preferred the piano, but Roger was entitled to his own interests. After a bit, she asked, "How did you like that song the children sang in the Sunday school opening, the one with motions about the wise man building his house on the rock?"

Jonah swatted the steering wheel. "That reminds me. Did you know Victor Flaming and Sarah Jost just got engaged? Problem is, they can't get married until he finishes the house he's building, and they save up enough money for furniture." He shook his head. "That'll take a while. She's always buying fancy new clothes, and he can't stay away from expensive tools and gadgets."

Annie leaned against the armrest on her door and studied him. He seemed to know as much gossip as the women in sewing circle. How could such a handsome guy be so shallow and boring?

As they reached a higher elevation, the road—shaded by evergreens—became more winding. Jonah sped up, swerving on the outward curves. Annie heard that guys did it to make the girls slide over next to them. It was a standing joke among the young people. But it scared her, and she didn't think it was at all funny. Now that the thirty-five mile-per-hour speed limit had been lifted, Jonah's foot was heavy on the accelerator.

At an especially sharp curve, Annie clutched the edge of the seat. "Slow down! You'll roll us over the edge."

But Jonah just grinned and waggled his eyebrows at her. Finally they reached a turnout, and to her relief he pulled over and stopped. "Okay, let's get out."

Standing near the cliff, Annie tried to calm herself, taking in deep breaths of pine. She stared down into the valley, wishing her life were as orderly as the neat squares of farms below. The scene reminded her of embroidery—orange trees looking like French knots, grapevines like stripes of backstitching, alfalfa fields like thick and solid satin stitching. Someday she'd make a quilt like that.

Then she thought about the quilt Jonah's mother would be making, and she turned to him. She had to tell him—now, before this went any further.

But he grabbed her hand. "C'mon. There's a better view on top of the next hill."

His hand was big and callused, his grip a command. She couldn't help comparing it with Donald's strong but gentle touch. She wanted to pull away, but the path was steep and covered with wet leaves and pine needles. Any wrong move, and they could lose their balance and slide down to the road.

Finally they came to a narrow, shaded trail, and he released her, taking the lead up the ridge.

When they finally reached the top, Annie gasped at the beauty. In a small glen, cows grazed peacefully. Birds flitted through the bushes along a wandering stream. From somewhere among the pine trees beyond, a plume of smoke added the faint scent of a campfire.

Jonah elbowed her. "Don't that look pretty? Someday I'll buy land here, build a cabin. Wouldn't that be swell?"

Annie nodded. "Sure. But it's awfully far from people. Wouldn't you be lonely up here all by yourself?"

He laughed and punched her lightly on the shoulder. "Always kidding. You know I mean *us.*" He slid a sideways glance at her. "We get along real good—why don't we get married, huh? What do you say? I've got money saved, so we wouldn't have to wait."

Annie felt as though she'd been punched in the stomach. She'd hoped to lead up to the subject gradually, to let him down gently, and now she'd walked right into this. "I just can't . . . we don't—"

He turned to her then and held up his hands in an I-give-up gesture. "Okay, okay, maybe that was too sudden. Think about it, huh? Let me know? But don't wait too long."

Annie nodded. What could she say without hurting his feelings? A cloud passed over the sun, darkening the scene. Wordlessly, she turned and started back down the hill. Jonah followed, his leather-soled shoes slipping now and then, forcing him to grab bushes and tree trunks to keep his footing. After a few slips, his suit pants were spotted with dirt. Annie knew his mother would have a hard time getting pitch out of that serge material. What could have possessed him to come here in his Sunday clothes?

But she knew the answer. He wanted to look his best for her. And she felt miserable, because no matter how good he looked, it wouldn't change her answer.

When they got back to the car, Annie headed for the passenger side. But Jonah leaned one hand against the door and wedged himself between her and the car. "If we're practically engaged, don't you think I rate a kiss?"

He didn't get it at all. She would just have to be blunt. "We're *not* engaged. Not even practically. So don't spread it around that we are." She stared at his hand pressed against the door.

Better get it over with, right now—no sense dragging it out. "I'm sorry. I don't . . . oh, Jonah. It just wouldn't work. You're a nice guy . . . I really like you . . . but you deserve someone who'll be a good wife to you. Not me."

He looked at her, his lower lip in a little boy's pout. "Hey, you haven't even given us a chance." He leaned his face close to hers. "If you'd only let me show you—"

Lord, help me to be strong. She shook her head. "No, Jonah. No." They stared at each other for a minute—she with determination, he frowning. His eyes narrowed with disbelief. "No," she said again, softly but firmly.

Then his eyes flashed with anger, and Annie felt suddenly afraid. He'd never been really mad at her before, but she'd heard about times when he'd lost his temper and gotten into fights. And here they were alone, miles from any help.

But she held his gaze, and finally he stomped over to his side of the car, his shoulders slumped. She heard him grumbling, "Boy-oh-boy. What does it take?"

As soon as Annie let herself into the car, Jonah twisted the steering wheel, and tires squealing, he U-turned and sped down the mountain curves. Terrified, she closed her eyes and hung onto the seat and the door handle, without saying a word. Their ride home was silent, except for Jonah whistling tunelessly through his teeth.

When Annie got home, her mother eyed her, smiling. "How was the drive?"

Annie couldn't meet her look. "Okay. The hills were nice and green." She glanced at her watch. "I've got to change. The quartet will be here in a bit."

Her mother's smile faded, then brightened again. "I better make some coffee. There's plenty of *tvehbock;* I'll open another jam."

In spite of her sadness, Annie felt a huge sense of relief. Jonah had been a good friend, but that was now in the past. It wouldn't be his nature to stay friends now. She thought of girls her age—and even younger—at church who were engaged. Some were already married;

one even had a baby. And here she'd just turned down the only proposal she ever had. But she knew she'd done the right thing.

By Wednesday night prayer meeting, most of the people at church knew that Annie and Jonah had broken up. Many wondered why. Some thought she was keeping him dangling and speculated how long it would take to change her mind. Nobody could understand why she hadn't jumped at the chance to marry a handsome Mennonite with a nice-sized farm and money in the bank.

Annie's mother was the last to hear. After they got home from prayer meeting, she came into Annie's room. "*Anchen, Anchen!* Is it true what they say . . . you told Jonah no? How could you do that? Are you *fe'rekt* . . . just plain crazy? Better make up with him before he changes his mind."

Annie took a deep breath. This might take a while. "I can't."

"*Ach, yauma,* why not? I moved to Rosemond just for you, and you turn down a good chance like this. He's got land of his own, a good future—"

"But I don't love him. I've tried . . . I really have! I've even prayed for God to give me that love . . . but it just isn't there."

Her mother stared at her soberly, then shook her head. "You better pray harder." She turned away and fussed with the doily on Annie's vanity, straightening the hand mirror and fiddling with the brush. Not looking up, she added, "I heard you were with a Jap out at the college on Saturday."

"Please, mother," Annie said wearily. "I keep telling you. 'Jap' is a bad word. As bad as cursing." She wondered who'd told her mother and how many whispers it had passed through.

"Then it's true?"

Annie shrugged. "I don't know what you heard. But I told you about Florence's brother. We were friends in school. He's just come home—"

"I knew college would give you all kinds of modernistic ideas. If your father hadn't insisted, you'd have settled down and given me grandchildren already."

Annie didn't answer. To her mother, anything not Mennonite was modernistic.

Her mother's eyes narrowed as she looked directly at Annie. "I think there's more to it. I think that Jap . . . Japanese boy is standing in your way. Maybe that's why God hasn't answered your prayer."

Annie sighed. She didn't want to admit she'd already struggled with that idea. Now that Donald was home, she knew it couldn't be true. "I've been studying my Bible. It says there's no difference between Jews and Greeks. Or any nationalities. God loves us all the same."

Her mother frowned. "You're just quoting Scripture to suit yourself. Of course God loves all mankind. But he also says not to be unequally yoked."

"With unbelievers. Donald is a Christian." Annie took the brush out of her mother's hand. Bending over, she drew the bristles through her curls. "And he's not an enemy of our country, if that's what's worrying you. He risked his life to stop Hitler—"

Her mother gasped and slapped the top of the vanity, staring at her in the mirror. "You mean . . . he was in the army? He carried a gun?" Her eyes bored into Annie's. "You know the Mennonite stand against war! *Kindt,* you think you have all the answers, but on this one you better study some more."

Annie flipped her hair back into place and ran the brush through it several more times. "Aren't you forgetting that some of our own church boys went into the army, too? Jack Schmidt, Roger Martens, Marlin Balzer—"

"Yes, and they'll have to answer to the Lord and the church council for that. But you forget something, too. They went noncombatant. That's not quite as bad."

"Marlin was a litter-bearer. He carried a gun, all right. He had to, going to the frontlines to rescue the wounded."

"Neh, obah!" her mother said with a mixture of disbelief, and scolding. "Are you sure? Praise God the war is over and he can ask forgiveness. But that's beside the point. It's just not right, against nature, you running around with a Jap . . . anese."

Annie bit her lip to keep from giving an angry answer. "Donald has better manners and is more deeply grounded in the Word than a lot of Mennonite boys . . . especially Jonah. I've talked about spiritual things with Donald. The Baptists believe the same as we do."

"Yes, well, maybe on the surface. You can't always tell. Sometimes other nationalities mix in their old heathen religions. It might be altogether different from the Americans who are Baptists."

"Mom! He *is* an American! And they don't worship idols, if that's what you mean."

Her mother became very still, staring at her. "How do you know so much about this person? How long have you been seeing him?"

"Just a little bit on Saturday. But I knew him and his sister from college. And he hasn't changed."

Her mother's eyes flashed with fear before she looked away. "I can't talk any sense into you. Better go see the preacher before you get yourself in any deeper."

Annie laid her brush back on the vanity and sat down on her bed to think about that. Rev. Loewen had always been friendly to her, especially when she went to his house for piano lessons with Mrs. Loewen. But this was a far more complicated matter.

A while back, an older girl had been dropped from membership for marrying someone not of the church. But that man was divorced, making it a big issue. And gossip said that when the preacher refused to marry them, the man had cursed him with unrepeatable words.

And a cousin of Jonah's had been written off for taking up with a woman who worked in a bar. A neighbor had seen him there, consorting with the drunks, bottle in hand, and quite *be'soped* himself.

But neither of those cases was like hers. And she and Donald had never talked about marriage. But the way she felt about him . . . maybe it was time to consider the future.

Finally Annie nodded. "Okay. I'll call Rev. Loewen tomorrow."

When she called the church the next day, there was no answer, so she called the reverend's home.

"I'm sorry, Annie," said Mrs. Loewen. "He just left for a conference in Kansas." He'd stay on several more weeks to give revival meetings in the area. "If it's urgent, you could talk to a council member or a deacon." She named several, and Annie decided to call John Driedger, one of the younger deacons. Being newly married, he'd surely understand—and his wife Thelma was a former Presbyterian who'd been rebaptized to join the Mennonites.

They lived a few miles out of town in a wood-frame house surrounded by a peach orchard. When Annie called him, he told her to come to their house after work the next day.

John welcomed her into the parlor, motioning for her to sit down. She sat on a brown corduroy couch in front of windows that were hung with white sheer panels. He sat in the straight-backed chair across the room from her. Thelma brought them coffee and slices of sponge cake, then left the room.

John said he had no problems with Donald being a Baptist. He agreed that they believed much like the Mennonite Brethren.

His race was another thing. Marriage—if it went that far—was a serious thing, and a hard enough adjustment even when both people had been raised alike.

He thought a while, rubbing his chin. "I don't know. I can't recommend it, but sometimes it might work out. . . . I have an uncle who married an Armenian, and they're still together after forty years. They seem happy. But Japanese—" His nose wrinkled as he continued. "They live different, think different. . . . Another thing . . . a lot of people don't know the difference between these honest, hardworking locals and those in Japan. There'd be a lot of prejudice. . . . He was sent to one of those camps?"

Annie nodded. "For a while. Then he joined the army and—"

John frowned and raised his palm. "Wait a minute. That opens up a whole new can of worms."

Annie remembered now that John had planned to go as a conscientious objector and counseled other young men in that direction. Then when the government discovered he was color-blind, they classified him

4-F and not eligible to serve. Had she made a mistake by coming to him?

Now his eyes turned cold. "You know how our forefathers fled Russia to escape being drafted. Were all our efforts for nothing?"

Annie stared at him, puzzled. She'd studied Mennonite history, too. "But Russia is communist. Of course our people wouldn't want to support that. But here, our army fought Hitler so America could stay a Christian nation."

John Driedger's face turned red. "God would have stopped Hitler in time. He doesn't need armies to help him out."

Annie frowned. "But what Hitler did to the Jews . . . the starvation, all those killed in gas chambers. I think God sent our armies to rescue them. Some of the Nisei regiment even helped with that."

John Driedger's lips tightened, and he shook his finger at her. "'Thou shalt not kill!' You college kids think you know everything. The more education you have, the more danger of straying from the Lord."

He stood up. Annie knew she'd already said too much and also got to her feet. John had left school after the eighth grade to take over the family farm. Unlike her father, education was a sore spot in John's mind. He couldn't see how more learning might have helped him.

Annie left the parlor, fighting back tears. Before she reached the door, however, Thelma was next to her. Had she been listening in? Would this also get spread all around church?

But Thelma put her arm around Annie and walked her to the front door. "I know how you feel. If you ever need to talk, I've got an open ear and a closed mouth."

Annie nodded. "Thanks." The unexpected sympathy made her feel like sobbing on the woman's shoulder, but she pushed back her emotions and left as quickly as possible.

The church people had taken Thelma right in and seemed to love her. She seemed to be happy, and had a bubbly personality. Was she just covering up for the hardship of adapting to the rigid Mennonite community?

Donald was friendly, too, and until Pearl Harbor had been popular with classmates of all nationalities and beliefs. He could easily fit into any culture. But if she married him, would her church welcome him, or would they whisper behind his back? Would he be allowed to use his God-given musical talents?

She thought again of John Driedger and knew there were many others like him.

Other army regiments had respected the Nisei combat team. The government had honored Donald with a jacket full of medals. He was considered a hero.

But not by the Mennonites.

Chapter Eight

THIS TIME ANNIE WAS PREPARED. When Donald picked her up at the furniture store the next Thursday at noon, she brought along two meat loaf sandwiches, a jar of lemonade, and cupcakes.

It was a cloudy day, with a bite in the air. Thanksgiving weather. After the heat of summer, Annie welcomed this cooler season and all that went with it. As they drove, she smelled burning leaves. People all over town must have been raking their lawns. She mentioned to Donald how that smell reminded her of her childhood, when she tumbled in the piles her father heaped up.

He grinned. "I can just see you jumping around, and your clothes and hair covered with leaves and twigs."

She wondered what his childhood had been like. "Didn't you do that?"

"Not that I remember. If I had free time, I played checkers with my sister. Or rode my bike over to friends' houses, and we'd play ball."

Annie imagined him as a little boy and envied his sister and friends. Being an only child, she'd missed out on a lot.

Donald drove into the country, up one road and down another until he came to one that had walnut trees on both sides. Their upper branches reached together in a natural arbor. Pulling off the road under one of the biggest trees, he said, "I think this'll be a good place. Almost as good as the college oak."

Annie laughed. "Better. This place doesn't have a janitor."

They sat in the car, sharing the lunch and chatting about nothing in particular. He told her about the odd jobs he was doing for neighbors—pruning, nailing boxes. She mentioned some of the interesting customers who came into the store, in particular the Hide-a-bed woman who still hadn't made up her mind.

Then Donald cleared his throat and looked into her eyes. Finally he said, "I have to ask you something."

She waited, holding her breath.

"Do you . . . how do you feel . . . about Jonah Krause?"

The question surprised her so much that her face grew hot. "Jonah? I don't understand. He's only a friend." At least he had been. "Why do you ask?"

"I just wondered. The day after I got home, I saw you with him—" He told her what he'd seen in the bank.

Annie drew back, staring at him. "Donald Nakamura! You mean you saw me that day and didn't even say hello?"

This time his face colored, and he looked down, letting his hands drop between his knees. "I was going to. I even started to leave my place in line. Then I saw *him* . . . and the two of you looked so cozy. . . ." He looked at her sideways. "I thought . . ."

She waited, but he didn't finish. "You thought he was my boyfriend?"

He just shook his head and looked at her sheepishly, without answering.

Her mouth dropped open. "You thought . . . we were married?" she asked in a near whisper, dumbfounded.

Donald nodded. "Then when you stopped by the church that Friday evening, I noticed you weren't wearing a ring." He hesitated. "I still need to know for sure. Are you . . . free? You're not in love with him?"

"Of course not. And I'm not going with anyone . . . especially not Jonah." She told him how they'd been thrown together at different occasions, and that she'd turned down his proposal. "I never really considered him. He's not my type."

She shuddered inwardly, remembering how she'd almost given up, resigning herself to taking someone she considered far below second-best.

"Who *is* your type?"

You, Donald. Only you. But she couldn't say it out loud. Not yet. "Someone who enjoys music, reads good books, likes to study the Word," she proclaimed, a smile sneaking across her face.

Donald smiled back, his face glowing. He slid his right arm along the back of the seat and looked at her face, his eyes moving from one feature to the other. As his eyes focused on her mouth, his lips softened and parted slightly.

Now, finally, he'll kiss me, she thought.

Instead, he took a deep breath, then whistled it out softly, shaking his head. "I've dreamed of you day and night, pictured your face, all through the years I was . . . gone. Even when your letters stopped coming and I lost hope. There was a hollow spot in my heart, and nothing else could fill it."

The intensity in his eyes thrilled Annie beyond endurance, and she had to look away.

He reached up and stroked her hair. "It's been so long. We've both been through a lot . . . matured a lot. In some ways, I feel like we're strangers. Would you be willing to put up with me . . . go out with me . . . so we can get to know each other again?" He rolled one of her curls around his finger. "Will you be my girl?"

Her heart thumped like a hammer and her head spun. All she could manage was a whisper. "Yes. I'd like that."

She'd loved him all these years, and now that he was back, her love was even stronger. But what he said made sense. There was so much she didn't know about him.

"Even though I'm Japanese?"

As if that made any difference! "You're . . . you!" she exploded. "When we're together, I don't think *German* or *Japanese.* We're both American."

He held up his left hand. "It's not that easy. Think about it. Real carefully." He stared out the car window. "Sure, legally, I'm American by birth. But my family . . . my people . . . most of them are still very

Japanese. They cling to a lot of the old customs. There'll be gossip. Prejudice. Even meanness. People around here aren't used to seeing mixed couples."

Annie thought about Thelma Driedger. Although she had some German in her background, she hadn't been raised Mennonite—and that made a big difference. At first people rolled their eyes at her lopsided *tvehbock* and snickered at her butchered *Plautdietsch,* that much-loved everyday low-German language. To insiders, it had incomparable descriptions and hilarious jokes that couldn't be translated without losing their punch. Annie was sure Thelma must have felt like an outsider, but she'd been good-natured, laughing at herself, too. Now she was accepted and loved.

If she and Donald didn't take themselves too seriously, Annie figured they could surely get along with both cultures. Couldn't they? "I know. I think I can take it."

He slid his hand around her shoulders and drew her close. "My sweet strawberry-blonde. I can't believe how lucky I am." This time he did kiss her, and his mustache tickled her all the way to her toes. She felt as though she were floating into the clouds.

During the next two weeks, Annie didn't see much of Donald. But one afternoon he surprised her, stopping at the store. He told her he was busy tying vines for neighbors and had just run into town on an errand. The expression in his eyes spoke promises.

The Sunday before Thanksgiving, Annie's church celebrated their first peacetime Harvest Festival. Everyone seemed especially happy. Missionaries spoke in the morning, afternoon, and evening. Special musical numbers and congregational singing were interspersed throughout the day's services.

Annie wore a new suit she'd made—green to match her eyes—and played for the quartet, sang in the choir, and played for a mixed octet.

In between services she practiced with groups for the next meeting. She often thought about Donald, and how he would have enjoyed being part of the program. But the church—especially people like John Driedger—wasn't ready for that yet.

At noon and suppertime, the social-hall tables groaned with food. Turkeys had been hard to find, but the *fest* committee had bought plenty of chickens. Now that most rationing was over, all the women brought their best salads and pies. And, of course, there were huge baskets of *tvehbock* with plenty of coffee and *prips,* the hot ground-barley drink the older people loved. Donald would have relished the food, too, and complimented the women and the *fest* committee.

Because she came in late after last-minute rehearsals, Annie quickly ate both meals with the servers. With such a crowd and all of her responsibilities, she hadn't seen Jonah at all. She felt people's eyes on her but, to her relief, with all that was going on, no one cornered her for explanations.

The Monday after Thanksgiving, Donald called her at work. His rich, warm voice thrilled her, and she closed her eyes, imagining his smooth face, his neat mustache.

"We've just had a phone installed at church. I had to try it out." He'd finished tying vines, and now he was painting the house and working at the farm by day, practicing a Christmas cantata with his choir several evenings a week. "Our church has never done anything like this before, and we want it to be a real tribute to the Lord—thanking him for bringing us through the internment and the war. We'll present it December 23 in the evening. Would you like to come?"

"Oh, I'd love to!" Then Annie hesitated. When was her own choir program? What if it was the same night? "But I'll have to check. My church—"

"It's okay. Just a thought. . . . You know, Annie, we've got to talk. I've done a lot of thinking. . . ."

That sounded an alarm in her heart, and Annie caught her breath. The church people, her mother, the deacon—all of them had warned her about Donald. What if he decided their relationship wouldn't work after all? A lump came to her throat, choking off her voice. He hadn't exactly said he loved her, but she knew he did. She just couldn't lose him again!

"Annie? Are you still there?"

She could barely whisper. "I'm here."

"When can I see you?" His voice was soft, caressing, and she felt better. But when they tried to set a time, either his farm duties or their church activities conflicted, and it seemed impossible. Then she heard a noise on the other end of the line, and Donald said, "Uh-oh. My dad just drove up with a flat tire. I'll call you later."

"Good-bye," she said to a dead phone, angry at herself for doubting him. If he were having second thoughts about her, he wouldn't have invited her to his Christmas program. If only she could attend!

But at choir practice the next week, her fears were confirmed. The church calendar had been scheduled, and her choir would be presenting its Christmas program on the evening of December 23—the same night as Donald's cantata. She'd promised to play piano for the toddlers, who would do their little motion songs at the beginning of the evening. Then she was to sing in a trio in the middle of the program, and accompany a male quartet near the end. There was no way she could get out of her commitments and attend Donald's church.

While the director explained how he wanted the choir members to sing the next song, Annie looked straight at him, but she imagined Donald leading *his* choir. She saw him standing straight and slim, his smooth strong hands guiding the singers through the hushed passages. Then the wide swings of his arms built them up into *fortissimo.* His broad shoulder muscles contracted to bring them into a finale. All through the song, he was one with the music. And she had to miss that! She breathed a silent prayer that it would work out, but knew there wasn't a chance.

Donald hadn't called since his invitation to his program, and she wondered if it was because he was too busy or if he'd changed his mind.

She wished she could call him, but only bold girls called boys, and her reputation was shaky enough already.

"Annie!" The woman next to her tugged at her arm. "Page one-sixty-three!"

The director gave the signal to rise, and Annie, her face getting hot, juggled her books to get the right one. She'd never been so absentminded at choir practice, and hoped no one else noticed.

But hoping did no good. Snickers drifted all the way from the back row of men and boys. News of her friendship with Donald had spread through the whole church and become the juiciest gossip in ages. Would it ever die down? How could she act normal with people watching her every move? Her mother had warned her about the gossip, but she never thought it would be this bad.

Well, she'd just have to get used to it. Ignore it, if possible. Their ridicule wasn't going to make her give up Donald.

It wasn't until late the next Saturday afternoon, nearly closing time at the store, that Annie heard from him. All day, she'd jumped at each ring of the phone, only to hear voices of customers and furniture representatives.

Her fingers spider-walked on the keys of the adding machine as she tried for the third time to balance the weekly credits with the cash register tape. As she rammed down the lever for the grand total, she heard someone clearing his throat. Looking up, she saw Donald. He was leaning on the counter, smiling, his dark eyes sparkling. She could barely breathe, and swallowed hard.

Whatever she said would sound dumb. "How long have you been here?" she stuttered.

He winked, and she melted inside. "Just a little while. Long enough to watch you battle the numbers."

She stood up, holding onto her desk for fear her legs would give way. Her hair was a mess, her nose shiny. She went over to the counter and spoke softly. "Have you . . . been real busy . . . with your choir . . . and the house?"

He ran his finger over her wrist, and she thought she would die. "Pretty hectic. The house is painted, but now I've been tying another farmer's vines. And with the cantata so close, we're practicing two, three nights a week."

"How's it coming?"

He leaned forward slightly and laced his fingers into hers. She wished time would stand still.

He shrugged, then nodded. "Pretty well. I've got the good singers shouting in the ears of the monotones. At least they've learned to follow me instead of blaring out in the wrong places."

He chuckled, and she smiled. His thumb caressed hers, reminding her of the first time he'd held her hand. It was three years ago, when he'd told her about the evacuation—the day she realized how much he meant to her. Tears pricked her eyes, and she blinked them away.

He tilted his head to look into her face. "Hey, what's the matter? Did I say something wrong?"

Annie shook her head. "I'm just so glad you came home safely. All the time you were gone . . . not knowing . . ."

"I'm glad too. And happy that Jonah, or any other Mennonite boy, didn't snap you up while I was gone." Donald glanced around. No one else was in the store. He leaned toward Annie, and as if in a trance, she watched his face move closer.

Just then the front door jangled, and two customers walked in. From the back office, Bob Taylor came to meet them. "Hello, Mr. and Mrs. Rogers! What can I do for you today?"

Donald quickly moved back, but Annie's lips tingled as though he'd kissed her, as though she actually felt the softness of his lips and slight brush of his mustache. She felt her face grow hot. Bob hadn't glanced their way, but that didn't mean he hadn't been watching.

Donald let out a soft whistle and reached out to touch the cuff of her long-sleeved blouse. "We've got so much to talk about. But not here. Let's see . . . how about . . . tomorrow afternoon? I have to be at the church at four-thirty to set up for a missionary film, but would you be free for about an hour, say . . . at three o'clock?"

She nodded. Tomorrow! How would she stand to wait that long? Little bubbles of joy danced through her. "Do you want to come to my house? Are you brave enough to meet my mother?"

He tilted his head to one side and gave a half-smile. "Is that a dare?"

Annie thought of all the objections her mother had to their friendship. Donald's good manners, his dignity and refinement—surely they'd work in his favor. "Yes. I dare you," she teased. *Mom can't help but see what a gentleman he is.*

"Well, I met the Germans head-on in Italy; I guess I can meet my sweetheart's mother in Rosemond." He blew Annie a two-fingered kiss and left with the same confident stride he had in college.

She took a deep breath and slowly let it out. He'd called her his sweetheart. And she'd been worried that he was having doubts about their relationship.

On Sunday Annie determined to keep her mind on the preaching. But the first sermon was from Ecclesiastes: "Do not be hasty in anger." She thought of the way Donald controlled his temper when the college janitor insulted him, how he was able to rise above the unfairness of internment and go into the army, distinguishing himself with bravery.

The second sermon was about the fear the disciples felt during the storm at sea and how Jesus calmed the waves. Annie thought of all the battles Donald couldn't talk about. In the medics he must have seen so many others die and must have risked his life, time after time, to save the wounded. There must have been times when he was terrified and the Lord helped him through. Silently, she thanked God for the wonder of him being safely home.

After the service, she barely listened to the chatter of her friends as they formed one of many clusters on the churchyard. A couple of the girls asked about Donald. "A college friend," Annie explained. But most of the talk was about Rebecca Jost's daring open-toed shoes, Virginia Entz's nylons—the naked-looking new seamless style—and the fur collars on coats displayed in stores. There were also whispers about suspected pregnancies and new couples.

Annie wondered if the gossip about her would die down—and if Japanese Baptists stood outside visiting after church as long as Mennonites did.

Somehow she couldn't see Donald going on about ordinary things like someone's new outfit, or even tractors or crops as the Mennonite men did. Not after listening to a sermon. He would greet people, ask about their lives, listen to their problems. And his mind would be full of questions: Why hadn't the disciples understood the Lord? Why did Jesus tell people not to broadcast his miracles?

As soon as she could without seeming rude, Annie broke away from the group and went to the car. Sliding behind the steering wheel, she hoped her mother didn't have quilting or bake sales to plan. Her main hope was that her mother hadn't accepted a dinner invitation.

A few minutes later, her mother came toward the car. Her eyes widened when she saw Annie waiting there. "What, are you mad or something?" She climbed into the passenger's seat and slammed the door, still staring at Annie.

"Mad? No. I just got tired of all the jabbering." She shifted into first gear and rolled out of the parking lot.

Her mother studied her a little longer, then reached over and felt her forehead. "You're not sick, are you?"

Annie swallowed a giggle. Lovesick, maybe. She couldn't let her mother know something was up. If she found out Donald was coming over, she'd have time to think up a lot of objections. "I'm all right. . . . Oh, by the way, did you know Tina Fachner is expecting?"

Tina and Bernard had been married exactly four months. As Annie had hoped, her mother's thoughts were sidetracked, and she was able to breathe easier all the way through dinner.

The steaming *borscht* was thick with potatoes and cabbage. Annie forced herself to eat normally, carefully avoiding the peppercorns. By the time the dishes were washed and dried and everything put away, it was still only one-thirty. How would she last until three o'clock?

Chapter Nine

ANNIE STRAIGHTENED THE DOILY ON the parlor table—again. She centered the vase and rearranged the scarf on top of the upright piano. She looked around for a conversation piece, then got her college yearbooks from her bedroom and put them on the table.

There was still more than an hour before Donald would come, so she curled up on the couch in the living room and tried to read *The Robe.* Although she could hardly put the book down last evening, she now kept looking at the same paragraphs over and over. Finally she set it aside and went to the piano. Before long she was pouring her heart into Beethoven's "Moonlight Sonata" and found it soothed her nerves.

When she finished the piece, she started another of his sonatas, the "Pathétique." While playing its dramatic opening chords, she heard the knock at the door. Her hands flew off the keys, flipping the sheet music to the floor. By the time she turned around on the piano bench to pick up the sheet music, her mother had hurried to the door.

"Who can that possibly be?" her mother wondered out loud.

The only time her mother had seen Donald was in the strawberry field several years ago, and he'd been wearing muddy work clothes. Now he was a grown man with a mustache, dressed in navy slacks and a white shirt, with a navy and white sweater.

Annie could see she immediately realized who he was, and watched her mother's face struggle between shock and good manners. The screen door was hooked, and her mother made no attempt to open it.

Donald spoke first. "How are you, Mrs. Penner? It's nice to see you again." He held out a little jar. "My mother's honey. Clover. I thought you might enjoy it on your wonderful *tvehbock*."

Annie's mother blinked and slowly unlatched the screen door.

Behind her, Annie smiled at Donald. "Come on in. . . . I didn't know your mother kept bees."

"It's a new venture. She just started after they came back from camp."

Annie's mother looked from Donald to Annie and back. Annie had never seen her so at a loss for words. Somehow that made her own confidence grow, and she took the jar of honey. "Thanks, Donald. That's very nice. Mom, you want me to put this in the kitchen?"

Her mother's head gave a little jerk as though she was just waking up. "Oh . . . ah, yes, thank you . . . for the honey. And thank your mother for me. I'll put it up, Annie." She took it in her hand, but still stood between them, looking from one to the other.

Donald moistened his lips. "Well, you were playing the piano, Annie. Don't let me stop you. I'd like to hear the rest."

Annie remembered he had only an hour to spend with her, and finishing the "Pathétique" would take up a precious third of it. "Some other time."

Instead, she went over to the college yearbooks and took out the one from the year he graduated. It fell open to the page of his senior picture.

"Hey, you never signed my annual," she proclaimed as she sat down on the couch with it and patted the cushion beside her. "Come on, have a seat."

He sat down and took the yearbook on his lap, turning the pages and shaking his head.

"Look at all those signatures! You can't imagine how I wanted to be there that last day of school, knowing all my friends would be tearing around, getting everyone to sign." He closed his eyes for a moment, then sighed.

She'd missed him an awful lot that day, too. "But the school did send you one?"

"In July. I nearly wore it out, looking at it so much. I could've had Florence sign, but there wasn't any point. So mine's all blank."

"Well, you'll just have to bring it over. Some of your friends are still around. We'll make up for it." On the end table beside the couch was a bowl full of pencils and pens. Annie fished out a pen and handed it to him.

He looked at it and clicked the end a few times. "Hmm . . . one of those new ball points. Nice." He poised it above his senior picture, then signed it quickly and turned to the last page to read through the notes other people had written. Then he found a blank spot and began writing.

She leaned over to see, but he covered the words with his other hand. Her knee accidentally touched his. Without looking up, he carefully moved his knee away.

Annie did look up. Her mother had noticed, but evidently his caution had eased her mind, because she turned and took the honey into the kitchen. But she left the door open.

When Donald finished writing, he closed the book and handed it to her. "Don't read it until after I leave."

"That bad?"

"No. Just . . . personal."

What if her mother read it before she did? Annie hugged it to her chest. "I'd better put it in my room."

"Why don't you get a sweater or something while you're there, and then we'll go for a little ride. Okay?"

She nodded. "Good idea."

After carefully putting the yearbook under her pillow, she threw a sweater over her shoulders, fastening the top button. As she passed the kitchen, she saw her mother sitting at the table, looking through a cookbook.

Before her mother could say a word, Annie assured her, "Don't worry. I'll be back about four." Then she joined Donald, who was standing by the front door.

This time he drove to the nearby Kings River, now running low and exposing sandy islands and a wide expanse of beach. They sat on a bench under wild olive trees and talked about their childhoods, the teachers they'd liked, the radio programs they enjoyed.

Annie was surprised how well he knew all the comedians, the serials. Henry Aldrich and Fibber McGee had been her limit—and those in only small doses. She hadn't even heard of the Green Hornet or the Shadow.

But Donald was equally familiar with the Old-Fashioned Revival Hour and Haven of Rest. The radio had been used far more in his home.

"'Showers of Blessings' just isn't the same without your father . . ." Annie told him. ". . . and your solos."

Donald nodded. "He misses it too. But his arrest is still too raw in his mind. And the counseling takes up all his time now."

"I guess you can help with that, too. All your experience . . ."

"I try. But sometimes I feel like I'm just mouthing the words. There was such a chunk taken out of my own life."

"I know you wanted to be a doctor."

Donald gave a short, bitter laugh. "Sure. Like the prophecy in the yearbook says: 'Donald Nakamura, famous heart surgeon.'" His shoulders drooped as he added, "What a laugh."

"Didn't you apply to medical schools?"

He shrugged. "Yeah. Quite a few."

"And?"

"Thank you, no Japs."

Annie stared at him, frowning. "They didn't say that. Did they?"

"Might as well have. They turned me down. At least, most of them. The others . . . well, it's been so long since I applied, they must have thrown my papers away." He sighed. "My father thinks I should just forget it and take over the strawberry farm. Help him in the church."

Annie shook her head. "Your father is a wonderful man, a great minister of God. But everybody needs to follow his own calling. Not someone else's."

He stared into space, biting his lip. "That's what I struggle with. How can I tell if it's God's will or just my own dreams?"

Annie thought a moment. Then she remembered a Sunday school lesson a few weeks ago and asked, "Have you ever set out a fleece?"

"A what?"

She reminded him about the story of Gideon, how he made sure his orders were from God by setting out some sheep's wool. If it was wet in the morning while the rest of the ground was dry, that meant he was on the right track. "Pray about it. Then reapply at those schools. That would be your fleece. If you're accepted, that means you're to go; if not—"

"That would mean my father is right." Donald nodded, and his eyes shone. "Annie, Annie, you're a wonder." But his eyes quickly sobered. "But the farm is our livelihood. Who else would run it?"

"Gideon set out two fleeces. Maybe your second one could be that your grandfather gets well and can take over," she offered.

"He isn't improving. Even if he does, he won't get any younger. And it would destroy my father if the place fell into strangers' hands."

"Then maybe . . . someone your father would approve of."

"That would be even less likely."

"Well, then. That's a great fleece."

"Sweet, Annie, you're asking for two miracles." He glanced at his watch. "I wish I had more time. But I need to get back to church." They went back to the car and he started the motor, then turned to look at Annie again. She met his eyes, and saw that they glistened with love and hope. He leaned over and kissed her tenderly—and time stood still.

"It's so hard for me to let you go." He sighed, kissed her again, then reluctantly shifted into gear and drove her home.

Annie walked into the house, nearly dancing with happiness. Her mother was in the parlor, reading the *Zionsbote*. "Well? What do you think of him?"

Her mother shrugged. "He's not bad-looking. Polite and mannerly." Then she frowned. "For a friend. Just make sure that's all he is."

Annie's joy wilted like a violet in dry soil. She'd hoped her mother would be able to see past his nationality. She picked up the book she'd left on the table and leafed through the pages for her place without looking up. "I'll be . . . going out with him sometimes," she announced.

"Going out? You mean on a date? In public? What will people think, seeing you two together? Everyone knows dating leads to marriage." Her mother set down the magazine and beckoned Annie to sit beside her. "*Kindt,* how well do you remember your father?"

Annie thought back. She'd been eight when he died. He never spanked her, rarely scolded her, and was always interested in her school activities and interests. "Enough to still miss him. He was so . . . so special."

"Do you know why he hardly ever came to church?"

Annie tried to remember. "No. But I once heard him say something about baptism. Something about the council—"

"They wanted him to be rebaptized. Immersed. He said he'd already had the blessing from sprinkling, so he refused."

"I always thought he was Mennonite, too."

"Yes. But not Mennonite *Brethren.*"

"He was a good Christian . . . I know he was. He loved the Lord." Annie remembered the line from his favorite song that he so often sang: "He walks with me and He talks with me, and He tells me I am His own."

"Yes . . . but we have to follow the church's rules." Her mother sighed. "I begged him: 'Do it for me, if for no other reason.' But all our life together, it was a thorn between us. I'd take you to church every Sunday . . . alone . . . and envy all the couples walking in together. I knew they felt sorry for me. I even hated visiting my family, knowing they looked down on him . . . and on me for marrying him. I don't want you to go through that . . . and much worse."

Annie frowned. People had always been nice to *her.* Or had they been making up for her dad's "failures"? She'd heard people comment to him, "Come to this special meeting, you'll see the light—" But he'd always changed the subject.

"Donald's a Baptist," she countered. "They baptize the same as we do. It wouldn't be a problem."

"But there would be plenty of other problems. No matter what you say, he's different. And that would set you apart. I don't want you to suffer like I did."

They stared at each other for a few moments—Annie unconvinced, her mother's face adamant.

"I . . . I don't understand." Annie thought her parents had been happy. Why had they let a point of doctrine come between them? "Couldn't you have just . . . gone to *his* church? *They* would have accepted you, wouldn't they?"

Her mother looked shocked. "I was born a Mennonite Brethren. I wouldn't have felt at home anywhere else."

That night, Annie searched her Bible for references to marriages. The only warnings she found were against marrying heathens and idol-worshipers. Many of the Israelite leaders—Joseph and Moses among others—had married women of other countries. Solomon also came to mind, but Annie thought he wasn't a very good example. But none of those patriarchs had been Mennonites, so there were no real comparisons.

It seemed that the church leaders had made up a lot of rules on their own. Almost like the Pharisees, who decreed that a religious service was only possible with a specified quorum, and that only so many steps—and no more—were allowed on the Sabbath, and that thing about symbolic hand-washing. With Mennonite Brethren, there could be no work on the Lord's day. Not even sports. And the list of forbidden things went from movies to makeup and short hair.

Donald had told her to think carefully about being his girl. The more she thought about it, the more she became determined to ignore the prejudices and unspoken taboos. If only she could persuade her mother to do the same!

She went to bed, but lay awake, her mind in turmoil. Legally, she was of age and could do whatever she pleased. If she and Donald decided to get married, they could elope.

But she couldn't do that. It was no way to start a Christian marriage.

Somehow, she had to convince her mother that Donald was the right man for her.

In the yearbook he'd signed, Annie found his note.

To the prettiest girl in Rosemond: Now that college and the war are over, we'll have to face life. It might go smoothly, or it might be hard. But whatever will be, wherever you go, with the Lord in your life there will be joy, excitement, and fulfillment. And I hope I can be with you to see it happen. Love, Donald

"I'll do my best to make your hopes come true," she whispered.

Annie didn't see Donald again for several days, although he phoned her a few times at work. He always called from the church and their conversations were short. Because he always spoke quietly, she knew his father must be nearby. When he asked about the Christmas program, she told him her choir had theirs the same night as his.

He hadn't seemed upset. Didn't he care? Somebody like Jonah would have gone into conniptions!

Then she realized it was probably Donald's Japanese way of coping—politely covering his feelings. There was so much to learn about his culture!

The Monday of the week before Christmas, Annie woke up with a sore throat, but the store was in the middle of holiday sales, so she went to work anyway.

By Tuesday she had a full-fledged cold and used up a box of tissues at her desk. She felt much better by Friday. But when the first customer of the day came to make a payment on her account, Annie opened her mouth and no words came out. She cleared her throat, but that didn't help.

The customer smiled. "Laryngitis, huh? I know what that's like. Better go home and drink some hot lemonade."

Annie grabbed a sheet of paper and wrote, "Thanks."

All that day she had to communicate in writing. By closing time, she still could only whisper or squeak.

With the final rehearsal for the Christmas program that very evening, she knew what she had to do.

She arrived early at the church in order to talk about her trio's number. "Sorry," she rasped to the soprano. "You'll have to get someone to take my place."

The young woman was sympathetic but dismayed. "I don't know . . . such short notice!" She thought a minute. "Maybe Bertha would do it."

Annie nodded, relieved. Bertha was a good alto. She'd have no trouble learning the part quickly.

By the time the practice started, it was settled. Bertha knew the song and agreed to fill in for Annie. "I might need a favor myself someday," she joked.

Annie gave her a hug and whispered, "Just let me know."

Singing in the choir was, of course, out of the question. But there were plenty of altos, and one less didn't make much difference. While she waited to practice with the male quartet, the choir director asked her to listen to the rehearsal from different sections of the sanctuary, to gauge the choir's clarity and effectiveness. Their voices sounded beautiful, but there were a few times she raised her hand to signal for better enunciation.

The quartet was another matter. The regular second tenor had the flu and someone else had to fill in. But instead of a reliable and experienced substitute like Bertha, this man had been chosen for popularity rather than talent. He was supposed to sing the lead, but kept drifting into the first tenor's part. The director sang in his ear several times to keep him on the melody. It was late before the rehearsal finished, and even then, the quartet asked if they could schedule an extra run-through the afternoon of the program.

Sunday, December 23, turned out to be a crisp, clear, and sunny day, and Annie had hoped to be free in the afternoon, just in case Donald came over. But she felt sorry for the men in the quartet and told them to come to her house for their practice session.

After two hours, everyone felt better about the music. Annie could tell that her mother loved having four young Mennonite men crowding around her daughter. Her mother fussed over them, sang along with the second tenor until he was confident, served them pie and coffee, and invited them to come again.

When they were gone, Annie braced herself for the inevitable lecture. She didn't have to wait long.

"See, you don't need to look elsewhere. Such fine, upstanding, hard-working men. And so nice-looking. How could you do any better?"

Annie laughed and shook her head. She managed to croak out, "Roger's married, Wesley's practically engaged, and Harry's clumsy. He'd stumble over a thread on the floor."

"*Ach,* he's probably nervous from being near you. What about Kurt?"

"Kurt's making eyes at the Friesen girl—you know, the one who just moved here. Forget it, Mom, these guys are not for me." The effort of talking made Annie cough, and she walked toward her bedroom.

Her mother tightened her lips, then called after her. "You've just set your mind against your own kind. What will it take for you to see reason?"

Annie didn't answer. What would it take for her mother to accept Donald?

That evening, the church was packed. Relatives and neighbors came to hear the Christmas program.

When Annie accompanied the toddlers in "Away in a Manger" and "O Come, Little Children," she felt as though she were playing a piano solo. The little ones froze, staring out into the sea of faces. A few did the motions, one cried, and the tallest boy in the back grinned and waved to his family. But everyone seemed to love having the children participate, and she heard several hearty amens.

Her duty over, Annie sat relaxed in the front row, ready to listen to the program she knew so well. First the narration, then three choir numbers, then a Bible reading. Two more songs, long ones—

She glanced at the clock. On Friday night, it had taken forty-five minutes to get to the quartet number. Subtract some time to get there and back—

Before she actually made the decision, her legs took her out the side door and she nearly ran to the car. The evening had turned cold, and the air hit her like an icy shower. But the Baptist church was only a few blocks away and the streets were deserted. Donald would be so surprised!

Chapter Ten

From a block away, Annie heard the joyful music. When she entered the church and peeked through the door, she saw the pews completely filled and extra chairs set up in the aisles. People even stood along the walls. Little wonder, then, so many cars lined the streets, and she'd had to park down the block.

Scanning the crowd, she saw almost as many Caucasians as Japanese in the audience; no one would notice her. She slipped through the door and stood in the back. From there, she could easily watch Donald leading his choir, their faces intent above their green robes.

Donald swayed with the rhythm, completely engrossed in the music, bringing in the tenors here, quieting the sopranos there. Then the tempo increased, and the song ended in a crescendo of praise. Annie's heart nearly burst with pride and humility for being loved by such a talented man.

An usher tiptoed over to her and apologized. He whispered that they'd run out of programs and that there were two more numbers.

Just then Donald turned to the audience and, in a hushed and mellow baritone, began to sing, unaccompanied, a spiritual she'd never heard before. "Sweet little Jesus boy," he sang. The pianist played a few soft chords, and then Donald's voice continued while the music wove around his words—"we didn't know who you was."

Annie wiped tears from her eyes and noticed many others doing the same. Even men were quietly blowing their noses.

When Donald finished, he bowed his head for a moment, then

straightened to look into the audience. Suddenly his eyes met Annie's, and he gave a noticeable start. His face glowed, and the hint of a smile played on his lips. He turned, nodded to the pianist, and motioned for the congregation to rise and join with the choir to sing "Joy to the World, the Lord Has Come."

As the voices swelled in praise, the choir marched down the aisle and out the front door. Donald followed, stopping only to grab Annie's hand and take her outside with him. Her pulse raced with the joy of seeing him, the thrill of hearing him sing, and the tingle of being near him.

He led her to the side of the church, where the light from inside filtered into a soft glow on the grass. "When did you come?"

She watched the choir march around the corner and into a side entrance. In their rush to get back inside, they hadn't seemed to notice her. She whispered, "Just before your solo. It was wonderful!"

"We can talk," he told her. "Nobody can hear us."

She rasped, "But . . . that's why I'm here. I lost my voice, couldn't sing. So I sneaked out—"

He pulled her toward him to give her a hug. "You didn't! Before your service was over?"

"I didn't know your program would be over this early."

"We started right at seven. Father's giving a short message and then closing. Can you stay and meet the others? There'll be refreshments in the basement."

Annie shook her head. "Our program is still going strong. I need to get back in time to play for the quartet. When you're through, do you want to come and join us for the *toots?*"

"The what?"

"*Toots.* They're packets of candy and nuts and fruit. The church always passes them out after the Christmas program."

"*Toots,* huh? Sounds great. I wish I could. But I have to get back with my choir. People will want to shake hands, and later we're going to the Home for the Aged and sing carols." He bent to kiss her, inhaling deeply, then drew back in surprise. "New kind of perfume?"

She laughed, then started coughing. "Sure," she sputtered. "Mentholatum."

"Better get back where it's warm. I don't want you to catch pneumonia." He pressed his lips softly on her forehead. "I'll call you tomorrow. Save me a candy from your—"

"*Toot,*" she offered. "I'll save you the chocolate kiss." They parted, their hands clinging, then sliding apart as she left.

It was so hard to be in different churches, with different schedules, Annie thought as she drove back to church. If they got married, which one would they attend? In her church, most men joined the church of their brides. But that was when they both were from Mennonite churches in different towns.

Donald so obviously enjoyed directing his choir. He was respected in his church. A leader. Would her church allow him to use his many talents, too? For Mennonites, it was such an honor to be chosen a song director, a Sunday school teacher, or even an usher or committee member. No one willingly gave up a position to another. Certainly not to an outsider. When one person needed to step down, three or four were always ready to fill in. How would Donald feel if he were not given a leadership position and had to sit idly in the congregation?

Back at the churchyard, her parking space was still open, and she hurried to the side door, hoping to sneak through unnoticed.

No such luck. As soon as she opened the door, the entire choir stared at her. To her horror, the narrator was reading the section right before the quartet sang, and the director glared daggers at her. Then his forehead smoothed, but his lips still frowned his disapproval.

Had she lost track of the time? She glanced at the clock. By her calculations, she should still have a good fifteen minutes.

As calmly as possible, she walked to the piano. But then she realized she'd forgotten the music. She started back to get it, her face growing hot. Luckily, a girl sitting in the front row brought it up to her, and with trembling hands Annie played the introduction.

Somehow, she got through the number. She didn't notice whether or not the second tenor found his pitch. When the song ended, she almost started another verse, but caught herself just in time.

After she went back to her seat in the front row, her knees shook uncontrollably. What had gone wrong? Had they skipped one of the numbers?

Then she realized that at rehearsal they'd gone over some of the numbers twice, taking up more time. How could she have been so careless as to forget that? And how was she ever going to live this down? She didn't even want to think about what her mother would say.

After the service, she thought of darting outside through the side door again, but found herself surrounded.

"Where were you?"

"What happened?"

"Why did you leave?"

Annie shook her head. How could she explain? She wormed her way out with the crowd, accepted her *toot* from the ushers handing them out. Seeing the boxes still piled high, she wished she had the nerve to ask for an extra one for Donald.

Outside, the questions started again. Annie took a quick breath, and ended up coughing. *Good timing,* she thought, and patted her throat meaningfully. That could be her excuse—let them think she had another coughing spell and left so she wouldn't disturb the program. *Forgive me, Lord,* she prayed silently. *Someday I'll confess.*

Monday was the day before Christmas, and the furniture store closed at noon. As Annie was getting ready to leave, Donald called. "I'd like to drop by. Do you have time?"

She always had time for him. "I'm through for the day—just need to stop at the five and dime," she said hoarsely.

"I'll meet you out front after you're done there."

As Annie finished her last-minute shopping, she saw Donald waiting outside. He looked around, then said, "I don't see your car. Did you walk to work?" When she nodded, he said, "Good. I'll drive you home. But I'm taking the long way around."

His car was warm, and she slipped off her jacket. His dark eyes gleamed, and she was glad she'd worn her favorite green slipover sweater.

As he backed out of the parking space he asked, "Did you get back to church in time?"

Annie gritted her teeth. "Just barely. The director nearly had a stroke." She told him how she'd handled it—the forgotten music and all. "I feel really guilty. But I'm not sorry I did it."

He shifted gears, then reached for her hand and squeezed it. "I was so thrilled to see you."

She snuggled a little closer. "Your solo was worth it all. And I loved watching you direct."

He drove on, his free arm around her, and for a moment they were quiet. It was a comfortable quiet, Annie thought, as though they could communicate what they meant to each other—even without talking. Then Donald described his choir's carol sing at the Home for the Aged, and before she knew it, they were parked at the college.

He went around to her door and opened it for her. Her cheeks tingled in the crisp and invigorating air, and she slipped her jacket back on. He took her hand and led her to the huge oak tree where they'd first met, the home of so many of their memories. The campus was deserted for the holidays—not even a janitor around—and it seemed they were the only ones in the world.

Donald cleared his throat and reached into his pocket. "I have something for you. It isn't much. Just something to keep you thinking about me."

She looked at the small rectangular box, then back at him, questioning with her eyes. He nodded. She opened it slowly—almost reverently. Inside was a red lacquered pendant, shaped like a strawberry with all its contours and bloom, and in its center rested a tiny diamond. She caught her breath in awe and held it up by the gold chain to admire it. "It's beautiful! I've never seen anything like it." He must have spent all his wages from tying vines.

"I had it specially made. The fruit of love, a symbol of my devotion." Donald lifted the pendant in his fingers and showed her that it opened like a locket. Inside were two tiny pictures—one of her and one of him.

She stammered, "But how . . . where . . ."

He smiled apologetically. "I mutilated my yearbook. Your picture is from the choir shot, and mine is from the science club. When we have newer ones to replace them, I'll paste these back in the book." He took the chain from her and opened the catch. "May I?"

She turned her back to him and gathered her hair out of the way so he could fasten it around her neck, thrilling to the touch of his hands. The pendant lay cozily on her green sweater, and the diamond, catching the sun, flashed up at her. She reached up, took his face between her hands, and kissed him. "Thank you. I love it. It's the best present I've ever had."

He returned her kiss. As she felt the locket pressed between them, she knew it would always be her most treasured possession. When she moved away to catch her breath, he said, "If I only could, I'd give you the world."

She sighed raggedly. "You already have."

When they arrived at her house she asked him to come in. Her gift for him was hidden in the bottom drawer of her dresser, and she wanted to present it to him.

As they went up the steps of the porch together, Donald asked, "What are you doing tomorrow?"

"We'll be at my grandparents' house for Christmas. Near Visalia. They always have a big family dinner and a gift exchange with all the cousins. What about you?"

"My father invited some of the church people over. Otherwise, it would just be my grandfather, my parents, and me. Florence was hoping to come home, but she's working this vacation and couldn't get enough time off to make the bus trip worthwhile."

Annie opened the door and Donald waited for her to enter first.

"I sent her a gift," said Annie, "some cologne. I hope she likes it."

"I'm sure she will. She said you'd been writing her." He winked. "About me, she said."

"Naturally! She's still my best friend, even though we lost touch for so long." Annie sighed. "I hope someday I'll know why. Maybe the post office sent my letters to Timbuktu by mistake, and they'll suddenly show up, all in one shot."

Donald gave a short laugh. "Sure. You bet."

The house was filled with the delicious aroma of freshly baked pies and rye bread, and Donald sniffed appreciatively.

"I guess Mom's already baked pies and *ruggebrot,* my favorite, for tomorrow's celebration." Annie motioned to the living room sofa. "Have a seat. I'll be right back." She didn't see her mother and wondered where she could be. Maybe at the neighbor's house.

Annie went to her bedroom, took out the record album she'd wrapped, and brought it to Donald. "I hope you don't already have this one."

Donald stood up as she entered the room. His jaw dropped when he saw the big package. "You shouldn't have spent money on me!"

She laughed. "I'm expecting to enjoy this with you." Then she blushed. "At least, some time."

He carefully removed the wrappings, folding the paper and rolling up the ribbon. "Oh, Annie . . . Beethoven! And Liszt's 'Liebestraum.' Chopin. Thanks . . . these will be the beginning of our collection. They'll give us hours of pleasure."

So . . . he was thinking of the future, too. Annie felt better about her bold remark and about choosing that particular album, especially since *liebestraum* meant "love's dream."

After Donald left, Annie noticed that her mother's bedroom door was closed. She opened it and peeked in. The window shades were drawn and her mother was resting on the bed.

Annie went to her and whispered, "Mom? Are you all right?"

Her mother rolled her head from side to side. "Just a headache. I hope it goes away before tomorrow. If it's still this bad, I don't see how I'll be able to stand all the noise and turmoil at your grandparents' house." Her voice was weak.

Annie wondered whether this was the start of flu, or if the thought of Donald was making her mother sick. If that were the case, this wouldn't be the time to show her the locket. But she felt guilty for being suspicious and patted her mother's shoulder. "You stay there and rest. I'll make supper."

She started to leave, but the light shining through the door must have reflected off the diamond.

"What's that on your sweater?" her mother asked, her voice sharp.

Annie clenched her teeth in dismay. "I'll show you later. First I'll go fix—"

Her mother held out her hand. "Come here." Her voice was stronger now, and Annie wondered if her suspicion was correct after all. Her mother sat up and switched on the bed lamp. "*Doch nicht!*" she exclaimed. "What have you there?"

Annie lifted up the locket. "A Christmas present. From Donald. It's a little strawberry on a chain." Put that way, her mother might not think it was too important.

"But . . . is that a real diamond in it?"

"I don't know. I didn't ask. Isn't it pretty?" She turned to go, but her mother held onto her arm.

"What does this mean? Have you . . . did he . . . you aren't talking about . . ." Her mother was standing now, looking horrified and searching Annie's eyes. "You're not wearing that tomorrow. What will the family say?" She sat down on the bed. "Maybe it's just as well we don't go."

Annie thought of Christmas, just her mother and her, glowering at each other over a bowl of leftover soup. She took a deep breath and straightened her shoulders. "Mom, I'm not engaged to Donald. Not yet, anyway. But you may as well get used to our friendship, because it could lead in that direction."

She started out of the room, then looked back and said firmly, "You've baked all those pies and *ruggebrot* I saw in the kitchen, and they can't go to waste. We'll go to the Christmas gathering and enjoy ourselves."

"That necklace—" Her mother's voice was weak again.

"If it bothers you so much that he's Japanese, just don't bring that part up. They'll find out soon enough."

Chapter Eleven

Annie's mouth watered. Carrying two of the egg custard pies, she followed her mother into Grandpa and Grandma Bartsch's large old farmhouse. Breathing in the delicious smells—ham, rich gravy, corn, sweet potatoes, and of course, *pluma mos,* that traditional thin plum and raisin pudding—years of memories swept over her.

This get-together with her mother's family had always been special to her. As a child, she never noticed any tension between them and her father. He laughed and joked with everyone. Had her mother been oversensitive, imagining slights? Or had she herself, busy playing with her cousins, just not noticed?

She set the pies on the kitchen counter, then hugged her grandmother, aunts, and older cousins, all jabbering as they stirred, tasted, chopped, and mashed. They'd come from all over—Shafter, Lodi, Orland—even from Washington State. Some of them she hadn't seen since gas rationing started.

The clamor didn't seem to bother her mother at all. She shoved things around on the counter to make room for the rest of the pies and grabbed a knife to slice the bread she'd brought. Laughing and adding to the chatter, she showed no signs of yesterday's headache.

Taunta Ruth, her youngest aunt, handed Annie a tray of dishes and silverware. Dutifully, she carried it into the dining room where the old claw-foot table had been opened to its full length.

While setting the plates out, she glanced through the open glass doors into the parlor. Just as she remembered from her childhood and on, evergreen boughs looped around the walls and on top of the upright piano, filling the room with mountain scent. Familiar glass ornaments, crepe-paper bells, and pine cones hung at intervals.

Her grandfather and uncles sat on the couch, rockers, and folding chairs. They argued about several questions at the same time. Who was the best horseshoe player? Was Hitler really dead? Would grandpa's John Deere tractor outperform Uncle Martin's Ford? Sprinkled throughout were the inevitable and hilarious *Plautdietsch* jokes that always made everyone laugh. "O Tannenbaum," playing on the console phonograph, faintly competed with all the other noise. Annie went in to greet the men, who patted her cheeks and told her she was pretty—all without missing a beat in their debates.

Taunta Ruth came down the hall with another tray of dishes. Annie left the men and took the tray from her. She carried it to a spare bedroom where a makeshift table of boards had been set up across two sawhorses. On the way, she dodged several toddlers, all giggling and screaming and chasing each other. She marveled at how much they'd grown in the past year.

When the tables were ready, she wandered outside. In the yard, the younger men and teenaged boys played one-sided baseball, working their way through the positions, while the girls watched from the wraparound porch and cheered them on.

The boys waved to Annie from their game. Cousin James whistled at her, and his brother Alvin shouted, "Hubba, hubba!" The girls clustered around her to show her their newest Christmas treasures. Now that the war was over, the celebration was the same as it had been before, and traditions were back in place.

It should have felt comfortable and settled, but Annie had a strange feeling, as though something was missing—as though she were not really there, but merely watching everyone from a distance.

Incomplete—that was it. She leaned against the porch railing, her eyes on the game, but her thoughts on Donald. What would it be like, with him here? What would he think about all the commotion? She remembered the way he'd been in college. He greeted everyone respectfully and knew all the right things to say, joining into whatever activity was going on. He knew how to fit in with any group. That was just the way he was.

But how would the family act? Would they be friendly? Or would they ignore him by gossiping about people he didn't know, or exclude him by speaking *Plautdietsch?*

She absently fingered the little bump that was her strawberry locket, hidden inside the bodice of her shirtwaist dress. Then she looked around to make sure no one had noticed. She'd compromised with her mother—she couldn't bear to take it off, but the family wouldn't see it.

"I *said,* 'How do you like my new Toni permanent?'" Cousin Luella hiked herself up on the porch railing next to Annie, then ran the fingers of her left hand through her golden waves.

Annie pulled her thoughts together and smiled. "Very pretty." She wondered what Luella's church in nearby Reedley thought of it. It must be more broadminded than Rosemond MB.

The other girls laughed, and Annie wondered what was funny.

Luella looked smug. "Don't you see something different?" She waggled the fingers still next to her hair.

Then Annie saw the diamond sparkling on Luella's left hand. "My goodness, how beautiful!" She tried to remember. Her cousin was now—only eighteen! She took the girl's hand in hers to admire the ring properly.

Luella bent her head coyly. "I beat you to it, didn't I? Your boyfriend must be really slow."

"My . . . boyfriend?" How did she know about Donald?

Luella turned her hand this way and that, watching the diamond pick up the sunlight. "Yeah, remember? Last time I saw you, you were writing to this guy at CPS camp, and I asked you which one of us would be the first to marry."

Jonah. "Oh . . . him. I didn't . . . he wasn't . . ."

"That's okay. Better luck next time. Are you going with anybody now?"

Annie shrugged. "Sometimes." What would Luella say if she knew that Donald was Japanese?

Why was she kidding herself? Luella—and all the others—would react exactly the way her mother had. And her grandparents—they'd be heartbroken. All because of tradition. None of them knew that Donald was a wonderful person, and more like her than Jonah—or any of the other local Mennonite men.

Then Luella asked, "What's his name?"

Annie swallowed hard. His name—that would surely give her away. "You don't know him."

"I met some of the older guys from your church at the last *Sangerfest.* You have some really good-looking guys with good singing voices at your church. Does he sing in your choir?"

Annie chewed her lip. If she wasn't careful, Luella could easily worm the information out of her. "Huh-uh." She looked around for something to distract her cousin. "Run, run, Wesley! Hey, nice catch, Alvin! Luella, did you see that?"

Luella wasn't put off that easily. "Well, if you'd just tell me his name, I'll know whether or not I've met him."

Annie's heart sank. The more secretive she was, the more curious her cousin would be. "He doesn't go to our church."

"He doesn't? Which MB church does he go to? Zion? Bethany? Wait . . . let me guess. That new MB church in Fresno?"

Annie shook her head.

"No? You mean he's—" she looked around, then whispered, "not even Mennonite?"

"Baptist." Should she take Luella aside, tell her the truth, and ask her to keep it secret? She looked around and saw the younger cousins staring at her too, eager to hear her answer.

Luella jumped off the railing, big blue eyes sparkling, legs poised to run and spread the news. "Well? Aren't you going to tell me his name?"

Just then a cowbell clanged and all the family members stopped what they were doing. "Dinner's ready!" someone shouted, and the cry was echoed by voices from the side yard, from out back, from the barn.

Annie was the first one inside. As the men brought in the folding chairs and everyone jostled for a place, she managed to find a seat in the dining room with the adults, next to her cousin Hulda, who was her age and married.

She'd just put down her six-month-old for a nap, and was delighted to visit with Annie. Hulda smoothed her blonde hair back and tucked the ends of the roll more snugly around its cotton rat. "I get so tired of talking about colic and the best soap for diapers," she whispered. She looked closer at Annie. "That's a pretty dress. Did you make it?"

"Uh-huh." Annie straightened her collar, making sure the chain of her locket was hidden. Her mother had been right—she shouldn't have worn it today. Just feeling it next to her skin kept her mind on Donald. She'd gotten away from Luella just in time—now if only she could think clearly and not blurt out something that would give herself away.

Grandpa Bartsch said grace, praying for the family, his church, the whole world and, finally, the dinner. At the amen, heads popped up and eager hands passed the food. Now that most rationing was over, the table was crowded with steaming hot dishes and luscious salads. Annie was sure each woman had brought enough food for the whole group. And, naturally, everyone had to sample it all, complimenting each dish and asking for the recipe.

Her mother's younger brother, Daniel, said, "Looks like we'll have enough to feed the five thousand, with twelve basketfuls left over!" That was said at every Mennonite festival, but they all laughed anyway. The joking and arguing continued, with each conversation louder than the one before it. People raised their voices just to be heard above the others, until Annie thought her ears would burst.

Hulda took a generous helping of candied sweet potatoes and asked her, "What are you doing these days? Are you through with school?"

Between mouthfuls of ham and watermelon pickles, Annie talked about her job and told little stories about customers and their problems with buying furniture.

Hulda helped herself to more creamed corn. "But what about you? Any man in your life yet?"

Annie laughed. "Speaking of men, I have to tell you this. The last time I went to the employees' restroom, there was a man inside! I backed out real fast, then realized it was only a life-sized cardboard figure of Bing Crosby. It had come with a shipment of record players, and the deliverymen had played a trick on me. You should have heard them laugh!"

Hulda laughed too, but then put down her fork and frowned at Annie. "You didn't answer my question."

Before replying, Annie passed the mashed potatoes and *ruggebrot.* "I have . . . friends."

"Just now, when you turned your head, I saw something shiny next to your collar. Is that a necklace? Why are you wearing it inside?"

Annie tucked the chain out of sight. "Didn't want to spill on it. You know how that is, you bend over your plate and down it goes into the gravy."

She looked around the table. Some of the men had finished and pushed their plates back, so she stood and collected the empty dishes nearest her. "I'd better go help cut the pies."

By the time everyone finished dessert, fresh cups of coffee, and *prips,* Hulda's baby was awake and crying. She left the table to nurse him. Relieved, Annie settled back in her chair and listened to the older folks reminisce about their childhood Christmases.

After the tables were cleared and the last pots and pans were washed and dried, Grandpa Bartsch shut off the record player. Everyone went into either the parlor or the dining room, the glass doors between them left wide open. The older women used the couch, rockers, and footstools, and the men used the folding chairs from the dining room.

First, Annie played Christmas carols on the old piano while the others sang along. Then Grandpa Bartsch quoted from memory the first twenty verses from the second chapter of Luke. Others recited with him as they were able. When he came to "And suddenly there was with the angel a multitude of the heavenly host, praising God, and saying," more voices joined in with "Glory to God in the highest." At this point, even the smallest children added their sweet voices: "on earth peace, good will toward men."

When Grandpa Bartsch ended the beloved story with the shepherds glorifying and praising God, Annie heard soft amens from around the room. No matter how many times she heard the story, it never failed to fill her with wonder.

Then came several prayers of thankfulness: for God's gift to man, for peace in their hearts, and for the peace that now had finally come to the world, which could be normal again. *Would life with Donald ever feel normal?* Annie wondered and checked her locket chain to be certain it was still hidden.

She left the piano bench to sit on the floor with the little ones and help them be patient. At least *they* wouldn't ask any nosy questions.

Then the youngsters who'd had a part in a church Christmas program stood and recited their little poem or verse, sang a song, or played an instrument. Some of the smaller ones needed some coaxing or bribing.

Finally, her grandfather and the other men brought in the presents from their hiding places—the cars, the barn, and the back bedroom closet. They piled them in the center of the parlor. Grandpa Bartsch picked up one gift after another, announcing the name on the tag and the giver, and a few chosen children passed them out.

Annie watched the women open packets of hand-embroidered dresser scarves or pillowcases and crocheted doilies or chair covers. Cousin Vera had given her a set of embroidered tea towels, for which Annie thanked her. She herself had sewed doll clothes for *Taunta* Ruth's eight-year-old Earlene, who happily changed the dress on her Betsy Wetsy and buttoned up the doll's new coat.

The men nodded thanks for socks, gloves, or ties. Boys grinned at their pocket knives or baseball gloves. Toddlers shrieked over their homemade wooden pull toys.

Grandma Bartsch had made sets of three embroidered handkerchiefs for each granddaughter, and Annie thought them too beautiful to use. But Earlene shouted, "Thanks! Just what I needed," and immediately blew her nose into one.

All the boys laughed, but the women looked shocked, and *Taunta* Ruth turned red as she apologized for her daughter.

When the last gift had been opened, all the handiwork admired, and the wrappings carefully folded for next year, the aunts poured boiling water over the used coffee grounds and filled the dining table with platters of *tvehbock*, ammonia cookies, and a huge bowl of hard little *peppaneht* cookies. It was time for an early light supper, the usual Sunday or festival *faspa*.

Finally, when everyone had finished eating their *tvehbock*, leftover salads, and cookies, when the last coffee cup was washed, Annie took a deep breath and let it out slowly. She'd made it through the day! Relaxing a little, she waited for the signal.

It didn't take long. Her grandfather slid out his pocket watch. "Just time for a quick nap before I milk the cows. Thank you all for coming. God bless you and keep you. And a joyful Christmas to all."

Thomas, her oldest uncle, asked, "*Bist rehd*, wife? Ready to go home?"

The women flocked into the kitchen to pick up their bowls and kettles. Girls scurried from room to room, looking for purses and jackets. Hugs were shared all around as the people left. When Earlene flung her arms around Annie and squeezed her tightly, thanking her again for the doll clothes, Annie felt the hard little bulge between them. She moved back and adjusted her collar, tucking the chain out of sight and hoping Earlene hadn't noticed.

But Earlene reached up, dipped her fingers under Annie's collar, pulled the chain free and lifted out the little strawberry. "What's this? Why are you hiding it?" She twiddled it in her fingers, then said, "Look, it opens! And there's pictures inside!"

Annie froze. Now she was in for it. All her caution had been for nothing.

Others noticed and came to look, but it was Earlene who said, "That one's you. But what's that Jap doing in there?"

The room became silent, and everyone stared at her.

Then *Taunta* Ruth spoke in a whisper. "Annie, you don't mean . . . you have a boyfriend who's . . . Oriental?"

Hulda's eyes almost bugged out, and she shook her head. "No wonder you wouldn't tell me."

What could she say? How could she explain? "He's . . . Japanese-American. A Christian. Studying to be a doctor." Well, that was premature, but with God's help it would be true.

The noise in the room built as the comments shot at her from all directions.

"I'm shocked, Annie."

"Annie! I've never known you to be dishonest!"

"And you were hiding the necklace?"

"Well, I'd be ashamed of it, too. A Jap?"

"Why were you hiding it?"

To avoid this very scene, she thought.

Annie felt rooted to the floor as the questions and accusations swirled around her, knocking her mentally off-balance.

"After Pearl Harbor . . . and what they did to us there?"

Donald's life was torn apart by Pearl Harbor, too. But she knew they wouldn't understand about that.

"Don't you know you can't trust any of them?"

I'd trust him with my life. He'd never treat anyone like you're treating me now.

"After all we've suffered because of the war?"

We suffered? We didn't have to be herded into desert prisons.

"Why? Were you that desperate for a man?"

This couldn't be happening. She knew they would disapprove, but to turn on her like this?

"Aren't Mennonites good enough for you?"

Luella smirked at her. "Baptist, huh? Don't you mean . . . Buddhist?"

Annie's mother was quiet, leaning against the wall just inside the dining room. Holding her empty pie pans, her mouth twitched. Grandpa Bartsch turned to her. "*Na*, Helena. I thought you'd learned your lesson well enough to keep your own daughter in the flock. But just the opposite. You took one step away from the faith. Now she follows your example and goes even farther."

Annie's mother clutched the pie pans closer to her waist and stared at the floor. "Thank you for the dinner," she said, her voice flat. "You all went to a lot of trouble. Come, Annie," she ordered as she walked to the door without looking back.

Annie followed her to the car. Her hands shook as she inserted the key into the ignition, and the car jerked as she ground the gears. She didn't dare look at her mother.

Neither of them would ever live this down. Might as well forget about seeing any of the family again. They'd never accept Donald. Never believe he was as good a Christian as any Mennonite. Nothing would convince them that she hadn't thrown her life away and was going straight to hell.

Chapter Twelve

"How was your family's Christmas?" asked Donald. It was Wednesday afternoon, the day after Christmas, and Annie was at the furniture store, typing a sales contract when Donald called.

When she hesitated, he added, "Don't worry, this isn't a party line. I'm at the church, and my father's out on visitations."

She'd cried all night, hardly sleeping at all. How could she tell him what her family said about him? How could she talk about it without breaking down again? Finally she offered, "Lots of people . . . busy . . . noisy . . . food galore. What about you?"

"Very quiet. We had some church people over. After they left, I listened to the records. They're wonderful. Thanks again. Did you have a good time at your grandparents' house?"

All Annie could think of was how they'd shamed her. "It was . . . ah . . . nice to see them again," she said flatly.

"Is there something you're not telling me?"

He knew! She couldn't stand it any longer. All her frustration and anguish burst out. "Oh, Donald. You told me we'd run into a lot of prejudice. I can't believe how unfair my family was!" she sobbed. Her tears gushed, and she wiped her eyes with the back of her hand, glancing right and left to make sure no one was watching. She was relieved to see Bob Taylor deep in conversation with a man and woman who were interested in a maple buffet.

Donald was silent a moment. "I take it they found out about me."

"Yes," she sniffed, and cleared her throat. "I told them you were a Christian, but they wouldn't even listen."

His voice was soft. "It might get worse. Can you . . . is it too hard . . . do you want to change your mind and just . . . be friends?"

Pain shot through her heart. What was he saying, this man who meant everything to her? Was she to pretend she didn't love him? But he was the one the prejudice was aimed at, and that was part of her pain. "Is that what *you* want?"

Donald was silent for a few seconds. Her hand ached from gripping the phone so tightly. She couldn't bear to break up with him.

"Oh, Annie. You wouldn't ask that if you knew how much I love you. I'd be lost without you. But I don't want you to feel obligated—"

She leaned back in her swivel chair, her body limp with relief. "I don't feel obligated," she glanced around to make sure no one was close enough to hear, "and I couldn't be just friends." *Not now,* she thought. *Not after those kisses, those wonderful times together.*

"I know. Me too. But I don't want you to have to choose between your family and me."

She'd thought long and hard about that—all the way home from her grandparents' house, and through the night. It would hurt, but she could stand not seeing her cousins. Even her aunts and uncles. Her grandparents—that would be much worse. They'd been a loving security in her life as long as she could remember. Now their disapproval of what she was doing—and what her mother had done—dragged her down like a millstone.

And her mother? For so many years, they'd had only each other. Although they had their differences, they'd been close. Yesterday, that closeness had been torn apart.

But she'd lost Donald once. Now that they'd found each other again, she couldn't live without him. "As for choosing between you and my family, I've already made my decision."

"And?"

"You won."

He let out a huge sigh. "Oh, sweet Annie. I was afraid I wasn't worth all the trouble." His voice dropped to a murmur. "The first time I saw you, my heart actually skipped a beat. And that's still the way you make me feel."

A thrill shivered through her, slightly loosening the knot in her stomach. Donald made the difference between darkness and sunshine for her.

Then his voice deepened. "This isn't enough. I have to see you. May I come to your house tonight?"

Annie thought of her mother's stony silence. She'd not said a word all the way home the evening before—not until they were walking together to the house. Her bitter words as she and Annie went into the house replayed in Annie's mind:

"*Why are you so stuck on that Japanese man? Weren't you listening all those years in church and Sunday school? Or are you doing this just to hurt me? Don't you even care what it does to me, to the family, to the church?*"

She'd answered all of those questions for herself, but knew it wouldn't do any good to answer her mother. It would only lead to an argument.

The silence at breakfast had been colder than the early morning frost. "Not yet," she told Donald. "My mother needs time to get over this. It really—"

"Made her lose face?"

"Yes. That's it . . . exactly." It was one of the things she loved about him—he was so quick to understand, to tie all the loose ends together. His remark helped her realize that being embarrassed before the relatives would make her mother's life miserable. And she'd had already faced that when she married Annie's father. This would make it worse.

The time she invited Donald to the house, he made a good impression on her mother. If only there were some way to build on that, some way to make her mother proud of him.

Donald cleared his throat. "There's something else. Even if your family approved of me, life would be hard for us. All those rejections from medical schools . . .you have to realize America doesn't want Japanese doctors. Would anyone in *your* family go to one?"

She knew they wouldn't. But that was because Mennonites naturally held to their own kind. Maybe other people would be more accepting. "What about the fleece? Have you heard from those schools?"

"Not a word. And I'm not holding my breath. It would be a real miracle if I were accepted."

"Then let's pray for a miracle."

She heard someone walking toward her and looked up. Bob Taylor was writing in his sales book as he approached the counter. The couple followed him as the man pulled a checkbook from his hip pocket. Annie reached for her receipt book.

"I have to go now," she whispered into the phone.

"Somehow, we'll work things out. So long, sweet Annie."

Because the customers were now at the counter, she murmured, "Mm-hmm. Bye" into the phone. Annie put the receiver down, her hand resting on it for a moment, still feeling its warmth. Then she smiled at the couple and joined them at the counter with the receipt book.

Donald left the church, and slumped behind the wheel of his car. His thoughts were in turmoil. Was he just fooling himself? Was it asking too much of Annie to share all the problems that were sure to come? She said she was willing, but she had no idea of the prejudice and rejections that could come. Things could get far worse than her day with the relatives.

He stopped the car at an intersection and leaned his face into his hands, letting himself feel the pain of his love. If he didn't make it into medical school, what would he do? He'd taught high school science at Gila River, but what public school would hire him? How could he support a wife?

The car behind him honked. He shifted gears and moved on, but his thoughts still churned. There was always the ministry. His father would be grateful for the help, pleased for him to follow in his steps. But that wouldn't earn a living either. The church people had lost so much, and most of them were barely scraping by. They couldn't support even one pastor. If it weren't for the strawberry farm, his family couldn't survive.

Here he was, with a college degree, and it wasn't worth the paper it was printed on. What did he have to offer Annie?

She mentioned the fleece. "Dear Lord," he whispered, "I see no way out. Only you can help me." He sighed in despair. "Please, Father, light my path and show me the way."

When he got home, he changed his clothes, took a hoe from the tool shed, and went out into the field. His mother was already there, chopping weeds, and he took the row next to her.

Seeing him, she straightened and flexed her shoulders. "Crop good now," she said with enthusiasm. "This spring maybe make some money. Pay bills."

He nodded.

And after that? he thought sadly. His mother couldn't do all the work alone. With so many people having problems adjusting to relocation, his father was busy counseling them. And his grandfather was still lost in his private world. That left just Donald to run the farm.

There's still time.

Donald looked around. Had his mother said that?

No, she'd moved on and was hacking away at a stubborn root.

He bent over to fasten down a stray runner and continued thinking: *There still* is *time. Maybe there's hope, too, of being accepted into medical school. But that doesn't solve the labor problem on the farm.*

That night when Donald went upstairs, he heard a sound from his grandfather's room. Looking through the open door, he was surprised to find the old man out of bed and standing by the window, just looking out.

He joined his grandfather at the window to see what had caught his attention. In the darkness, Donald saw the shapes of several cars driving past, slowly, like a funeral procession. But in a funeral, cars turned on their lights. These hadn't.

His grandfather turned to him. "Bad."

Donald nodded. The people in those cars were up to no good.

Since coming back from the camps, a lot of Japanese homes had been struck. Mostly in the coast areas, but recently, in nearby towns. Someone had fired shots at the houses, burned barns, and slashed tires.

He stared out the window, wondering if he should go downstairs and mention this to his father. But the cars went past without stopping. Although he stood there with the old man, watching a while longer, the cars didn't come back. Donald pulled down the window shade and snapped on his grandfather's bedside lamp. Time enough to tell his father tomorrow.

Then he realized—his grandfather had spoken for the first time since he'd come home. He hugged the old man. "You're going to be all right."

But his grandfather broke loose and turned away. Without another word, he climbed into bed. Donald sat down on the chair beside the bed and talked to him very quietly.

He talked about the good days before the evacuation, before the war with Japan, when life was comfortable, and food and goods weren't rationed. Bread was nine cents a loaf and gasoline fourteen cents a gallon. He and Florence often squabbled over who got to use the family car. Then his dad insisted he use his four hundred dollars in savings to buy the Plymouth coupe from Takanishi's used car lot.

Donald talked, too, about his grandmother. Although she'd been small, she was strong and healthy and, before the internment, spent her days working the strawberry field alongside his grandfather. She chopped vegetables in the kitchen and scolded Donald for stealing chunks of carrots, pared peaches for his mother to can while he watched the peelings coil down into the sink. She often slipped him an extra sausage from his grandfather's breakfast plate when Donald, a growing boy, had gobbled his own too fast.

While he talked, his grandfather lay there with his eyes shut. He didn't respond, and Donald wondered if he even heard.

But suddenly the old man squeezed his eyes closed even tighter. A tear rolled down his cheek, then another, and he reached up and wiped them away. "You grandmother, she good woman."

A real breakthrough! Donald felt like shouting for joy at his grandfather's response, but didn't want to destroy the fragile moment. He answered softly. "Yes. She was the best."

Then his grandfather opened his eyes and turned his face toward Donald. "Not belong there."

Donald shook his head. "I wish I could have come for the funeral. But I didn't know . . . by the time I got the letter it was too late to get a pass."

Florence had written later that the old man changed from a cheerful companion to a silent, brooding shell. He no longer played dominoes or the game of *goh* or told jokes with the other elderly men. Instead, he laid on his cot, staring at the bare rafters and leaky ceiling, until the day that the bus left for Rosemond. He had to be pushed aboard, against his will.

"Someday I'll take you back there, *Jiichan.* We'll take flowers and decorate the grave. Say a final good-bye."

The old man rolled his head from side to side. "Here." He pointed to the window, his hand trembling. "Bury here. With me."

Donald felt emotion well up, tightening his chest. His grandparents' love had been much stronger than he'd realized. He cleared his throat. "Maybe we can move her here. I'll look into it; see what I can do." He pulled the covers up to the old man's neck and patted his shoulder. "Try to sleep now, *Jiichan.* Goodnight."

He hoped his grandfather wouldn't retreat from the progress he'd made tonight. Making a mental note to mention this to his father, Donald went to his own room and laid on his bed.

But he couldn't sleep, thinking about his grandmother. Ever since he and Florence were little, *Baachan* had told them how proud she was of them. She didn't understand the significance of the good grades and honors they received at school, but applauded each little success.

At Gila River, even when she wasn't well, she was interested in every small improvement—the shelves he put up, the chairs and table he helped his grandfather build, the solos he sang in church. And when he was asked to build up a choir, even though she could barely walk, she insisted on coming to the church barracks to hear them and watch him direct.

But then she took a turn for the worse. The camp doctors, lacking skill and experience, could only give her painkillers, and she slept the days away.

One afternoon, he had a day off from the hospital and slipped into their room to write a letter to Annie. He'd just helped his mother carry bundles of dirty clothes over to the laundry. With long lines waiting to use the washtubs and scrub boards, he knew she'd be there a while. Florence was off with friends, and his father was in the chapel, studying the few books he'd brought along. His grandfather was playing dominoes or *goh* with his friends, talking about better days. Nobody stayed in the cramped barracks longer than necessary. Just his grandmother, and as usual, she was asleep.

But now she stirred and looked at him. "*Gohan?*" she asked weakly, maybe thinking he'd brought her food.

Donald took her frail, outstretched hand between his. "Not time for rice yet, *Baachan.* Two more hours." He lifted her up a little, gave her a sip of water, helped her lie back down and then smoothed the hair off her forehead. She murmured something he couldn't understand and then closed her eyes again.

He took out his tablet and a pen, sat on the plank floor, and leaned against his lumpy straw mattress. Halfway through the letter, he sighed, and his grandmother turned to look at him.

He put down the letter and felt her cheeks; they were hot and dry. Taking a cup of water, he poured a little on a washcloth, and gently soothed her forehead. She smiled at him, and he wondered what his grandmother would think of Annie. The two had been friendly when Annie and her mother had come to buy strawberries that one time just before the evacuation.

He moistened the cloth again and used it to touch his grandmother's eyelids, her temples, her cheeks.

"You good boy," she said. "Good doctor."

He was surprised—he hadn't thought she was aware of his ambition. Or could this be a prophecy? He kissed her forehead. "Someday, *Baachan.* Someday, I promise."

But now, Donald wondered if he'd be able to keep that promise.

As he drifted off to sleep, he was back in Italy. *Bombs were falling, people were running and screaming. He reached for his bayonet, but it wasn't there. Then an atomic bomb exploded next to him, its glare blinding his eyes. He scrambled out of his foxhole.*

He looked around, confused. *This isn't Italy; it's my own bedroom.* A spotlight shone through the window, and voices jeered and hooted. "Get those dirty Japs! Kill them all." He heard the noise of cars gunning their motors, spinning hookers with their tires—then a loud crash, and a large jagged rock landed inches from his bed. He leaped over the glass splinters and took refuge behind the door, his ears ringing with the violence and hatred.

After a long time, the cars revved up. Tires screeching, they sped away, and the yelling faded into the distance.

Donald hurried into his grandfather's room and found him standing by the window in the dark, shivering. No damage had been done here. He took the old man by the arm and led him back to bed. "It's all right, *Jiichan.* They're gone. Go back to sleep, okay?"

His grandfather rocked his head from side to side. "Bad, bad."

When Donald went back into the hall, his father was coming up the stairs, his mother right behind, hanging on to a wad of his father's nightshirt. "What was all that noise?" she asked.

Donald didn't want to worry her. "Just a broken window. It's getting a little gusty . . . maybe a tree branch hit it."

She looked toward the grandfather's room and Donald said, "He's okay. I just got him back to bed." Then she noticed the glass on the floor, and scurried downstairs, coming back with a broom and dustpan.

"I'll do that," said Donald, but she elbowed past him and quickly swept up the shards.

His parents both saw the rock at the same time. His mother shrieked, and his father's lips tightened. "Tree branch, huh?"

Donald's shoulders sagged. "I'm sure it was just drunks having fun." But he realized that his parents knew as well as he—this was only the beginning of trouble.

Chapter Thirteen

ANNIE HADN'T HEARD FROM DONALD since his phone call on Wednesday. *Well . . . it's only Saturday,* she thought. *Probably busy on the farm.* He'd said something about getting more work, pruning trees and tying vines for neighbors. It had been cold, cloudy, and windy. She hoped he had warm clothes to wear, and wondered if he was thinking about her as constantly as she did about him.

She'd made several mistakes in her bookkeeping ledger the past few days, and her boss had asked her if she was feeling all right. "I'm fine," she told him, but she meant physically. Emotionally, her moods swung wildly from the wonder of being in love to a deep sorrow for the wedge that had come between her and her family.

She'd written to them. A thank you to her grandparents for the luscious dinner and the beautiful handkerchiefs her grandmother had embroidered, a thanks to Vera for the tea towels, and a letter to Luella to wish her God's blessing on her upcoming marriage. But she'd heard nothing from any of them. She really hadn't expected to; still, it would have been nice.

She hoped against hope that after their initial shock they'd remember she'd always been a true Christian, a faithful Mennonite, and a loyal member of the Bartsch family. Or didn't any of that count? What had happened to all their smiles? The pats on her head, telling her she was pretty? The whistles and "hubba, hubba" from the boys?

She was still mulling over those questions when the phone rang. "McGinnis Furniture."

"Oh, really? I thought it was Annie." The sound of Donald's voice always made her feel good.

"I wondered if you'd forgotten me."

"Impossible. I just haven't had a chance to get to church before. Don't want to give the old ladies on our party line something to gossip about. How are things going for you?"

"The same."

"Your mother?"

"She won't look me in the eye and doesn't talk any more than absolutely necessary. What about you? What have you been up to?"

He was quiet for a bit, and she wondered why. "Just . . . working a lot. I've been noticing the snow on the mountains. Would you like to take a ride up there tomorrow afternoon?"

Annie thought. Did she have any commitments? Quartet practice at 6:30—they were to sing in the evening service. "Sure! As long as I can be home by . . . oh . . . six o'clock at the latest." From the corner of her eye she saw her boss come out of his office. "I've got to hang up. What time?"

"Two? That okay?"

She breathed out slowly, letting the thrill in her heart settle before answering. "I'll be waiting."

That evening, Annie looked through her closet, trying to decide what to wear. Could she still fit into the warm brown slacks that she'd made last year for Christmas caroling?

Last year. That seemed a lifetime ago. She'd been a different person. Jonah was home then, and somehow she'd gotten paired with him. This year, no one had even mentioned caroling to her. With her cough still hanging on, it probably was for the better. But it hurt just the same, and she wondered if it was because of Donald. Didn't they know Japanese could sing too? She thought of his solo at the Christmas program and the times he sang snatches of songs to her. If they only knew what a beautiful voice he had!

The slacks still fit, and she looked through her closet and drawers, wishing she had something sporty to go with them. Everything she owned had been bought or made with church and work in mind. Then she saw something almost hidden behind some old dresses she should've given away a long time ago. It was a jacket she'd worn in college. Heavy wool, green and white—the school's colors.

Perfect! Donald had liked it then. He'd teased her about it—said it was her version of letter sweaters, that she should sew on a "C" for CLOC Club. She wondered if he'd remember that now.

The next morning, the sun was bright and the air crisp. On the way to church, Annie could see a blanket of snow low on the mountains. It reminded her of whipped cream on cake, and she smiled when she thought about being there with Donald later that day. She thought she'd have trouble keeping her mind on the sermon.

Rev. Loewen spoke on 2 Corinthians 6, stressing that Christians must stay away from the world. When he emphasized "Be ye separate," he seemed to be looking straight at her. And from the corner of her eye she noticed other people darting looks at her.

She had her own Bible open and saw the rest of the verse: "and touch not the unclean thing." Well, that certainly didn't include Donald. Surely Rev. Loewen didn't think—What would it take to convince people that Mennonites weren't the only Christians in the world?

She thought back to the days before the war, when most of their services were in German. When the church leaders talked about using English instead to show they were not enemies of the country, a dear old lady had insisted that God was German. "After all," she declared, "the Bible says so. In the first book of Moses, verse 3, when God speaks, it says, '*Und Gott spracht*'!" People realized how illogical her reasoning was, so couldn't they also change their minds about other nationalities? And denominations?

Trying to stay unflustered, Annie dared to meet Rev. Loewen's eyes. She wished she had the nerve to talk to him privately. She respected him and hated to think he might be hearing ugly rumors about her. Once she told him what kind of man Donald is, he'd understand—wouldn't he?

But after her talk with Deacon Driedger, she couldn't be sure of anything.

After church she went right to the car and waited for her mother. She didn't have to wait long. Evidently her mother wasn't anxious to answer questions about her daughter.

They ate lunch quietly, finishing the leftover *schaubel sup* Annie had made the other evening. The smooth hot soup was one of her favorites. Chunks of ham and onions, a bay leaf, simmered with summer savory tied-up in a bunch, giving just the right flavor to the green beans and potatoes in it. She wondered if there was enough ham left in the refrigerator for sandwiches to take along on the ride to the mountains.

She'd told her mother yesterday about the snow trip. "But I'll be back in time for quartet practice," she promised. Her mother had just sniffed and turned away.

But now, as Annie rummaged in the refrigerator, her mother spoke in a grudging tone. "There's still oatmeal cookies."

When Donald came to the door, Annie's mother went to her room for a nap. But Annie was ready in her slacks and sweater, the sandwiches and cookies in a bag. She'd put a pair of galoshes, mittens, and extra socks in a larger bag.

Donald's dark eyes glowed. "You look very pretty. I've never seen you in slacks before." When she showed Donald the lunch bag, he grinned. "You think of everything."

As they walked to the car, he stared at her sweater. "Now *that* I've seen before."

He tapped his chin with a finger, his forehead creased in thought.

They said it at the same time. "CLOC Club!" He added, "Your letter sweater. You're even cuter in it than you were in college."

Annie held out her little finger.

Donald looked at her quizzically. "Huh?"

She laughed. "When people say the same thing together, they have to hook little fingers and make a wish."

"Mennonites do that? It's not against your religion?"

She batted him on the arm. "Everyone does it. I learned that in grammar school. Come on. I have a good wish."

He joined his little finger to hers, and electricity shot through her body. He pulled her around and held her to him, their fingers still joined. She could feel his heart pounding as fast as hers.

She glanced at her mother's bedroom window, but the shade was drawn. "We'd better go before the neighbors start watching," she whispered.

He took a deep breath, released her, and opened the car door for her. "What did you wish?"

She shook her head. "Not supposed to tell, or it won't come true."

Donald helped Annie into the passenger side, put the two bags on the back seat, then slid behind the steering wheel. "Mine better come true." His eyes, now sober, looked deeply into hers. "It has to." He started the car and turned his attention to the road as they drove out of town and past orange groves, vineyards, and turkey farms.

Just as in college, they had lots to talk about. Their growing-up years, their favorite foods, special honors and awards in school. He told her there'd been two older brothers, who died before he was born.

She told him about her father—his work in construction, his kind nature, the walks he took with her when she was small. How she couldn't weep at his funeral, and then she worried that people would think she hadn't loved him, so she squeezed out a few tears and then couldn't stop crying.

"He would have liked you; I know he would." She told Donald about the difference in her father's and her mother's churches, and the problems it had caused for them. "That's why my mother objects to me dating someone not of our denomination. She says she doesn't want me to go through all that heartache."

Donald's jaw muscles flexed. "We both know it won't be easy. But no one else can live our lives for us. We have to trust the Lord to keep us from harm."

Annie touched his sleeve, and he put his arm around her. "Just until it gets winding," he said, cuddling her close.

He started to hum. She recognized the tune of "Sunshine in My Soul" and hummed an alto above it. At the chorus, they both broke into the lyrics, harmonizing, "Oh, there's sunshine, blessed sunshine, when the peaceful, happy moments roll. . . ." They went from one song to another. "Joybells in My Heart." "There's Within My Heart a Melody." "Great Is Thy Faithfulness." When they came to the words "strength for today and bright hope for tomorrow," Donald gave her an extra squeeze, and Annie's heart soared. She hadn't known anyone could feel such happiness.

As soon as they were in the foothills, Donald kept his word and drove the curving mountain roads slowly and carefully, both hands on the steering wheel. Annie watched the farms in the valley below turn into the familiar patchwork, reminding her of the quilt she wanted to make. She smiled, and in her mind added a few touches to the pattern—rich golden brown stripes between the rows of dormant vineyards, with a border of the same color.

Donald glanced at her. "What are you thinking about?"

It was too soon to mention the quilt. "I'm just . . . happy. I've been looking forward to this."

"Me, too. I thought about it so much I could hardly get my work done."

Laughing, Annie told him about her bookkeeping mistakes. "I'd better settle down or my boss will fire me."

"No danger of that. He knows he's got the best, the smartest, the prettiest bookkeeper in all of Rosemond."

Annie felt her face get hot. No one had ever been that complimentary to her before. She was so lucky—

No. Luck had nothing to do with it. God had brought their lives together, and together they would serve him wherever they went. If the Mennonites wouldn't accept Donald, she would join his church. If his church didn't want her, they'd find one that would accept them both.

It was three-thirty before they reached the snow—white patches under trees and rocks at first, then solid drifts over the slopes. As soon as they spotted an untouched snow bank at a turnout, Donald stopped and parked the car. Annie slipped on her galoshes and mittens, then jumped out of the car to toss a snowball at him. But he beat her to it.

After a wild flurry of crossfire, Donald took a cardboard box and a camera out of the car trunk. They flattened the box and took turns sliding down the hill on it, taking pictures of each other. They romped and slipped and tumbled, somehow always ending up tangled in each other's arms. He kissed her, and her cold lips warmed deliciously.

Suddenly she noticed the setting sun and looked at her watch. "I need to get back!"

While Annie changed into her dry socks, Donald picked up the wet, battered cardboard and threw the pieces in the trunk.

Opening the lunch sack, Annie fed Donald the ham sandwich and cookies while he drove, giggling as he licked the crumbs off her fingers. She'd just crumpled the wrappings into the paper sack when a car full of laughing and yelling boys drove up from behind and passed them on a blind curve.

Donald slowed down to give them more space, and the other car rocked back into the right lane just before oncoming traffic zoomed by.

Annie sighed in relief, but her relief was short-lived. Just as they reached another curve, the car ahead braked and slowed to a crawl. Donald was forced to slam on his brakes and inch along after them. It was getting dark, but Annie could see the boys wrestling around, leaning out the windows, and making obscene gestures at them. As soon as the road straightened and the other lane was clear, Donald moved to pass. But the other car sped up.

"Oh," Donald muttered, "so you're playing games with me."

Over and over, the boys kept up their fun, slowing on curves, speeding on the straight road. Annie peeked at her watch and realized with a sinking heart that she'd be very late to quartet practice—if she got there at all. She knew Donald must be furious, but his face was smooth with only a slight paleness to betray his emotions.

It was past six-thirty when they finally dipped down into the valley and could see the road for miles ahead. Donald tried again and again to pass, but the other car sped up each time. There was just enough oncoming traffic to prevent Donald from making a dash around the teenagers.

"I'm sorry," he said.

"I know. It's not your fault. Those crazy guys!" Finally, as they came to the city limits, the other car turned off onto a side road and was gone.

"If I'd been alone, I would have out-raced them. I couldn't take chances with my precious cargo."

She nodded. "Thanks. It would've really scared me." She couldn't help thinking of Jonah. He wouldn't have cared. He would've raced, swerved, and landed them both in a ditch.

By thc time Donald pulled up at Annie's house, it was almost time for church. The car was gone, and Annie was glad that her mother hadn't stayed home, waiting for her. Donald came in, waited while she ran into her bedroom and changed, and then he dropped her off at her church before going on to his.

She walked into the sanctuary just after the opening prayer, and sat on a back bench. The song director announced the quartet, and Annie started up the aisle. Then she noticed another girl walking to the piano. It was Barbara Goertzen, a girl barely out of high school and part of a group of popular kids.

Annie gulped. She hadn't even known Barbara played piano! She slipped back into her seat, her face red, hoping not too many people had noticed.

The girl performed all right, although she played too loudly and overused the sustaining pedal. But the boys sang well, and when they finished the number, several men approved with hearty amens.

Annie left the church right after the closing prayer, wondering where her mother had parked the car. She'd have a lot of explaining to do, but at least she could prove she'd been in church. How else would she know Barbara had played for the quartet?

The next day, she phoned one of the boys and apologized. But before she could explain, he brushed her off.

"You don't need to put yourself out for us any more. Barbara said she'd be glad to do it from now on."

Annie hung up the receiver, her heart aching. Little by little, the church people were shutting her out. Just as her family had.

Chapter Fourteen

I've really done it now, DONALD THOUGHT. Sitting in the back row of his church, he was glad that a visiting speaker stood at the pulpit—glad he didn't need to look into his father's eyes just yet.

Grace sat in the front row, which meant she'd played piano for the opening songs—songs that he should have led. He knew he'd disappointed his father.

Getting Annie to services late wouldn't earn him any points with her mother either. Nor anyone else in the Mennonite church.

He should have known better and kept a closer watch on the time. *I could have made it if it hadn't been for those crazy kids!* he fumed.

When the car first passed him, he'd thought: *I'm a Jap . . . with a blonde. Will they throw a rock through my car window, too?* But then he realized that they probably couldn't tell what he looked like. All he saw of them were their heads bobbing around. He didn't make out their features until they leaned out the windows to yell or gesture. *They were just idiots having fun,* he concluded. It had been all he could do to keep his temper, to keep from ramming them off the road. If Annie hadn't been with him—

Donald focused on the speaker and tried to follow his message: Take courage, trust in the Lord, and rebuild your lives. Don't be discouraged.

His father had probably led the songs, all the time watching for him, wondering why he wasn't there. He'd surely hear about *that* when they got home. It was his God-given responsibility to lead the singing in church.

Donald sighed. He would be twenty-six in the fall. A man that age should be free to come and go as he pleased. But as long as he was still living at home—his education still uncertain, no career, the farm in his name as the only male American citizen in the family—all he could do was put his feet under his parents' table and show filial respect.

He did respect his father. He loved his parents. He was very fortunate to have an educated father who had Caucasian friends and was respected in the community. His mother did her best to make their home pleasant, as well as working hard in the fields.

But in spite of the anger and guilt, his thoughts wandered back to the afternoon. He couldn't keep from smiling. It had been worth it. Watching Annie sail down the slope on the makeshift toboggan . . . running . . . tumbling with her in the snow . . . kissing those inviting lips . . . and he'd snapped some great pictures to make the memories last even longer.

He wondered where he could take her next time. A movie maybe? Although his church frowned on going to movies, he and some of his friends had gone to a few. *Going My Way* was playing at the town theater. He'd seen it when he was on R&R after being wounded, so he knew it was good. But with all the rules in Annie's church, he was sure Mennonites weren't allowed to go to movies.

The college would have interesting events, ball games, maybe some concerts. Youth for Christ every Saturday evening. In spring they could go to a high school play or two—

Donald pulled his attention back to the message: "Let us forgive those who wronged us, as Jesus forgave his tormentors, 'They know not what they do.'"

He wondered if he could ever do that. It seemed like those who'd wronged the Japanese certainly knew what they were doing—and didn't care! But as he listened, he understood. They knew exactly what they were doing, but didn't realize the far-reaching results of their actions: the careers wiped out, businesses ruined, relationships torn apart, lives destroyed.

Later that evening, as soon as he heard his father come home and go into his study, Donald knocked quietly on the door. "I'm truly sorry I was late. There were circumstances beyond my control—" he explained as he sat down.

His father's eyes bored into his. "One must make allowances for unexpected delays. It was a poor decision to while away the afternoon. I assume you were with Miss Penner?"

"Yes. The snow in the mountains looked so beautiful. We went up to enjoy it."

His father nodded. Donald knew he appreciated beauty and had commented on the "frosted mountains" himself. "Only surpassed by Mount Fuji," he'd once said. But now he sighed. "Son, is your memory so short as to forget the violence of the other night? If people see you with a Caucasian girl, you will only incite more hatred. Is that what you want?"

Donald lowered his eyes in respect. "No, sir." It would do no good to argue that the guys in the other car probably hadn't realized he was Japanese.

"You remember the dynamite found at a farm in Parlier? Not once, but twice. The shots fired into a home in Madera, narrowly missing an old grandmother holding a child."

Donald nodded. What could he say in his defense: *"I love Annie; I want to marry her and make a life with her"? What kind of life would that be, the way things are now?* He hoped that now the war was over, the threats and vandalism would die down. He hadn't told Annie about the rock thrown through his window and that for a few nights his family had been sleeping on pallets in the back part of their house.

He hadn't heard of anyone else in Rosemond being harassed since the incident at his house. But with more Nisei men coming home from the army—more people trying to reclaim their property—would more violence break out? Couldn't people see they were just trying to be good Americans, doing the best they could to rebuild what they lost?

His father's anger was spent now, and the eyes looking at him were sad. "Believe it or not, son, I know what it is like to be young and vigorous.

But be careful. Weigh your pleasures against the danger." He rose, and Donald stood too. The lecture was over and he left his father's study.

On the way to his room, Donald thought back to college days, when no one except the janitor seemed to mind seeing him with Annie. Life was good then, simpler and easier. But no matter how he regretted what his ancestral country had done, there was no going back. The only thing he could do now was be more careful about being seen with Annie in public. For her sake, if not for his own.

Annie's mother had been silent since Christmas, but she certainly made up for it now. "What will people think of you, dragging in late to church? You said . . . you *promised* . . . you'd be home in time for quartet practice. You had your chance to play piano for that nice group of men, and now you've thrown it away. Nobody's going to ask you again, if you can't be depended on. There are too many girls just hoping for an opportunity like that. If you don't—"

"Mother, I've been trying to tell you. We would've made it on time, but some kids were acting up and not letting Donald pass their car."

"That's what you get for being with a Japanese. People will treat you as if you're one of them. It's just plain dangerous to be seen with him! Haven't you heard about the shootings—"

Annie sighed. "That wasn't around here. The community knows Donald. They know his father is a pastor. The family has a good reputation."

"Don't fool yourself. That's not worth a cent to a lot of people around here. They don't trust Japs. You've just had your head up in a fog, or you would've noticed it."

Annie left the room, rubbing her temples. Arguing wouldn't help. But at least her mother was speaking again. Once this was out of her system, maybe she'd listen to reason.

But her mother seemed to bottle her anger back up, because the next day she went back to her silence, muttering complaints whenever Annie was around. The towels were folded wrong, the doilies set crooked, a crusty spot left on a dish.

The next Sunday Donald picked Annie up again, and they drove to Three Rivers.

Sitting close together on a large rock overlooking the Kaweah River, they soaked up the sunshine, listened to the water gurgle, watched the splash of white foam. Donald had bought a felt hat to hide his dark hair and shadow his eyes, and she wore a scarf around her head. Friends might recognize his car, but a passing stranger wouldn't be able to make out their features and be shocked to see them together.

Donald finally told her about the violence two weeks ago, about the rock thrown through the window. She agreed to be as unnoticeable as possible. He said nothing had happened since then, and that it probably was just some drunks out of control—but she knew better. The unreasonable hatred that had started with Pearl Harbor would take a long time to die down.

All week long Annie looked forward to the Sunday drives, wondering where they would go. On foggy days, Donald drove up into the hills, above the fog. While they enjoyed the sunshine, they looked down on the thick gray blanket that covered the valley.

As they walked in the sunshine one of those afternoons, he told her stories about his life in the army and some of the crazy things that happened in boot camp. "A bunch of us were sent to Alabama to guard some German prisoners. They'd been put to work harvesting peanuts. We thought we were really big. *Hey, the government trusts us now!* They even put us in a unit with Caucasians! Then we noticed—those Caucasian troops were guarding *us!*"

"Did you get to do anything special on holidays?"

"Once, while I was in training, people in a nearby town invited us into their homes, in groups of three and four, for Christmas dinner. That was nice. We were out in the field on Thanksgiving and got canned turkey served into our mess kits." He rolled his eyes and added, "But, of course, in combat one day is the same as another—we were lucky to get *anything* to eat."

He talked about the early rivalry between the Hawaiian "Buddhaheads" and mainland Nisei "katonks." "You know, the sound 'katonk'? Like when a coconut hits the ground. That's what they called us." He rapped his knuckles on his forehead to demonstrate. "Empty heads."

Then he sobered. "But once we got into combat, we were one team. Like this," he laced his fingers together to illustrate. Looking into the distance he added softly, "I lost a lot of brave buddies. I'll never forget them."

Annie slid her arm around his waist and held him close while he talked about the surprise German attacks, the land mines, the wounded he ran out to rescue. The men he watched die, their bodies shattered beyond repair. She felt honored that he could share these dark memories with her, and hoped it would help him recover from those awful days.

One rainy afternoon, Donald took Annie to the home of another Nisei. He'd recently been discharged and had come home to his young wife and a baby boy, who'd been born while he was gone. The couple welcomed them and was courteous to Annie, who enjoyed playing with the happy little Japanese boy. Donald smiled as he watched her with the little one. *Maybe someday,* he thought.

One afternoon he took her to Millerton Lake where they sat on the grassy bank and enjoyed the view. A breeze rippled the waves, and the mountains rose just beyond the water. Tents nestled among the pine trees and live oaks on the other side of the lake, and a small marina perched at the water's edge.

As they walked across Friant Dam they saw the bass just underneath the glassy surface. Laughing and walking in step with their arms around each other's waists, they sang silly songs about little fishies and their mama, and "Mairzy Doats."

Wherever they went, they both watched the time carefully and got back in plenty of time to go to their evening church services.

In the middle of February, the weather warmed up and daffodils and lilies-of-the-valley popped up in yards. Camellia bushes grew thick with blossoms, and buds peeped from the rose bushes. All through the countryside, orchards, thinking it was spring, burst into bloom and tried to outdo each other in masses of pink, red, and white. As they drove past them, Donald stopped so they could take pictures of each other leaning against the peach trees, their faces framed by branches of lush, deep-pink sprays.

But on the last Sunday of that month, it turned cold and cloudy. Donald told Annie to dress warmly, and this time he took her to a large park in the country. Mooney Grove featured a shallow lagoon that wandered through the tree-studded lawns, and visitors could use rowboats from the shelter.

Her church usually held their Sunday-school picnic there in the summer, but Annie had never been there in winter. The park was now deserted, the trees bare, and no one tended the dock. But Donald knew the caretaker and had wrangled permission to use one of the boats.

They sat side by side, each with an oar. A chilly breeze rippled the water, but Annie cuddled against Donald and his head leaned on hers as they rowed lazily. She'd ridden in these boats so many times before, but it had never felt like this.

"We make a good team," he declared.

Ever since picking her up that afternoon, he had a mysterious twinkle in his eyes. Annie's heart beat faster. Would he ask her?

Without looking at her, he deadpanned, "Maybe we should sign up on a slave galley."

She stopped rowing, cupped her hand in the cold water and splashed it at him, rocking the boat. "You . . . you . . ." For once, words failed her.

He held up his oar. "Don't shoot! I surrender!" Then he lay the oar down in the boat and laughed. "You know what this reminds me of? After we finished with the Germans, some of us were sent to the Philippines. Oh boy, you wouldn't believe all the rain! We'd dig in for the night, deep in the mud, two guys together so we'd have one poncho to sleep on and one for cover. It poured so hard, the poncho on top of us would fill with water, like one big pond. When it got too heavy to hold up, we'd punch up with our fists to dump it out."

Donald laughed harder, and she looked at him, puzzled. "It just slopped down into the next foxhole. You should have heard the cussing!"

Annie laughed with him, but shuddered inwardly at the thought of him spending the nights in those muddy holes. She was glad *he* could find something funny about it.

They paddled on a while. She stopped rowing when he did and they drifted against the bank, the boat bumping to a stop. He tilted her chin with his fingers and kissed her softly, then more urgently. Annie forgot his jokes, thinking she might float into the sky like a balloon unless she held on to something—and the only solid thing in reach was Donald.

Then he released her and reached into his jacket pocket, bringing out a letter. Annie was still in a daze from that last kiss as he unfolded the letter. He solemnly cleared his throat and read aloud: "We are pleased to inform you that you've been accepted to the Chicago General Hospital Medical School for the fall of 1946."

He stared at her, waiting for her response. Slowly, the words sank in. "Medical school . . . Chicago . . . you've been accepted!" she exploded.

His smile lit up his entire face. "Yep."

"Oh, Donald that's wonderful! I'm so excited for you. I knew there was something you weren't telling me. That look in your eyes—" Then she caught her breath. That meant he'd be going away again. Her joy at the news dissipated, and she felt guilty for being selfish. He wanted this so badly, and she wanted it for him, too. *But Chicago! That's so far away.* "What does your father say about it?"

"I think he's happy for me. He said he's always wanted the best for me. He just didn't want me to be disappointed in case they turned me down like the other schools had."

"What about the money? Can you get a scholarship?"

"The GI Bill will take care of it." He stopped and looked at her, searching her face. "But I have to tell you something. I put a rider on that fleece."

"A rider? What do you mean?"

"That's a legal term . . . an added condition." When she still looked puzzled, he said, "The rider was that if I got accepted, it meant I could ask you to marry me."

He looked deeply into her eyes. "I love you, Annie . . . more than life itself. I don't ever want to be separated from you again." He looked down at his feet. "I'd get down on my knees to propose, but there's water in the boat, and I'd probably dump us both out."

Annie felt like laughing and crying at the same time. She loved him so much it hurt. But marriage would mean a lot of changes. Moving all the way to Chicago . . . "What about your parents? What do they think about me?" *And what about my mother . . . my church?* she asked herself.

"When they get to know you, they'll love you, too. They won't be as big a problem as your family." He sighed. "We'll just have to take one thing at a time." He took her hand. "You haven't given me an answer. Do you need more time to think about it?"

She smiled into his eyes and saw the yearning there. "No . . . I mean . . . I don't need more time. I'd be proud to marry you. Oh, yes, Donald! Yes!"

He hugged her so tightly she could hardly breathe. "Thank you, sweet Annie." He touched his lips to hers, skimmed up to her cheeks, her nose, her forehead, then slid down to the pulse on her neck before settling back on her lips. His kiss was so passionate it rocked the boat, flipping his hat onto the wet wooden floor.

She grabbed the sides of the boat to keep from falling off the seat, and from the corner of her eye saw an oar slide into the water. But she didn't care. She was engaged to the man she adored, and nothing else mattered. When she finally gasped for air, the oar had floated around a bend. Laughing, Donald paddled after it.

"Can't get in bad with the caretaker," he joked as he scooped up the wayward oar. "We'll want to come back here sometime to celebrate."

By now a cold breeze had picked up. Wind rustled the bare branches and tugged at their clothes. But before they rowed back to the boathouse, they held hands and thanked God for Donald's acceptance into medical school and for bringing them together. They asked for his help over the hurdles that blocked their happiness, and for the grace to follow wherever he led.

Once at the dock, Donald jumped onto the landing, secured the boat, and helped Annie up. They walked back to his car, arms around each other. He kissed her again, this time tenderly.

But when they pulled up at Annie's house, she felt as though a rock had settled in her stomach. How would she tell her mother?

Evidently, Donald had similar thoughts. "Maybe we should keep this between ourselves," he said, "until some of the problems get untangled."

Relieved, she nodded. "If this is God's will for us, the rest will fall into place, won't it?"

"I hope so. I've loved you ever since the first time I saw you."

She smiled, remembering that day. "There at the college, under the oak tree?"

"You were with my sister. I thought . . . I still think . . . you're the prettiest girl I've ever seen."

Annie's face grew hot. "The day you sang about a strawberry blonde?"

"You heard that?" he asked sheepishly. "I thought it was my secret."

"I watched you swagger away—"

"I didn't swagger!"

"You did! Florence said you thought you were too grown-up for us lowly freshmen. But then you came back that next day—"

"And the next. And the next. I couldn't stay away from you. The guys all teased me—"

"I didn't know that!"

"But I didn't care. And pretty soon they were all in love with you, too, and I had to do some fancy maneuvering to get close to you."

"They didn't hold a candle to you," Annie said, shaking her head. "I thought, *When Donald is a famous doctor, I'll be able to say I was his friend in college.* And now—wow! I'm going to be the famous doctor's wife!"

Donald ran his fingers through his hair. "There's still a very big hurdle before I can go to medical school."

"The strawberry farm."

He nodded.

Annie said firmly, "God wouldn't give you a scientific brain and then not let you use it. He'll make a way."

"Sweetheart, I hope you're right."

He got out of the car and went around to open her door. But when he started to walk her to the door, she told him, "Not this time," and waved him off.

Chapter Fifteen

"You look like the cat who got into the lard," Malinda said to Annie. "What did you do today?"

That evening, Annie had gotten to church barely in time to walk in with two of her friends. It had taken her a while to comb her tangled hair and press the wrinkles from her skirt. No wonder her mother glared at her when she burst through the door and dashed straight to her bedroom.

Now, she sat next to Malinda in the fourth bench from the front. Annie turned to the announced page number in the hymnbook, biting her lip to keep from laughing. If Malinda only knew! "Oh," Annie answered Malinda, "just . . . messed around."

"With who? Not Jonah . . . I heard he was with Barbara Goertzen today."

Annie gasped. *Barbara! That girl really takes the cake.* Not only had she snapped up the chance to play for the best quartet in church, but she also had grabbed Jonah to boot. And he sure didn't waste any time before jumping to another girl.

Well, Barbara was welcome to him. Donald was worth a dozen Jonahs.

But what will people think of me? Annie's upbringing warned.

Her happiness answered, *What do I care.*

She grinned, glanced around to see if anyone noticed, then added her alto to "Count Your Many Blessings." It was a blessing that Jonah was out of her way. And a huge blessing that Donald had been accepted into medical school. But the best blessing of all was that he'd asked her to marry him! Annie lifted her head and poured her heart into the song.

Malinda stared at her exuberance. Bertha, sitting on Annie's other side, looked at Annie, a question in her eyes. Annie was glad that there was no time to explain. After that one song, the program started.

It was *Jugendverein* night. Annie thought it was funny that the church called it "Youth Society," because the old people were a big part of it. But her mother had explained. It had started by featuring things to interest the young. Now, though, the high school kids had their own earlier meeting and called it "Young People's Meeting," but no one had bothered to change the name of the Youth Society. *Jugendverein* was simply kept on as a program night, with no preaching. Everyone took turns presenting some sort of musical number, poem, or Bible quiz.

First on tonight's program was a duet, then a number on a musical saw. The music from the saw was sweet and pure, but still some of the youngsters on the front benches giggled into their hands at the unusual instrument. Donald would have appreciated it; Annie decided to mention it to him the next time he called.

Then old Mr. Kruger recited a long poem—in German, with a lot of expression. All around, the older people soaked it up, and at the end many murmured their amens.

Last year, they wouldn't have dared speak in German, but now that the war was over, it was all right again. And before Sunday school, the older folks even had a separate German message. *Then why,* Annie wondered, *were people still so suspicious when the Japanese spoke in their own language?*

During the war, there'd been whispers about a fifth column and spies among the Japanese. All because the older people still spoke in Japanese. Donald told her that his father still didn't subscribe to Japanese newspapers—even those printed in the United States—for fear of being arrested again.

But there wasn't time to dwell on that. Tonight old Mrs. Klippenstein had the quiz, and she had a talent for finding the toughest questions in the Bible. She showed no mercy. Her victims stood up as soon as their names were called and then slouched back into their seats if they didn't know the answer. In the past, Annie had been able to answer almost every time she'd been called upon. But she hoped she wouldn't be called tonight. It was hard enough just to keep her mind on the program.

Mrs. Klippenstein went through at least a dozen questions, and her eyes were at the bottom of her paper. Almost finished. Then—

"Annie Penner!"

Annie took a deep breath, rolled her eyes at Malinda, and slowly stood up.

"What was the name of Moses' father-in-law?"

That was easy. They'd just finished Exodus in Wednesday night Bible study. Annie had looked up Moses' marriage to a Midianite woman, Zipporah. A mixed marriage there, too. He'd fled to her country after killing the Egyptian who'd struck an Israelite. There were several daughters in the family, and he'd helped the women water their sheep. But what was their father's name?

Annie's mind went blank. *Gershom . . . no. That was Moses' son.*

The whole church was looking at her. "Japheth?" Annie stammered.

"Wrong! Barbara Goertzen!"

Annie slid back into the seat.

Barbara stood up and smiled sweetly. "Jethro." She pronounced the name clearly, letting her tongue slide over the "th."

"Correct. Exodus 3:1."

Of course. Annie turned to Malinda, and barely moving her lips murmured, "I knew that."

Malinda shook her head and whispered, "I've never seen you so *be'duzzled.* Right after church, you'd better tell me what's up."

Annie couldn't look at her. Donald had said to keep their engagement secret for now. But she'd burst if she didn't tell *somebody.* Could she trust Malinda?

Ever since Annie and her mother came to Rosemond, Malinda had been friendly to her, and now Annie considered her a best friend. Her boyfriend, George Regier, was now back from his alternate service—the mental hospital in New Jersey—and ever since then, they'd had eyes only for each other. If anyone would understand, it would be Malinda. But she'd always been a homebody and very careful to follow all the traditional ways. It might be smart to keep quiet.

After church Annie tried to slip away to the car, but Malinda followed her.

"Okay, what's going on?"

"Can't I be in a good mood without something 'going on'?" Annie tried to keep walking, but Malinda planted herself in the way.

"I heard you were running around with a Japanese guy."

Annie cringed at her tone of voice and looked around. They were alone in the darkness of the parking lot. "What about him?" she challenged.

"Just that . . . you mustn't think I'm gossiping . . ." Malinda sighed. "But they say you couldn't hold on to Jonah and got desperate."

Annie pushed her way around Malinda and kept going until she reached the car, then turned around and leaned against the door. "I guess you didn't hear that it was I who quit Jonah . . . *not* the other way around."

"He sure didn't look heartbroken tonight. When Barbara answered the question you missed, he grinned as though the price of raisins just went up."

Annie shrugged. "One girl or another . . . doesn't seem to make much difference to him."

"Well, I think you're brave to hold your head up and act as though nothing's wrong. But really . . . a Japanese?"

Annie felt anger and frustration boiling inside her. Why did everyone make such a big fuss about his nationality? "He's a Christian. And he's going to be a doctor. How many guys in our church have the brains for that?" She opened the car door and put one foot inside. "He's the nicest and most respectable person I know, and I'd be proud to marry a man like that."

Immediately, she realized she'd said too much.

Malinda clutched Annie's arm. "You're actually serious about this guy?"

When Annie pressed her lips together and didn't answer, Malinda's mouth dropped open. "Annie, are you crazy?"

Annie took a deep breath and exhaled slowly. "Maybe." Not for loving Donald, but for blabbing their secret. What would he think of her now?

That evening, Donald offered to drive his mother home from church. No sense in making her wait for his father to finish with his counseling. It had been a special service to encourage evacuees who were relocating, and a lot of people needed his advice.

With his own good fortune that afternoon, Donald thought he'd be too excited to concentrate on the message. But as several people told of their experiences, he got caught up in their plight in spite of himself. Most had been lied to and cheated of income that was legally theirs; many had lost everything they owned. And they all faced scorn and ridicule. When the meeting closed, these troubled people had many questions.

He, too, had stayed a while to talk with men who were newly discharged from the army. Some needed jobs and housing, and most were confused and upset. In spite of their bravery in the United States Army, they met people who were afraid to hire them or to live next to a Japanese family.

He could relate to that. He advised them not to take it personally and to concentrate on the areas where they were accepted, doing their best to build friendships and confidence. He told them to stay in the valley's small towns. Rosemond was one small pocket where Japanese-Americans could live. Here, they could find some tolerance and relief from the hatred shown in the larger coastal cities. He told about the neighbor who had been kind enough to watch over his own farm.

He wished he could also mention Annie, but was afraid he'd say too much too soon. As it was, he hoped his own happiness and enthusiasm wouldn't give them false hopes.

So many families were divided. Parents still dreamed and reminisced about the old Japan, and the younger people despised anything—including their elders—that set them apart from patriotic Americans.

He realized again how lucky he was. Although he and his father didn't agree on everything—especially Annie—they could still talk things through. His father had an open and discerning mind; he'd come around. Someday. Wouldn't he?

Donald was also glad he'd saved his service pay—sent some home, bought bonds, and spent very little on himself. Many others had saved, too, but some wasted their money whenever they had a chance. A few gambled their money away. They said they'd done without for so long, now it was their turn to do as they pleased.

As he drove home, he noticed that the wind had picked up, and tree branches waved against the sky. Dried leaves and bits of trash skittered along the road and the clouds scurried across the moon. In the distance, lightning zigzagged over the mountains. As he turned into the yard, Donald noticed the shed door slapping against its metal latch. After driving the car in, he fastened the latch more tightly.

"Air smell like rain," his mother commented as they walked to the house.

He nodded, glad that the weather had held through the afternoon. "The fields could use a good soaking. Not too much though. We don't want the strawberry plants damaged." A big crop would ensure his family's welfare. But then what? Who'd take over the farm so he could leave for medical school without worrying about his parents and grandfather? They couldn't impose upon Menno Bartel again. He recently bought more land and had enough to do. *Lord, I depend on you to provide.*

Donald thought of traveling with Annie to Chicago, finding an apartment, a good church, meeting new friends.

He followed his mother into the house, wondering what she would say when she learned he and Annie were engaged. He turned on the kitchen radio, flipping the dial until he found romantic music. The song "It Had To Be You" struck him right in the heart. *Oh, yes, Annie, there are no two ways about it. It has to be you,* he thought, dreaming about their times together.

He grabbed his mother around the waist and spun her into a slow dance, dipping and swaying until she pulled away, sputtering. "What's the matter, you crazy, you?"

He laughed, and she looked into his eyes. "Something happen today. I think maybe . . ." She raised her eyebrows, and looked at him over her glasses. "You see Annie, yes?" She shook her head and clucked her tongue. "Not go too fast. You whole life ahead. Lots of school now."

Donald turned away. If she could read his eyes that well, how was he going to keep any secrets? "Don't worry," he told her. "I'll be a good boy. I won't do anything you wouldn't do."

She swatted him lightly with her purse before he leaped out of her reach and took the stairs two at a time.

His grandfather stood in the upstairs hall, watching. Donald gave him a hug, nearly knocking him over, then told the astonished old man, "Good service tonight. You should have been there."

"Next time, maybe."

"I'll hold you to that. Your old buddies at church miss you." His grandfather's hands still trembled, and he tired easily, but it was a relief to see him standing straight, looking alert, and coming downstairs for meals. The depression seemed to be easing. He often took part in conversations and occasionally initiated them on his own. On sunny days he sometimes went outside and pulled a weed or two in the yard. By fall, maybe he'd be strong enough to work in the fields again.

The old man went back into his bedroom, and Donald followed him. Through the window, he saw the moon had a ring around it. "Looks like rain, *Jiichan.* It's really windy out."

His grandfather sat down in the rocker. "Bones say yes." He rubbed his knees. "You *Baachan,* she always know. Now I, too."

Donald went to the dresser, found a jar of ointment, and helped his grandfather to a chair. He pushed up the old man's loose trouser legs and rubbed some of the salve into the bony knees. Then he knelt and worked his way down to his ankles, massaging his feet and each of his toes.

His grandfather sat with his eyes almost shut. "So good, so good. You fine doctor."

"I hope so, *Jiichan.* Someday." Donald helped him to his feet and then into the bed. "Lie on your stomach." He worked salve into his grandfather's shoulders and down his back. By the time he finished, the old man was asleep, and Donald put an extra blanket over him.

He crept out of his grandfather's room and went to his own, where he prepared for bed. Picking up his Bible, he knew that his exhilarated mood called for the Psalms. "I will praise thee, O LORD, with my whole heart. . . . Bless the LORD, O my soul: and all that is within me, bless his holy name. . . . O give thanks unto the LORD; for he is good; for his mercy endureth for ever."

He read on and on, his soul overflowing with joy. His prayers had been answered—medical school was a reality, and Annie had said yes. The rest would work out, too.

Outside, the lightning flashed, reflecting on the window shade, and thunder rattled the house. Then the rain came, at first crashing down from a cloudburst, then slowing into a steady, gentle patter on his window. Donald relaxed, put his Bible away, and settled into his bed. He closed his eyes, but knew he was too excited to sleep.

He heard his father's car drive into the yard, heard him slam the back door shut. Voices, the words muffled, floated upstairs. His father's low tones mingled with his mother's higher and softer ones. He wondered if his mother would say anything about Annie.

It started to rain harder again, the rain providing an even, monotonous lullaby.

The planes came roaring over Rosemond, diving over the college, weaving in and out of buildings. Donald wallowed through mud and brush, trying desperately to reach the barracks. But when he got there, the barracks were gone. Instead a man stood pointing a bayonet at him, shouting, jabbing, cursing. Then the planes dove again, their engines whining, louder, louder, louder—

Donald sat up suddenly. He was awake, but the noise didn't stop. He got out of bed and without turning on a light, tiptoed to the window to look out. The rain had stopped, and a bit of moon peeked from a cloud. In the moonlight, and almost out of his view, something glinted. Staring, he made out the rear reflector of a car.

He went to his bed stand to get his flashlight and shone it on his alarm clock: 3 A.M. Had the guys who'd broken his window come back to finish off their job?

But what was that noise? It sounded like . . . like . . . a car's motor racing, wheels spinning.

Some drunk had run off the road and gotten stuck in the mud, that was all.

He went back to the window. Down below, he saw his parents' bedroom light flash on. If some poor guy were in trouble, his father would go out to help him. He'd better go downstairs and lend a hand.

Donald pulled on a pair of work pants and stuck his arms into an old jacket. Stepping barefoot into work boots, he grabbed his flashlight and hurried downstairs. His father had just turned on the yard light, and suddenly sucked air noisily through his teeth.

Beyond the light, in the middle of the strawberry field, barely visible in the thin moonlight, a car was sunk in the ground up to its fenders. The car doors popped open, and two figures jumped out. They slogged through the mud, straining toward the road, where two more cars were parked. Several more guys darted around those cars, some held doors open, others gestured wildly. When the mud-jumpers reached the road, everyone piled into the cars and sped off, tires squealing.

Donald took a huge breath and let it out. "What now?"

He heard a soft noise behind him and turned. His mother held the phone receiver out. "Call police."

He looked back at his father. "They'll want to know the license number. I'll go take a look."

"No!" His mother held the receiver to her chest. "They come back!"

"I don't think so." His father seemed unusually calm, and Donald knew it must be to keep his mother from panicking. "Hang up the phone. Donald and I will go only far enough to make out the license number and be right back."

The clouds had blown away, and a few stars glimmered. Moonlight reflected in the puddles that had formed in the yard. Some tree branches were down, and trash littered the yard. Donald turned the flashlight beam toward the stuck car.

It was a black Chevy sedan. Twin ruts were gouged out in front and behind the tires where the vandals must have rocked it before giving up. But the worst damage was in the field itself. The joyriders had left a pattern of swirls and loops, smashing the tender strawberry plants.

His father's shoulders slumped, and he bowed his head. "The windowpane was easily replaced. But this . . . this will be most difficult to remedy."

Donald stared at the destruction. It was more than careless vandalism. Was it his fault? Was someone punishing him for loving Annie? No. Mennonites were nonresistant. They would never do something that violent. Unless—

What about Jonah? What about that time in the bank when he'd seen Jonah looking at Annie? He didn't know Jonah well, but he knew that look. Maybe Jonah had decided not to give up that easily.

Donald trained the flashlight on the license plate: 1H4970. He'd never seen the car before. He hadn't been back long enough to know everyone's car, but he did know it wasn't Jonah's. For some reason, that made him feel better.

His father broke into Donald's thoughts. "I guess now we can call the authorities."

"You want me to do it?" Donald hoped they wouldn't laugh it off as a prank. Would they joke among themselves: "After all, they're only 'Japs'"?

But his father said, "They know me. It's better if I do it."

Once inside, Donald added information as his father talked on the phone. It sounded as though the conversation was polite, and he was again proud that his father was respected in the community.

"They said many other places were vandalized tonight," his father reported as he hung up the receiver. "All Japanese, including our church."

How could they desecrate a church! Even if it was Japanese. But he realized that meant the attack was aimed at Japanese in general and not him personally. So it probably wasn't because he'd been with Annie.

But that put a new slant on the incident. At church, he'd assured the men that Rosemond was a safe place for Japanese to live. Now he'd need to eat his words. No matter how loyal they were—not even if they'd risked their lives for the country—there wasn't any place where Japanese-Americans were welcome.

His father went on, "Someone will be out to impound the car. They were glad for the license number. Said they can trace it right away."

Donald knew he wouldn't be able to sleep any more. His mother must have had the same idea, because she started frying bacon and scrambling eggs.

Before eating, his father prayed, "Lord, forgive the vandals. They also know not what they do."

Donald felt a tightness in his throat. He still couldn't pray that prayer—to ask God to forgive them—much less forgive them himself.

Chapter Sixteen

THE POLICE ARRIVED AT NINE-THIRTY that morning, followed by a photographer. They said they'd already stopped at several other places where there had been damage.

Someone had driven through the Takanishi vegetable garden. The Watanabe seafood store's windows were smashed and the glass cases smeared. And the Sasaki barn was burned down, destroying all the tools and equipment. Donald realized that all of those families were from the church.

The police mentioned that tires had been slashed and car windows broken in town. All of the vandalism, of course, had been to vehicles and property owned by Japanese people. According to the officers, the damage at the church included red paint splashed on the building and several broken windows.

Donald's father signed a statement for the police. As the officers left, they thanked him for his cooperation and promised that the tow truck was on its way.

His father also left to visit the other families whose property had been vandalized.

As promised, before long the tow truck arrived and hauled the car out of the field. It left still more—and deeper—tracks in the muddy field.

All this time, the sun shone in a blue sky. In the clear air, the white-capped mountains looked deceptively close. Most of the puddles in the yard had already soaked in. Any other time, Donald might have thought it a perfect day.

But now he trudged numbly into the ruined field and bent over to pick up a ragged strawberry plant. Using his fingers, he dug a hole for its naked roots, tamping the muddy soil around them again. He reset another plant, then another, and another. Looking down the long rows, he realized how futile it was—one person trying to salvage the crop.

His crop—his fruits of love—ruined. Was this the way his whole life—the life he'd asked Annie to share—would be? He went back to the house, sat down on the back steps, and buried his face in his arms. How could God allow this to happen?

A rustling sound behind him made him turn around. His grandfather had come down the stairs and was now looking out the screen door. He wore a pair of loose trousers and a blue work shirt.

"*Jiichan!*" Donald said in surprise. He stood up and pulled open the screen. "Come outside, the sunshine will do you good."

His grandfather shuffled out. As he looked at the strawberry field, his face puckered. "Bad, very bad. I go fix."

Donald and his grandfather worked side by side, replanting the tattered little seedlings, throwing aside the ones that couldn't be salvaged. The soil was too wet, and Donald knew he ought to mix in some peat, maybe more fertilizer as well. But because the sun was now surprisingly hot for February, all he could think of were the little roots lying exposed and drying. No use looking ahead at the acres in shambles. Better to concentrate on one plant at a time. And there was no time to waste.

As it got closer to noon, Donald noticed his grandfather lagging behind. But that was all right. At least he was showing an interest—for the first time since the family had returned from camp. It was a relief to see him move around and work with his hands. And to hear him talk again. But how ironic that it took the devastation of the farm to jolt the old man further out of his depression.

In a flash of hope, Donald wondered if this was the answer to the second fleece that Annie suggested. Was it possible his grandfather would regain his full strength by fall and be able to take over the fields? That is, if they could save enough plants to make a crop for next year.

The next time he looked up, the sun was high, and his stomach was growling. "Time for lunch," he called to his grandfather. "We'll drink lots of tea. Can't afford to get dehydrated."

His grandfather didn't respond. Donald turned and saw him kneeling, his hands on the muddy ridge, his body stiff.

Donald went to him and lifted him up by his arms. His grandfather looked at him vacantly, then blinked. "*Gohan?*" He took a step, but stumbled against Donald.

He shouldn't have let *Jiichan* get so tired. "Yes. Time for rice. Maybe my mother will have some pickled radishes for us." His grandfather loved their spicy tartness. Putting his arm around *Jiichan's* thin waist, Donald moved slowly, helping him shuffle to the house.

At the door, he brushed the mud off their knees, took the old man's shoes off, and slid the gnarled feet into slippers. Donald then led him to a chair at the table. His mother stood at the stove watching her son tenderly care for her father-in-law. "I should have brought him back in sooner. He's overtired," Donald apologized.

She frowned. "Too soon. Must take easy. What you expect, you doctor boy? Dance already?" She shook her head. "All lost anyway. No use." Her eyes were red, her mouth trembling.

Donald laid his arm across her shoulder and gave it a squeeze. "Maybe not. We'll do our best to save what's left." But he knew she was right.

His mother sighed as she lifted the lid of the kettle on the stove. Dipping in her index finger, she tested a few grains, then took down bowls and filled them with the steaming rice. She added some chopped vegetables and shreds of roast pork from a pan on the back burner, then tossed in a few slivers of almonds. "Eat. Get strong." After watching them for a minute, she reached in the cupboard for a jar of pickled vegetables and poured a few into a small dish.

Donald grinned at his grandfather. "See? She knows what we like."

He winked at his mother, glad that she'd always gotten along so well with his father's parents.

Then he noticed the old man's hands. The left one lay relaxed on the table, but the right, reaching for his bowl, moved with a rhythmic tremor. He remembered his grandfather's stumbling walk, and a chill ran up his spine.

The shaking palsy. He'd seen enough cases in the camp hospital to recognize the symptoms. But there were other causes for that kind of shaking, so he could be wrong. He'd have to take his grandfather to a specialist to find out.

After eating, he pushed his chair back and stood up. "You need to rest now, *Jiichan.* Father will be back soon; he can help."

But as he made his way back to the field, the old man followed him. Before long his mother joined them. Then his father came home, bringing peat moss and fertilizer, and the four of them worked steadily and silently until it was too dark to see.

At the store that same day, Annie muddled through her work, her mind far away. Part of her was still in Mooney Grove, thrilling to Donald's proposal and his expressions of love. But another part was sunk in worry and guilt. He'd call today—she knew he would—and she'd have to admit she'd broken her promise and told Malinda their secret.

He'd be disappointed. But would he also be angry? Would he ever trust her again? Why hadn't she been more careful? Oh, what was she going to say to him?

Every time the phone rang, she answered at its first little jingle, her hands shaking. Each time it was someone complaining about a refrigerator freezing the lettuce or the men delivering the wrong couch. Throughout the day, she watched the front door. But the only people to come in were customers—most of them just browsing—the mailman, and a linoleum salesman.

That afternoon she was at the counter taking an installment payment when the phone rang again. As her hand jerked to answer it, she nearly swept her ledger onto the floor. Mr. McGinnis happened to walk by just then. He didn't say anything then, but just before closing time, he hiked himself onto the corner of her desk.

"I notice you're a little jumpy today. Expecting a special call?"

Annie felt her face grow hot. "I'm sorry. I didn't mean to be so clumsy."

"That's okay. We all have our days. But if there's a problem, I'd like to know about it."

Annie shook her head. "Just . . . something personal."

Her boss gazed across the showroom. "Bob Taylor tells me he's seen you with one of our Japanese boys, just out of the army. The preacher's son."

The hair bristled on the back of her neck. Bob *had* been watching her. Not only was she the talk of the church, now she was the store's favorite subject. Well, she wasn't going to make the same mistake twice. "We knew each other in college." If her boss objected, she would sooner give up her good job than part with Donald.

"He's a nice kid. I've heard a lot of good things about his regiment. Too bad some idiots can't get past the fact that his people look like the enemy we fought against."

She stared at Mr. McGinnis. He sounded more broad-minded than she'd realized. Or was he warning her about something? "What are you talking about?"

"This afternoon I had coffee with a friend of mine from the police department. He said there'd been some damage done to Japanese farms and businesses last night. Some vehicles vandalized. Paint thrown at the church."

Annie turned cold all over. "Which farms?" If something had happened to Donald—

"I guess it was bound to happen sooner or later. You've heard what's gone on in other towns. But I thought our community was above that. They ought to know our Japanese here are as patriotic as any of us."

Annie couldn't stand it any longer. She reached out and touched Mr. McGinnis's arm. "What farms? The Nakamuras—"

"You didn't know? That was one of them." He clicked his tongue. "Too bad. Those were the best strawberries around." He slid off Annie's desk and headed for the front door, taking the store keys out of his pocket to lock up for the night.

What had happened to Donald's field? Had he been hurt too? Annie grabbed the phone and asked the operator to ring the Nakamura number. Who cared if only bold girls called men? This was an emergency.

Seven rings brought no answer, so she hung up, grabbed her purse, and hurried out of the store with her boss. But he'd already told her everything he knew. She ran all the way home, wishing she'd taken the car to work.

Her mother had taken a group of women to Fresno to buy supplies for the sewing circle, and she wasn't home yet. Annie let herself into the house and tried calling again, but there still was no answer. She then tried the Baptist church, with no luck there either. If the damage was as bad as Mr. McGinnis had said, probably everyone was outside working.

She turned on the local radio station, but there was no news flash—only an interview with a man who had invented a device to control gophers.

To keep from falling apart, Annie set the table, then started peeling potatoes. By the time her mother came home, there were meatballs simmering in the iron skillet, and supper was almost ready.

Her mother actually smiled. "You made *klopps!* Just what I was hungry for."

While they ate, her mother chattered about the quilt materials they bought, other shoppers they met, and what skimpy clothes people in Fresno wore. Finally Annie cleared the table and washed the dishes. She worked so furiously that her mother commented, "What's the matter? Are you mad about something?"

Annie dried her hands on the towel that hung over the oven handle, then turned around and faced her mother. "Yes, I am. Somebody tore up the fields around here, broke windows in a store, and threw red paint at the Baptist church."

Her mother sat back down at the table, her face pale. "*Doch nicht!* Are you sure? Why would they do that?"

"Just because they're Japanese."

"Oh . . . you mean those fields . . . that church. What about your friend . . . was their . . ."

Annie glanced at her. Did she really care, or was it her own jam she was thinking about? "Oh, yes. Your favorite strawberry fields, all ruined."

"What will they do now?"

"What can they do? All their hard work is for nothing. And Donald was just accepted into medical school. But how can he leave his family without any income? His father doesn't get support from the church . . . most of the people lost everything in the evacuation."

Her mother sighed. "*Ach, yauma.* What's this world coming to? I thought the war was over."

"Well, some people still have it in for them. They don't realize that our American Japanese helped bring the peace." Now would her mother see that?

"Didn't I tell you? That's what you have to look forward to, getting mixed up with Japs—"

"Mom! Don't call them that." Nothing had changed.

"Well, but it's true. If you want to be around them, you'll have to take the consequences. People aren't all as accepting as we are—"

"Accepting? I don't see that acceptance," Annie scolded back through tightened lips. "You're talking as though they deserve to have their fields destroyed. What have they done against you?" She felt as though her heart was bleeding.

Her mother's lips trembled. "Don't shout at me. The Bible says to honor your mother—"

Annie knew she couldn't say she was sorry, but she did lower her voice. "A terrible thing has happened, and it's got to be made right. I don't know how, but it has to."

Her mother sat frowning, her chin cupped in her hand. "We must pray about this. Give it over to the Lord."

Annie shook her head. "There's a time for praying and a time for doing."

Her mother gasped. "That's sacrilegious! The Bible says to pray without ceasing."

Just then the phone rang and Annie grabbed it. But it wasn't Donald. It was Mrs. Bartel, a neighbor of the Nakamuras. "I guess you heard about all that damage to the farms? Menno's getting together a group for the Mennonite Disaster Service. He figures if they help all over the world, they should also help those in our area. Do you suppose you and your mother could take a carload over there? There might be others in the community joining us, too. We'll meet at our church tomorrow morning at eight."

Annie covered the mouthpiece and repeated the message to her mother, adding, "See? Even the church knows there's a time to put muscle behind our faith."

Her mother shook her head. "The MDS is for natural disasters, not to get mixed up with someone's squabbles. If we get involved, the offenders might come after us, too."

Annie couldn't believe her ears. "There's no squabble. This involves the whole town. And I'm going."

"No!" This time her mother shouted. "You can't miss work for something like that. And I need the car for sewing circle."

Annie gritted her teeth. She couldn't control what her mother did, but she was old enough to make up her own mind. She turned back to the phone. "I'll go. Just me. And I'll need a ride."

Mrs. Bartel was quiet a few seconds. "Okay. I'll put your name down and get back to you."

Annie hung up the receiver and turned to her mother. "I have to. It's the right thing to do. Donald's a good man, and I'll help him and his family any way I can. And the other Japanese, too."

Her mother wiped tears from her eyes. "*Kindt,* I have nothing against the Japanese. But I love you. I see nothing but disaster ahead if you don't break off with this man."

Chapter Seventeen

The fog swallowed up a person and set him in a world of his own. And at five in the morning, it was so thick Donald couldn't see more than a few feet in any direction. In unspoken agreement, everyone in the Nakamura family was back in the strawberry fields. There was no sunrise—just fog. With all the traffic accidents it caused, dense morning fog after a cold rain was the thing valley people hated and feared the most. Donald hadn't expected it this late in the season.

But in a way, he liked it. Being unseen made him feel protected, safe from all the outside evils.

This time, trying not to be obvious, Donald worked close to his grandfather in order to watch him. His heart sank when he noticed that the old man's right hand still shook. No matter what the cause, he'd never again be as strong as he'd been before the evacuation.

At eight o'clock, Donald's mother went into the house and brought back a thermos of tea and some hot oatmeal. They sat together on the damp soil, shivering. His father asked God's blessing not only on the food, but also on the damaged plants. "Lord, again we seek your help. To us this is a hopeless task, but with you, nothing is impossible."

After they ate, Donald's father trudged over to the farthest part of the field while his mother took the empty bowls into the house. Donald heard the screen door slam as she came back out. Then he heard the roar of motors and his mother's scream.

He looked back toward the house. The fog had lifted slightly, and he could barely make out lights and dim outlines on the road. Car after car, pickups, trucks—all squealed to a stop. Car doors slammed. Footsteps pounded. People shouted and laughed.

It was happening all over again. Just like Sunday night. He needed to protect his mother, help his grandfather, get some kind of weapon for defense. But his feet stayed anchored to the ground. How could those hoodlums attack them openly, in the daytime, rushing at them, grinning, carrying—

What? They were brandishing hoes, shovels, and trowels, carrying boxes of strawberry plants!

Donald's mouth fell open in disbelief. He tried to make out the faces. German, Armenian, Mexican, Japanese. Men, women, boys, girls, and even a few children. They were all beaming, laughing at his astonishment.

Some were strangers, but he recognized the young men he'd counseled in church Sunday evening. Many friends from college days and several businessmen from town were among the group, and some of the ministers his father had met with regularly before the evacuation. Neighbors from all around had come. The Mennonite preacher got out of a truck while a group of young people jumped from the back of it. And then *she* appeared—his own dear Annie, in rolled-up overalls, carrying a trowel. She'd never looked more beautiful.

"What? . . . Why?" Donald asked as he walked toward the group.

Rev. Loewen laid his hand on Donald's shoulder. "We've come to help you . . . in the name of the Lord."

"But . . . how did you know?" he asked, glancing at Annie.

Rev. Loewen told him, "One of your neighbors heard the commotion and then overheard your call to the police on the party line. She and her husband drove by and saw the damage to your fields. And then—"

"Then we called everybody on our line and got the word out," Mrs. Bartel chimed in. "We would've come sooner, but it took a while to get organized."

Her husband looked around. "Okay, just tell us what to do and where to get started."

Donald took a deep breath. By now, the sun had filtered through the fog, and he saw his father approaching. "Well, how about if six or eight people go over to my father, and I'll get another group transplanting the first-year plants here." To demonstrate what he needed them to do, he tamped the soil carefully around the tender roots, shaping the ridges evenly. Then he took another group farther into the field and showed them what needed to be done there. Leaving them to their assigned task, he started yet another group.

After everyone was working, he went over to Annie, who was down on her knees near his grandfather. "I'm just . . . flabbergasted. Why are all these people being so kind to us?"

She smiled into his eyes, and his heart melted. He had to steel himself not to take her into his arms right there in public. "Just like our preacher said, we're doing this to help you, in the name of the Lord. It's part of our Mennonite Disaster Service. We help people because we love the Lord and that's what he would do. And once we got organized, a lot of other people wanted to join us. They like you and respect you."

She went back to work on the plant in front of her, but Donald continued to stand there, bewildered. She looked up at him again as she moved on to the next plant. "They feel terrible about the evacuation, all you've been through. Everyone knows it was wrong." Then she looked over the field and added, "Well, almost everyone. Have you found out who did this?"

"Not yet." He told her about the stuck car. "The police are tracing his license number." Donald straightened a furrow nearby and kept pace with her.

"I hope they put all the vandals in jail. It would serve them right."

He shrugged. "Yeah . . . well . . . that's for the police to decide. My biggest worry right now is my grandfather." He told her how he'd thought the old man would be strong enough to take over the fields, until he noticed the tremor.

She was quiet for a few minutes, then said, "Oh, Donald. I'm so sorry." Her voice trembled, and again he wished they were alone. To control his quickening pulse, he excused himself and stepped across the ridges to the next group of workers.

"That's good," he told them. "Cover that last bit of root, too . . . build up the furrow just a little higher . . . that's it . . . wonderful." He went around, checking on the progress and encouraging the volunteers, eventually going back to Annie.

They worked steadily until noon. Suddenly he wondered if there was enough food in the house to feed all the people. God would have to do another miracle like the loaves and fishes to feed the five thousand!

Then, as the sun dissipated the last of the fog, two more cars drove up. Four ladies got out, carrying sacks and jugs. They spread a tablecloth in the back of a pickup, laid out a lunch, and then blew a whistle.

Annie straightened up and shaded her eyes with her hand to peer at the women. Then she gasped. "I don't believe it."

Donald followed her gaze. "Your mother!" He looked back at Annie. "Didn't you know she was coming?"

"No. She . . ." Annie sighed. "Last night, she didn't even want me to come."

By now all the workers were straggling in from the fields, brushing off their clothes. Donald led them to a faucet in the yard, where they could wash their hands.

Rev. Loewen asked God to bless the food, the workers, and the strawberry fields, and then they lined up for the sandwiches—ham and cheese on thick homemade bread—sliced fruit, and bar cookies. And plenty of coffee and lemonade to wash it all down.

Donald's thankful smile moved over the servers, but settled on Annie's mother. He wondered what had changed her mind. When he moved up in line closer to her, he said, "We'll never be able to repay you for your kindness. God bless you."

Mrs. Penner's face turned red, and her eyes didn't quite meet his. "Well . . . it just wasn't right . . . what happened." Then she straightened and stuck out her chin. "Besides, *somebody* has to feed the workers." She turned away and poured coffee for the next ones in line, then busied herself setting out more sandwiches.

The people settled themselves in shady spots, on the ground under trees, along the house and shed, joking and laughing while they ate. Donald's grandfather sat on the back porch steps, away from the crowd, but Donald noticed that Annie had slipped away to take him some food. She sat down beside the old man, smiling and talking with him. He seemed responsive, even alert. And from the distance Donald couldn't see any shaking. Maybe working in the sunshine would repair his grandfather's weakened nerves and muscles.

He thrilled at Annie's thoughtfulness, and wondered what she and his grandfather were talking about. But he didn't want to break into their conversation or make his affection for Annie too obvious. Instead, he moved among the groups, thanking them, asking about their own families and work.

Several of his old college friends had also been in the military, serving in New Guinea, the Philippines, Italy, and France. They gave him news about other mutual friends who were still in occupied Japan and Germany. Donald seized the opportunity, hurried into the house and brought out his yearbook. Laughing and joking, they passed it around, scribbling signatures and notes and remembering those carefree days.

The men he'd counseled at church thanked him again for his advice and said this was the only way they could show their appreciation.

Even the strangers were courteous and sympathetic, and before long Donald felt as though they, too, were old friends.

He saw his father engaged in a lively discussion with the Mennonite preacher and a few other older men, and Donald was proud of his father's ease with people of different cultures. He remembered that after his father had been released from prison, he became a liaison between the families at camp and the authorities. That terrible time must have also been a time of growth.

The sun was shining brightly now. Encouraged and uplifted, Donald took a deep breath of the fresh, clean air. Annie loved him, there was hope for a crop, his grandfather seemed to be stronger, and the townspeople supported them. God really could do the impossible!

That evening, Annie soaked in a tub of Epsom salts and thought she'd never be able to move again. Every joint ached, and her fingernails were ragged and packed with dirt.

It'd been worth it, though—and wonderful—to be able to work beside Donald. Amazingly, she'd been able to keep up with him. Or maybe he'd worked slower for her sake.

There'd been no chance to tell him of her broken promise, that slip of the tongue. In a way it was a relief, but it only postponed what she knew would be his disappointment in her. Evidently Malinda hadn't told anyone else about her involvement with Donald. At least, in the field, none of the people had mentioned it.

But it was too much to hope that the news wouldn't eventually spread like floodwater, and then she'd have to pay for it.

A knock at the bathroom door brought her out of her thoughts. "Aren't you done yet? Supper's ready."

When Annie had come home from the Nakamura's, she'd asked her mother about her change of heart.

Her mother had said, "They needed more hands, and I couldn't very well say no."

Now at the supper table, with her fingernails scrubbed and her wet hair wrapped in a towel, Annie reveled in the hot *heyna sup.*

The tasty chunks of chicken mixed with spices, broth, and thick homemade noodles were just what she needed. She wondered if her mother's participation today meant that she was softening toward Donald. She darted a look across the table, wondering how to bring up the subject, when her mother beat her to it.

"You don't need to think I've changed my mind. I still say you're ruining your chances for a happy life. What decent Mennonite man would want a woman who's been playing around with a Japanese guy?"

Annie tried out several answers in her mind: *I'm not playing around, I'm serious. Why would I worry about a Mennonite man, decent or otherwise, when I'm marrying Donald?* But she knew that no matter what she said, it would be the wrong thing.

Instead, she remembered what her mother had said—*"I couldn't very well say no"*—as an explanation for her decision to help with the lunch. "So . . . you just came out there today to make people think you were kindhearted? Not to help the needy, but just for show." As soon as she said it, she regretted it. But the words couldn't be taken back.

Her mother pursed her lips and rose from the table. "The day will come when you'll see what you're doing to yourself. Let's just hope it won't be too late."

And maybe it will be the other way around, Annie fumed. She stretched her sore back and arms and rose to do the dishes. What would her mother say when she learned her daughter was already engaged to Donald? And that she had kept it a secret?

Or had she? If Malinda gossiped, and her mother heard about it third or fourth hand, she would be even more hurt.

Annie sighed. Keeping secrets was a complicated business.

The next day, Donald called her at the furniture store and thanked her for helping in the strawberry fields. "After I finish the rest of the field," he said, "I'll help clean up the Watanabes' fish market. I also promised to get together a crew of volunteers to paint the church." Donald paused only a beat. "I was happy to see you with my grandfather. Did you have a good visit?"

"Yes. He's such a nice man. He told me about your grandmother, and how proud she'd been of you." Would this be a good time to tell Donald about Malinda?

She looked around the store. Mr. McGinnis was heading toward the counter with some customers and the deliverymen were hauling a stove out to their truck. She'd be needed to write out a sales contract. Definitely not a good time.

Donald called again Friday afternoon, and this time his voice sounded strangely different—not cold, but sad. "I really need to see you. I'm at the church . . . can't be gone for long, but I have to pick up more paint. Would you be able to get away from the store for a little bit? That new sandwich place next door to the hardware . . . Sweets and Treats . . . can you meet me there?"

Annie shivered. He must have learned of her blabbing. Why hadn't she confessed sooner? "I'll be there."

Chapter Eighteen

The three blocks from the furniture store to the sandwich shop were the longest Annie had ever walked. She fully expected Donald to be there ahead of her—the church was only two blocks on the other side of the shop. But no customers were there when she arrived. She went to the counter and ordered two sodas.

The waitress, her gray hair in a snood, smiled at her. "Meeting someone?"

Annie nodded and took the glasses to a booth.

Within minutes, Donald, wearing faded jeans that had white spots on one knee, slid in next to her. "I'm waiting for the hardware store to mix the paint for me. It'll be ready when we leave," he explained. Although the waitress stared at him, he ignored her.

His face was smooth, his expression calm, but Annie knew that didn't mean anything. He was very good at hiding his feelings. She watched him bite his lip, and he wasn't looking at her. Something was very wrong.

"I know we agreed not to say anything—" she blurted out. She glanced at the waitress before continuing. "About us, I mean," she whispered. "But I think one of my friends suspects. She—"

Donald still didn't look at her. "It doesn't matter. Nothing matters. I just don't know how to tell you."

A chill went up Annie's spine. "What is it? Did the medical school—"

He faced her then, his eyes full of sadness. "Worse. Have you ever heard of . . . miscegenation?"

"No. What is it?"

An elderly couple entered the shop and went up to the counter, distracting the waitress. Under the table, Donald took Annie's hand in his and caressed her fingers with his thumb. He whispered, "Marriage between different races. A friend of mine has an uncle who's a lawyer." The calm mask slipped, and his face twisted. "This lawyer says it's illegal."

Puzzled, Annie stared at him. "Why? We're both American citizens."

"That's why I didn't consider it before. I even had to sign an oath to prove my loyalty when I joined the army. That was supposed to restore our rights. Our citizenship." He ran a hand through his hair. "Lot of good that did me. All that I've been through for our country, the medals I earned . . . none of it means a thing. Just because my parents are Japanese, it's against the law for us to marry."

Annie felt numb. She couldn't be hearing right. All her dreams, her happiness—everything she hoped for—came crashing down around her. If she couldn't marry Donald, what use was there in living?

He closed his eyes and sighed heavily. "I'm so sorry, sweet Annie."

She knew he felt as miserable as she, but that didn't ease her pain.

"I'd do anything to change it," he said, slipping his arm around her waist. "But I don't know what it could be." They sat in silence for a little while.

Then she frowned. "But . . . I know Mennonites who married English people. They're different races."

"Color is what matters. They were all whites. Seems the law was first made to keep Negroes from marrying Caucasians. Then the government got worried that yellow faces might take over the country," explained Donald with a crooked smile. "They added Japanese to that law . . . so we untouchables wouldn't pollute the national purity.

"We don't have a chance," he sighed dejectedly. "I heard of a Nisei named Ohara who was hired to work, sight unseen. The boss thought he was Irish. But one look at him, and no more job." He shrugged. "Another guy had plastic surgery on his eyes to escape evacuation. Told people he was Italian. It didn't work. They caught him anyway, locked him up."

Annie felt tears burn her eyes. Angrily, she wiped them away. "Some people are so ignorant. What does it matter how faces are shaped or what shade their complexion is? You're so handsome, Donald Nakamura . . . in your heart as well as your face. And I love every bit of you."

Her mother's comment echoed in her thoughts: *No decent Mennonite would want you after you've been with a Japanese.* But she'd rather be an old maid the rest of her life than marry anyone else!

A group of teenagers came into the shop, jabbering and laughing, shouting orders for hot dogs. After filling their order, the waitress came to the booth. This time, she wasn't smiling. "Do you want anything else?"

Donald moved away from Annie and shook his head. He'd barely touched his soda.

Still watching them, the woman went back to the counter. Annie felt like asking her, *Haven't you ever seen a Japanese-American before?* But she didn't want to embarrass Donald.

Annie glanced at the wall clock. She'd told Mr. McGinnis she'd be back in thirty minutes—it had now been almost forty. But she couldn't bear to leave. Not now, thinking she might never be with him again—or that he might get arrested just for wanting to marry a German girl. She gave the waitress a hard look, as though it were all her fault. The woman turned abruptly and scrubbed at the counter.

Donald cleared his throat. "I have to get that paint back to the church."

Annie nodded. "If I don't show up, Mr. McGinnis might send the deliverymen to find me." Still, they sat there. The waitress kept scrubbing and glancing their way.

Finally, Donald sighed and got up. Annie slid out after him. He gave the waitress a little nod and a polite wave. Her steely eyes stayed glued on him as she lifted her fingers ever so slightly to return his wave. Donald opened the door for Annie and followed her out.

In front of the hardware store, he stopped and looked at her. "My sweet Annie. I love you so much. You're so precious to me." He looked into her eyes, and she felt she could see straight into his soul.

"I just can't understand it," he said, slowly shaking his head. "Would God bring us back together just to tear us apart?"

Annie knew what her mother would say. That they'd misunderstood God in the first place. Substituted their own desires—she'd probably use the word "lust"—for his will. She looked up at Donald's face, memorizing each feature, and whispered, "Will I see you again?"

His gaze wandered over her face, and then he nodded. "Sunday afternoon. Two o'clock. No matter what."

Donald watched Annie walk away. As she turned the corner, she gave a little wave before heading toward the furniture store.

For Annie's sake, thought Donald, *it would be better to break it off.* It would be torture to keep on seeing her, knowing that it could never go any farther.

But he couldn't give her up. Wasn't there some way—some loophole—that would allow them to marry?

He went into the hardware store, signed the bill for the paint, and picked up the cans. Slowly he walked back to the church, hardly noticing that the handles of the heavy cans bit into his palms. Was he being selfish, thinking only of how much he wanted her? If somehow he figured out a way to marry her, would their life be so hard that she'd resent him?

He thought of all the ups and downs in his life. College had been happy, especially after meeting Annie. How sweet those noon hours had been under the oak tree, all the talking, arguing, and laughing as he got as close to her as possible. How heady it had been to breathe in her beauty.

Then came the disgrace and humiliation of Pearl Harbor—the evacuation, grinding him and his people into the dust. His despair when the letters from Annie stopped. The excitement of release from the internment camp, even if it was to army barracks.

There'd been good times mixed with the bad. He'd made a lot of friends, lost some of the best, survived the war, and maybe helped make a difference in the world. But the snubs and rejections on the way home should have warned him. The cars slowing down, then speeding away when they'd seen his face.

Annie's love had shot him high as a rocket. The joy of acceptance into medical school, the unbelievable support from the community after the vandalism—none of it was enough. No matter how loyal, how educated, how *American* he was, he could never be a full citizen.

"Hey, where you going?"

Donald stopped and looked around. He'd been so deep in thought he'd walked right past the church. His neck grew hot as his friends laughed at him. He felt like lashing out, taking out his anger and disappointment on them.

Instead, he walked back to them, drew on all the Japanese control he could muster, and put on a grin. "Just wanted to see your work from a distance." He set the paint cans down.

One of the men he'd counseled in church Sunday evening, Sho Kimura, sat on the front steps. "Took you long enough. We finished one coat and had time for a game of checkers. I won, too." He got up and stretched, then took a screwdriver out of his back pocket and opened one of the cans. "Hey, I went in to the county office like you told me to. They said I'll get twenty dollars a week. It'll sure help me get on my feet. Thanks for clueing me in."

Donald poured paint into his empty bucket and tried to focus on the other man's problems. "You're entitled. But, remember, you have to keep applying for work. It won't last forever."

"Fifty-two weeks, the clerk said. I'll find something by then. I heard that Super Save Grocery needs box boys. And there's always packing houses and the cannery."

Donald climbed a ladder and began painting. Sho had seen a lot of rejection, too. He was a good worker, but had just a high school education. If only someone would overlook his race and give him a chance.

"Wasn't much fun standing in line for an hour, though," Sho continued. He dipped his brush into Donald's bucket, scraped off the drips, and began working around the window frames.

Donald nodded. "Next time, take a book along," he suggested.

Sho laughed. "Me? I'm not much for reading books . . . especially not standing up."

For a while, the only sounds were the swish of brushes, the rattle of a pickup going by, and the occasional chirp of a bird in a nearby tree. Then Sho said, "The guy in front of me took the longest. They almost turned him down . . . said he'd quit his job without good reason. He argued that he had plenty of reasons."

"Did he say what they were?"

"Oh . . . boss cut his hours . . . gave him the dirtiest work . . . watched him every minute and made him so nervous he couldn't help making mistakes . . . that kind of stuff."

"Hmm. Did it do any good . . . the arguing?"

"He just kept at it. Had an answer for everything they said. Took three agents to hash it out, but finally they worked out a way. Said he'd have to wait a couple of weeks extra, but promised him the money."

Another friend, Tom Ichiba, had painted his way over to Donald. "Hey, Nak, when you gonna settle down and get married? You're making it hard for us younger guys. All the pretty girls are trying their best to get your attention."

"Don't worry." Donald felt his neck getting hot again. "I'm going to medical school this fall. You'll have an open field." And he'd be all alone again, Annie hopelessly out of his reach. He felt his teeth clench and forced himself to relax.

Sho laughed and winked at Tom. "I'm betting on Grace. He needs her for his singing." He crooned a few off-key bars of "I Love You Truly," eyes closed, his free hand over his heart.

Tom added, "Yeah, and with her good looks and his brains, they ought to—"

"She's dating a guy from Fresno State," Donald said quickly. He hoped it was true. She mentioned something awhile back about a play she'd seen with a guy at the college. "Besides, I've got . . . other plans." Plans that had just been smashed.

The two men stared at him, their eyebrows raised. When Donald didn't explain, Tom whistled. "Someone said you had a German girlfriend, but Nak, you wouldn't be so crazy as to get serious . . . would you?"

How dare they talk that way about Annie? His friends were just as bad as all the rest of them. All the bitterness rushed back into Donald's heart. "Haven't you heard? That's illegal," he shot back, then he turned and slapped paint onto the wall, brushing with furious strokes.

But as he painted, he remembered the man Sho told him about—the man at the county office who hadn't given up, even though the laws seemed against him.

A thought hovered at the edge of Donald's mind. *Maybe there* is *a way . . . maybe we* can *get around that anti-miscegenation business.*

Donald's breathing slowed and his paint strokes became more even. *Maybe there's hope after all.*

Chapter Nineteen

ANNIE'S MIND WANDERED IN CIRCLES. Back at work, her fingers flew over the adding machine. Donald said he would see her Sunday. Without fail, he said.

She wanted to see him, to be with him. But if they couldn't marry, couldn't even tell people how they felt about each other, had to sneak around—what kind of life would that be? As it was, he had so little time for her. Always busy with the farm, his choir, or helping other Japanese adjust to life after the war. And no matter what, he was going to medical school.

She closed her eyes as the pain overpowered her. After he left, she'd probably never see him again. Even though he loved her, he'd adjust—the same way he adjusted to all the other hardships in his life. A wonderful man like him wouldn't stay single just because he couldn't marry a Caucasian. To her, his solution was obvious—he'd simply marry someone of his own race. And then it would be easy for him to forget about her.

But her life was over. Everything in Rosemond reminded her of him. Day after day, she'd see the places they'd been and be reminded of their happiness, their love. The mountains, the country roads, and the college and their favorite oak tree. Even the town sidewalks, especially in front of the hardware store where she just left him. The sandwich shop. Right here in the furniture store, where he'd leaned over the counter to catch her attention. Her own living room!

And Mooney Grove where he proposed to her. The church would be having their annual picnic there. She wouldn't be able to look at the lagoon and the rowboats without bursting into tears.

If Donald left her, she'd just have to leave, too. Go somewhere she'd never been before, where nobody knew her.

Emptiness flooded her heart and she lay her head down on the desk. Her little strawberry locket tapped against the wood, and she curled her fingers around it. Every little curve and contour of it brought Donald closer.

"Hey, you sleeping?"

Annie raised her head quickly and brushed tears away. "Malinda!" She pushed her chair back and went to the counter.

Malinda looked worried. "Are you okay?"

Annie shrugged. She'd already told her friend too much.

But Malinda kept staring at her. "Did something happen? With your . . .uh . . . Japanese friend?"

Annie smiled bitterly. "I guess that's spread all over church by now."

Malinda's eyes opened wide. "You don't think . . . I wouldn't repeat what you told me! Annie! If that's all you think of me . . ." She shrugged and looked at Annie from the corner of her eye, ". . . I guess I'll just have to go somewhere else to pick out a cedar chest."

"Cedar chest? You mean . . . a hope chest?" Annie couldn't help feeling a pinch of envy. *Is Malinda thinking of marriage too?*

Malinda bit back a smile. "I've kept your secret. Now you have to keep mine. I haven't even told my folks yet."

Annie gasped. "Did George ask you?"

Malinda nodded. "He hasn't bought a ring yet. We won't get married for at least a year, but he said to come pick out the cedar chest so I can start getting ready. I'll have to get busy quilting."

Annie wanted to congratulate her. She walked around the counter and hugged Malinda, but no words came out. Instead, all the despair and frustration flooded over her, and she couldn't hold back the tears. Why couldn't her own life be that normal, that easy to work out?

Malinda patted Annie's back. "Hey . . . hey . . . it can't be as bad as all that?"

"It is. Oh, Malinda, you just don't know."

"Of course I don't. Tell me. Maybe I can help."

Annie dug a tissue out of her skirt pocket and blew her nose. "Nobody can help."

"Well, tell me anyway. Did you break up with your . . . Japanese boyfriend?"

"No. I mean . . . it's not him . . . I can't . . . we can't . . . it's illegal!" Annie explained the anti-miscegenation law to Malinda. "When it comes to marriage, the government doesn't recognize Donald's citizenship." She felt tears threatening again and blinked them back.

Malinda's eyes widened. "You really love him, don't you." It was a statement, not a question.

How could she explain? "I've dated other guys . . . you know . . . Jonah, Pete Ediger, Andy Kroeker . . . but Donald . . . he's head and shoulders better than any of them. He's so kind, so honest, so smart . . . he's just the right man for me. He'll make a wonderful doctor. And you should hear him sing!" Annie lifted her locket and opened it. "Here's his picture. Isn't he handsome?"

Malinda looked at the little photo for several moments. "He *is* good-looking."

Annie waited for the rest—"for a Japanese"—but Malinda seemed sincere, so she snapped the little strawberry shut and held it snug in her hand. Then she shook her head. "Now, I don't think I'll ever get married. I'll never meet another person like him."

"Have you prayed about this?" Malinda's voice was sympathetic.

"Not yet. Donald just told me this afternoon. Anyway, what's the use . . . if it's illegal?"

"You never know. Remember the Bible says if two or three people agree to pray about something, God will answer. I'm one, you're two, and if Donald loves you as much as you love him, he'll be praying too. And if it's God's will, it'll happen. Okay?"

Annie blew her nose and gave a weak smile.

"Now," said Malinda. "What about that cedar chest?"

"Let me show you a beautiful one that just came in."

Annie led the way to the polished honey-toned chest, then opened the curved lid so Malinda could smell the wonderful scent of cedar and admire the compartments.

"Mark it sold," Malinda announced. "I'll tell George, and he'll come put it on layaway."

She put her arm around Annie. "Look. I'm sorry I gave you a bad time about dating a Japanese. It was just . . . I can't imagine being with someone not in the church . . . someone raised differently . . . looking so different. Don't hold it against me."

Annie squeezed her friend's arm. Malinda might never understand, but she wasn't as quick to judge as some of the others.

By mid-afternoon Saturday, Donald and his crew had finished painting the church, and put up barriers and "wet paint" signs. They cleaned the brushes, put away the cans and buckets, and stowed the ladders at the side of the church. A little after four o'clock Donald headed home. There, he found his grandfather hoeing in the strawberry field.

"*Jiichan!* Better let me do that." He led the protesting old man to the house, steadying him so he wouldn't stumble over the ridges. Donald helped him take off his shoes before they went into the kitchen.

Couldn't take a chance on him overdoing and slipping back into depression. He'd been through so much all these years.

Baachan had told Donald how his grandfather bravely came to the foreign country of America as a young man. He slaved in the fields for many years, lived on practically nothing until he saved enough money to send for his wife and son, Donald's father. He hired himself out, sharecropped, rented, and then finally bought the land—only to find that he couldn't own it because there was no hope of his becoming a citizen.

But by that time, Donald's father had sent for a wife, Donald had been born in this country, and when he was of age his grandfather put the land in Donald's name. The strawberry field, however, had always been *Jiichan's* special love, and he considered it his own.

"You rest now, okay? Then maybe tomorrow you'll feel good enough to go to church. See your old buddies again. You can watch me lead the choir." Donald waved his arms, exaggerating the directing motions. He then bowed from the waist in several directions, coaxing a smile from the tired old man.

His mother, chopping celery at the counter, watched his antics, smiled, and shook her head at him.

He winked at her, then said quietly, "Don't let him come back outside. I'll finish up. And father said he'd be home pretty soon. He'll be hungry. Don't wait supper for me."

He hoed and chopped, working hard and fast in an effort to clear his mind of the anger and despair of losing Annie. It wasn't until nine o'clock that he gave up and went inside.

His mother had kept a plate of food warm for him. "You work too hard," she said. "Getting skinny."

He flexed his aching muscles. "But look how strong!"

Before going upstairs to his room, he stopped at his father's office to check the order of service for Sunday.

"Is your choir well-prepared?" his father asked as Donald entered the room.

"I think so. We've started working on Easter things, too." He scanned the list of congregational hymns his father had chosen to support the sermon. All familiar. That was good. Grace would have no problems—she knew most of the songs in the book—and the people would sing heartily.

"Goodnight," he said with a yawn. After all that physical work, he shouldn't have any trouble sleeping.

Upstairs, his grandfather was snoring. Donald prepared for bed, then reached for his Bible. By now, after his usual reading, he'd developed a habit of reading a few psalms every evening—some for encouragement, some for their expressions of sheer joy. All this time, the thirty-seventh psalm had been his favorite: "Fret not thyself . . . Trust in the LORD, and do good; so shalt thou dwell in the land. . . . Delight thyself also in the LORD; and he shall give thee the desires of thine heart." Now he wondered, *Can I still hang on to that promise? Is there a way out?*

He read on. "Trust also in him; and he shall bring it to pass."

A thrill shot through him. He slid to his knees beside his bed. "Oh, Lord, I do trust in you. And I ask you to show me how I can marry my beloved Annie." It still seemed impossible, with all the restrictions and roadblocks. "I don't know how you'll work it, Lord, but I'm counting on you."

He got into bed and lay thinking, his arms supporting his head. Tomorrow he would be with Annie, would hold her, smooth back her soft hair, kiss her sweet lips. . . .

It took a long time to fall asleep.

The next morning Donald helped his grandfather put on his best clothes. He had to punch another hole in the old man's belt to cinch up the waist of his brown trousers.

His choir sang well, although Sho and the other basses missed one of their cues, and the voice of one soprano cracked on a high note. When he sat down on the platform with them, he glanced at his grandfather, who nodded solemnly to him. It felt good to have his approval. And good to see him with his old friends—the few that were still living.

His father's message was helpful and encouraging, and after the service several people went forward for rededication.

Donald thanked his choir, put away the sheet music, then stopped to chat with several people. When he finally walked out the front door, he saw his mother with a group of parishioners. They were clustered around the steps, murmuring, gasping, wringing their hands—

Then he saw they were huddled around someone who was lying across the steps—someone wearing brown trousers.

"Jiichan." He rushed forward. "What happened?"

People all talked at once.

"He fell—"

"Hit his head on the step—"

"I tried to catch him—"

"He's not moving!"

His grandfather's eyes were shut, his arms hung limp. A gash in his forehead stained his shirt with blood. Someone leaned over and lay a folded handkerchief over the cut.

Donald pushed people aside to feel the pulse in the old man's throat. It was weak and uneven. "Somebody tell my father," he shouted.

One of the old man's legs lay at an awkward angle, and Donald felt carefully for broken bones. He hoped his grandfather's hips were all right—those took a long time to heal.

His mother crouched beside him, her face pale. "What we do now?"

Donald looked around, thinking. The clinic in Rosemond was closed on Sundays, and the nearest hospital was in Fresno. He couldn't leave his grandfather sprawled across the steps, but how could he move him without risk of more injury?

If only he could call an ambulance. But they'd never come all the way from Fresno. Not for a Jap. Besides, how would he pay them?

His father ran from the side door of the church. He nearly tripped over the ladders that were still lying where they'd been left Saturday.

The ladders! Donald pointed to them and Sho brought one to him. Others rushed to scrounge church tablecloths, a blanket from a car, a shawl. Donald folded them all, attached them with donated belts, and made the makeshift litter as soft and smooth as possible. But now, how would he get his grandfather to a hospital?

When a panel truck drove by, Tom waved down the driver. After some shouting and explanation, the driver, a florist, agreed to drive the injured man to the hospital. He maneuvered the truck onto the lawn, close to the steps, then opened the back doors and jumped inside to clear a space.

With the help of his friends and his father, Donald slowly, carefully, lifted his grandfather onto the ladder and eased it into the truck. He then helped his mother to a place by the litter, turned to his father and said, "Follow us in the car, okay?"

His father nodded. "Where to?"

"Fresno County Hospital. Cedar and Ventura."

Donald climbed into the back of the van, pulling the doors shut as the truck eased onto the road. Still it lurched and bumped, and Donald gritted his teeth, hoping the jostling wouldn't worsen his grandfather's condition. The strong scent of flowers permeated the enclosed compartment, an uncomfortable reminder of funerals.

Sitting on the floor beside him, his mother rocked back and forth, weeping silently into her hands. "I *told* him wait," she said over and over. "He want to go."

"Shh," Donald told her. "He'll be okay." Silently, he prayed this was true.

It was all his fault. He was the one who had urged his grandfather to come to church. He wanted to show off the choir, his directing. He kneaded his fists into his forehead.

His mother wiped her face and looked up at him. "Your father. He come?"

Donald nodded and felt again for a pulse. It was still weak, but steadier. Relaxing a little, he realized that a few minutes ago, for the first time in his life, he had given orders to his father—and his father obeyed. He actually felt like a doctor, as though he knew what he was doing.

Now if only the hospital would be willing to help his grandfather. Ease the pain, set any broken bones, and take the necessary tests. He'd talk to the doctors there, and tell them—

Suddenly he realized. There was no way he'd see Annie at two o'clock.

Chapter Twenty

WHAT COULD BE A MORE COMMON BOND? Annie and Malinda—both in love, both engaged. And nobody else's knowing made their friendship extra special.

At church that morning, they'd sat together. Malinda told her not to worry about that marriage law. Somehow, it would work out. They'd prayed about it, hadn't they? But how could Malinda be so sure? How could Annie be sure?

Now at noon, Annie's mind was in a daze as she set plates on the kitchen table for her mother and herself. Keeping the bad news bottled up had just made her feel worse, but now that she'd shared her secret with her friend, she felt some relief.

Could Donald be mistaken about the law? Since the beginning of the war, all kinds of crazy rumors had floated around, especially about the Japanese. They'd gone through such terrible times they probably took it for granted everyone was against them.

Donald had said he'd be over at two—no matter what. A thrill went through her at the thought of seeing him again.

She put down two water glasses, two knives, and two spoons. The way she would if—*when*—she and Donald were married. In the center of the table would be a bud vase holding a red rose from their garden. She'd dish out his favorite meal, and they would clasp hands for the blessing. . . .

But Donald said the information had came from a lawyer. A lawyer would know, wouldn't he? And Donald, always honorable, always reliable, wouldn't have mentioned it if it wasn't true.

Annie's hopefulness sank back into despair. By September he'd be gone, and she'd never again see him smile, hear him speak, never again listen to his rich baritone voice, feel his gentle touch, or thrill to his kiss. The pain was an arrow through her heart.

"*Na, Anchen.*" Her mother tied on a flowered apron as she came into the kitchen. "Why are you standing there so *be'duzzled* with the gravy bowl in your hands? Where is your mind?"

Annie looked at the dish in surprise. She didn't even remember taking it out of the cupboard. Quickly she set it on the counter and went to the refrigerator for the *pluma mos.*

Her mother still stared at her, but Annie pretended not to notice.

"Are you seeing your Japanese friend today?" asked her mother, stressing the word *friend.*

Annie nodded. "At two." Glancing at the clock, she noticed it was after one. The sermons had been long that morning. "Are the *verenikya* ready?" she asked.

Her mother adjusted the burner under the iron skillet. "Almost." She waited a few minutes, then turned them. "You can slice some cucumbers and pour a little vinegar over them."

Annie peeled the cucumbers, her mind still churning. She would take some leftover *verenikya* for Donald to try. She loved the large dough pockets full of cottage cheese, especially when boiled ahead of time and then fried and covered with ham gravy.

It would give them something to talk about. But what else could they talk about—she and Donald—now that their relationship had nowhere to go? Would they spend the whole afternoon together, or was this going to be a "good-bye-and-it's-been-nice-knowing-you" short afternoon?

No, that wasn't like Donald. He loved her as much as she loved him. Didn't he?

Somehow she got through the meal, not even aware that the *verenikya* tasted flat until her mother made a face. "Forgot to salt the dough. I'm getting as absentminded as you, *kindt.*"

Annie wished her mother wouldn't keep calling her that. Granted, she *was* her mother's child, but she'd soon be twenty-three—a grown woman. Older than most unmarried girls. Old enough to make her own decisions and run her own life.

She took the dishes to the sink and washed, then dried them. Some people she knew left them in the drainer to air-dry, leaving an embroidered tea towel over them. They said it saved time and was more sanitary. Her mother, though, had always insisted on a tidy counter. "You never know when company might drop in. Even the preacher." Everything depended upon what other people might think.

And now, Annie thought, *I've sure given people something to think about.* If they only knew the whole story! Annie Penner and her Japanese boyfriend, wanting an illegal marriage.

She gave the counter a furious wipe-off, then set the dish rack under the sink, hung the folded rag over the faucet, the tea towel over the oven handle. Everything was clean and tidy, the way her mother liked it. She'd have no reason to complain.

Should she wrap up some of the *verenikya* for Donald? They *had* been a little flat, so maybe she should wait until the next batch. She'd hate to feed him something that was less than perfect.

It was a quarter to two, and Annie went to her bedroom to change clothes and comb her hair. She quickly dabbed on a few dots of lilac cologne and smoothed her hands with Jergens lotion. It wouldn't do for them to be rough when Donald held them.

At the stroke of two, Annie went into the living room and sat down in the easy chair closest to the front door. Picking up a book from the nearby table, not even looking at it, she turned the pages.

After a few minutes, she realized what she was staring at. It was her mother's copy of *Martyrs Mirror,* a history of the Anabaptists in Switzerland and Holland. They had been persecuted and tortured because they broke away from the state religion. Annie had heard sermons about them, those dedicated people who followed Menno Simon's example and accepted a believer's baptism. Because of that they'd been the first ones to be called Mennonites. The book contained illustrations of the awful deaths suffered by the martyrs—people being drowned, burned at the stake, and executed in other ways.

She shuddered. What brutal persecution those people had accepted rather than give up their faith. Clapping the book shut, she put it back on the table, not realizing her mother had been watching from the doorway.

"*Ya*, you see what your forefathers went through in order to cling to their faith. And just like that"—her mother snapped her fingers to emphasize her point—"you want to throw your heritage away. Just for a . . . a . . . Jap!" She stared at Annie defiantly. "I know, I know. You don't like the word, but it comes down to that. That's what other people call them . . . and that's what they'll call you—a Jap lover."

Annie glanced out the window. What if Donald was at the door and heard her mother's outburst? But he wasn't, and she drew herself up as tall as possible and looked her mother in the eye. "The time will come when you'll be judged for your hatred of God's people. Mennonites aren't the only Christians. Donald was saved when he was sixteen, old enough to understand what he was doing."

Emboldened, she continued. "How many in our church got baptized just because they were twelve years old and their friends were going through it? How many glibly made promises not to go to shows or drink or smoke—not even to cut their hair—and just as easily broke those promises? Do you see a lot of girls with real long hair in our congregation? Don't you wonder how they get around that promise?"

Annie touched her own hair. She was glad she'd been baptized before moving here, in a church where the promises required had more to do with following Christ than a list of taboos.

"*Kindt*, what are you saying?"

"Just that it's more important to follow the Lord's teaching than a whole lot of rules that aren't even mentioned in the Bible." Annie looked out the window again. Why wasn't Donald here? He'd *promised.*

"Well, the Bible says to honor your father and mother. I don't see that in your life. You've torn the whole family apart, all the relatives—" Her mother fumbled for the handkerchief in her apron pocket, wiped her eyes, then blew her nose loudly and left the room.

The relatives. Annie regretted that part. She especially missed her grandparents, and wished she could sit down with them and help them understand. Wished they could meet Donald and see what a wonderful person he was. She tasted salt and realized tears had rolled down her own cheeks, too. Now her face would be puffy, her nose red when Donald came. *If* he came!

He'd never been late before. Maybe he changed his mind. Maybe he decided there was no use to keep on seeing her.

She went into the bathroom to freshen up, and as she looked in the mirror she saw the hopelessness in her eyes. That brought more tears, and she turned on the faucet in the sink to cover her sobs.

When her watch ticked past two-thirty, Annie went into her bedroom. She felt exhausted, dry, and empty and threw herself onto the bed, pulling her knees to her chin, not caring if her clothes got crushed.

At the hospital, Donald had spent the last hour sitting beside his mother in the emergency room. He talked softly to her, trying to shore up her spirits. His father paced up and down the hall, sometimes stopping to stare out the window, hands linked behind his back.

They'd been lucky in having his grandfather accepted as a patient. When they arrived at the hospital, the florist ran into the building first, coming back with two orderlies and a stretcher. By the time the men realized it was a Japanese man they were carrying, the florist had left, refusing any pay from Donald for his help. The orderlies had no place to take the stretcher but inside.

The receptionist had been curt, and for a while Donald wondered if she'd tell the orderlies to take his grandfather out and leave him to die on the sidewalk. Then an older doctor walked past and saw what was going on. "Put him in room four," he said sternly. "I'll take a look at him myself."

He turned to Donald's father. "I'm Dr. Robbins. This man will get the best care we can provide." He glanced back at the receptionist, but she'd turned away and picked up the phone.

Donald had been hoping to use that phone to call Annie, but after the way the woman had acted, he knew there was no use asking.

After an examination and X rays, the doctor cleaned the old man's head wound and splinted a finger. He sent his patient upstairs with a nurse to put him into a room. "I want to keep a close eye on him," he explained to Donald and his parents. "I need to make sure there's no swelling or pressure on the brain."

As soon as *Jiichan* was settled into a bed, Donald and his parents were allowed into the room. Although they spoke to him, rubbed his hands, and stroked his cheeks, there still was no response. The nurse finally sent them into the waiting room.

Donald saw a phone there, but several people sat close by, talking idly. What he had to say was private. He and his parents took seats the farthest away from the jabbering visitors. To keep his hands occupied, Donald picked up a *Saturday Evening Post* and leafed through it, barely noticing the contents. His father sat wordlessly, leaning forward with folded hands between his knees, while his mother stared at the wall.

Donald knew they were praying silently, hopefully—wondering, as he did, what would happen now? Was this the end for *Jiichan?*

The clock on the wall seemed to stand still, but after an hour, the doctor came into the waiting room. Donald and his parents rushed forward to meet him. At first the doctor directed his comments to Donald's father, glancing only occasionally at Donald and his mother.

"Your father has had a concussion," he explained. "And there's some swelling in the brain, but I've ordered intravenous medication to bring it down. If that works, there should be some real improvement soon. But for now, you'll just need to be patient and let him rest."

There was hope! "Is the edema unilateral?" Donald asked.

"Yes. Just at the site of trauma."

"What about his white cell count?"

"Near normal." The man's eyes widened. "Are you a doctor?"

"Not yet." Donald told him about his acceptance into medical school.

The man shook Donald's hand. "Congratulations! When you go into practice, give me a call. Fresno needs good Japanese doctors." From then on, he directed most of his comments and instructions to Donald. When asked about broken bones, the doctor said that the old man had been very lucky in that respect, with only bruises on one leg and hip.

Finally the doctor looked at his watch. "I need to make rounds. Why don't you take your parents out for something to eat? You'd better keep up your strength." He nodded at the others, then left.

Donald stared after him, hardly daring to breathe. Had he heard correctly? Had the doctor really meant what he said, or was he just being polite? Would people around here actually accept a Japanese doctor? If this was true, it was the best encouragement he'd had in a long time. Maybe there was hope for him after all.

As he looked out the window, his gaze followed a row of tall palm trees lining the street. In the distance a plum orchard gleamed in full white bloom. Beyond, the foothills rose to the mountains, their snowcapped peaks sharp in the sweet, clear air.

California. The San Joaquin Valley. After the dust of Gila River, the muck of Camp Shelby, the rocky hills in Italy, and the muddy foxholes in the Philippines, Donald was sure the best place on earth was right here. And if there was a chance to go into practice here, that was what he wanted most to do.

He looked at the clock again. Nearly four. As soon as possible, he had to find a phone booth, apologize to Annie, and tell her what the doctor had said.

He heard a slight cough and noticed his father standing next to him.

"The doctor was right. We must have food. There may be a long wait until your grandfather shows any improvement. Come, wife."

Donald's mother shook her head. "You two go. I stay."

His father looked at her pointedly, tapping the car key against an outstretched finger. But her lips were tight, her eyes stubborn. Finally he said, "No use arguing. We'll bring something back for her."

Donald nodded. Maybe there'd be a phone booth at the restaurant.

They found a Chinese restaurant a block away, but it had no public phone. When he and his father finished eating, Donald bought a carton of steamed rice with vegetables and a container of hot tea for his mother. But when he gave her the bag in the waiting room, she thanked him and set it aside.

By now, the waiting room was crowded, mostly with Caucasians. Donald realized she was embarrassed to eat in front of them, so he took her by the arm. "Come, we'll go to the car. Father can stay here. If there's any change, he'll come get us."

She looked around and smiled apologetically, her face flushing. But the other people were too busy in their own conversations to notice. Donald urged her a little more firmly and his mother went with him.

After finding their car in the parking lot and helping her in, Donald handed his mother the bag of cartons, then looked around. In the opposite direction from the restaurant, at the end of the block, was a service station. He spotted a phone booth outside near the sidewalk.

"Will you be all right if I go make a call?" he asked his mother, pointing toward the station.

She looked around. Children played in a yard across the street, and families sat on lawn chairs next door. "Go," she said.

He approached the phone booth, digging in his pocket for change, but he found only three pennies. Frustrated, he leaned his forehead against the metal phone box and pounded its top with his fist.

Clink . . . clink . . . clink.

Donald drew back. Unbelieving, he snaked his finger into the coin return. A quarter, a dime, and a nickel. Whoever had used it last forgot their change.

He held the precious coins in his hand. Would it be stealing to use them? But there was no way to know who left them. He could walk around asking, "Who lost these?" and a hundred people would claim them. They had to be a gift from God. Manna from heaven.

He gave the operator Annie's home number and listened to the rings. Two longs and three shorts. Once, twice—then he heard a click. "Annie?" His voice cracked and he cleared his throat.

There was no answer, just another click, and the operator kept ringing. Someone else on the party line must have picked up, then hung up.

"No one answers," said the operator.

"Please keep trying," Donald urged.

He had almost given up when he heard Annie's voice, breathless and shaky. "Hello?"

Donald swallowed hard. "Oh, sweetheart."

"Donald? Is that you?"

"It's me. Are you all right? Were you worried?"

"I was . . . a little anxious." Her voice broke then. "Oh, Donald. I must have cried myself to sleep."

His heart ached from causing her pain. "Sweet Annie. I'm so sorry." He told her of his grandfather's fall and the trip to the hospital in the borrowed truck, about his search for a phone that wasn't surrounded by people. "I don't know when I'll be back. But I want you to know that I love you. More than anything in the world, I love you."

He knew his time was nearly up, and quickly added, "I'll tell you more later. But I think God is working things out for us. Somehow, our problems will work out."

Chapter Twenty-One

ANNIE HUNG UP THE RECEIVER and noticed her hands were shaking. Limp with relief, she sank into a kitchen chair, going over the conversation in her mind. Had Donald really said there was hope for them? Did he mean they might be able to get married?

One thing she knew for sure. He still loved her.

She heard a footstep and saw her mother come into the kitchen. "Did I hear the phone?" Her hair had straggled loose from its *schups,* making Annie think she must have been asleep, too.

Annie nodded. "Donald." She told her mother what had happened. "I hope his grandfather will be all right. He's such a nice man. You saw him, didn't you, when we went there for strawberries?"

Her mother's expression was hard to read. Then Annie realized she'd only seen the old man from a distance, and he'd been wearing dirty old clothes and a wide-brimmed straw hat, stooping over the plants. But someday she'd get to know him, too.

"They'll be ripe again in a couple of months," Annie reminded her. "I'll help you make jam."

Her mother shrugged. "After what happened, the Nakamuras' plants probably won't bear this year. We might have to buy somewhere else."

"Donald says they're doing fine, thanks to all the help from the community. And he's mentioned several times how much he appreciated your bringing food that day."

Not waiting for a response, Annie went into the living room and took several books and sheets of music out of the piano bench. She chose "His Eye Is on the Sparrow" first. After playing the introduction, she sang the first line of the refrain from a full heart. "I sing because I'm happy." When she got to the last line, her voice was a near-whisper. "And I know he watches me."

Pouring her soul into the music, she modulated into one song after another, improvising, adding runs and cadenzas, trills and arpeggios. Her fingers seemed filled with a spiritual energy all their own as she created arrangements and variations—some dramatic, some lilting, some peaceful and soothing.

More than an hour passed, and still Annie played on. She jumped when she felt a hand on her shoulder.

"*Na, kindt.* It's six-thirty already. You better come eat something. *Faspa's* on the table." Her mother went to the windows, reached behind the sheer panels, and pulled down the shades. "You're coming to church this evening, aren't you?"

Annie dropped her hands to her lap and stared at her mother. She'd never been given a choice before. Should she stay home in case Donald called again? Surely he wouldn't leave the hospital until visiting hours were over, probably nine. She'd be home soon after that.

She nodded and smiled. "Sure. I'll go with you. Are we having *tvehbock* and *eiyah* pie for *faspa?*" She loved her mother's egg custard pie; it was peacefully smooth, just right for her mood today.

A nurse came into the hospital waiting room. "Nakamura?"

Donald stood up. "Yes?"

She looked at Donald's parents, then back at him. "Your grandfather is beginning to stir, and he opened his eyes once, for just a moment. You may want to be with him in case he wakes."

"Thank you." Donald helped his mother to her feet, and they followed his father to the room.

Standing by his grandfather's bedside, Donald lifted the thin wrist and felt for the pulse. It was steady, so he focused his attention on the man's breathing. That was slow, and he checked the carotids. Reassured, Donald lifted one eyelid, then the other. The pupils were large but not fixed. He stroked his grandfather's cheek. "Can you hear me, *Jiichan?*" He took the old man's hand in his own. "If you can hear me, squeeze my hand."

Nothing happened. Donald glanced up at his parents, who were standing on the other side of the bed, watching. After several long minutes, he felt a twitch in his grandfather's fingers.

"Good!" he exclaimed. "Can you do that again?" This time the movement came a little sooner, a bit stronger.

Donald nodded. "I think he's coming out of it."

The nurse bustled in and took out her stethoscope and blood pressure cuff. When she was finished, she smiled. "It's stable. He seems to be doing just fine." She turned to Donald's parents. "Dr. Robbins is quite impressed with your son. Thinks he'll do well in medical school."

His father nodded. "Thank you. He's always hoped to become a doctor. Now it looks as though his dream will come true."

Donald's heart swelled with joy. Trying to hide his pleasure at the compliments, he shrugged. "I'll do my best." His father's comments indicated that he'd come closer than ever before to accepting Donald's goals. And to think the doctor had even mentioned him to the nurse!

He straightened his shoulders, then heard a sound from the bed. "*Jiichan?*"

His grandfather mumbled something in Japanese—it sounded as though he was calling for his wife—and then his eyelids fluttered.

Donald picked up the old man's hand again, and this time felt a weak but definite squeeze. "Come on, *Jiichan.* The strawberries are setting. We need you to get better and come help us in the field."

His grandfather's eyes opened. He blinked a few times, then looked at his family, who stood around the bed. Then he frowned down at his covers, and at the IV stuck in the back of his hand.

Donald's father said, "Praise the Lord," as his eyes glistened with tears.

"What this?" *Jiichan* spoke in Japanese, his voice hoarse. "Why you here?"

"You fell," Donald told him. "At the church steps. Remember that?"

"Fell?" He wrinkled his forehead, then winced.

Donald could tell he was in pain. He looked for the nurse, but she'd left the room. He reached for the buzzer, then dropped it as he saw her come back in.

"How are you feeling?" she asked his grandfather. When the old man slowly reached his free hand up to his forehead, she told him, "Yes, your head hurts. Just lie flat. I called the doctor, and he'll be here soon. He'll prescribe something for the pain, and then you'll want to sleep. That'll help get your strength back."

She rolled up the window blinds. "It's been a beautiful day. Look out the window. Can you see the sunset glow against the mountains?"

His grandfather blinked. "*Hai,*" he said weakly.

"He said yes," Donald interpreted. He wondered if the fall made the old man forget how to speak English. Then he realized that his grandfather had understood the nurse, that it was only his weakened condition that caused him to lapse into the more familiar tongue.

While growing up, Donald had always spoken to him in English, encouraging him to improve his language. But now, as they waited for the doctor, Donald and his parents chatted with him in Japanese. Donald was glad that as a kid he'd attended the Saturday Japanese school and could still speak the old mother tongue. Whatever the language, the more his grandfather talked, the better the doctor could gauge the damage to his brain.

Within an hour, Dr. Robbins came in. He examined the bandages, checked his patient's reflexes, eyes, and vital signs, then talked with him. Donald translated when necessary.

He told Donald, "He seems to be responding well. Tomorrow I'll take further tests, and we'll have a better idea of his condition. The nurse will give him a shot, and he'll sleep naturally tonight. By tomorrow evening, you'll be surprised how much better he'll be. Why don't you all go home and get some rest?"

Donald glanced at his parents. Now that the crisis was over, the worry they'd tried to hide came out in tired lines in their faces. He knew they'd be smart to follow the doctor's suggestion. But his mother said, "I stay. You come back tomorrow. Maybe I go home then." She fluttered her hand at Donald and his father. "Go."

Donald shook his head. "If anyone stays, it'll be me." He took his grandfather's hand and asked in Japanese, "Would you feel better if I stayed?"

His grandfather looked down and chewed his lip. Finally he nodded. "*Hai.*" He turned his face away, and Donald could see his lips were trembling.

The doctor shook hands with Donald and his father, and nodded to his mother. "I'll be back on rounds about midnight. Meanwhile, if you need anything, the nurses' station is to your left down the hall." He patted his patient's shoulder and left the room.

Then Donald realized there was something he needed to do. He told his father, "Say your good-byes to *Jiichan*; I'll be right back."

He hurried down the hall after the doctor. "Dr. Robbins, I didn't want to say this in front of my parents, but I should mention something about my grandfather."

The doctor turned. "Yes?"

"Even before his fall, I'd been noticing something. A tremor in his right hand."

Dr. Robbins raised his eyebrows. "Hmm. I'll make a note of that. It might not mean anything, but it's worth taking into consideration. Thank you."

That night, after his grandfather had gone to sleep, Donald tried to get comfortable in the bedside chair. He was drained, tired enough to sleep in any position. He'd had enough experience doing so during the war—burrowed in muddy foxholes, taking turns sleeping and watching for the enemy. But although his body was at ease, his mind stayed at attention.

What a relief that his grandfather was better! If only that shaking could be controlled. He hoped he was wrong. Palsy was incurable, a miserable condition that would only get worse. Dr. Robbins would know. Tonight there'd be a chance to talk more with him.

Just thinking about the doctor filled Donald with awe. Dr. Robbins had treated them with respect, as though they were no different from other people. In spite of the doctor's busy schedule, he took an interest in Donald's future plans, speaking as though Donald's ambitions were realistic and not just wishful thinking.

Also—and maybe because of that—even his father had shown a change of attitude. He'd acted proud that his son hoped to become a doctor.

Donald realized his father's change had started earlier. He'd accepted his suggestions on how to deal with the accident, followed his directions. Maybe he would also come to accept Annie.

Donald closed his eyes, imagining the sweet curve of her lips, the smile in her eyes. He could almost feel of the soft ringlets of her beautiful strawberry-blonde hair curling around his fingers.

Tomorrow he'd ask questions. Find out if there was a place—any place, even if they had to fly to the moon—where they could legally marry.

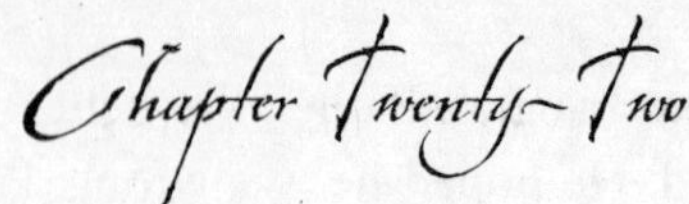

Chapter Twenty-Two

The screech of metal rings and the curtains *whooshing* open woke Donald. A bit disoriented, he struggled to his feet and realized he'd fallen asleep in the hospital chair.

His grandfather snored softly, and his breathing sounded even. The doctor was making midnight rounds and stood at the foot of the bed, studying the chart. He felt for a pulse, checked the IV, then lifted the covers and felt the old man's feet. Looking at Donald, he nodded. "Seems to be doing well."

Pulling up another chair, the doctor gestured for Donald to sit back down. "You mentioned a tremor in his hand. Just the one hand, or both?"

"I noticed it mostly in his right; I can't be sure about the other."

"Is this in motion or while resting?"

Donald thought a bit. What had his grandfather been doing that first time? "He was reaching for something."

"Does he drink much caffeine? What about alcohol?"

"Tea. Fairly weak. He used to take a little *sake.* But that was before the . . . war. Not lately."

"What about walking? Does he have any trouble?"

Donald remembered helping his grandfather out to the strawberry field. "He was a little unsteady."

"Did he take small, shuffling steps?"

"No. More like . . . staggering. As though he were drunk, but I know he wasn't."

"He lives with you?"

"Yes, with my parents and me."

"So you are able to watch him on a regular basis?"

Donald nodded. "Now that I've been discharged from the army. When I came home—"

The doctor raised his eyebrows. "You were in the 442nd regiment?"

"Three years. In the medics. Italy, France, then the Philippines."

"And before that, an internment camp?"

"Gila River. Worked in the hospital there."

The doctor whistled softly. "Young man, you are commendable. I wish you well in your pursuit of medicine. Here, I'll leave my card with you. If you have any problems or need a recommendation, use my name."

Donald swallowed hard. He hadn't been mistaken about the doctor's sincerity. "Thank you, sir. You're very kind."

The doctor shrugged. "It's the least I can do." He stood up. "Thank you for the information on your grandfather. I'll keep an eye on him." When Donald rose, too, the doctor shook his hand, pulled the curtain shut, and left.

Donald's heart thumped rapidly. What if the doctor knew about Annie? Would he still be sympathetic, or would his attitude change?

He looked down at the doctor's card and saw his own hands shaking. He wondered again about his grandfather's tremor. Was he making too much of it? Maybe, like his, it had just been excitement.

By the time Donald's parents came back in the morning, Donald had given his grandfather a bath—the nurse had been delighted when he offered—combed his sparse hair, and helped him manage his breakfast.

Donald had watched for the tremor, and saw it both while his grandfather rested and when he reached for the glass of orange juice. And it was in both hands. But maybe that was good—a sign that it wasn't palsy after all. Since the doctor had questioned him, he remembered reading that palsy was most noticeable during rest and, usually, in only one hand.

Donald's mother didn't come empty handed. Along with a vase of purple and yellow iris, she brought Donald some toast, two hard-boiled eggs, and a thermos of tea. "Eat," she told him. "Make more muscle."

He hadn't felt hungry before, but the pungent aroma of the tea made him realize that he was starved. He dug in with relish.

After the night's rest, Donald's grandfather was more alert, in good spirits, and speaking in English again. He wanted to know all the details of his fall, who'd seen it, and how he'd gotten to the hospital. "A ladder? You carry me on *ladder?*" He jabbed Donald with his free hand. "I don't fall through?"

"No, we padded it good. Shoved you right into the panel truck."

His grandfather stared at him. "Who got panel?"

Donald couldn't remember the name of the florist. He didn't even know if the man's shop was in Rosemond, or in a neighboring town, or whether the ladder had been returned to the church.

Everything happened so fast. When he got home he'd ask Tom, see if he could locate the shop and thank the man properly. When he told his grandfather about the fast talking it took to persuade the driver, the old man laughed. But then he clutched his side and groaned.

"Does it hurt badly?" Donald gently ran his hand over his grandfather's taped rib cage. "You probably cracked some of them. It'll take them awhile to heal. I'll ask the doctor to give you something for the pain." He helped his grandfather sip some water through a straw and plumped the pillow for him. "You probably should rest a little now."

His father had brought the newspaper, and Donald decided he'd read to his grandfather after the old man had rested.

As soon as he felt up to it, they would bring his *goban* to the hospital. That game board had traveled to Gila River and back with them. Besides the Japanese Bible, which had been confiscated, it had been the only thing his grandfather treasured. Almost every day in camp, the older men had spent hours over the board and stones, playing the game of *goh. Jiichan* had earned a reputation throughout the camp as someone hard to beat. But Donald hadn't seen the board since he'd been home. He hoped he could find it in his grandfather's room.

The next time the doctor stopped by, he brought along the X-rays. Donald had been right; three of the ribs were cracked. He studied the films with the doctor, taking note of all the places the doctor pointed out. His grandfather's right shoulder had been dislocated but was now popped back into place. And a bone in his elbow had been chipped. But Donald was thankful, too, when the doctor reported that the swelling on the brain seemed to have lessened.

"I'd like to keep him here a few more days . . . for observation. Before he leaves, I want to get him walking and check his reflexes. There's no need for all of you to stay. He's doing just fine."

After talking it over, Donald's father insisted on staying. Donald and his mother got ready to leave, promising to return in the early evening.

On the way to the parking lot, he asked her, "Shouldn't we let Florence know?" Although phone calls were expensive, surely this was a great enough emergency.

"You father send telegram. Say no worry, letter follow. You write?"

"Sure. I owe her a letter anyway." Earlier, he'd written her about his acceptance to medical school, but maybe it was time to tell her how close he and Annie had become. If she didn't suspect already.

He sang while driving, smiling to himself. "Count your many blessings—"

"You happy?" His mother poked him in the ribs. "Act like doctor, look at pictures, know everything. Someday you want to cut. But not cut me. Uh, uh."

Donald winked at her. "I don't know what field I'll go into. Probably not surgery." He thought about his grandfather's shaking hands. It would be good to know what caused it. "Maybe neurology. See what makes people tick. If I last that long in medical school."

"You last. You be good doctor. I know in heart." His mother looked down at her hands, rough and callused from fieldwork and housework.

Donald's heart sank. Here he was eager to go away to school, to better himself. But that meant his mother would be left to tend the strawberries. His father could help a little, but his ministry would always come first. Even if his grandfather didn't have palsy, he'd never be able to work like when he was younger—before the war, before the prison camp.

When they got home, the first thing Donald did was head for the telephone. As he waited for Annie to answer, he felt such a craving for her that he wanted to hang up, jump into the car, and go on to the furniture store. But his duty to his mother held him back. He impatiently drummed his fingers against the wall.

"McGinnis Furniture."

Her voice sent a shiver through him and for a moment he couldn't speak.

"Hello?" This time her voice was sharper.

"Sweet Annie. It seems like years since I've seen you. I'd like to come riding on a white horse and swoop you up with me. Ride away into the mountains and live on mushrooms and wild honey."

"Donald?" She was laughing now. "Did the doctor make a mistake and give *you* a pain pill instead of your grandfather?"

"I'm just so happy to hear your voice. "

"How is he . . . your grandfather?"

Donald told her about his injuries, but added that his grandfather had been cheerful this morning, eaten a good breakfast, and that Dr. Robbins was pleased with his progress. "And that's not all. I told the doctor about my plans for medical school. You know what he said?" He told her of the encouragement, the offer of reference. The doctor's accepting attitude. "Just as though I were a Caucasian."

Annie's voice softened. "See? I'm not the only one who thinks you're wonderful. You wait. When you set up your practice, people will wait in line at your office door, just like we line up for nylons at the stores."

Donald promised her he'd call again and come to see her as soon as he could get away. After saying good-bye, he immediately changed into work clothes. His mother was already out in the field.

Donald shook his head, marveling how well the crop was doing after the beating the field had taken. He and his mother worked late into the afternoon, weeding, guiding the runners back into line, and tamping up the rows.

By the time they cleaned up and ate a quick supper, it was time to return to the hospital and take food to his father. His mother had found the *goban* in his grandfather's closet. Although Donald knew playing a game might be too strenuous, he thought his grandfather might be cheered by the sight of it—and by the memories of all his victories.

And maybe the doctor would be there. It would be exciting to talk to him again.

Chapter Twenty-Three

TUESDAY MORNING WAS PERFECT FOR the strawberries. The sky shone bright and sunny, with fair weather predicted for the next few days. Donald looked over the field and breathed a prayer of thanks for all the beautiful green plants, all the reaching suckers that would take root and begin new life.

He thanked God, too, for the encouragement from the community and their help in restoring the field, for his acceptance into medical school, for his grandfather's recovery. That fall could have been so much more serious, even fatal.

Donald added thanks for Annie and their love for each other. "And oh, Lord, please help us find a way to get married." God was good. He was opening so many doors; surely he wouldn't close the door on their happiness.

When Donald and his parents went to the hospital that evening, he watched his grandfather closely. The old man's color was good and he seemed to enjoy the visit, although he still complained of a headache if he sat up. Donald read him news from the *Rosemond Recorder*—the strawberry crop was estimated to be 35 to 45 percent higher than the year before, and plans were in the works to dam Kings River up by Trimmer. He told him the latest Red Skelton radio jokes, using the voice of Clem Kadiddlehopper. It was good to hear *Jiichan* laugh without as much pain.

The next evening, with prayer meeting at church preceded by

committee meetings, Donald's parents were unable to go with him to visit his grandfather. Before leaving for the hospital, he phoned Annie, hoping she would be at home, hoping she'd be the one to answer.

Annie did answer, and she sounded so happy to hear his voice. He knew he had to see her soon.

"I have to come into town tomorrow about noon," he told her. "It looks like we're . . . uh . . . nearly out of nails. For strawberry boxes . . . you know." He could tell by her soft laugh, she knew it was only an excuse. "May I see you then? Have lunch with you?"

"I'll be waiting," she promised. "I'll fix something tonight and bring it to work."

After they said good-bye, Donald held the receiver against his cheek, picturing her face, her smile, her lips. But he knew his grandfather would be waiting and, reluctantly, he hung up the phone and went out to the car.

Arriving at the hospital, Donald was surprised to see his grandfather sitting up with the *goban* on his tray, ready to challenge him to several games of *goh*.

Donald didn't take any handicap, thinking the old man wouldn't yet be up to his usual level of skill. How wrong he was. Even though he led with black, in every game his grandfather captured more of his stones and conquered more territory. And his leathery old hands had been no shakier than before. Maybe even a little less.

"Tomorrow I teach you tricks," said *Jiichan*. "You get smart."

"You'd better watch out. I might get so good I'll beat you yet." Donald grinned. "Like grandfather, like grandson, you know."

"*Jiichan* not worry. He still have more tricks." The old man tapped his forehead and nodded. "You see." He slid the black and white stones off the board and into their wooden storage bowl. "Strawberries be okay?"

"They're happy . . . but I think they miss you!" Donald settled his grandfather back on his pillow. "Keeping me busy. They sure like this sunshine."

He knew the days must be long for the old man. Donald wished someone could be with his grandfather during the afternoon, for the two hours when visiting was allowed. But they were so far behind with the field work, and it took so much time to get to the hospital and back, once a day was the most they could manage. And Donald knew how much *Jiichan* loved his farm—he'd want it to be well-kept.

On Thursday morning, Donald's mother caught up with him in the field. "You write Florence?"

"Sure, mom. It's in the mailbox. If the postal truck driver doesn't see the red flag, he's too blind to be driving." Besides telling Florence about their grandfather's fall, he spent at least two pages confiding his and Annie's hopes and plans. He also mentioned his worries about leaving the family to tend the strawberry fields. She already knew about his acceptance to medical school, so he just mentioned his excitement to be digging again into solid studies.

His mother nodded. "Mailman stop. Come harvest, he want free berries."

Donald worked until nearly noon, then hurried to the outside bathhouse to clean up and change. It seemed an awful long time since he'd seen Annie.

At the furniture store, Annie glanced up with each slight noise—a customer moving a chair, the salesman opening a dresser drawer, even her own knee bumping the metal wastebasket under her desk. After her disappointment Sunday, would something happen again to keep Donald from her?

Then the door opened and in he strode, shoulders thrown back, his step almost a swagger—the way it had been in college. He smiled and fixed his eyes on her, his love reaching out like a tangible force.

She met him at the counter, and silently he took her hands. They stood that way for several moments, just looking at each other, and her heart sang with joy.

Donald suddenly released her hands and leaned slightly away from her. For a split second she was puzzled, until she realized Mr. McGinnis had come out of his office.

"Well, Mr. Nakamura," said her boss. "How are you this fine spring morning?"

Donald cleared his throat and shook Mr. McGinnis's outstretched hand. "Fine, thank you. Your store's looking good. Are you able to stock enough merchandise now that the war's over?"

Without his touch, Annie felt empty. Still, she had to bite back a smile. Donald had such a talent for words, but she doubted that he'd noticed anything in the store besides her.

"It's starting to look up. Plastic's really big," said Mr. McGinnis, "but we can get some metal appliances already. Companies are whipping things out so quickly they sometimes cut back on quality. . . . By the way, did they ever catch the vandals who tore up your field?"

Donald nodded. "They sure did. That license number helped a lot. Seems it was a stolen car from up north . . . Modesto, I think. The guys were from some small town around there. . . . Mr. McGinnis, may I borrow your bookkeeper for a little while?" He winked at her. "I need some help on my . . . accounts."

Mr. McGinnis smiled, his eyes knowing. "It's up to her. She has an hour free for lunch."

Annie grabbed her purse, then went into the back room and brought out a large string bag she'd been storing in the refrigerator. She walked out with Donald, wishing his arm were around her and her head nestled against his shoulder. But she knew they needed to be discreet. There would be time later.

He helped her into his car. "I thought we'd drive toward the foothills. There's a big oak tree right off the road, nice shade. I brought pickled vegetables and some apples—"

"And I fried some chicken and made a potato salad." Annie patted the bag by her feet.

"I wondered what smelled so good." Once out of town, he glanced through the rearview mirror. There were no other cars in sight, and he pulled over to the side of the road and stopped.

Annie wondered if he had car trouble. But he just looked at her for a moment, smiling, then drew her to him and kissed her until she gasped for breath. Breathing hard himself, he ran a finger lightly over her lips. "Sweet Annie, my beautiful girl. I've waited so long for that."

Her lips tingled with his touch, and she lifted her face for more. He hadn't been the only one who'd waited. This time she moved closer to him, her arms around his neck, her fingers tangled in his luxurious black hair. Her hunger for him made her forget everything else, until finally he gently released her. Bending his forehead against hers, he squeezed his eyes shut.

"Oh, sweetheart, you don't know what you're doing to me." His voice was hoarse, and he turned away and started the car. "We'd better go have our lunch before I eat you up."

He drove slowly, his arm around her. They were quiet for a while, and then Annie asked about his grandfather.

Donald told her about the shock of his fall, the dash to the hospital, their worry, and the great relief when he came to. "Last night he actually felt good enough to play *goh.* I thought it'd be an easy win for me, since he was so weak, but before I knew what happened, he had me surrounded. After that, I was more careful, but he's good. Really, really good."

When he saw the puzzled look on her face, he explained the game, describing the board with the black and white stones, telling her about the struggle for territory and capture of prisoners.

It sounded very complicated to her. "I guess I'd have to see it to understand."

"I'll teach you after we're married."

Annie sighed. She loved him so much it hurt. But how could they get married? When he went away to school, she wouldn't be able to go with him—not legally. How would she ever stand it? She knew of girls who ran off with their sweethearts, lived together without marrying.

But she couldn't do that. Even if she'd be willing, Donald wouldn't consider it.

She had to ask. "Did you find out anything more about that law? Miscegenation?"

"Anti-miscegenation. Not yet. But somehow I know it'll be all right." He was smiling, his face shining.

Just thinking about all the legal problems and the prejudice against the Japanese made Annie's hopes plunge. How could he be so sure of himself, after all the terrible things that had happened to his people?

He gave her shoulder a squeeze. "There's a chapter in the Bible that seems like it was written just for me." He told her about Psalm 37, how it had answered some of his questions. "'The desires of thine heart.' I'm claiming that verse for us. If I made a list of all the things in the world that I desire, you'd be the first. And God has promised you to me. So how can we lose?"

His faith is so strong. She believed the Bible, too—all of it. *But is every verse written for anyone who reads it?* It was so easy to pray about lost keys, test grades, unbalanced columns, even the healing of relationships. But something as serious as this—did she trust God to answer yes? The people who made laws didn't use the Bible for a guide, or they wouldn't have made that ruling in the first place.

Donald pulled off the road under the oak tree. Its branches spread their shade over them, and they sat on the running board of the car, eating their lunch. It felt almost like those carefree, happy days back in college.

"I wrote to Florence last night." Donald handed Annie an apple. "Told her about us. Do you mind?"

Annie looked down, then peeked up at him through her lashes. "She already knows. I had to tell someone or bust. I made her promise not to say anything to you."

He threw his head back and laughed. "Oh, you little rascal! When she reads my letter, she'll giggle all day." Then he looked at Annie sideways. "Did you tell anyone else?"

Annie took a deep breath and let it out slowly. Then she nodded. "Just one person."

His smile faded. "Jonah?"

"No. I haven't talked to him for weeks. He's out of my life and going steady with another girl. No, I mentioned it to my friend Malinda. She just got engaged, too."

Annie told Donald about Malinda's cornering her one night after church, telling her the gossip she'd heard, begging Annie to tell her what was really going on. She told him, too, about her friendship with Malinda and how she felt their secret would be safe with her.

Then she mentioned Malinda's coming into the store to choose her cedar chest, how supportive her friend had been when Annie shared her despair over the marriage law. "She's praying for us, too. I guess we have a lot going for us."

Donald took a bite of chicken thigh, chewed it slowly, then nodded. "Besides that, you're such a good cook . . . there's no way around it. You *have* to marry me."

Annie snuggled closer to him, pushing away her doubts. "I can sew, too."

"Yeah, but can you make . . . what were those things again . . . *veronicas?*"

Annie laughed so hard she nearly choked. "*Verenikya.* I thought you didn't know what they were."

"I didn't. But I asked my friends. Aren't they some kind of dumplings filled with cottage cheese?"

"Yes. Sort of like giant, flat ravioli. We serve them with ham and gravy."

"Sounds good. And there's something called *plumes*—"

Annie was touched. He really had studied up on German food. "*Pluma mos.* That's a thin pudding with prunes and raisins. Hey, you might turn into a regular Mennonite before you know it."

"Maybe. Have there ever been any Japanese Mennonites? I might be the first."

"You'll be the best . . . that's for sure." Annie gathered up the chicken bones and wrapping papers and put them into her bag. If they could be together, she didn't care whether they were Mennonites or Baptists. Or . . . or . . . even Presbyterians! She leaned back against Donald and looked up at his face, into his shining dark eyes so full of love.

He tipped her chin up and brought his lips to hers. She closed her eyes and lost herself in the soft sweetness of his kiss and the caress of his mustache, wishing the moment would last forever. If he believed that verse in the Psalms paved the way to their marriage, and if Malinda went by the promise of answered prayer, Annie would have enough faith, too.

Donald went back into the strawberry field that afternoon, full of energy. If this year's crop was good, and paid as well as predicted, maybe he could make a down payment on an engagement ring. If Annie had any problems with wearing it, he'd buy a chain for it and she could wear it around her neck.

He thought of all the people in the Japanese community who'd be surprised, shocked, even horrified when they announced their engagement. But once they knew Annie, they'd realize how well-suited he and his sweetheart were to each other. It was so hard not to say anything, especially to his mother and grandfather. *I've got to say something to* Jiichan *when I visit him tonight—*

Then he remembered—that night was his regular choir practice, and he'd not yet gone over the songs for Sunday. He usually planned ahead a little, and right now the group had one special number almost ready. But the second song they'd been practicing was more difficult and needed a lot more work.

What shall I do? His grandfather was expecting him, and he couldn't let the old man down. His father had a board meeting and his mother wouldn't want to drive alone to Fresno. The church people often asked about his grandfather, but he doubted any of them would drive all that way.

Then he had an idea. *I wonder if Grace would lead choir practice tonight?*

Donald ran into the house. He remembered Grace's mentioning that she'd found a job at the Charm Curl beauty parlor, washing hair and sweeping up. He asked the telephone operator for that number.

When Grace came to the phone, her voice was sweet. "Well, hi, Donald! What a surprise to hear from you!" He heard giggling in the background, and knew the women must be teasing her.

"I wondered whether you'd take over for me this evening at choir practice," he said hurriedly. It wouldn't do to give her a wrong idea.

She hesitated for a moment. "Who . . . me? I'm no director." Now her tone was sharper.

He told her about his grandfather, and suggested she choose two easy hymns for Sunday's specials and let the choir sing through them a few times. "I'll go over the songs with them right before church on Sunday," he promised.

"Well . . . okay."

"You're a doll. I really appreciate it."

"You'd better!" she teased.

When Donald and his mother got to the hospital, they found his grandfather walking unsteadily around his room. "They say not lie down too much."

Donald's mother straightened the sheets on his bed and refilled his water glass. When the old man dropped into a chair, she helped him take off his slippers. Sighing, he crawled back onto the bed.

"It'll take a while for you to get your strength back. But they know best," Donald reassured him. "Moving around will keep you from getting pneumonia."

"I go home. Get strong there." His grandfather glared up at the ceiling. "Food no good . . . jiggly red lumps."

Donald's mother looked around to see if anyone else had heard his comment, but no one was close enough. "That's Jello," she told him. "Try it. You might like it."

The old man kept grumbling. "Nurse wake me up, make me wash face. Stick me too much."

Donald laughed. "I've never heard you complain like that before. Sounds like you're getting better. I'll see what the doctor says."

Donald was glad that he'd chosen to come visit, and hoped he could cheer *Jiichan* up.

When the nurse came to check on her patient, Donald asked, "Do you think grandfather will be released soon? He's getting pretty restless. And I can help him at home if the doctor gives me instructions."

The nurse said the doctor wouldn't be on rounds until after visiting hours, but she would phone him and find out. When she returned she said, "He feels your grandfather is making good progress, and if he keeps it up, he can go home Saturday morning. But it will take him at least a month to fully recover, and he'll need to come in for weekly check-ups."

When she left the room, Donald got out the *goban*, and his grandfather brightened up. True to his promise, he led Donald through a few quick capturing games, giving him tips on which stones were in the most danger. Then, when they played the full game, Donald saw where he'd been making mistakes—but he still didn't win.

Donald then opened the *Saturday Evening Post* he brought along, and the three of them laughed over the jokes and cartoons as Donald explained them. By then the old man was in much better spirits. Donald promised to come again the next evening, and his mother said she'd bring along some food he'd like. But it still hadn't seemed the right time to announce his engagement. *When Jiichan comes home,* he promised himself.

When Donald and his father brought *Jiichan* home on Saturday, Donald's mother had the old man's bed freshly made and the room ready. She'd even set a delicate flower arrangement on his dresser, and he grunted his appreciation.

Donald hoped that now, without all those trips to Fresno, he'd have more time for Annie. But his grandfather was still very weak, and between helping him and doing the farm work, he was busier than ever the next two weeks. The weather turned cloudy, and intermittent sprinkles brought out new crops of healthy weeds for him to attack.

Even his time on those precious Sunday afternoons was eaten up. His father had arranged for an evangelistic service, and asked him to call extra choir practices on Sunday afternoons to prepare special numbers for it. It seemed like everything was conspiring against his time with Annie.

He had to be satisfied with a quick phone call to her now and then, and a short pop-in at the furniture store when he dashed into town for farm supplies. Each time, she seemed happy to hear his voice or to see him, but he sensed an undertone of wistfulness—a hesitancy—in her voice. He hoped she wouldn't give up on him.

Chapter Twenty-Four

THE LAST WEEK OF MARCH, THE valley thrived. The weather turned warm and sunny, and the strawberry plants grew lush and full. Most of the fruit trees in neighboring farms had dropped their petals, stippling the ground beneath them in pink or white. Some of the young peaches, plums, and nectarines were almost ready for thinning. Grapevines leafed out in fresh greenery.

Wild poppies and lupine bloomed along the shoulders of the roads, and the camellia bush by the Nakamura's back steps was full of gorgeous red blossoms. Donald's mother often floated one or two in a saucer of water on the kitchen table.

Day by day, Donald tended the strawberries lovingly, guiding the runners back in line, sifting a little mulch over them, and pulling out invading weeds. *Goh* wasn't his grandfather's only specialty—he was a master gardener, too, and Donald was determined to follow the old man's methods. He missed having his grandfather in the field with him but was glad the old man was now home to offer advice.

If the weather held, the first picking could start about the middle of May—as long as he could get pickers and a bank loan to pay them. And when the season was over, with the land prepared for fall, he'd leave for medical school.

Although it had been a whole month since he'd proposed to Annie, he still hadn't found a way for them to get married. He tried several times to contact his friend's lawyer uncle. The one time he'd reached the man by phone, all he got was, "Oh, it's illegal all right. Since 1920. But what Japanese would want to marry a Caucasian anyway? Aren't our own girls good enough?"

It wouldn't be fair to ask Annie to wait for him to finish school—he couldn't wait that long himself—only to come back to the same restrictions.

He'd been so sure God was leading in his life and had spoken to him through that psalm. Had he misunderstood?

No. There *had* to be some kind of loophole in that law so they could get married.

Hearing the familiar rumble and rattle of the postal truck, Donald looked up from the plants—and his thoughts. He wiped his hands on his work pants and jogged down the driveway. The old gray mailbox looked like a metal lunch box perched on a splintered wooden post. Before he reached it, the mailman stuffed a handful of mail into it, waved, swerved back onto the road, and drove on.

Donald pulled out the usual bills, a flyer from Rosemond Car Sales, *The Sunday School Times* magazine his father enjoyed, and a letter from Florence—addressed not to his parents, but just to him! He ripped it open, leaned against the mailbox, and grinned at the salutation. *Hi, you fast worker. You really are making up for lost time. Tell Annie you both have my blessing, and I pray that it all works out for you.*

He nodded slowly. The more people praying, the better.

Florence sent greetings to their parents, especially their grandfather, expressing her sympathy for his accident and wishing him a speedy recovery. She was sorry she wasn't there to help. She asked about the strawberries, and said she'd miss the valley's fruit season.

She went on to tell about college life—the parties, the sports. In previous letters she'd mentioned dating a young man named Sam Nagawa. Now a lot of her sentences began, *Sam thinks . . . Sam likes to . . . Sam and I went . . .* Smiling, Donald tapped the letter against his chin. His little sister sounded pretty serious about this guy.

Then he wondered where the man was from. If Florence married him, would she move even farther away? He missed her teasing giggle, her friendly advice. They had always been close—especially since Annie had come into their lives.

Then she wrote, *This might interest you. I went to a symphony concert in town. One of the flutists was East Indian. Later I learned that she's the wife of my English teacher, who's Caucasian.*

He read that part again, and his pulse throbbed in his throat. Were mixed marriages all right in Kansas? Surely a college wouldn't hire a teacher who was breaking the law. Were some states more liberal than others? He'd look into that at the very first opportunity.

Donald crammed the letter into his pocket and lifted his face to the sky. "Thank you, Lord, for giving me a ray of hope."

He hurried back to the field and bent to his work, his mind racing even faster than his hands. If there was any way he and Annie could get married, they'd find a small apartment in Chicago, something just big enough for the two of them. Anything in the city would be better than the barracks at Gila River. With the GI Bill and odd jobs—maybe he could tutor or help with research—and staying on a budget, they should be able to make it financially.

Annie would sew curtains and do all the little womanly things that made a place feel like home. Probably she'd want to work at first. That was something they ought to talk about. In the evenings, they'd have supper together—American, Japanese, or Mennonite food—and talk about their day apart. And then . . . at evening's end . . .

Donald breathed hard and worked a little faster, pulling out the stubborn weeds as though they were the only things keeping him away from his beloved. Softly, he sang "Girl of My Dreams," the words expressing just what he felt. For him, Annie *was* the girl of his dreams, the only girl in the whole world.

And when he finished school, he'd set up his practice and they'd raise a family. Sweet little children—a boy with black hair like his daddy—and a girl with strawberry-blonde curls, toddling around after their mother as she took care of the house. She wouldn't need to work anymore, because he'd be Dr. Nakamura with enough patients to support a family.

He heard a soft gurgling and turned to see his mother beside him, pouring tea from a thermos into its cup. She offered it to him, steaming hot. "Drink. Keep juices flowing."

He hadn't realized how thirsty he was. When he'd had enough, she dipped into her apron pocket and handed him two cookies.

"You want to keep my sweet tooth chewing, too, huh?" he teased.

When he found a state where he and Annie could marry, he'd tell his parents of their plans. But looking at his mother as she smiled at him, seeing the love and pride in her eyes, he suddenly realized—if he had to go far away to get married, she would not be able to attend the wedding. And she'd be very hurt—even more disappointed than his father.

Donald's heart sank. Whenever one problem seemed solved, another cropped up.

On Wednesday, the temperature dropped ten degrees and a brisk wind whipped through the trees and chased dark clouds across the sky. The radio warned of rain.

Donald turned from one station to another, listening to each weather bulletin. A nice gentle shower would do the strawberries good, might even save one watering. Cooler weather would slow the ripening process, but a few days of hot sun would take care of that. A hard rain, though, especially with strong winds—that could be disastrous.

On Thursday the dark clouds passed and emptied themselves over the mountains. More came though, and early the next morning Donald woke up to a crashing noise. His first thought was that the vandals were back to finish their destruction, and his heart nearly stopped.

But as he lay propped on one elbow, looking out the window, lightning turned the sky into a silvery sheet. A few seconds later, a blast of thunder shook the house.

Donald scurried out of bed and padded to the window, watching the display until the noise died down. Then came the rain, first in a light sprinkle, then spates of heavy downpours alternating with more gentle showers. Each time the rain beat on the roof and rattled down the gutters he was sure it was hail, but it was too dark to see.

There was no use going back to bed. He knew that even when the rain slowed to a soft patter on the roof, it wouldn't lull him back to sleep. Not when his crop was at stake.

He checked to make sure his grandfather was still sleeping, then pulled on his work clothes and went downstairs. Just as he reached the bottom step, his father came out of his room.

"Looks pretty bad, huh?" Donald said.

His father nodded. "We're in for a rough time. But we've weathered other storms. God will help us through this one." He went into the kitchen and turned on the radio just in time to catch the 5:30 A.M. weather report.

". . . Storm passed through last night, leaving hail the size of marbles . . . frost in some areas . . . another storm on its way." Donald's father shook his head, then went to the table and knelt beside his chair.

Donald followed his lead, and at first the only sound was the steady torrent and the plinking of water against metal drainpipes.

His father prayed, quietly at first, then more and more passionately. "Lord, Thou knowest our needs . . . we trust in Thee completely . . . Thou art our only hope. We beseech Thee to save us from disaster."

When they rose from their knees, Donald's mother came in and headed for the pantry. "Today no go to field," she said briskly. "Have time eat pancakes. Big American breakfast."

But Donald looked at her eyes and could tell she'd been crying. Trust his mother to be cheerful even when her heart was breaking. "Don't make too many," he told her. "Our stomachs aren't awake yet." He wondered if he'd be able to eat at all.

It would take a miracle to save the strawberries this time. He glanced at the clock on the counter—5:55 A.M., nearly sunrise. But the steady rain sounded like it would not stop any time soon. From the window he saw the sky grow lighter in the east, but he knew the sun probably wouldn't break through the clouds all day.

He went out to the screen porch and turned on the outside light. It reflected in puddles all over the yard as the slanted rain made little pocks in their surfaces. He tugged on rubber boots and a slicker, took a flashlight from a drawer, then went outside, dreading what he'd see.

There were no signs of hail in the yard, and although some tree branches had fallen, there didn't seem to be any real damage.

In the field, the furrows were deep in water and the strawberry plants flattened, but he was relieved to see that most of them could possibly survive. As soon as the rain stopped he'd do whatever repair was necessary.

He went back to the house and met his father at the door. "Could be worse." He reported what he'd seen, noting that he hadn't seen any hail.

By the time they finished eating, the rain had slowed to a drizzle, and the three of them slogged through the mud, shoring up the plants.

But by midmorning the clouds opened again. The heavy downpour undid all their earlier work. Donald's father was to meet a despondent old man at the church, and said he'd stop at the bank on his way home. "We can't expect the Mennonite Disaster Service to help us this time," he remarked as he left. "All the farmers have their own problems, maybe worse than ours."

Donald stood by the back screen door, watching for a lull in the rain. His thoughts went in circles—Annie, marriage, medical school, *Jiichan*—but through it all was his silent prayer: *Please, dear Lord, answer our prayers. Spare our field from hail and ruin.*

He heard shuffling footsteps and turned to see his grandfather coming to join him. "Too much, too much," the old man said, shaking his head. "Strawberries not like."

Donald nodded. If only there was something, *anything*, he could do to help the crop.

His mother finished a load of laundry and began feeding the clothes through the wringer. He strung up the thin rope lines, glad for something to keep his hands busy, crisscrossing them through the rooms, connecting them to nails at the tops of window frames. Donald then helped his mother clip the wash to the line.

It was nearly noon when he glanced out the window and saw his father pull into the yard. Donald met him at the back door and saw the discouragement in his face.

"I guess rainy days are no good for borrowing money," he told Donald. He cleaned the mud off his shoes, using the metal scraper by the steps, and shook the rain from his felt hat.

Donald stared at him, his heart sinking. "No luck?"

His father shook his head. "They said it was too risky. If our crop were destroyed, how would we repay the loan?" He ducked under the clothes as he entered the kitchen, and Donald followed him.

His mother had rice ready, and after saying grace, they all ate their lunch in silence, only their eyes betraying their feelings.

Finally, Donald said, "Maybe if the sun shines hot for a week . . . dries things out . . . we can try the bank again."

His father shrugged. "Maybe. Now, we'll just wait."

Wait. That was the hardest part. Not knowing if they had a crop. If they did have one, would they have money for pickers? And if that all worked out, would he be able to marry Annie? Donald turned back to his food, but his appetite was gone. For a man who claimed to trust God, he had so many questions.

He had to get out of the gloom of the house, to think things over. "Please excuse me," he said to his father. "I need to look over some Easter music at the church."

His father peered at him over his glasses. "Why don't you take Grace along? She could play them on the piano, help you decide."

Donald pretended to think that over, but actually was choosing his words carefully. "I'm sure she's at work. Besides, I'd concentrate better alone. I can hear the music in my head just by looking at the notes."

"You do that?" His mother stared at him. "You hear little black dots?"

"Sure! If they move up, the music goes up." He demonstrated, his voice following the upward swoop of his fingers. "The same when they go down."

"My boy too smart for me." She picked up the dishes and took them to the sink. "I clean up. You go hear dots. And you," she pointed at her husband, "read book till mouth fall open and snore."

Donald's father looked sternly at her. "Disrespectful to your pastor."

But Donald saw the twinkle in his father's eyes. He was lucky to have parents who, after all these years of hardships, still loved each other. And who loved him. He just hoped they would learn to love Annie, too.

As Donald opened the door to the back porch, he looked back. "*Jiichan*," he said, "I'll be back in time to play a couple of games of *goh* with you this afternoon. Maybe this time I can beat you."

An hour looking at music, fifteen minutes talking to Annie on the church's private line—that would work out just fine. Grabbing his hat from its nail in the back porch, Donald slapped it on his head and ran through the rain to the car.

Annie answered the phone, using her professional voice. Instead of softening it, though, when she realized who was on the line, she continued to speak in a businesslike tone. "Yes, this is she. I beg your pardon?"

"Annie, what's the matter?" His voice sounded hurt. Then he caught on. "Are you . . . are there people with you?"

Annie glanced at the group of men standing around her desk. "Yes. May I call you back later?"

"Oh, sure, sweetheart. I'm at the church. I'll be waiting. Bye!"

She dropped the phone into its cradle and took a deep breath, letting it out quietly. The lawyer next to her closed the store's ledger book and asked, "May I have the accounts previous to these dates?"

"Sure." She reached under the counter and brought out three more heavy gray books. The men—two lawyers and an accountant—had first come to Mr. McGinnis some days ago, claiming he was running an illegal contract business.

He wasn't, of course—Annie knew that. All the long-term contract accounts were entered in ledgers under a different name to keep them separate from the open accounts, which weren't charged any interest. The name was registered, but the lawyers claimed it was fictitious and, therefore, fraudulent.

Mr. McGinnis had reasoned with them until he was angry, then argued until he was livid. They'd left—that first time—but today they came back with a warrant.

When Mr. McGinnis saw them come through the front door, waving that paper, he told Annie, "Let them see anything they want. But if they try to take anything away, call the police." Then he strode into his office and slammed the door.

When Donald called, Annie had just started going over the accounts with them, explaining the rules and guidelines the store followed, showing them how the system worked. Now, she patiently went through it all again, repeating again that the terms were explained to the customers, too, before they signed anything. The interest was figured on a yearly basis, and if they paid in full ahead of time, they ended up paying less interest than had been scheduled.

After a while, the accountant was satisfied. Bored, he wandered around the store, trying out the sofas and recliners. One lawyer studied the pictures on the walls, but the other still hovered over her, seemingly unconvinced.

Annie got up from her swivel chair and stretched her shoulders back. "Why don't you sit down, Mr. . . . uh . . ."

"Patterson."

"Mr. Patterson, I can get some more ledgers if you need them."

"That won't be necessary. Tell me, young lady, are you in charge of all these accounts?"

"Of course. I'm the only bookkeeper."

He continued to stand, looking around her office space—the neat counters, the orderly shelves. The once-tidy desk was covered with ledgers, his briefcase, and tablets filled with his scribbled notes. A bud vase holding two roses, and a glass paperweight filled with multicolored sand, had been shoved dangerously close to the edge.

"So you know pretty well what goes on here. Could you swear in a court of law that all these accounts are legitimate?"

Annie put on a polite smile and shook her head. "Why, Mr. Patterson! I'm a Mennonite. Mennonites don't swear. We give our word, and we don't lie," she said most firmly. Then she bit her lip. "We might gossip and poke fun at people who are different from us," she dared to joke, "but we're honest to a fault."

The man almost smiled back, then nodded. "I wish I could say the same for lawyers!" He glanced through the ledgers again, then finally closed them. "You've been very helpful. Thank you."

Trying to hide her relief, Annie stacked the ledgers back on the shelf. Then she eyed him sideways as she straightened her desk. "Have I been helpful enough for you to do me a favor in return?"

His near-smile vanished. He stuffed the notebooks back into his briefcase without looking at her. "Depends. What do you have in mind?"

She glanced at the other two men. They'd begun drifting back toward the counter.

"What do you know about the laws against miscegenation?"

Attorney Patterson leaned his head back, as though surprised she even knew the word.

She stared him down, and he shrugged. "Mixed marriages are illegal in some states. Why?"

Annie's heart began to pound. "Only some states? In which states are they legal?"

He frowned as he thought. "I'd have to look that up. Probably some of the states back East. See, on the East Coast they didn't have the same influx of Orientals as California did. As for the Negroes, that was a problem more in the South." He went on to explain how the law specified the Chinese on the West Coast and then eventually targeted the Japanese as well.

"Which states do you *think* might not have that law?"

"Oh, I'd say probably New York. Indiana, maybe. I'm pretty sure Illinois never had any law like that, and maybe—"

"Illinois?" Annie caught her breath. "Thank you, Mr. Patterson, thank you!" She grabbed his hand and shook it vigorously while he stared at her, looking completely puzzled. The other lawyer gawked at the whole scene, and the accountant's eyes practically had question marks in them. But Annie had no intention of letting them in on her important secret.

She dropped his hand, composed her features, and announced in the most professional tone she could muster, "Well, if we're finished, I'll get back to my work."

The lawyer gave a nod, then motioned with his head to the other men. Walking out, he glanced back at her again and saw that she was watching him. He quickly turned his head, grabbed his waiting umbrella, and followed the other men out the door.

Annie waited until the door closed behind them before she picked up the phone. She ought to go rescue her boss, but first things first.

When Donald answered, she could hardly get the words out. "Guess what . . . ! That anti-miscegenation law . . . ? Illinois doesn't have one!"

Chapter Twenty-Five

"TELL ME AGAIN. HOW DID YOU FIND OUT?" Donald sat across the table from Annie at Sweets and Treats. No other customers were there at the moment, and when the waitress turned her back, he reached across the table for Annie's hand.

He'd rushed over to the store right after her phone call and found Mr. McGinnis exulting over Annie's handling "those lousy no-good snoops." With her boss's blessing, Donald had swept her off to celebrate her good news. His heart nearly burst with joy, and he felt like a high school kid on a date with the prom queen.

She told him about the lawyers and accountant at the store. How they'd poked into financial business that was perfectly legal and none of their concern. How she'd been so syrupy nice to them, she felt she earned the privilege of asking a legal question. "Now, he wasn't absolutely, positively sure, but he said some of the eastern states weren't that concerned about mixed marriages, so they didn't bother making those kinds of laws. And if Illinois really is one of them, well, doesn't that solve our problem?"

Donald nodded, quickly releasing her hand as the waitress returned and brought over their order: one milkshake with two straws. Strawberry, of course. Anything to create more demand for the fruit.

The waitress eyed them—first Donald and then Annie—then put the glass down so hard, a little slopped over the sides. Donald smiled at the woman. "Thank you," he said in the extra polite voice he reserved for rude people. The waitress' mouth twitched as she went back to the counter.

Ordinarily Donald would have walked right out, determined never to go back, but the woman wasn't important right now. He turned his attention back to his wonderful, clever sweetheart. "Wouldn't it be swell if we could take our families and friends to Illinois for the wedding?"

"If they'd even approve of our marriage." As Annie sipped at the milkshake, concern wrinkled her forehead. "My mother is still pretty upset. The last I heard, she and I are the black sheep of the Bartsch clan."

Donald toyed with the idea of his parents traveling to Illinois. It would be too hard on his grandfather. His friends? Even if he could pay for their transportation, they'd lose wages for the time off. And then there'd be housing—

His heart sank. It didn't do any good to dream. If anything else happened to the strawberry crop, he'd be hard pressed to come up with the fares for himself and Annie.

But Florence—she might be able to come. Kansas was closer, and she'd probably still be working there. She'd always been loyal to both of them, encouraging their friendship and love. In fact, he realized, she'd started it all!

From the way Florence and her friends had talked while growing up, Donald figured that all girls had their hearts set on a big fancy production. Bridesmaids, a church full of flowers, a huge decorated cake. Lots of people congratulating them. Gifts.

If Annie married him in Chicago, away from all the family, she wouldn't have any of that. Years later, would she look back and resent him for it?

Surely the prejudice would die down someday. The laws would eventually change. They could come back to the San Joaquin Valley and throw a big anniversary party—Dr. and Mrs. Donald Nakamura.

He studied Annie now. Her curly hair glistened with a few raindrops from their walk to the snack shop. When she leaned forward to sip and stare into the glass, he envied that straw next to her tempting lips, and slid his feet to capture hers between them in the privacy under the booth, thrilling to the contact. If her news proved to be true, soon they could be open about their love.

The shop door opened and three men with briefcases entered, shaking the rain off their umbrellas. The waitress headed for their table. After placing their order, they looked over at Donald and Annie, then leaned together and whispered.

Annie blushed and her eyes clouded.

Donald whispered, "Do you know them?"

She nodded. "The ones who were in the store. Now they know why I was asking all those questions," she whispered. Clearing her throat, she spoke a little louder. "Wasn't that storm awful? How did your strawberries do? I heard a lot of peach orchards were ruined by the hail."

He knew she was making small talk, even though she *was* truly interested. It wouldn't fool anyone—the shared milkshake gave them away. "The rain beat them down pretty badly but, thank God, the hail seems to have skipped us."

"Will this delay the harvest?"

"Probably. And some plants won't make it, but that's to be expected. If the weather clears soon and we get some sunshine, we'll be okay." He thought again of his father's rejection at the bank and ran his hand through his hair. If they couldn't pay pickers, they'd just have to plow most of the crop under.

Annie pushed the glass toward him. "Go ahead and finish. By the way, how's your grandfather?"

"He's getting stronger. I need to take him in for a check-up on Monday, but I'm pretty sure the doctor will say he's nearly back to normal."

"What about his shaking? Did the doctor ever figure out what causes it?"

More people had come into the shop, and with all six of the little tables full, the waitress pointedly stared at them.

Donald finished the milkshake, reluctantly freed Annie's feet, and rose from his seat. Pulling out a few coins, he glanced at them, then left them next to his crumpled napkin. "The doctor doesn't think it's palsy. My grandfather's condition doesn't fit the pattern . . . his shaking affects both hands and stops when he rests them."

"That's a relief, isn't it?" Annie asked, sliding out of the seat.

Donald held the door open for her, and from the corner of his eye, he saw the lawyers and accountant still looking at them. None of the three was smiling.

Annie's face was still flushed as she started out the door. She turned slightly and waved at the men, who quickly looked away.

"It certainly is," he answered as he let the door swing shut after them. Glancing back at the men through the fogged up window, he was proud that his Annie was brave enough to weather the silent criticism. She'd do okay, this sweetheart of his. "But whatever the problem is," he continued, "I doubt if he'll ever get strong enough to work much in the fields again. Not like he did before. I don't know who'll take charge when I'm gone. It's too hard for my mother, and my father has his hands full with the church."

Once past the sandwich shop, they walked under the store awnings for shelter. Donald took Annie's hand, gave it a little squeeze, then released it and moved discreetly a few inches away from her. No sense pushing their luck—it wouldn't be right to give her a bad reputation. Although it was still raining, people passed by on the sidewalks. In a town the size of Rosemond, people gossiped.

When they were nearly back to the furniture store, Annie looked at him, her forehead furrowed in thought. "Have you ever thought of selling the farm and moving to town? If your father has the church—"

Donald stopped walking and stared at her. "Sell? After all the problems we've gone through to buy land . . . ? Working around the alien landlaw, forming a corporation while I was still small . . . My father had to persuade the neighbor to join until I was of age and could take ownership as a citizen. . . . Sell? . . . No . . . Never . . . Out of the question!"

Then he was ashamed of his outburst, smiled at her and spoke softly.

"Property is better than gold. It can stay in the family and increase in value through the years. It'll be security for our children and for generations after."

She looked down, blushing a deeper red. "Our children?" She gave a little laugh. "I wonder what they'll look like."

He laughed, too. "With lots of *borscht* and *tvehbock*, they'll probably look like fat little Sumo wrestlers." Then he sobered. "Annie—what if they look very Japanese? Straight black hair and slanted eyes? How would you feel?"

Then she faced him, her eyes sparkling. "I hope they look just like you. Handsome, smooth ivory complexion, beautiful lips. Dark brown eyes so deep and mysterious. I love the way you look."

He took a deep breath, his heart galloping as though he'd been running. To calm himself he grinned at her. "Was it Lincoln who told the story about the woman who said she wanted a child with her beauty and his brains?"

Annie laughed. "Actually, my English teacher said that was George Bernard Shaw. He shut her up by saying the child probably would have *his* looks and *her* brains."

They reached the store and stood in the doorway. Donald stared at her, memorizing her features. "Well, God blessed you with enough beauty and brains for both of us, and talent besides. Our children can't help but be wonderful. But do you think . . . would you mind . . . if we wait to have them until I finish school? Or at least close to the end? It's not going to be easy for either of us."

"Hey, I'll get a job. I'm sure Mr. McGinnis will give me a good reference. I wouldn't want to sit around all day while you're at school studying your head off."

"You don't mind working?" Donald felt as though a load of rocks had just rolled off his back. "I wouldn't want you to feel I was taking advantage of you, letting you support me through school." It wasn't only the job. He'd need to study late at night, and children would be an added distraction. When they did have children, he wanted to be able to spend time with them, play with them. Show them his love. His and Annie's children—

He sighed. "If we hadn't been dragged off to camp, I'd be through all that and have a good life to offer you. The sensible thing would be to wait so I can catch up on those lost years." Then he moved closer, greedy for contact, but still under control. "But I don't think I could stand that."

She clasped her hands and playfully propped her chin on them. Her green eyes were shining pools, swirling him into their depths. "Donald Nakamura! If you'd go off and leave me again, I think I'd die."

His control evaporated, and he had to kiss her. But just before his lips reached hers, the sound of footsteps brought him back to his senses.

"Good afternoon, Mr. Nakamura!" Mr. McGinnis said coolly as he came down the sidewalk. Swinging around them, he pushed open the door to the furniture store and said, "Annie, did you ever find that Gregory file?"

Annie gave Donald a look of apology and slipped through the door. "I'll get it for you right now."

Her heart still racing, Annie found the file and laid it on her boss's desk. She couldn't believe how bold Donald had been, trying to kiss her in public. What if someone—those lawyers, maybe—had seen?

She settled into her work, posting the day's sales and payments into their proper ledgers. Shaking her head ever so slightly, she realized more and more how much trouble a public kiss could have caused for him. He must really love her to take a chance like that.

People in Rosemond bragged about how broad-minded they are. The past weeks, however, had shown her that most of the acceptance was merely superficial—something people said, or did, just to be nice. Helping Japanese farmers recover from vandalism was one thing. Kissing one of them was as unthinkable as walking through town in a nightgown.

She thought about the rudeness of the waitress at Sweets and Treats. She and Donald wouldn't go back there again! *When Donald is a successful doctor, people will see how intelligent and capable he is,* she thought, *and be ashamed of the way they treated him.*

From the corner of her eye, she saw the Gregory file sliding over her ledger. She looked up to see Mr. McGinnis perched on the corner of her desk. He was studying her and frowning. "Should I scold or apologize? Was Nakamura bothering you?"

Annie shook her head, her face growing hot. How could he think such a thing about Donald? Her boss was no better than that waitress! "We'd just gone for a milkshake," she explained.

"Just you two? Pretty girl like you . . . you could have your pick. Lots of guys are coming home from the service, just aching to meet someone like you. Why are you chasing around with a Jap?"

Chasing around? *Jap?* Annie's pulse pounded in her temples, and she bit her tongue to keep from lashing out. With the war over and all the servicemen looking for jobs, she couldn't risk being fired. Now, more than ever, she needed to save every penny she earned.

She chose her words carefully. "Donald was in the service, too. He earned a lot of medals for bravery. People," she paused a bit, "shouldn't use the term 'Jap.' He's an American. A good citizen."

Mr. McGinnis cleared his throat as she went back to the work on her desk, but he didn't apologize—nor did he get up. Glancing up, she saw the look of disapproval still on his face. What would he say if he knew she was going to marry Donald? She wished she had the courage to tell him, but now was definitely not a good time—not before she and Donald told their parents.

She forced herself to add in a level tone, "His sister was my best friend in college. A bunch of us . . . all nationalities . . . hung around together. The others . . . I guess they've scattered. Some are still overseas. One was killed in action. Maybe you know his family—Billy Garabedian?"

"George's son? Yeah, I'd heard. Tsk. Too bad. Those who came back in one piece were awfully lucky. If our Harold hadn't made it, it would have killed my wife."

Annie forced a smile. At least she'd sidetracked her boss's thoughts. "How's Harold doing? Has he found a job?"

"He's with Security Bank in Visalia. Likes it real well. Has a new girlfriend; she seems very nice. Hey, whatever happened to that other guy you were going with? The one in your church?"

"Who?" She knew he was talking about Jonah. But she'd never been serious about him. Not really. And she hadn't thought about him in ages. "Oh, you must mean Jonah. He's got a new girlfriend, too." She opened the file Mr. McGinnis had returned. "Did you find everything in order? I added carbons of the letters you sent the company—"

"Sure. Fine. I just wanted to be sure we were within the deadline for payment. Don't want more lawyers bouncing in, trying to make trouble." His eyes crinkled in a smile. "Appreciate the way you handled the last ones." He patted her shoulder, slid off the desk corner, and headed for his office.

She took a deep breath and let it out slowly. All the time spent with those lawyers had been worth it, if only to get Mr. McGinnis's mind off her private life. She smiled wryly to herself. It had paid off in more ways than one—she got the information she and Donald needed. He'd promised to call the Fresno courthouse to verify the facts, and she was sure the information would prove to be correct. With all the prayers that had been going up for them, this had to be their answer.

Illinois. Would she and Donald go there together? Would they be allowed to sit together on the train? Maybe he'd have to go first, get settled, then send for her. And then they'd get married, probably at the courthouse in Chicago. Then they'd start a completely new life together.

Chapter Twenty-Six

TROUBLED, ANNIE SAT IN THE CAR, unable to move. She'd just left work and slid behind the wheel when it suddenly hit her—she'd been considering only her own feelings and the reactions of those who cared about her—her mother, her grandparents, all the relatives, her boss. If all of *them* were against this marriage, how would strangers react when they saw Donald and her together? People like the waitress. Or those lawyers and the accountant. A lot of people still suspected any person who was Japanese.

She and Donald couldn't live in a dream world built just for them, where they'd be safe from criticism. Every day they'd see neighbors, store clerks, bosses, professors—not to mention all the strangers on the streets of Chicago. Even if Illinois didn't have an actual law against mixed marriages, the people there might not be any more accepting than those in her own town—and in her own family.

Would she and Donald even be able to rent an apartment? She thought she could stand up to ugly comments from strangers, but what about making friends? Donald enjoyed people, liked being with groups. If they couldn't have friends, would he still be happy? She loved him so much, but would her love be enough?

She thought back to the year they'd spent together in college. Donald got along with all sorts of people. His classmates liked him, and the CLOC Club members respected his leadership, his teachers enjoyed talking with him.

Those days had been so much fun. She could still see Donald's confident grin, his easy way with all the other kids. Her innocence at the time made her smile. Thinking it was just coincidence that he always managed to sit next to her at club meetings, football rallies, jamborees. She was so proud that such a swell guy liked her, enjoyed being seen with her, wanted to walk her to class.

And when their brown-bag lunch group gathered under the oak tree—joking, teasing, arguing—he'd usually sit leaning toward her. She recalled the electric jolt each time his hand grazed hers or his sleeve brushed her shoulder. Each time she acted calm, as though she didn't notice, while her heart beat faster at the thrill.

Their oak tree. Annie drove past the college and parked. She gazed at the living monument, huge and lonesome in the rain. A few branches had broken off in the storm and were lying on the ground.

She imagined herself sitting there with Donald. All the other memories—so sweet, so painful—swept over her. Donald's news of the evacuation, and the first time she'd realized her deep feelings for him. Their reunion picnic when he came home after all those years apart, and the joy of finding their love still strong and growing.

What would her life be like if he hadn't come back? What if she'd married one of the young men in her church, simply because she didn't want to be an old maid? There were several nice guys. She liked them, respected them. Without Donald around, she might have even learned to love one, on some level.

But it wouldn't have been the same. She and Donald were meant for each other. With anyone else, her life would be hollow, just a pretense of happiness.

No. Whatever life had in store for them, they'd work it out. In spite of prejudice and criticism, their marriage would be happy.

Finally, she started the car and drove home. Her mind was made up. She'd tell her mother. Tonight. She'd plan her words carefully and be firm without sounding rebellious.

Ever since her dad died fourteen years ago, she and her mother had depended upon each other. When she left, her mother would be all alone to face the relatives' and the church's reproach—even condemnation. She loved her mother, and didn't want to hurt her. But she couldn't give up her whole life just to please others.

That evening after the supper dishes were washed and put away, Annie took her mother by the arm. "Let's sit down for a minute. I need to talk to you."

Her mother drew back. "*Kindt!* You're not—" Her face turned red and her lips squeezed into a tight pucker.

Annie smiled and shook her head. "Don't worry, Mom. I'm still a good girl." She pulled out a kitchen chair for her mother and sat down beside her.

Her mother eyed her warily. "Does this have to do with your Ja . . . Japanese friend?"

Annie took a deep breath. This wasn't going to be easy. "He's . . . asked me to marry him."

"*Doch nicht!* No! Surely you turned him down? Mennonites don't marry outsiders. You know that!"

"I've given it a lot of thought. I know that your parents didn't want you to marry Dad . . . that it was a hard time for you . . . and you want to spare me that. But you and Dad loved each other. I know you did. And you still miss him a lot."

Her mother nodded, her face clouded. "But that's—"

Annie held up her palm like a stop sign. "Please. Let me finish." She thought a minute, then smiled. "Remember that old man with sloppy clothes? What was his name . . . the Bible salesman who stopped by every week? Mr. Hooge, wasn't it? I could tell—the Bibles and tracts he was selling were just an excuse to see you. And that guy . . . Mr. Schindel . . . he'd bring over lugs of tomatoes and peaches . . . said they were just culls even though they were perfect. He had more than fruit on his mind. Why weren't you more friendly to them? They were good Mennonites. They would have gladly married you, if only for your rhubarb pie!"

Her mother shrugged one shoulder, then the other. "Well, I wasn't going to marry just to please some silly old *schuzzle.*"

"But if there'd been someone nicely dressed, with good manners and a sense of humor—someone you could talk to, laugh with—wouldn't that have been different?" Annie watched her mother's eyes turn wistful. "Someone like Dad?"

Her mother dabbed at her eyes with the corner of her apron. "There wasn't anyone else like him."

It was now or never. "Mom . . . that's how I feel about Donald. He's everything I've ever wanted in a husband. He's smart, he's kind, and he's a good Christian. We think alike about so many things! And I've agreed to marry him." Before her mother could react, she added quickly, "I'm not a *kindt* any more. I'm nearly twenty-three. I know it'll be hard. I've seen how the Japanese have been . . . *still* are . . . treated. But I'd rather live with love than have an empty life just to be dutiful."

Her mother sighed and shook her head. "Oh, *Anchen.* I wish I could give you my blessing. You may think you're grown up, but you just don't know what you're getting into." She got up and left the room, muttering, "What will people say?"

"Stay there," Donald ordered. "Don't go off on your own." Bending over the strawberries to capture a stray runner and anchor it in place, he felt like a parent training a mischievous little child.

I sound like my father, he thought, and his grin turned into a sad smile. *And I'm like this runner.* Donald knew he'd disappointed his father by choosing a different path in life, although he now seemed resigned to it.

The rain had eased during the night, but earlier that Saturday morning, it was still too wet to work outside.

Jiichan had awoken with a headache and sore throat, and Donald spent the morning reading to him and telling him stories of army life.

By noon the sun broke through and, in spite of the cool breeze, the weather was warm enough to dry out some of the strawberry leaves. After lunch, Donald came out to work in the field, hoeing the ridges and getting rid of the weeds. His heart soared as he thought about Annie. He was constantly amazed that, in spite of their different backgrounds, they thought alike about so many things.

Tonight at supper, he'd tell his parents that he'd asked her to marry him. He already knew his mother liked her. He was almost sure *Jiichan* would approve, too. Annie had made friends with the old man that day she'd come over to work.

But my father, thought Donald as he coaxed another runner into line, *he'll need some convincing.*

In his role as a pastor, he was still hoping Donald and Grace could work together as a team, serving God in their church—and later in one of their own. Donald knew that, as an infant, he'd been dedicated to the Lord's work.

But the medical profession was a highly esteemed vocation, and it was possible to serve God there, too. If enough patients would be willing go to a Japanese doctor. If Dr. Robbins was right in thinking this valley was ready for one, maybe other areas were, too.

But people like the waitress at Sweets and Treats wouldn't allow him to touch them. Although she hadn't said, "We don't serve Japs," her behavior said she was thinking it. And those lawyers had looked at him and Annie as though they were ready to take him to court.

When Donald's mother came out to the field to help, he smiled at her. "It's a miracle," he told her. "I've found no hail damage."

"Thank God," she said. "Plenty work anyhow." Together they hacked, smoothed, and straightened, guided stubborn stragglers and rescued buried runners.

Tomorrow, although a Sunday, he'd have to replace the mulch washed away by the rain. And tonight at the dinner table, right after grace, he'd have the courage to make his announcement.

The sun warmed his back, and a stray tune wandered into his head.

He hummed under his breath, then the words came, and he found himself singing, "Oh, there's sunshine, blessed sunshine, when the peaceful, happy moments roll . . ." He remembered the day he and Annie sang it together, and wished she were there next to him.

His mother said, "You happy boy. See Annie yesterday, maybe?"

He stopped singing and tried to look composed, but couldn't keep the smile out of his eyes. "You know me too well."

"She like you too? Get serious, hmm?"

He cocked his head to one side, studying his mother. "Could be," he shrugged.

Her eyes wouldn't let him go, and he couldn't help grinning.

"You ask her marry you, maybe?" she prodded. "You pray God's will be done?"

What was the use? His mother had always been able to see into his heart. He nodded.

"She say yes?"

He nodded again, slowly. "I believe she's the one God chose for me."

Suddenly he found himself hugged tightly by muddy hands. "She good girl. Make you happy."

So much for keeping it a secret. "I'd planned to tell you tonight at supper. All of you."

"I keep quiet. Big surprise." She considered for a moment. "Maybe bake big cake for your wedding. Lots of sugar now."

With a mother like that, how could he have a wedding she couldn't attend?

The first Sunday in April dawned sunny and warm, almost hot. Mount Whitney was picture perfect, its snowy peak touching the clouds. In the clear air, it seemed almost close enough to touch. In the country, grapevines reached from post to post, full and green, on their neat wire trellises. Fruit trees had all finished blooming, the early peaches were beginning to size, and the nectarines were starting to color. Wild poppies, purple clover, and wild iris decorated the roadsides.

The San Joaquin Valley was so beautiful. Annie knew she'd miss it—all except the fog. But in spite of prejudice, Chicago would be an exciting adventure. She'd listen to Donald talk about his classes and his training in medical school. They'd do things as a couple—shop for groceries and have people over for coffee. Maybe even serve them *tvehbock*.

She and her mother had been attending church as usual. In public, both acted as though nothing had changed, although Annie could see disappointment and resentment in her mother's eyes. At home, her mother spoke only when necessary. Nothing Annie said or did seemed to please her. It had been a relief finally to be open about her love for Donald and her plans to marry him. Annie wished, though, that her mother could have peace about it. Annie decided to make that a matter of fervent prayer.

"Do the Japanese believe in engagement rings?" was the only question her mother had posed about Annie's announcement.

Annie had shrugged. "Probably. It's not the most important thing on our minds right now." Getting ready for the strawberry harvest and working in the vegetable garden were Donald's biggest worries right now. She hoped the good weather would hold. If it looked like the strawberry harvest would go well, his family would be encouraged, making it easier for Donald to break the news of their engagement.

She knew he wouldn't be able to see her this Sunday. He had extra music practices for his Easter choir program. But on Monday, after he'd taken his grandfather to the doctor, he went to the church and called her at work. She told him about her mother and how she'd taken the news about their engagement. How the tension had built between them. "She hardly says a word to me. All she does is mutter to herself about how wrong it is . . . that I'll always regret it. I hope that once she gets used to the idea, she'll be okay."

Donald hesitated a little, then said, "My mother knows."

Annie stared into the phone. "How did she find out? Did Florence—"

"No. She said she could tell, just by seeing how happy I am. I think she likes you. She won't be a problem."

Annie was glad to hear that; at least someone might be on their side. "But your father . . ."

Donald sighed. "He's still trying to match me up with our church pianist. I've been trying to get up the courage to tell him, but there never seems to be a good time." He paused for a moment. "I don't know about Mennonites, but we Japanese have this thing called *On*. Respect . . . I guess you'd call it. Obligation. It's ingrained in us from birth. Obedience to parents, to our Japanese community. Anything different is swimming upstream."

Annie felt a tug at her heart. She was willing to give up her own culture. But what if his *On* was stronger than his love for her? "It's kind of like that with us, too. Certain things are expected, so we do them. The church expects us to marry our own kind, and if we choose someone else, it causes a big fuss."

"Exactly. The younger kids, though, don't seem to have as strong a tie to the old ways. The high schoolers are now the third generation here, and they're a lot less respectful. Maybe the farther we grow from our roots, the less we hang on to them. Don't know if that's good or bad. Maybe a little of both."

"Ha-rumph!"

Annie looked up. Mr. McGinnis stood next to the desk. How long had he been there? What had he heard?

Chapter Twenty-Seven

DONALD STUDIED HIS CALENDAR, feeling a measure of anxiety. Easter was April 21—less than two weeks away—and his choir would be presenting a full program. He'd been so busy the past few weeks, time had slipped away. All the choir members were busy, too, with their jobs and farm work—how many practices could he ask of them?

He'd hired Sho, Tom, and a young boy to nail strawberry boxes, to tie onions and chop weeds in the vegetable garden. Several other choir members worked at neighboring farms, and some of the younger women did housework for the wealthier families in town. Grace worked at the beauty parlor, performing her usual duties as well as running errands and unpacking supplies.

By evening everyone was exhausted. But so far their commitment to the church had kept them attending every rehearsal. Even so, the tenors were shaky in their parts, and the altos needed more confidence. Maybe he could work with individual sections for half an hour each. If only they had two pianos, he could work with the men while Grace took the women.

Grace had been so cooperative, so patient, and so helpful whenever he needed a pianist. Everyone said they'd make a perfect pair, and he was afraid she'd started to believe it, too.

They'd often been thrown together because of their involvement in church music, and they got along well. Still, he didn't think he'd done anything to give her reason to think he had special feelings for her. They joked and laughed; a couple of times, he'd playfully jabbed her shoulder. While they were going over the music, he sat close to her on the piano bench, and on occasion had accidentally brushed her arm. He thought of her as a sister.

But what if she made more of it than he did? Lately, she hadn't mentioned dating that college student.

What if she's waiting for me to make a move? Donald wondered.

It wouldn't be fair to lead her on. It was time she knew about Annie. But before he told Grace—which would be the same as announcing it to the whole church—he had to tell his father. And that's what he dreaded most.

The past few nights at the dinner table, he'd cleared his throat, ready to speak up. But just then his father would introduce yet another subject—the co-op being formed to give the Japanese farmers more buying power, the truck they were using to take produce to the cities, the shortage of housing for returned evacuees, the rising prices of food and goods.

His father had never been easy to approach with personal problems. Behind the pulpit he was a dynamic speaker, and on the air he'd spoken with ease. As a counselor, he was ready with solutions when others came to him with their problems. But at home, where life touched more closely, his mother was the one who gave advice, soothed hurts, and settled quarrels.

Donald and his father had worked side by side in the fields and discussed farm issues and finances. At church they were both professionals—minister and choir director—and acted their parts. But when it came to matters of the heart, Donald had never confided in his father. In the past, he'd always answered personal questions with answers that were expected—words that wouldn't ruffle their surface relationship.

Shikata ga nai. It can't be helped, grin and bear it. Make the best of things.

That was the Japanese way of life. Donald knew, from hearing his college friends talk, that American fathers—at least some of them—

listened to their children. And they took time to do things together, go fishing, play ball, or go to the snow on the mountains.

When he and Annie had children, they'd do things together as a family.

Annie. Donald wondered if he should approach his father alone, in his study.

Yes, that would be best. After that, since his mother already knew, it would be easy to tell his grandfather. His grandparents had always been indulgent and, now after Donald had helped his grandfather through depression and his accident, their relationship had become even closer.

On Tuesday evening Donald's father relaxed at the desk in his study. He seemed refreshed from a hot, soaking bath and a stomach full of savory noodles and chicken. Donald had just picked at his own food. He felt like a nervous wreck at dinner and was even more tense now.

The door to the study stood slightly ajar, and Donald decided now was the time to approach his father. Steeling himself, he tapped lightly on the door.

"Yes?" His father turned a page, keeping his eyes on the book. A biography of Abraham Lincoln. "Come in."

Donald studied his father, breathed a quick prayer, then said, "I'd like to speak with you, if I may." He kept his voice low and respectful.

Without looking up, his father gestured toward an empty chair.

Donald glanced around the room, then focused on a picture that sat on his father's desk. It was of Florence in her high school graduation cap and gown. She was smiling and squinting against the sun. "I really appreciate the support you've shown Florence and me. All the years you've encouraged us to do the best we could, in whatever we did." He hadn't always been thankful, especially when he was little and wanted to play instead of work or study. But now he knew the effort had been valuable.

His father carefully inserted a bookmark and laid the book down. Lowering his eyebrows, he peered into Donald's eyes. "God gave both you and Florence good brains. It was right you should excel in school."

Donald took a deep breath and eased it out. Now that he had his father's attention, he mustn't stumble over words. "I also appreciate your encouragement to become a real American and feel comfortable in mixed groups. You've given me a good example, the way you associate with ministers and professionals of other nationalities."

His father leaned his elbow on the desk and cupped his chin with his hand. "Your courtesy is admirable, but as an American, you may dispense with Oriental preliminaries. Son, what exactly is on your mind?"

Donald felt his neck grow hot. "I . . . I wanted to tell you . . . I would like to get married."

His father nodded. "That would be a good thing. Would you like me to suggest an acceptable girl?"

Donald knew exactly who that acceptable girl would be. "Thank you, but I've made my choice."

His father raised his eyebrows. "I see. And is it too much to hope that the girl is Grace Miyamoto?"

Donald straightened his shoulders and clenched his jaw. He felt as though he should salute. "I'm sorry, Father. Grace is a fine girl, but not for me. I've asked Annie Penner to marry me, and she's accepted my proposal."

His father's face sagged as he slumped back in his chair. For a long time, he didn't respond. Without looking up, he finally said, "I had hoped you'd given up that foolishness. Behind my back, knowing my convictions, you have already made a commitment. My son, my only son. You cannot know how disappointed I am." He lifted a hand and waved Donald away. "I must commune with the Lord about this."

There was so much more Donald wanted to say—to explain—but this was not the time to insist. His time was up, and he had lost face. He'd survived the evacuation, the war, hatred, and prejudice, only to be crushed by his own father. Feeling as though his heart were bleeding, Donald went up to his room and made his own contact with the Lord.

After an hour, Donald felt strengthened. But he knew he wouldn't have peace until his father accepted Annie.

He stayed up in his room that evening, and when he came down the next morning his mother told him that his father would be meeting with pastors in town that day, and then had a bank appointment. Donald was already in the field when his father drove off.

Donald still felt stung by his father's dismissal, but he prayed for his success at the bank. He hoped that his father's persuasiveness and charm would influence the manager to grant the farm loan. The friends who worked on their farm were doing so on faith that they'd eventually be paid.

At lunch his mother served to Donald and the workers rice-ball soup and pickled vegetables with leftover chicken wings. Sho and Tom chattered about the annual picnic the Japanese youth club was planning—an all-day event to be held at a ranch in the foothills—volleyball, tug of war, races, plenty of good food, soda water. If Hiro Takanishi brought his portable radio, later in the evening they could sing along with some *Hit Parade* songs. Maybe even dance a little, if they could get by with it. Hiro knew some jitterbug steps.

Donald wondered if he should ask Annie to the picnic. They needed to get used to each other's cultures, but was it too soon? How would the other young people react to her? If only Florence were here to give extra support.

He tried to remember, had Annie ever come to church programs with Florence when they'd been friends in college? He couldn't remember seeing her there. She'd always been so busy with her own church doings. The Mennonite church seemed to be like his in that way. Their entire social life revolved around their culture and church activities.

In the middle of the afternoon, Donald heard the mailman's truck coming, and left the field to meet him.

The mailman handed him the mail folded into his grandfather's Japanese newspaper. The paper came from Livingston now, and was printed entirely in English. "I see they're publishing it again. I hear there's quite a large group of Japanese in that area."

Donald nodded. "Three different colonies. Nice people. They were smart enough to get a corporation to look after their farms, so they didn't lose everything like so many others."

Donald's church had met with the Presbyterian Japanese from the Livingston area before the evacuation. They'd even had song festivals together, just like the Mennonites. Maybe now they'd start up again.

The mailman pointed to the thriving strawberry plants in the field. "You were pretty lucky yourselves."

"I don't know what we would've done without our neighbor, Bartel. He's been so good to us." Donald flipped through the letters. Two for his father, one for him from the medical school, and two from Florence—one addressed to him, the other to his parents. He waved as the mailman drove off and then quickly tore open the letter from the medical school.

He'd written to them about housing for married students. A very brief answer told him there was none—he'd be on his own in that department. His heart sank. But then he saw a note at the bottom. Apparently on her own, the secretary who typed the letter had added a list of people to contact about housing. She even included addresses and a hand-drawn map to several large houses that had been converted into apartments.

Donald tapped the paper, thinking. There was no mention of restrictions for nationality, but that didn't mean anything. They surely could tell by his name that he was Japanese, but they didn't know about Annie.

He folded the letter, slid it back into the envelope, and then opened the one from Florence.

Her first sentence nearly made him drop all the mail. *I'm getting married, too! Remember I've been writing about Sam Nagawa? Well, we've set the date for November. That is, if our parents agree to it. I've written them about it too, so it's okay to tell mother. But please don't mention it to father until he reads that other letter.*

Donald felt a twinge of envy. Florence would have no problem convincing their father. Not after the bomb *he'd* just dropped. Would she come home for the wedding? Where would they live—California or Kansas?

He read on: *Sam is an ag major so he wants to go into farming, but he's from Oregon and not interested in the corn and wheat farming here in Kansas. I was wondering—have you found someone to work the strawberries?*

Donald felt a chill down his spine and didn't know whether to laugh or cry. Instead, he pumped his fists into the air and shouted, "Halle-LU-jah!" The men working in the field looked up and stared at him.

He couldn't explain; he didn't have the words. Again, God had come through. This was the second fleece, someone to manage the farm. He folded the letters into the newspaper and ran to the house.

With shaking hands, Donald put the mail on the kitchen table and motioned for his mother to sit down. "Florence," he managed to say. "Read it."

One positive result of the internment was that his mother had used her spare time learning to read English. Florence's typing was clean and free of mistakes, so he only helped his mother when she had problems with the longer words.

His mother didn't have any trouble knowing how to feel. She cried. Donald was sure most of the tears were from joy.

She read the letter through three times before putting it down. "She come home! Get married in church here. Good, good. You both . . . make a double?"

Donald sighed. "I wish we could. But Mom, Annie and I can't get married here. California laws won't let us. We have to go to a state where it's legal. And then we'll be in Chicago for my school when Florence and Sam get married in November."

His mother frowned. "Not marry here? No fancy clothes, no big dinner, no high cake with teensy groom bride dolls?" She shook her head. "Not good. Bad way to start home. Maybe father can fix."

His father would be the last person to fix that problem. "Right now, I'm not in his good favor. He has his heart set on my marrying Grace."

"Grace pretty girl. Plenty boys for her. Maybe too many, maybe not so good wife." His mother shrugged. "You wait. Father be okay. I talk to him."

Donald knew it wouldn't be that easy. His father and Annie's mother were still the two biggest obstacles to his and Annie's happiness. If they went ahead and got married, it would split both of their families apart.

Chapter Twenty-Eight

ANNIE FELT AS THOUGH SHE HAD ACTUALLY entered Jerusalem, waving branches and rejoicing. The Palm Sunday and Easter choir programs had been thrilling performances. She'd been transported to the foot of the cross to witness her Savior's heartbreaking death. And, with Mary Magdalene, she'd experienced the wonder and joy of her risen Lord, bringing her to tears.

But all the practices and high emotions had left her drained. By the next Sunday she was glad to relax in the congregation while the male chorus sang. As she listened to the male voices blending in beautiful four-part harmony, she thought of Donald's rich baritone, and thrilled with the thought of finally having a carefree afternoon with him.

He'd been so busy the past few weeks; she'd seen him for only a few stolen minutes here and there—when he came into town on errands and stopped at the furniture store. But he assured her, as soon as the harvest was over they'd spend more time together.

During one of their quick phone calls, he told her about the progress he'd made on their plans: "I've written to several places in Chicago about housing, the ones suggested in the letter I got. Haven't heard back yet, but it's still early." He also told her about Florence's engagement, and Sam's interest in the farm; they'd marveled together at God's answer to Donald's fleece.

That afternoon, Donald arrived promptly at two, and they drove to Smith Mountain, a solitary little mound near the foothills.

He showed her the caves he and his friends explored when they were in high school. Arms around each other, they sat under a scrub oak that overlooked the cemetery, the orange groves, and the pasturelands beyond.

Scuffing a clump of grass with his toe and looking toward the cemetery below, Donald said quietly, "My grandmother is buried at Gila River, at the camp." He cleared his throat. "I promised my grandfather to bring her here so they could be together again."

Annie felt sweet peace flow over her, and she silently thanked the Lord for this wonderful, considerate man. The time went all too fast, and as they left she had to satisfy herself with dreams of the next Sunday afternoon with him.

But that week, the weather turned hot. By Tuesday the temperature shot up to a record ninety-four degrees, twenty degrees above normal. When Donald called her at work that afternoon, he had bad news.

"I hate to tell you this. Of all times, this Sunday is the only day I'm allotted ditch water. I'll have to spend the afternoon irrigating. The plants are in the middle of flowering and this is a crucial time."

Annie tried to swallow her disappointment. "I understand. I know it's important to get a good crop. There's always the next Sunday."

But they realized that would be Mother's Day and, especially now, they both needed to spend that time with their mothers.

Then Donald remembered the Sunday after that was the Japanese youth club picnic. "Somehow I got roped into taking charge of the activities," Donald told her, his voice begging for her understanding.

"It's not just the kids from our church," he said. "There'll be groups from other towns." He apologized for not inviting her along. "I'll be running here and there, directing games and stuff, and it just wouldn't be fair to you."

They'd seen so little of each other in April—now it seemed that May would be the same. After she hung up the phone, Annie felt a twinge of resentment. *He could have turned down the picnic assignment,* a little voice whispered in her mind. *Sunday afternoons are supposed to be our special time together.*

But then she felt ashamed. With Donald's God-given ability for organization, it was only natural for him to take on that responsibility. In college, he always seemed happiest when he worked on committees and was active in other areas of leadership.

Maybe his father's attitude was also part of the reason he didn't invite her to the picnic. He'd said his father now treated him as a stranger, speaking to him extra politely and avoiding him as much as possible. His mother had told him not to worry, that things would work out. "Give it time," she'd said. But time was flying.

Annie wondered if his love for her was stronger than the *On* instilled in him. Would he someday resent her for coming between him and his father?

She knew that Donald longed for—needed—his father to understand and to give his blessing. But if that didn't happen, he'd assured Annie, they definitely would still get married. "Nothing will keep us apart."

She often found herself imagining married life with Donald, and she wished she could confide in her mother as she had in earlier days.

What will it be like, just the two of us, so far away from family and friends? If only I could talk to Mom about wedding clothes. About my trousseau. What I should take along.

Since first starting to work at the furniture store, Annie had saved most of her salary, so she had some money to buy things. But how could she plan ahead, not knowing what the weather would be like, what people wore? *I'll need linens. Bedding.* The thought of sharing a bed with Donald made her face grow hot.

Their three Sundays apart had passed slowly. But the special Mother's Day program at church and the extra time she'd spent with her mother hadn't helped their relationship. If anything, it seemed to widen the gulf between them. Every mention of "honor" and "obedience" at the service had felt like a stab wound in her heart. Although her mother didn't actually scold, her eyes were accusing, and Annie could almost hear the resentful thoughts.

Why couldn't her mother accept her happiness?

Donald called her the morning after his picnic. The bank loan had come through and they'd started the first picking of strawberries at dawn. He'd just rushed into the house to call her before changing clothes and taking a truckload to stores in Fresno.

When she asked him about the picnic, he said, "Oh, you know, all kinds of races, tug-of-war—boys on one side and girls on the other—and a volleyball tournament. Lots of pop and homemade ice cream. Sure wish I could have taken you. You would have loved it."

Annie thought, *If you only knew how much I'd wished that.* But she was glad to hear that the harvest had started. Now it wouldn't be long until they could spend more time together.

All that week, it was hard to keep her thoughts on her work. In spite of the thermometer zooming into the high nineties and beyond, her mother plunged into spring housecleaning. Annie took Friday off to help her wax the floors. She wondered if her mother was scrubbing and polishing so hard in order to work off her resentment of Donald.

It was lunchtime when they finished. After they ate, Annie's mother stayed at the kitchen table, fanning herself with a piece of cardboard. "Bartels say they bought strawberries already," she said.

Annie's heart skipped a beat. That meant Donald's family was right on schedule, maybe a little ahead. They usually let the public buy after they'd filled their orders to the stores. She tried to answer calmly. "I guess we should get some next week so we can make jam."

"No." Her mother stared at the calendar on the wall. "We need to get ours before they're picked over too much. I hear the Goertzens have a patch. Maybe we should try some of theirs this year."

Annie reminded her, though, of her reputation among the women at church for making the tastiest strawberry pies and jams. "You know the Nakamuras have the best fruit. And this year's crop is just as good. It's amazing how it recovered from the shock. You can't go to all that work and have your preserves turn out *niedrich.* You'd never be satisfied with second-rate."

Her mother shrugged, and went into her bedroom. She came out in a fresh housedress, ready for the drive to the Nakamura farm.

Near the road by the strawberry field, a flatbed truck was parked beside a standpipe. The truck-bed was partially loaded with stacks of full crates, and the rows of lush green plants were polka-dotted with red. Instead of the usual large crew of pickers, only a few people, wearing straw hats, were bent over the plants in the afternoon heat. Annie wondered if one of them was Donald.

As she parked beside the road, Donald's mother straightened up, went toward the house, and washed her hands at the water hose beside the porch steps.

"Allo, Annie, Missy Pennah," she called out. "You want berries? Cheaper if pick yourself."

Annie and her mother looked at each other. Her mother never could resist a bargain. And they'd come in everyday clothes, so a little dirt wouldn't matter. They each took a flat crate filled with empty berry boxes and headed for the rows that Mrs. Nakamura pointed out.

As Annie walked, she scanned the workers. They all wore blue work shirts and bandanna scarves around their necks, but she soon picked Donald out by his quick and agile movements. He stopped for a moment, as a boy handed an empty crate to him. The boy traded it for Donald's full one, then ran back toward the truck. Donald stood up to stretch as the youngster scampered away. Then he saw Annie. Her eyes met his, and her pulse raced. He waved and came toward her.

Stopping in the row next to her, he wasn't close enough to touch her, but his eyes expressed his longing. He looked around. Her mother was turned the other way. Putting one finger to his lips, he kissed it, then pointed it at her. "That's a down payment for later," he whispered. His look made her knees tremble.

Then his face turned businesslike, and he dropped to a squat. "Let me show you the best way to pick these berries."

The nearness of Donald was even more intoxicating than the fragrance of the ripe fruit, and Annie had a hard time concentrating. But she made herself look for the largest berries. It was true—this farm had the best strawberries. No other fields had such big luscious fruit. She commented on that, and Donald said his grandfather had a secret method and had passed it down to his family. But it took months of hard work.

"I see he's out in the field, too. He must be feeling a lot better."

"I can't keep him away. At least we've convinced him to rest when he's tired. Tell you what—if he comes this way, tell him '*Konnichiwa.*' See what he says."

"What does it mean?"

"It's a Japanese greeting." He made her repeat it until she pronounced it just as he had.

At first he kept pace with her as she picked, sometimes correcting but always encouraging. Then he worked up to his own rhythm, and by the time he finished his row she was only half through hers. He came back, carefully laid some of his berries in her crate, then said, "See you later," and went back to the other field.

Annie watched him go, and remembered his happiness about Florence, and her fiancé's willingness to take over the farm. But would their father use that as an excuse to change the ownership from Donald to his sister? Would he go as far as to disown Donald, his only son?

Annie thought that the financial part wouldn't bother Donald as much as the emotional wound. At least now, he and his father were still speaking to each other; a complete break would tear him up. Why did life have to be so complicated?

On her other side, her mother was ahead of her, too. Annie shook off her daydreams and picked faster. When her crate was full, she noticed that her mother had already straightened up. Her cotton dress was stuck to her back, and wet half-moons appeared under the arms.

When she and her mother took their fruit to the truck, Mrs. Nakamura met them there, wrote some numbers on a scrap of paper and smiled at Annie. "Good, sweet. You taste?"

Annie hung her head. "Just one. Maybe two. I couldn't resist."

"That okay. You make sure ripe, yes?" She turned to Annie's mother. "That one dollah. Enough? Want more?"

Annie's mother picked up a berry that had rolled onto the truck bed and placed it in one of her baskets. She wiped the perspiration off her forehead with the back of her hand. "I think we'll get another crate. We can work together this time."

Mrs. Nakamura pursed her lips and looked at her sideways. "Purty hot day. You sirsty? I get you tea."

Please, God, Annie prayed, *please let her accept.* It could be the beginning of friendship.

Annie thanked Mrs. Nakamura, loving her for her thoughtfulness, but her mother shook her head. "No, thanks. We'll hurry and finish up. I want to get that jam made. Come on, Annie."

When they reached their rows, Annie noticed Donald's grandfather a few rows over, heading toward the house. She waved at him, and he waved back. He swerved a little, stumbled, but caught himself and headed her way.

As he came near them, he gave a little bow and said, "Allo."

Annie smiled. What were those words Donald had taught her? "*Konnichiwa.*"

The old man laughed and bowed three more times, his eyes shining. "Velly good. You learn!" He glanced at Annie's mother, but she was busy picking and didn't look up.

He walked away, murmuring, "*Konnichiwa.*" He nodded, looking back at her, still grinning. "*Konnichiwa.*"

Annie watched him make his way to the house. He seemed a little unsteady, but he straightened his shoulders proudly, and she noticed a little lilt to his walk. Donald had said he knew about their plans and loved to tease him about getting married. She imagined the old man at Donald's age, and wondered if he'd been as handsome and confident. As romantic.

He leaned over and turned on the faucet by the back steps to get a drink out of the hose.

"No! No cold! Get sick." Donald's mother came running, amazingly fast for the short gliding steps she took. She went into the house, pushing the old man ahead of her. When they came out a few minutes later, he was carrying a steaming cup and sat down on the steps to sip from it.

She wished her mother had taken up Mrs. Nakamura's offer of tea. Wished she herself had insisted—her throat was getting awfully dry. She picked faster, glancing up only occasionally. If they had all this jam to make, they'd better get home soon.

They had nearly filled the baskets when Annie stood up to stretch her back. How could people do this day after day? She'd be glad to soak in a tub of hot water. Maybe even a bubble bath. With a glass of lemonade to sip. "Wow, am I—"

Her mother's face was pale, with red spots high on her cheeks. Annie had seen her like that when she was angry, but she didn't seem angry now. She was crouched on hands and knees over the crate of berries, staring—

Annie jumped over the row to her side. "What's the matter, Mom? Are you all right?"

Suddenly her mother collapsed onto the edge of the crate, scattering some of the berries.

"Mom!" Annie screamed, and bent over her mother, trying to lift her, but she was in too awkward a position.

Annie raised her head to call for help, but Donald was already on his way. He felt her mother's forehead and sucked in a breath. "She shouldn't be out in this heat." He picked her up as easily as he would a child and carried her to a shade tree in the yard. Annie followed, leaving the crate of berries.

Donald settled her mother in a grassy spot under the tree and looked around. "Do you have a pillow in the car?"

Before she could answer, his mother came out of the house with a cushion.

"Towels," he said. "Wet."

His mother ran back into the house and came back out with a basin and a stack of towels. Before his mother filled the basin, Annie soaked two of the towels at the hose, squeezed them out lightly and handed them to Donald. He stroked her mother's cheeks and forehead with one of them. "Loosen her dress at the collar."

Annie did as he said, and used the other damp towel to pat her mother's throat and neck.

"Take off her stockings and put a wet towel between her legs."

Annie's mind shut down, and all she could do was obey him. "Will she be okay?"

Donald felt the pulse in her mother's throat and nodded. "Mrs. Penner?" He patted her cheek. "Can you hear me?" He took the towel from Annie and squeezed a few drops onto her mother's lips. "Wet it some more."

After a few more drops, Annie's mother swallowed. She opened her eyes, looked straight into Donald's face, and moaned. Then her eyes rolled back.

Chapter Twenty-Nine

Annie bent over her mother's face as the wet towels brought her back to consciousness. Her mother blinked in the sunlight that filtered through the leaves, turned her face, then groaned. "Oh . . . my head. I can't . . . Where am I?" She tried to sit up, but Annie gently pressed her shoulders to the ground.

"Just lie still and rest, Mom. You got too hot in the sun and passed out." She hoped that's all it was—just a faint. "You need to cool off a little before you try to get up."

Donald, crouching behind her mother with a basin of wet towels, cleared his throat and passed Annie a cup of water. "Get her to drink some water. The more the better." He spoke quietly, but her mother seemed to recognize his voice.

She reached toward her throat, knocking the cup out of Annie's hand. Touching bare skin where her collar should be, her fingers scrabbled in vain to pull the buttons of her dress together. "What's going on?" She reached toward her legs. *"Ach, yauma,"* she moaned. "My stockings! What have you done?"

Annie moved closer and reached across to keep the towel between her mother's thighs. "Mom, you have to stay cool. Don't you understand?"

Her mother stretched out her hands and touched the dirt and clumps of grass around her. "Why am I on the ground?" She moved her shoulders. "And all wet?" Her breath came fast and shallow.

Annie sighed. How could she help her mother if she wouldn't cooperate?

Donald put a fresh damp towel on her mother's forehead. "She needs to get to a doctor as soon as possible. They'll stabilize her and send her to a hospital if necessary. What's your doctor's name?"

Annie tried to think. Her mother always used home remedies; neither of them had seen a doctor in years. But there was one in their church. Maybe he'd help them. "Dr. Entz. He's on Main Street, next to the gas company."

Donald nodded. He chewed on his lip and stared at Annie's car parked nearby. "Let's put her in the back of your car so she can lie down. Someone ought to notify the doctor so he'll be ready for her." He looked at his mother, but her eyes slid past his and she motioned with her chin.

He turned and saw his father coming. "Mrs. Penner is in danger of heatstroke," Donald announced. "We're taking her to a doctor."

"Have you called to let him know you're coming?" Rev. Nakamura glanced at Annie, then back to Donald.

"Not yet. We need to get there as fast as possible. I was hoping you or Mom—"

Annie moved closer. "Please, Rev. Nakamura—would you please call Dr. Entz? I don't have his number, but I'm sure it's in the phone book. I'd really appreciate it."

He gave one quick nod. "You go quickly. God be with you."

Donald picked up Annie's mother, wet towels and all, and hurried to the car before she could squirm away from him. Annie got there first and had the back door open. Mrs. Nakamura pushed the cushion in and Annie settled it under her mother's head again.

Donald crouched on the floor beside his patient, fingers on her pulse, then said, "Let's go." Annie jumped into the front seat and drove off as fast as she dared.

When they arrived at the doctor's office, the receptionist was waiting and held the door open for them. Donald carried Annie's mother into an examining room and put her down gently on the table. "Let me know when the doctor arrives," he whispered to Annie, and then he went back to the waiting room.

Annie helped the nurse undress her mother, then they slid ice packs under her arms to replace the towels. The receptionist stood with a clipboard. "Name?"

Annie glanced up. "Hers? Helena Penner."

"Age?"

Annie had to think. Was it fifty-one or two? Her mother moved a hand to her forehead and murmured, "Fifty-two."

"Height and weight?"

"Mother's an inch or two taller than I . . . five-four, I think. Maybe . . . about a hundred and forty pounds?"

Annie had never seen her mother undressed and she'd been discreet when she undid her mother's stockings under the tree. Now she stared in shock. Why was her mother wearing a full corset? On Sunday, sure, but something so tight on a hot day like this? And while picking berries out in the sun? No wonder she got overheated. How would they get her out of it?

The nurse, noticing Annie's hesitation, quickly unhooked the side fastenings. She deftly removed the corset, flipped a cotton gown on her patient, put an ice pack between her thighs, and covered her with a damp sheet.

Just as she slid a thermometer into her patient's mouth, Donald came in with Dr. Entz, explaining what he suspected and what had been done.

"Good, good," said the doctor. "You did the right thing."

Donald watched quietly, leaning against the door, as the doctor took Mrs. Penner's blood pressure and felt her pulse. "Eighty over fifty. Pulse 120." The doctor pulled out the thermometer. "Hundred three. Set up an IV."

The nurse did as he said, then changed the ice packs.

Dr. Entz turned to Annie. "She needs to get to a hospital."

Annie's mother rolled her head from side to side. Her face was still pale, with the bright red blotches on her cheeks. "No hospital. No! Annie, take me home. I'll rest a little." She gasped for air. "I have to . . . I have to make jam." Then she opened her eyes wide. "Where are my strawberries?"

Annie glanced at Donald. What was wrong with her mother? How could she think of jam at a time like this?

Donald moved to the side of the bed. "They're all right. We'll save them for you."

Her mother squeezed her eyes tight, then opened them again. "Why are *you* here?" She clutched Annie's arm. "Annie, I *told* you Japs couldn't be trusted."

Annie frowned. "Mom!" She glanced at Donald, but he lifted his palm and shook his head.

Dr. Entz took her mother's hand. "Mrs. Penner, this Japanese man saved your life. If it weren't for his quick action, you could have died."

Her mother frowned. "He didn't—"

Annie bent over her mother. "Donald knew it might be a sunstroke. He's treated cases like this at the internment camp. He knew just what to do." She leaned in closer. "It would be best if you went to a hospital now."

Her mother flailed a hand to dismiss that idea, and Annie had a thought. "Maybe . . . maybe the doctor would let you come home . . . if you agree to have Donald come check on you and report back to the doctor."

Annie looked up at Donald. A smile lurked at his lips and his eyes shone. He nodded and gave her a thumbs-up. She felt so proud of him she could have hugged him. But now was not a good time.

Dr. Entz took her mother's temperature again, looking thoughtfully at Donald, then at Annie, and back at Donald. "Down almost a degree." He felt her pulse, then said, "Mrs. Penner, do you trust *me?*"

Her mother looked puzzled. "Sure! You're Mennonite, of course I trust you."

Dr. Entz gave a wry smile, then turned sober. "Then you must do exactly what I say."

"*Yo,* I will."

"This young man has had medical experience and knows what problems to look for. I want you to follow his instructions to the letter." He repeated: "To—the—letter! Promise? If not, it's got to be the hospital."

Her mother looked at Donald, her lips trembling. Then she looked up at Annie.

Annie waited, her eyebrows raised in question. She felt as though their roles had been switched. She was now the parent and her mother the child—a child who needed to learn a hard lesson.

Finally, her mother nodded. "All right." She closed her eyes and added in a whisper, "If that's the only way." A tear rolled down the side of her cheek. Annie took a tissue out of her pocket and blotted it.

Dr. Entz turned to the nurse. "As soon as the IV is finished, if she's down at least half a degree more, get a robe for her to wear home and help her on with her shoes. No stockings, no corset. Put them in a bag for her." He turned to Annie and Donald. "Both of you, come to my office. I'll give you instructions."

Sitting at his desk, he motioned for them to be seated. "I've heard about you two. People talk a lot." He looked at Donald. "After watching you, hearing your opinions, I'm impressed. You'll make a good doctor, and I wish you well in medical school." He reached into a drawer, brought out a stethoscope and blood pressure cuff. "You've used these before, yes?"

Donald nodded. "Lots of times, at camp. The medics, too."

Dr. Entz handed the instruments to Donald. "I'll need a report every two hours. Keep the ice packs on until her temperature's normal. If she worsens, call me immediately." He turned to Annie. "Do you have a thermometer?"

"Yes."

"Make sure she rests until she's been without fever a whole day. Can you keep your house cool?"

"We have a room cooler in the parlor and a plug-in fan."

"Good." He stood up and shook hands with Donald, then Annie. Then he gave a half-smile. "No jam-making until the day *after* she's completely well."

The doctor held open his office door, and as they went out he added, "God bless you. I wish you much happiness."

When they got home, her mother settled into bed with dry towels to protect the sheet. The crisis apparently over, Annie's legs were so shaky she could hardly stand.

Several thoughts churned through her mind. What if her mother had died? Why was she willing to pick the berries herself just to save a few pennies? Why had she been too proud to be seen without a corset?

When her patient was comfortable, a light quilt up to her chin and her arms folded over her chest, Annie plugged in the fan and then called Donald.

Her mother's eyes widened as he came to her side, and she opened her mouth—but Annie slipped the thermometer in before she could object. "Remember what the doctor said," Annie warned. "Donald knows what heat can do to you. He and his people were in Arizona . . . in blazing sun, with no trees and not much water. If he hadn't come running when you fainted, if he hadn't put on the wet towels, you wouldn't be here now." She wouldn't mention the corset in front of Donald, but her mother would hear about that later.

While Annie was talking, Donald took her mother's pulse and blood pressure. Then he smiled. "Better." He looked at the thermometer. "Down another two-tenths. I'll call the doctor if you'll show me where the phone is."

Annie smoothed her mother's hair back, adjusted her pillows and quilt, then followed Donald out of the room and led him to the kitchen.

"I'm so proud of you, so thankful," she told him. "In spite of the way she's treated you, you took care of her. Even Dr. Entz could tell you were a notch above most men."

He dropped into a chair, pulled her onto his lap and kissed her. "You've been a wonderful help, too. The way you solved that hospital problem—you're a real jewel, my sweet Annie." He lay his cheek against her soft hair and held her close.

Finally he squirmed his way out of the chair and stood up. "I better call the doctor. Then I'll get my father to pick me up. I need to get home and help with the crop. Be back in two hours."

It was seven o'clock that evening when Annie heard Donald's car. She opened the front door before he could knock. "Mom's sleeping."

He'd changed into khaki pants and a clean shirt, and smelled of spice. He looked tired, but when he took her face into his hands and looked deep into her eyes, his were glowing. "You're so beautiful." He kissed her forehead, her eyelids, and finally found her lips. When they came up for air, he said, "Better wake her or she won't sleep during the night . . . and you won't get any rest."

But when Annie went in to check, her mother was sitting on the edge of her bed, her feet searching for her slippers. "I'm all right now."

Annie sighed. This wouldn't be an easy recuperation. "Mom, you promised. Donald is here to check on you. Let me tuck you back in." While talking, she eased her mother back under the covers, then called, "Okay, she's ready!"

Donald came in, the stethoscope around his neck, his manner as professional as a real doctor. "How are you feeling, Mrs. Penner?"

"I'm fine. There's no need to go through all this."

Donald slipped the cuff around her arm and pumped it up. "Maybe not. But we have to make sure. We don't want you to have a relapse. It can happen, you know." He watched the dial closely, then released her arm. He checked the thermometer, and said, "Looks good. Still going down. What's your normal blood pressure?"

Annie's mother stared at him. "I don't know. I haven't had it taken since . . . since Annie's father died."

"That must have been a very hard time."

She nodded. "Worst time of my life. I still miss him so much. It's not easy, raising a daughter alone." She turned her head away.

While Donald phoned in the report, Annie stayed with her mother. She fingered the quilt edge, studying the little pieces of her childhood dresses and her father's shirts. "You loved Dad a lot."

"Of course! You don't know what it's like to lose a husband. My whole life was torn apart."

Annie ran her finger around a little square, feeling the stitches so neat and even. "Yet, that's what you want for me." Her mother started to protest, but Annie went on. "I'm not a child with a crush. I've loved Donald for more than four years. Most of that time, he was gone. I don't know why he stopped writing . . . he thought that *I'd* stopped writing. But when he came back, we both knew we were meant for each other. We've prayed about it, searched the Word, and are at peace."

She lifted her mother's head, plumped the pillow, then put it back under her head. "If I lost him now, it would be like you losing Dad. Do you want my life torn apart, too?"

Her mother was quiet a long time. Then she rolled her head from side to side and tears flooded her eyes. "Oh, *kindt,* my heart is so heavy. There's something I haven't told you."

Chapter Thirty

DONALD'S HAND FROZE. HE'D JUST RAISED his knuckles to rap on the open door of Mrs. Penner's bedroom. Then he heard Annie say, "What is it, Mom? Is it something about Dad?"

Mrs. Penner turned and noticed him, and he saw tears in her eyes. He cleared his throat. "Excuse me. Dr. Entz gave me a message for you, but I'll wait until later."

To his surprise, Mrs. Penner reached out and beckoned him in. "Stay. You need to hear this too." She took a handkerchief from the bedside table and wiped her eyes. "First, I want to thank you . . . Donald . . . for what you did for me. Now that my head is more clear, I realize the danger I was in. You really did save my life."

Donald nodded his acceptance of her thanks and waited for the rest of her sentence. There had to be a "but"—as in, "but now you must stay away from my daughter."

Mrs. Penner went on. "You helped me and have been kind and . . . I'm sorry for the way I spoke to you. Please forgive me. My brain must have been curdled by the heat."

Again Donald nodded, still waiting, his eyes fixed on hers.

When Mrs. Penner hesitated, Annie looked puzzled. "What about Dad? Did he have some kind of sickness, something I might have inherited?"

Her mother sighed heavily. "No. It's not about your father." She blew her nose, then struggled to sit up. Annie helped her and propped pillows behind her.

"It's about you . . . and Donald." She closed her eyes and shook her head, and the next words came out in a rush. "I'm so ashamed. I have no excuse. Except that I love you, Annie. I truly wanted the best for you. And I was so afraid."

Annie backed away from the bed, reached for Donald's hand and held it tightly. Her fingers were cold, her face pale. "Mom . . . what are you saying?" She glanced up at Donald, a horrified look on her face. "No . . . the letters . . . you weren't the one . . . you couldn't—"

Mrs. Penner nodded as the tears ran down her cheeks. "All these years I've felt so guilty. Over and over, I've asked the Lord to forgive me, but felt no release."

Donald frowned. "I don't understand. How could you have intercepted all those letters? Mine, hers—" He shook his head. "That's impossible." But watching her, seeing her unable to look him in the eyes, he knew she would've gone to any lengths to keep them apart. How she must hate him! He felt a cramp in the pit of his stomach and wanted to leave. But he knew there was more, and he had to hear it all.

Mrs. Penner wiped her face. "That first summer . . . Annie, remember how you told me what Florence had written, the conditions at the camp, all their hardships? Well, one day when I was putting away the laundry, I saw her letter on your dresser. It had been opened, and I took it out and read it."

Annie gasped, and her mother held up a hand. "I know. I shouldn't have. But I wanted to tell the ladies in my sewing circle about the hardships at the camp so we could pray for Florence and her family. Since you already told me, I figured you wouldn't mind me looking at it once more. What difference would it make?"

She shook her head, then looked at Donald. "That's when I saw your letter. At that time, Annie hadn't told me she was writing you, too . . . so that worried me. And after reading it, I was shocked. I could tell there was something going on between you . . . something much more than friendship. I was . . . horrified."

Donald drew his arm around Annie. He was afraid, too. Afraid that this would be the turning point, when Annie would be forced to choose between her mother and him. Was her love for him strong enough? He felt her muscles tense, and he looked around, found a chair and pulled it up for her. He stood behind her, his hands on her shoulders.

But Annie pulled forward and leaned toward her mother. "Why did you have to be so sneaky? Why didn't you just discuss it with me?"

Her mother shook her head. "What good would it have done? I was so upset that all I could think of was to stop the romance before it was too late. I thought . . . if you didn't hear from him, you'd stop writing and, with all the nice Mennonite men around, it wouldn't take you long to forget him. So I made sure I got to the mailbox first."

Annie looked around. "Where are the letters now? Where did you hide them?"

Mrs. Penner hung her head and spoke so softly Donald couldn't believe he heard right. "I burned them."

He felt as though he'd been kicked in the stomach. "You . . . burned them? Even the ones from overseas? While I was risking my life to keep our country safe, you destroyed the only things that kept me going?"

Annie grabbed her mother's arm. "What about mine? Why didn't he get the ones I sent?"

"I watched you put them in the mailbox and took them out before the carrier came."

"And I guess you read all of those, too." Annie's voice trembled and red spots showed on her cheeks. Donald had never seen her so angry.

"No. I didn't want to know what they said. I'd only read the one I mentioned . . . the one that had been opened. The one I thought you'd told me about." Her mother reached out and touched Annie's hand, but Annie jerked away.

"I mailed some at the post office," Annie said. "What happened to them?"

"I don't know. Maybe those got through."

Donald nodded slowly. "Those were the ones that didn't quite make sense. No wonder . . . you hadn't gotten my questions."

Annie got up and stood beside Donald. She shook her head. "Mom, you say you love me, and still you could break my heart like that?"

"I was desperate!" Mrs. Penner leaned forward in her intensity, palms turned up. "What else could I do? I thought it was for the best. You'd get over it quickly and settle down to a normal life." Mrs. Penner looked at Donald and sank back. "You have to understand. I have nothing against you personally. It's just that all our lives, we Mennonites are taught to avoid the rest of the world. It was bad enough that I married a man from a different branch of Mennonites."

She signed deeply and shook her head. "When my husband died, Annie was small. My life revolved around her, and I tried to raise her the best I could. But our church only had a few other children her age. So when she finished high school, I wanted her to have an opportunity to meet suitable young men. Her own kind."

Her eyes flickered, then focused again on Donald. "I chose to move to Rosemond . . . *specifically* for the big Mennonite Brethren church. It had a large group of young people, and I wanted Annie to have good Christian friends."

"And marry a good Mennonite farmer," Annie said bitterly. "Problem was, those who were interested in me didn't care that I had a brain. All they wanted was a *husfrue* . . . someone to keep house for them!"

Donald gently guided Annie back to the chair. The anger and fear that still boiled in him was mixed with a little understanding. "Mrs. Penner, I know what you're saying. My people feel the same way. My father would love to see me married to a nice Japanese Christian girl. But when Annie and I met in college, we found more in common with each other than with our own kind. And in spite of being apart so long . . . three whole years . . . and in spite of not hearing from each other, our love lasted."

Annie added, "Race doesn't matter to us. Our love goes beyond barriers like that. *God's* love isn't limited."

"I know that. But what about . . . children? If you marry, they'll be a mixture. They'll be different. Where will they fit in? What if other children don't accept them?"

Donald felt his neck getting hot and fought to get himself under control. Until the internment, he'd felt accepted. He'd grown up thinking he was American. But now, no matter what he did, he still wasn't good enough. And people like Mrs. Penner would pass that idea down to his innocent children.

Annie spoke before he could. "Our family's already a mixed bunch. German, Swiss, Dutch, Flemish—even a little French thrown in somewhere."

"But all Mennonites."

Annie gave a short laugh. "Mennonites aren't always perfect. Didn't one of our uncles run a brewery in his shed during Prohibition? And another one, wasn't he kicked out of church for running off with the choir director's wife?"

"*Na, kindt.* That was a long time ago."

Annie shrugged. "And I remember a story about your grandfather. His wife died just before they were to leave Russia and come to America. He took another woman with him on the ship—a Russian woman. And didn't he pretend she was his wife so they wouldn't lose their place on the ship?"

"Well, those were dangerous times. They had to leave quickly before the Communists found out. I think they did have a secret wedding with a minister before they left Russia. They were married in the sight of the Lord. As soon as they arrived here they were married legally."

Annie's mouth fell open, and she looked at Donald. He stared back at her and, in spite of his misery, felt a smile creeping over his lips. Was she thinking what he was thinking? He nodded at her. They'd talk later.

He looked back at Mrs. Penner. "The important thing is, Annie and I are both Christians, willing to serve the Lord in whatever capacity he leads us. If not in a Mennonite church, then in a Baptist one. Or even nondenominational . . . as long as it's true to the Word."

She looked at him a long time with great sadness in her eyes. Then she nodded. "I know you're a good man and that you and Annie love each other. I have to accept that."

The cramp in Donald's stomach eased. He took a deep breath and released it slowly, then quietly said, "Thank you." He waited, sensing that something was still bothering her.

She slumped deeper into the pillows and turned her head. "But if you take her away to Chicago, how will I stand it? She's all I have. I may never see her again."

Annie leaned and whispered to her. She stroked her mother's forehead, gave her a drink of water, and helped her settle down in bed.

Donald slipped out of the room and went into the parlor, where he sank down on the couch, exhausted.

What a day, what an emotional strain! He'd always considered himself in good condition. He thought back to the war, when he hauled many a litter, even lugged a dying man on his back for miles. But working since five this morning, carrying his sweetheart's struggling, resentful mother, trying to keep the woman alive—that was something else.

He still found it hard to believe that Mrs. Penner had stopped their letters. He didn't know if he could forgive that.

But he had to grant her this: It must have taken a lot of courage to admit that she'd wronged them. It hurt to see her pain now, but what could he do about it? Chicago *was* a long way from California, and their marriage wouldn't be legal here. For Annie's sake, should he offer to take her along with them?

His own mother was still old-fashioned enough to stay in the background. But Annie's mother was outspoken. Although she claimed now to respect him, she must still have a lot of doubts.

What would it be like, her living with them, always there? Could he stand that, knowing that she had once kept them apart? Would she be tempted to do it again, in other subtle ways?

He stood up when Annie, wearing a tired smile, came into the room.

"I got her calmed down. Told her we'd write often, and she could come visit."

"Good." He pulled her into the circle of his arms, and she burrowed her face into his shoulder. He sighed, relieved. He wouldn't need to make that offer. If Annie's love was strong enough to survive everything that had happened, their marriage would be all right.

"Oh, Donald," she whispered. "How could she do a thing like that? My own mother!" He felt her tremble and realized she was crying. Her pain stabbed him right through the heart, and he got even angrier with her mother for being the cause.

But for Annie's sake he needed to swallow his own hurt. His lips tightened, and he nestled his face in her hair as he stroked her back. "She thought she was protecting you."

"I know. She didn't realize what she was doing."

If Annie could forgive her mother, he ought to do the same. It was the only way to begin a Christian marriage. He took a deep breath. Sometimes, the Lord gave very difficult assignments. But he'd pray about it. With God's help, he'd be able to forgive her, too.

Then he snapped his fingers and turned Annie to face him. "I nearly forgot. Dr. Entz's message! He wanted me to tell your mother, if she continues to improve, and you check on her during the night, I could wait until morning to report to him. But . . . what if she has a setback . . . especially after all this emotional upset?"

Annie wiped her cheeks with her fingers, but there were still tears shining on her lashes, and she was more beautiful than ever. "I think she'll be okay. Now that she's confessed about the letters and it's off her conscience, she should feel a lot better. I think she'll sleep pretty well tonight. I'll put up a cot in her room, and set the alarm. If there's any problem, I'll call the doctor."

Her lips trembled again, and she shook her head. "Why did she have to *destroy* them? If only she'd kept them . . . at least I'd be able to read what you were going through in the war."

Donald led her to the couch and pulled her down beside him. "Actually, I didn't write much about the war. It would have been censored anyway, and you would've received a letter full of holes."

She looked into his eyes, her lips temptingly close. "What *did* you write?"

"Well, I said I'd like to do this—" He hugged her tightly. "And this—" He smoothed her curls, letting them wind around his fingers. "And this—" He kissed her once, then again.

Her fingers slid over his neck, tickled past his ear, and crept around his shoulders. Shivers ran down his back, and he could hardly breathe. A few moments earlier he'd felt exhausted, but now his heart beat so fast he wondered if he'd sleep tonight.

Finally, he moved away a little, raked his fingers through his hair, and tried to calm his hungry heart. He had to look away from her face—those lips were just too sweet.

She reached for his hand and smoothed out his fingers. Her touch made him wild, but he covered her hand with his other one and held it tightly.

He cleared his throat, not sure he could speak. "Annie," he said, his voice intense. "When we were with your mother just now, she said something about her grandfather having a secret wedding."

She grinned and nodded her head. "Yes!" then she looked around the room speaking quickly and with excitement in her voice. "We could do something like that. Right here in the parlor. With just our family and best friends."

"My mother would love that. She was sad that she wouldn't be able to attend our wedding."

"This way we can have the nice clothes, cake, flowers, and all—"

"And as soon as we get to Illinois, we'll find a justice of peace and make it legal!" He could hardly believe his life was falling into place after all.

Annie's eyes sparkled at him. "Mr. and Mrs. Donald Nakamura."

"For the rest of our lives." Who could wish for anything better!

"Forever and ever."

He sealed that with another kiss. Just then, Annie's mother called. Annie sighed and went to check on her.

Annie was gone for quite some time. When she returned she smiled at Donald, her expression like that of a mother who'd just put a reluctant child to bed. “I needed to help Mom get settled for the night. Do you mind helping me put up the cot?” she asked.

“Be glad to. I’ll check her once more, and then I’d better leave.”

When Donald drove away, his heart sang. Mrs. Penner was recovering, she more or less accepted their marriage and, in spite of the hurt, at least the mystery of the letters was solved.

Then he sobered. If only his father would come around. It would be so wonderful if he would conduct that special ceremony.

Chapter Thirty-One

On Sunday, Annie and her mother stayed home. Although her mother seemed better, she was still weak. They'd miss the *kinderfest*—the children's day picnic—an all-day outdoor event. But being around people and answering their questions would be too much of a strain, and Dr. Entz had said for her to rest a few more days.

Although the picnic, held at Mooney Grove, was called *kinderfest,* it was for the entire family. The children would recite their pieces in the morning service, which was held in the pavilion. After lunch the young people would get as far away as possible from the adults and gather in small groups to take pictures and play circle games—Two Deep, or maybe Flying Dutchman—games that allowed boys and girls to stand close or hold hands while running, with no one objecting.

But the rowboats were always the biggest attraction, and girls from grammar school on up gauged their popularity by how many boys invited them for a ride.

Every year, Annie'd had her share of boat rides. But she never dreamed that someday she'd receive a marriage proposal in one of those boats.

She sighed. Those childhood memories now seemed so silly. After that cold day in February—the thrill of riding in a boat with Donald and having the park all to themselves—the place would never be the same for her.

She'd wondered about asking him to the picnic. But then she thought about the two of them, eating alongside the others, walking together along the lagoon. She could almost see the shocked faces, hear the whispering, the older people taking offense at seeing them together.

In the past, she'd always enjoyed the *kinderfest.* But without Donald along, she didn't mind missing it. Instead, she and her mother had a little service of their own in the parlor. Annie played hymns on the piano, many of them her mother's requests. "In the Garden" was one of her mother's favorites—it was the one her father had loved to sing. For herself, she chose "Great Is Thy Faithfulness." When she came to the phrase, "strength for today and bright hope for tomorrow," she thought of the time she and Donald had sung it together on the way to the mountains. God had really answered their prayers and had given them hope for the future.

Sometimes her mother sang along softly, but mostly she just hummed. Then she asked Annie to choose Scripture to read. Annie had no trouble picking a chapter. Next to the Psalms and the Gospels, she loved Romans, and she read the first thirteen verses of the tenth chapter.

When she came to verse 12 and read "the same Lord . . . is rich unto all that call upon him," she noticed tears rolling down her mother's cheeks.

"Oh, *Anchen,*" she said. "Can you ever forgive me? All along, I knew I was wrong. I just didn't know *how* wrong. What it was doing to you . . . and to Donald."

Annie tried to swallow the lump in her throat. She loved her mother dearly, and the thought of almost losing her to heatstroke had been frightening. But those three years she and Donald were apart had been so hard. All those agonies of wondering where he was, why he hadn't written, if he'd forgotten about her. And Donald himself. What about the hardships *he'd* gone through? Torn away from his home—stripped of his citizenship, his career, and his dignity, then risking his life in the war—

None of that was her mother's fault, but it *was* her fault that Annie hadn't been able to give him comfort and encouragement—the hope he'd needed so badly during that time.

Her mother still looked at her, waiting for an answer.

Annie thought of the Lord's Prayer. *Forgive us our debts, as we forgive our debtors.*

Suddenly she realized that she wasn't without blame either. If she'd been honest with her mother—had admitted her friendship with Donald and her growing feelings back then—if she'd ridden through the disapproval and rebukes and taken a stand right away, maybe none of that would have happened.

She knelt down beside the couch and took her mother's hands in hers. "Let's pray the Lord's Prayer together."

When they came to the forgiveness part, they both burst into tears, and Annie threw her arms around her mother. "I forgive you. I don't want any hard feelings between us. Our time together is too short."

At that moment, Annie sensed that their relationship had changed. They'd always be mother and daughter, but now they were also two adult friends who could be honest with each other. Maybe her mother wouldn't call her *kindt* anymore! She knew the two of them would enjoy planning the special wedding ceremony.

But there was a more urgent problem. What should she do about Monday? If she left her mother alone, a little burst of energy might make her decide to cook, wash, or even do more canning. And there was still that jam to make.

It was a bad time to take another day off work. Mr. McGinnis had hired a new salesman and needed her to help him with the contracts and layaways.

Did she dare call Grandma Bartsch and ask her to come and stay a few days? She hadn't talked to her grandparents since that disastrous Christmas get-together, and her mother had been too upset to get in touch with them.

If she asked her mother about it, she'd say no. She might even get angry. But the more Annie thought about it, the more she felt an urge to phone them.

It was the right thing to do. Her grandparents ought to hear about the heatstroke, and it was a big enough concern to warrant a long-distance call.

When her mother was napping after lunch, Annie placed the call. On the other end, the phone rang once, twice, three times. She wondered if they'd gone visiting. But after the fourth ring her grandfather answered. "Bartsch here."

It was so good to hear his voice again. But she tensed up, wondering how he'd respond to her. "Grandpa? This is Annie."

Silence. Then she heard him clear his throat. "*Yo?*"

"It's Mom." She couldn't keep her voice from shaking. "She's had a heatstroke."

"*Neh, obah.* How bad is it?"

"She's some better now. But I have to work tomorrow, and—"

"I'll put Grandma on." But she still heard him breathing. "It's . . . good to hear from you."

Her heart swelled with love for him and her voice cracked. "I've missed you and Grandma so much."

"Yes." His own voice trembled. "Well . . . here she is."

"*Liebchen,* how are you?"

Annie's tears flowed, and she didn't bother to wipe them away. After she explained her problem, her grandmother sounded eager to come and stay a few days. "I'll just throw some things together and your grandpa will bring me. Don't worry." In a lower voice she added, "I'm so glad you called us. So many times I've thought of you. It takes courage to make the first move in healing a break . . . courage I didn't have."

Annie wondered if that lack of courage went as far back as her mother's marriage. Had it been her father's death, when she was little, that allowed them back into the family's arms? No wonder her mother was upset. For a long time, she'd been caught between her parents and her husband. And now the same thing had happened with her own child. Why couldn't her grandparents see that God's love could reach beyond the Mennonite Brethren church?

"Annie, let your mother know we'll be there in an hour or so. And thank you again for calling," her grandmother added.

They hadn't asked about Donald, and she hadn't brought up the subject. It would be better to tell them in person. But she did explain to her mother that she'd called them and that they cared enough to come.

When they arrived, Annie's mother was lying on the couch with a thermometer in her mouth. She smiled around the thermometer, but only lifted a hand in greeting—because Donald was on one knee beside her, taking her blood pressure. To Annie's surprise, he'd stopped by a little while ago, still wearing his Sunday trousers, starched white shirt and tie.

Now he took the stethoscope from his ears and stood up. "Very good. One hundred twenty over seventy, pulse sixty."

Annie introduced her grandparents, and he shook hands with them. "I'm glad you could come. I know Annie appreciates it."

Her grandfather said, "It was kind of you to make a house call, Dr. . . . uh . . . I didn't catch your name."

Annie swallowed hard. She should have warned them. But if she had, they might not have come at all. "This is my fiancé, Donald Nakamura." What if they turned around and left?

Her grandfather took a step back. His Adam's apple moved but no words came out. He looked at Annie's mother, at the blood pressure cuff Donald was folding into a case. "I . . . didn't know you were a doctor."

Donald smiled modestly, tilting his head. "Not yet. I start medical school in the fall. But Mrs. Penner didn't want to go to the hospital, and I have experience with cases like this, so Dr. Entz worked out a system for me to keep him informed of her progress. If you'd like, I can call him so you can speak to him."

Her grandfather looked from Annie to Donald and back again. "I know Dr. Entz. He's a good man. If he made that arrangement, it must be all right." He lowered himself into an easy chair.

Donald took the thermometer from Annie's mother, and she sat up. "Donald saved my life. If it weren't for his quick thinking and help, I wouldn't be here."

Annie added, "He worked at the camp hospital. It was awfully hot in the Arizona desert, so he saw a lot of people with the same problems."

Grandma Bartsch sat beside her daughter on the couch. "But what were you doing on such a hot day? Even I know enough to stay inside with a glass of lemonade."

"I wanted to make jam."

Grandma still looked puzzled, and Annie thought again about her mother's corset. But now was not the time to bring it up. Instead, she explained that they'd wanted to save a little money by picking the strawberries themselves.

"Well, you should have waited for a cool morning."

Annie nodded. "I know." But she also knew some good things had come out of it. "Donald was right there, giving her emergency treatment. He even carried her to the car."

Her mother gave a wry smile. "I was so far gone, I didn't know what was happening."

Annie glanced at Donald, and he shrugged. "I only did what I could."

Her grandfather nodded. "We're much obliged to you." Then his brow wrinkled. "Nakamura? Wasn't that the name of the minister who gave sermons on the radio?"

"That's my father. He pastors our Japanese Baptist church."

"I used to listen to him. Very good, sound doctrine. Do you attend there?"

Annie couldn't resist putting in a plug for Donald. "He's the choir director. You should hear him sing! He had a few solos on his father's program, too."

"*Na, yo.* And you're a Christian, *yo?*"

Donald's expression was pleasant, his posture relaxed. "Accepted the Lord when I was sixteen." Annie was proud of him for being neither defensive nor pushing too hard.

Grandpa Bartsch nodded. "That's what's important. Ephesians 4 tells us there is one God, one Father of all, and unto every one is given His grace."

Donald nodded and smile crinkles emphasized his dark eyes. "Does that include Japanese?"

"I guess so. It does say everyone, doesn't it?"

Annie had to know. "Grandpa, would that also go for other kinds of Mennonites? Like my dad?"

His bushy eyebrows lowered and his face wrinkled into sadness. "*Ach, kindt,* that was a different time."

Her grandmother shook her head. "The church was so strict on forms of baptism back then, the leaders couldn't see any farther. Backward, forward, kneeling, standing, once, twice, three times . . . it's a wonder the Lord didn't give up on all of us. We should have followed Jesus' example instead of the Pharisees'."

Annie's grandfather looked surprised at his wife's outburst, and she hunched her shoulders, her face coloring. "Sorry. I shouldn't have spoken out like that. But it's true."

Annie was glad. It needed to be said.

Her mother had been following the conversation with pursed lips, and now asked, "Would you do things differently today? Not turn your backs on me as though I was trash?"

Grandma Bartsch hugged her daughter. "Many times I've prayed for pardon. But I know now that wasn't enough. We wronged you, Helena. Your father and I, the church council . . . all of us." She wept into her handkerchief. "And now I ask your forgiveness."

The two women cried together, and Grandpa Bartsch blew his nose loudly. "I, too, am ashamed of those stubborn years. If you can find it in your heart—"

Annie's mother motioned impatiently. "Of course, those were harsh times, I know that. It's easier to forgive than to forget the hurts. But now we must think of Annie. Do we want her to go through the same hurt?"

Grandpa Bartsch stood up, looked at Annie, and opened his big strong arms. She went into them, and his deep voice rumbled into her hair. "You've always been precious to us. I can't bear the thought of losing you."

Losing her? "Grandpa, what do you mean? You couldn't lose me if you tried." She took Donald's hand and brought him close. "All you have to do is welcome the man I'm marrying."

Her grandfather turned to him, shaking his head. "Marriage is a lifetime of adjustment. It's hard enough when two people have been brought up the same, and when there are such differences—"

Donald's eyes sobered. "We've discussed that and prayed about it. Annie and I feel the Lord has brought us together, and we're determined to make our marriage work. We'll gladly embrace each other's culture."

Annie thought about the Bartsch Christmas celebration—the horrified reaction to Donald's picture in her strawberry locket. If she and Donald ever came back from Chicago, would the rest of the family welcome either of them?

She said, "It's strange, Grandpa, but Donald and I are more alike than different. We enjoy the same things, agree on almost everything."

"*Yo,* you think so now . . . time will tell." He stroked his chin as he looked from one to the other. "But maybe you're right. Maybe this time I was too hasty in judging before I saw the whole picture." He nodded slowly. "One thing I *can* see. This young man will make something of himself, Lord willing." He sighed. "*Ach, yo.* The world's shrinking, and we all have to learn to get along." He reached out his hand and Donald shook it. "I'm glad I met you. I'll go home and chew things over in my mind while doing chores. An old man like me can't change my way of thinking too suddenly."

Strange, Annie thought. The radio sermons—with the few words of Japanese at the end to encourage the old people who didn't speak English—the same program that caught the ears of the FBI and sent Donald's father to prison—was now the very thing that made her grandfather respect Donald.

When Donald got home, he was surprised to see his mother bustling around a hot kitchen, the counter filled with small glass jars. The smell of sweet strawberries filled the air. "Mom, what are you doing? Sunday's a day of rest."

She wiped sweat from her forehead with the back of her hand. "No waste. Your father preach that Sunday okay pull mule from well. These berries one big mule."

"You mean . . . these are the Penners's strawberries? You made all this jam for them?"

She nodded. He picked her up and whirled her around.

"Naughty boy, you." She straightened her clothes. "You think they like?"

"Sure!" At least, he knew Annie would. He hoped her mother would appreciate the effort, too. Maybe Japanese-made jam wouldn't be up to Mennonite standards. "I'll take you over there so you can give them to her."

She giggled, covering her mouth with her hand. "No, no. You take. I too ashamed. Maybe no good."

"They're good all right. I can smell how good. Hey, listen . . . you'll be related soon. Might as well get to know each other."

She pushed his shoulder. "No. Plenty time, that. This you take."

He finally gave up, and after church that evening he delivered the jam. His mother had put the jars in a large box, carefully padding each jar with newspaper.

Annie was touched. Her mother was speechless but finally said, "Tell your mother thanks ever so much. She didn't have to do that!"

"I'll pass that on," said Donald. "But I think she'd be really pleased if you told her yourself."

Mrs. Penner's eyes widened. Donald knew it would be hard for her, as it was for his mother, to make that first contact. But he also knew she'd do the right thing.

Annie's grandmother sat in a rocker with a German magazine open on her lap. Donald's eye was drawn to a picture, an institution of some sort. He pointed to it and asked, "Is that a Mennonite hospital?"

"Bible Institute. A new one, just three years old." Mrs. Bartsch looked at it again. "They're looking for a matron for the girls' dormitory."

Annie laughed. "There's a job for you, Mom. A matron job. Instead of missing me, you could mother fifty other girls."

"What would I do with fifty girls? One is bad enough."

Donald asked, "Where is it?"

Mrs. Bartsch held the magazine up to him. "Terrance, Illinois. Near Chicago."

Mrs. Penner stared at her. "Near Chicago?" With a twinkle in her eye, she looked up at Annie. "I wonder if I *could* do something like that."

Donald asked, "Why not?" That might solve one of the problems. If she was that close to them, she might not feel so abandoned. And she'd still be far enough away to have her own life.

After Annie's mother and grandmother went to bed, Donald and Annie made a few more plans for their ceremony. Who to invite, what kind of clothes to wear. She said she didn't want a formal wedding dress, but a nice suit she could wear often. Donald said that Japanese weddings usually included a full meal in a restaurant, but Annie said her mother would be more comfortable with a light *faspa.* Just *tvehbock,* cold cuts, maybe salads, and the cake."

"Well, okay. But the cake has to have the tiny bride and groom dolls on it. That's what my mother's looking forward to."

Annie raised her eyebrows. "Don't know what my church would say. They might think it's idol worship."

Donald laughed. "I promise . . . we won't pray to them. Not even a Japanese bow. Besides, how many from your church will be here?"

They counted. She wanted Malinda and her fiancé, of course, and Dr. Entz. Her grandparents, if they'd be willing, and any close relatives who might come around by then. But nobody who opposed their marriage.

He wanted Sho and Tom, and a few other friends. They still teased him a lot, but seemed happy for him. "If we wait until August, Florence will be home." Then he frowned. "But . . . won't you regret not having a big church wedding, with a bridal gown, all the trimmings?"

Annie shook her head. "No. Not at all. This'll be so nice. Nothing fancy, and just the people we love. And for music, you can sing to me."

He grinned at her. "About the strawberry blonde?"

She batted his shoulder. "Oh, you! What about 'Great Is Thy Faithfulness'?"

He hugged her close. "Okay. But I've also got a song buzzing around in my head. Maybe by then I can get it down on paper."

When Donald got home that night, he was surprised to see his father still in his office. He knocked on the open door and asked, "Is everything all right?"

His father raised his head from the book he was reading and took off his glasses. "Well, yes and no. How is Mrs. Penner?"

"Much better. She's still weak but on the mend."

"Dr. Entz called. He had many good things to say about you."

"He did?" Donald felt a burst of joy. "He was very friendly in the office."

"He said you show signs of becoming a good doctor."

"That's reassuring." If he accepted Japanese people, maybe others in the community would learn to get along with them.

His father leaned back in his chair. "Dr. Entz is a good friend of mine. I think highly of his opinions. Before the war, it was he who first suggested I give sermons on the radio."

"I didn't know that. Will you ever be able to do that again?"

"That was the reason he called. They want me to prepare a series for this fall. Subject to editing, of course."

Donald knew that really meant censoring, since those sermons seemed to be the main reason for his arrest. But at least this was a start in the right direction.

His father steepled his fingers and leaned his chin on them. Donald waited, sensing there was more.

"He spoke well of Annie Penner. He says she is sincere and thoughtful, not one to make foolish decisions." Donald started to speak, but his father held up his hand. "Your mother says Annie is a fine girl, even though she is not Japanese. She has been kind to your grandfather, and he is pleased with her. It seems I am the only one with doubts."

Donald sighed. "I wish I knew how to ease those doubts."

His father rose and walked around the desk. He stood staring at his bookshelf, his back to Donald. Finally he said in a muffled voice, "You are my only son. If you marry out of our culture, will you turn your back on us? Will Dr. Nakamura become so American that his family means nothing to him?"

"Oh, Father." Donald's voice choked. "Never, never. You and mother, *Jiichan,* Florence . . . you are all part of my heart. I love and honor my family, and Annie will too. We will never lose touch. And I promise to teach our children the Japanese *On.*" He walked to his father and stood beside him. "My greatest hope is that someday our marriage will be recognized in California, and I can set up a practice right here in the valley."

His father turned around, and they embraced, awkwardly at first, but then fervently, patting each other on the back.

His father cleared his throat. "I will miss you as a choir director, too."

"There are others who can take my place."

His father nodded. "But not as talented." He sighed. "*Shikata ga nai.* Time moves on, and we must move with it. No one is indispensable . . . except in our hearts."

Donald hesitated. Was now a good time to ask?

His father raised his eyebrows. "You have a problem?"

"A favor to ask." *Please Lord, let him consent.*

"Yes?"

"Since we must go so far away to be legally married, Annie and I would like a private family service before we leave. At Annie's home." He mentioned some of their plans.

His father's eyes lit up, and he nodded. "That would please your mother."

"I know. I think we'd all feel better. It would represent a blessing of the marriage. My question is . . . would you be willing to conduct the ceremony? We would be truly honored."

"My son, my son." His father had tears in his eyes. "It is I who am honored. Yes. And every day I will pray that the laws will change, and that you two can move back to this valley."

Chapter Thirty-Two

Annie wore a mint-colored suit. She'd pulled her curls back into a matching snood that her mother crocheted for her. The diamond engagement ring sparkled on her finger as she picked up her bouquet of yellow roses. Then taking Donald's arm, she walked beside him to the arched doorway of her living room. She felt as though she were floating on air.

It was Sunday afternoon, the eleventh of August, and the war seemed far in the past. She looked up at Donald, so strong and healthy, eager for medical school and their new life together.

Finally, everything had fallen into place and their dreams had come true. No matter what was ahead, she and Donald were together. With God's help their love would carry them through.

The people gathered in the living room were those most special to Donald and to her. Her mother had splurged on a stylish lavender crepe dress with a flounce on one side of the skirt. She now sat in the easy chair, smiling through her tears. Annie knew she was still struggling with the idea of a Japanese son-in-law, but today she seemed more at ease with Donald.

Her grandparents had come, bringing a beautiful handmade quilt and a generous check. Her Grandpa could hardly tear himself away from his discussion with Donald's father—baptism, the Millennium, President Truman—and had to be reminded that Donald and Annie had a train to catch.

Taunta Ruth sat in a chair next to Annie's mother, but Uncle Martin had a heifer coming fresh and couldn't leave his farm. None of her other relatives had come either, but maybe someday they'd soften. Annie would do her part and send Christmas cards from Chicago.

Donald's mother, in her best brocade silk, sat on the couch beside *Jiichan,* who smiled every time Annie glanced his way. She would miss him; she'd grown to love him dearly. She'd started to call him by that Japanese term, too. It was a good way to distinguish him from her own grandparents. If only *Baachan* had lived long enough to be here. She'd had a friendly greeting for Annie when they'd met. Now, their next greeting would be in heaven.

Annie and her mother had decorated the parlor and dining room with vases of asters and dahlias. Baskets of freesias trailed snowy blossoms over the top of the upright piano. Between the two rooms, ivy—twined with strands of yellow jasmine—framed the doorway where she and Donald stood.

Florence and Malinda now came and stood next to Annie. She regretted that she and Donald would have to miss their weddings. But Annie knew there was no other choice, and they'd promised to send many pictures.

On the other side of Donald stood his friends Sho and Tom, outfitted in new suits, grinning bashfully.

Donald's father stood between the wedding party and the family, and opened with a prayer for Donald and Annie that brought her to tears. "Lord, we beseech thy loving hand upon this pair. Protect them, guide them, let them daily seek thy wisdom and follow thy precepts. We know the life they have chosen will be hard, and yet we trust thee to keep them strong and help them overcome any adversity."

Annie handed her bouquet to Malinda, then turned back to Donald. He took both her hands and unaccompanied, sang to her alone, the love in his eyes shining deep into her heart.

Beneath an oak one wonderful day
You caught my heart, right from the start.

I asked the Lord, "Show me the way
To win her love, dear Father above."

Annie listened, tears streaming down her cheeks, thrilled with the beautiful words and melody composed only for her by her wonderful, talented bridegroom. The song went on to tell the story of their separation, their despair and, finally, their joyful reuniting.

She thought back to the years of heartache and felt the echo of that pain. But now, the only thing that mattered was that God had brought them back together, that Donald loved her and this was the beginning of their life together.

Not war, nor strife, nor separate life,
Can keep us apart, dear love of my heart.
The Lord has brought us together again
Oh wonderful joy that none can destroy!

Donald gently pressed Annie's hands before releasing them. Florence handed her a tissue, and Rev. Nakamura took off his glasses and wiped his own eyes. Murmurs and amens drifted over the room, and then everyone settled to hear Rev. Nakamura's short message of encouragement. When he finished, Annie and Donald knelt and he placed hands on their heads for a final blessing.

"The Lord bless thee and keep thee; the Lord make his face shine upon thee and be gracious unto thee; the Lord lift up his countenance upon thee, and give thee peace."

To Annie, this ceremony was the real thing. It meant far more than the "I do's" they'd say when they reached Chicago, or the piece of paper stamped by a stranger.

After they rose, Rev. Nakamura asked everyone to join hands. In a trembling voice he started singing "God Be with You Till We Meet Again," and the others joined in.

As she sang, Annie looked around the circle, wondering if she would see her loved ones again. Her mother had decided against applying for the matron job—it would be too hard to leave her family, church, and sewing circle to go live with strangers.

Grandpa and Grandma Bartsch were growing old, and Chicago was so far away.

Taunta Ruth was a favorite of hers; Annie would miss her. And she was just getting to know Donald's parents better; his mother, especially, had been kind and friendly.

Jiichan, so loving, so frail.

By the time they got to the final chorus, several of the voices had dropped out, others had weakened, and many trembled. Her mother was openly sobbing into her handkerchief.

Annie knew she'd never again sing that song without tears. Only her unwavering love for Donald made her able to leave all these dear people.

"God be with you till we meet again."

As the last line faded, there was complete silence, then hugs and kisses all around, tears and laughter, whispers of love and loyalty. Annie even hugged Sho and Tom, although they seemed embarrassed, and she hoped they didn't think she was too bold.

Taunta Ruth helped Annie's mother set out the *faspa,* and once the coffee and *tvehbock* with strawberry jam took effect, everyone was talking and laughing. Grandpa Bartsch's eyebrows raised when he saw the little bride and groom on the cake, but Donald put his arm around Annie's waist and they posed behind it as Tom manned the camera.

Tom clicked so many other shots that Annie was nearly blinded by the flashbulbs, and Donald finally told him to take snaps of the guests.

Donald's mother lifted off the little top layer of cake that held the figures and set it into a box before she sliced the rest of the cake.

"Take along, save in freezer," she whispered to Annie. "After one year, eat, for luck."

Annie smiled and nodded. If they depended upon luck, they'd need it long before the year was over. But they were in God's hands, and he would care for them. As for the cake, they'd probably finish it on the train.

Her bags were packed and ready, and some of their things had been crated and sent ahead to the apartment Donald had leased. He'd help her find her seat on the train, then go on to a different car. He promised that, once they were out of California, he'd find her again.

Annie remembered that he always managed to be with her at college. She knew he'd find a way for them to sit together.

Epilogue

In 1948, California repealed its anti-miscegenation law. Eight years after that, Donald and Annie, with their three children, returned to the San Joaquin Valley. Donald had become a neurologist, well-known for his articles in medical journals, and the friendly doctor who treated *Jiichan* helped Donald get established in Fresno.

Annie never regretted marrying him. They had prayed through troubles and adjustments, encouraged each other in the Word, and their love had grown even stronger through the years.

Prior to 1956, they paid just two short visits to Rosemond: In June of 1949, Annie's mother married a widower, a deacon in her church; two years later they returned for the beloved *Jiichan*'s funeral. Now that they were home to stay, Donald vowed he'd pull every possible string to move *Baachan* back from Gila River so his grandparents' graves could be together.

At each visit, Annie was surprised to see the changes that appeared in the Mennonite Brethren church. And now it was more obvious, with the latest dress styles, permanent waves on both young and older women, some makeup, and a few earrings. The church even included other nationalities in their membership and occasionally had fellowship with several other denominations in town. Most of the Bartsch clan by now had accepted Donald; the others, though still wary, were at least polite to him.

Donald and Annie still used their music in the Lord's work. Together, they did presentations in various churches, singing solos and duets. Donald would also tell how the Lord had led him through the internment, the war, to Annie, and into the medical profession.

He'd always conclude his remarks by saying, "There may always be some hurt, way down deep. But the hatred is gone. The Lord has given me all the desires of my heart."

Then he and Annie would close with the hymn, "Great Is Thy Faithfulness," their voices soaring on the phrase, "Strength for today and bright hope for tomorrow."

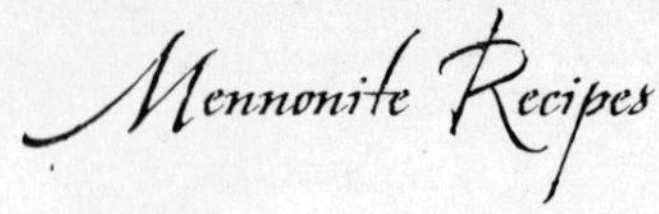

Tvehbock

(A double-decker roll also known as zwiebach.)

1 cake yeast
1 tablespoon sugar
⅓ cup lukewarm water
2 cups whole milk
¾ cup shortening (some butter)
3 teaspoons salt
6 cups flour (have an extra 2 cups on hand in case more flour needed)

Set yeast in a small bowl. Sprinkle sugar over yeast, and pour the water over that.

Set aside.

Scald milk. (Heat on stove just until bubbles form at the edges.)

Add shortening and salt to milk. Pour into large bowl and let cool to lukewarm.

When milk is lukewarm, add the yeast mixture and salt, and gradually add flour, stirring well, until the dough is smooth. When dough is firm enough, use hands to knead until very smooth and elastic. Cover bowl with slightly dampened tea towel or a lid and let dough rise in a warm place until double, usually 1½ hours.

Punch dough down and, while holding a chunk of dough in both hands, use a thumb and forefinger to pinch off round egg-sized balls. (This is an art handed down from mother to daughter. I find it easiest to pick up a handful of dough in my left hand, pushing with my right, then pinch off with the left fingers and pluck loose with the right.) Place about 1–2 inches apart on lightly greased baking sheets. When one sheet is filled, pinch off slightly smaller balls and place on top of the other balls. Press down with hand to hold balls together. (Some people anchor them by poking a thumb through the center.) Let rise in warm place until double (about 20–30 minutes). Bake at 425° for 10 minutes, then turn oven down to 350° and bake until golden brown. Makes about 3 dozen, depending on their size.

Serve with jam or honey. After three or four days, if any are left, take balls apart and roast in a 225° oven about an hour or until brown and very crisp. They taste wonderful crumbled up in hot salted milk or coffee.

Rollkoaka
(Crullers)

1½ cups flour (add more if needed)
½ cup whole milk
1 egg (do not beat)
2½ teaspoons baking powder
3 tablespoons butter or margarine

Mix well with hands, adding extra flour if needed. Roll out to about ¼-inch thick on lightly floured board, and cut into 2" x 4" strips. Cut a two-inch slit in the center of each, and twist one end through the slit. Deep fry in hot oil, three or four at a time, depending on size of pan, turning them once. Serve with ice cold watermelon.

This was considered a full meal, with the last few rollkoaka spread with jam for a dessert.